THE
CHÂTEAU

ALSO BY PAUL GOLDBERG

FICTION

The Yid

NONFICTION

How We Do Harm (coauthored with Otis Webb Brawley M.D.)
The Thaw Generation (coauthored with Ludmilla Alexeyeva)
The Final Act

TRANSLATION

To Live Like Everyone by Anatoly Marchenko

THE CHÂTEAU

PAUL GOLDBERG

PICADOR

NEW YORK

THE CHÂTEAU. Copyright © 2018 by Paul Goldberg. All rights reserved. Printed in the United States of America. For information, address Picador, 175 Fifth Avenue, New York, N.Y. 10010.

picadorusa.com • picadorbookroom.tumblr.com
twitter.com/picadorusa • facebook.com/picadorusa

Picador® is a U.S. registered trademark and is used by Macmillan Publishing Group, LLC, under license from Pan Books Limited.

For book club information, please visit facebook.com/picadorbookclub or email marketing@picadorusa.com.

Title page illustration of man by David Curtis Studio

Designed by Steven Seighman

Library of Congress Cataloging-in-Publication Data

Names: Goldberg, Paul, 1959– author.
Title: The Château : a novel / Paul Goldberg.
Description: First edition. | New York : Picador, [2018]
Identifiers: LCCN 2017028305 (print) | LCCN 2017030203 (ebook) | ISBN 9781250116109 (ebook) | ISBN 9781250116093 (hardcover)
Subjects: LCSH: Reporters and reporting—Fiction. | Fathers and sons—Fiction. | GSAFD: Black humor (Literature) | Mystery fiction.
Classification: LCC PS3607.O4434 (ebook) | LCC PS3607.O4434 C48 2018 (print) | DDC 813/.6—dc23
LC record available at https://lccn.loc.gov/2017028305

Our books may be purchased in bulk for promotional, educational, or business use. Please contact your local bookseller or the Macmillan Corporate and Premium Sales Department at 1-800-221-7945, extension 5442, or by e-mail at MacmillanSpecialMarkets@macmillan.com.

First published by Picador.

First Edition: February 2018

10 9 8 7 6 5 4 3 2 1

For Susan Keselenko Coll

Мы живем, под собою не чуя страны . . .
—Осип Мандельштам

We live not feeling the country beneath us . . .
—Osip Mandelstam

PART I

||||||||||||||||||||||||||||||||||||||||||||||||||||||||||||||||||||||||||||||||||||||||||||||||||||

I like to think big. I always have. To me it's very simple: if you are going to be thinking anyway, you might as well think big.

—DONALD TRUMP
The Art of the Deal

||||||||||||||||||||||||||||||||||||||||||||||||||||||||||||||||||||||||||||||||||||||||||||||||||||

1

THE BUTT GOD

Let us not focus on the events that sent Zbignew Wronski over the railing of a forty-third-story balcony of the Grand Dux Hotel on South Ocean Drive in Hollywood, Florida, on January 5, 2017. Salacious rumors are usually true, but it's unlikely that everything said about the man known as the Butt God of Miami Beach could be.

It is plausible that immediately prior to the plunge, Zbig was with two women, only one of whom was his wife. The sometimes-Pygmalionic sometimes-Oedipal ethics of cosmetic surgery being what they are, it is plausible that the other woman—if she existed—was a "patient." "Client" would be a better word. To qualify for the moniker "patient," one should be ill, which no one in Dr. Wronski's care was. He was an exterior designer. A posterior designer.

Consuela Ramirez-Wronska unquestionably was a client. Her taut buttocks, tanned, set like jewels in a black thong, continued to grace the Web site of Zbig's practice for many days after their maker's fatal plunge. A "before" picture was not provided.

Big Zbig collaborated with a specialist in vaginal tightening. This partner didn't seek to be known as either the Vagina God or the Vagina Caesar. A little man who liked money, he would have been fine with Vagina Elf.

For years, rumors circulated that Zbig's clients tested their rejuvenated nether regions with their tall, handsome, broad-shouldered Slavic surgeon.

Had the ancient, some say outmoded, Hippocratic rules of medical ethics been applied, that test would have been regarded as problematic. Some might suggest that it would have been more appropriate to utilize a simple device that faithfully mimics the human organ. But even if these rumors were grounded in fact, it was clearly agreeable, even upon reflection, to all parties involved. Zbig's disciplinary file at the Florida Board of Medicine in Tallahassee was pristine.

An artist must either love or hate his or her medium in order to reimagine and reshape it. Men's butts left Zbig indifferent. He didn't do men; this might as well be established early.

Before drilling deeper into Zbig's life and his death in a search for clues about his final flight, we will consider the flight itself:

You are over the edge, you versus gravity, uninsulated, unparachuted, with nothing to forestall the shattering of the atrium's nine-foot glass panes, a gentle bounce off a steel girder, the breaking of the pipes of the sprinkler system, the final fifty feet of flight in the halo of glass shards and streams of water, toward the indoor palm trees and bar stools. Do your thoughts focus on the circumstances that caused your flight? Does it matter whether the genesis of flight is voluntary, accidental, premeditated, impulsive, or the consequence of foul play? Do you experience fear, a fleeting mourning for your life, or do you swallow the swill of salty air, morning mist, cloud and fog, stretching the boundaries of ecstasy, surrendering to rapture, convincing yourself of your power to deploy your exaltation as a mystical tool for changing the inflection of your gravitational doom?

Decades earlier, when Zbig was a student at Duke, his roommate—a fellow Slav—was obsessed with the raspy-voiced, screaming Muscovite poet Volodya Vysotsky, the kind of bard who uses exclamation marks more than any other form of punctuation:

Я коней напою,
Я куплет допою,-
Хоть мгновенье еще постою на краю!

I'll water the stallions,
I'll finish the song,
I'll stand on the edge for a moment more!

The roommate's name was William M. Katzenelenbogen.

The dateline changes to WASHINGTON.

We are at Martin's Tavern, a storied Georgetown bar, where we find William M. Katzenelenbogen.

Martin's is not an imitation pub, not faux English, not a dive. Washingtonians have come to Martin's for generations, sometimes several times a week. It is said that JFK proposed to Jackie at a Martin's booth (Booth No. 3), that—presumably on a different night—Dick Nixon poured ketchup over everything, and that J. Edgar Hoover was seen playing footsie with

Boyfriend Clyde or perhaps trawling the place for cute, clean-cut boys. Martin's is what a pub should be: you can bring the family if you've got one, or you can sit at the bar and be as withdrawn as you wish. Martin's treats gin with respect.

Bill's appearance evokes the image of an outsized terrier. He is six feet tall on the dot. Lean, with no trace of a middle-age paunch, he sports a closely trimmed beard and an identically cropped head of coarse hair. His hair color was never static. It turned from straight and blond to curly and light brown sometime before college. Now, fifteen minutes past middle age, it looks like a fragment of the coat of an elderly Airedale. Not the back of an elderly Airedale, which is salt-and-pepper, but a front paw—an arm—which turns salt-and-cumin, or some such.

Bill has ordered Tito's and regular Bombay (not Bombay Sapphire), a vodka and a gin, mixed 1:1, shaken, with not a thought of vermouth. Rinse out the shaker. He fucking hates vermouth.

It's January 6, 2017, 6 p.m.—two full weeks to go before inauguration, installation, ascension, coronation, sanctification, consummation, or putsch—whatever is the right name for this thing that history has dragged in.

The image of the president-elect is on two of the television screens above the bar, a silent montage of his puppet hands, his pouting lips, his aggressively orange face topped with the mop of misshapen yellow hair.

The third screen serves up grainy images of the massacre du jour, this time at the Fort Lauderdale–Hollywood International Airport. A crowd on the tarmac waits, panicking in place. A high school yearbook mug shot of the shooter flashes on the screen. Not ISIS this time—just a baby-faced psychotic, being a good boy, obeying commands from the voices that whisper in his skull.

On second thought, it's possible that inner voices do not whisper. They may toll, like bells, for thee, and thee—and thee. Possibly, some of these voices are more legitimate than others. Some may be healthful, even beneficial; how is one to know? As a science writer—make that a former science writer—Bill doesn't have a blessed clue. No one to ask, no place to look for answers, no reason to.

A Twitter icon pops up on one of the Trump screens. It's about Putin ordering the hacking of the election and celebrating—dancing like a Cossack, presumably—when his boy prevailed.

Fuck it, all of it, Bill declares, looking away, turning his attention to the wood grain of the bar, his eyes contemplating the complexity of its gentle waves, seeking solace, escape even. Of course, Bill is mistaking these asymmetrical shapes for nature's assurance that this episode of search for simplicity shall pass, as it has at various times in Italy, Germany, Spain, the USSR, for nature itself gravitates toward democracy and social justice, self-correcting, inevitably, conveniently.

The act of reading reassuring, determinist messages in the wood grain is yet another indicator of being intensely in need of a drink, and, fortuitously, a drink is precisely what is about to happen in Bill's life.

The bartender is new and needs to be instructed.

"Tito's and Bombay—is there a name for this?" he asks, filling the martini glass with the liquid he has expertly clouded via intensive interaction with ice in the shaker.

"TB," Bill improvises.

"Would a twist make it better for you?"

"Worse."

It would take more than a twist or even an olive to make things better for William M. Katzenelenbogen.

Bill is a science writer and an investigative reporter: an investigative science writer, one of the best of his generation, a serial finalist for the Pulitzer Prize and the Loeb Award for Excellence in Financial Journalism as well as a laureate of a boxful of lesser prizes, most of them dispensed by the Association of Health Care Journalists and something called the Washington Professional Chapter of the American Society of Professional Journalists.

A top-flight journalist in his thirties and forties, he flew into turbulence after crossing into his fifties.

Two hours ago, he was discharged, unceremoniously—for cause—presumably to be replaced on *The Washington Post* payroll by three low-paid, tech-savvy youths.

He marched out of the newsroom brandishing a broomstick, which, witnesses said, he held with pride and devotion, like a cross at an Easter procession. A two-man Easter procession this was: a rent-a-cop followed. All of Bill's friends had taken buyouts or been fired years earlier. He was the last of the generation. There should have been music. Incense should have been burnt.

Why the broomstick? you might ask.

Reporters of Bill's ilk get lectured about the need to stop using the word "nail" as a verb in discussing targets of inquiry. At thirty, shortly after joining the *Post,* he stopped making references to castrations with dull, rusted blades. By forty, he mellowed a bit more and stopped likening the art of writing stories to the act of shoving broomsticks—indeed, entire brooms—up the recti of people who had betrayed the public trust: corrupt government officials, avaricious CEOs, data-cooking scientists.

At one point, Bill proposed developing a scale for measuring impact in inches shoved, and in 1998, a group of interns presented him with just the broomstick he proposed. It was a fond gift for what amounted to contributing to delinquency of newsroom minors.

This broomstick was to be aimed at *proverbial,* as opposed to corporeal, assholes. In the newsroom parlance of the post-Watergate era, a broomstick salute seemed to be a fitting punishment. A good investigative story is a weapon, the enemy is the enemy, and denying humanity of the enemy is a requirement in all combat, including the combat that is journalism.

For nearly two decades Bill kept the broomstick hidden behind a filing cabinet near his desk, a time-capsule-preserved artifact from the days he thought such things were funny. He moved and rehid the broomstick when the *Post* relocated to its techy new quarters.

The first inch shoved was marked "Denial of all Allegations"; two inches—a "Letter from Lawyers"; three—"Acknowledgment of Minor Clerical Errors"; six—"Tearful Apology"; eight—"Resignation"; eleven—"Restitution"; fourteen—"Conviction"; eighteen—"Meaningful Change." Arrows near the tip of the broomstick pointed in the direction of "Revolution," indicating that an additional broomstick will be required.

Bill was not about to leave this time-honored journalistic artifact, this totem, in enemy hands. The other aged memento he took was his Rolodex, which he dropped into the bike messenger's bag that served as his briefcase. He hadn't updated any of the yellowed cards in two decades, but the Rolodex was in perfect working order: it spun.

Being jettisoned by your profession—for insubordination, let the record show—was the biggest betrayal in a life rife with them.

The firing was simple: an officious, heavyset, middle-aged woman with long fingernails (from Personnel, presumably) read the verdict. There was no editor in the room. They were busy chasing details on the Fort Lauderdale airport shooter.

There was a paper they wanted Bill to sign and an envelope containing a check he would earn by agreeing to various crap the *Post* wanted him to do and not do, but Bill said "Fuck You." He didn't sign shit. He had neither grounds nor plans to sue; the Fuck You was a matter of principle.

It's difficult to be fired for cause at the *Post*. It means somebody up high has generated paperwork and the Newspaper Guild was asleep. Being fired for cause means no severance package. (The check dangled in front of him was a pittance, he presumes.) His upcoming paycheck will be his last. And "insubordination" is just another word for being moved to a stultifying beat and being forced to write stories that need not be written and demoralizing you enough to force you to phone it in for a few years and finally quit. What do you expect when you dispatch someone like Bill to Fairfax County, the place he doesn't know how to find or what to do with once he is there?

After the Easter procession, Bill heads to Martin's, and here he is, on his beloved bar stool, in the southwestern corner, his broomstick leaning like a personal flying device against the bar. He is receiving an ice-cold TB.

If wine at a communion symbolizes the blood of Christ, a TB at Martin's symbolizes Christ's spinal fluid.

"I'll have what he's having," says a young woman, sitting down, and in the same motion, Yogically, lifting the broomstick. She handles it with care, reverence even, like a fragile artifact from the distant past.

"Another TB coming up," says the bartender.

"TB?"

"TB."

There is no hug, no handshake, not even a tap on the shoulder, just the raising of the broomstick. She lifts it, turns it over, admires the scale. There is a boundary between them, perhaps professional, perhaps personal.

"Gwen, a pleasant surprise," says Bill, staring at the nadir of the cone of his martini glass. She is in her midthirties, a redhead, freckles. She settles in, crosses her legs.

Gwen was once a gonzo take-no-prisoners reporter. A star straight out of Harvard, she went from intern to Style at twenty-two. She was the princess of Style, pounding booze, banging out Salingeresque copy by the yard, covering social Washington—reporting from parties—producing dross about misbehaviors of people convinced of their larger-than-lifeness. No one since Sally Quinn had a better ear for quotes or eye for mischief. Bill thought she wrote like a dog eats—fast, gasping, grunting, hiccupping, with emanations of saliva—but it was young, energetic prose. And she was a hoot to drink with. His thoughts about her were mostly chaste. They'd slept together only once.

"I heard," she says, awkwardly placing her hand on the back of his neck and leaving it there. "I thought I'd find you here."

Bill takes the first sip of TB, its coldness deadening the nerve endings as it seeps toward the absolute darkness of his aching Russian soul.

"I almost forgot: it takes eighteen inches to get 'Meaningful Change,'" she says, running the broomstick through her loosely clenched fist.

"This seemed hilarious at the time," she adds upon reflection. "It's deeply offensive, actually."

She should know. She was the lead author of the scale, one of the interns who produced this object.

"Gwen, our president-elect would dismiss your reaction as political correctness."

"An argument for political correctness, in my book."

"Was this a flavor of 'locker room talk' then—'newsroom talk'?"

As Bill considers her legs through the prism of the martini glass, his peripheral vision registers the amused look on the face of the bartender. They are nice legs, draped in black tights, with lots of distance between the knee and the herringbone tweed hem. He reflects on the freckles that live beneath those tights.

In 2008, Gwen was dismissed, publicly, humiliatingly, for fabricating a story. Then it turned out that many stories over many years were tainted. As of today—January 6, 2017—they have something in common—discarded by the *Post*; she for fabrication, he for insubordination. Both guilty as charged.

Bill takes another sip.

"Remember what you told me when I was shit-canned?" she asks.

"No."

"You said, 'Write a fucking memoir. Take responsibility for things you did and things you didn't do: going down on French poodles, smuggling baby pandas to private zoos. Apologize for slavery, apologize for the Holocaust, apologize for the loss of habitat of gorillas and the clubbing of white baby seals. Accept all responsibility, falsify backward if you must. You are no longer a reporter; it doesn't matter anymore—the worse the better.

Nobody has ever gone wrong by taking too much responsibility. Own your guilt, own your unmooring, reach for more, more, more.'"

"Sounds like my voice."

"It was quite an oration—and good advice. It saved my life."

"How would you have done it?"

"The big *if?* I lived in a high-rise across the river—thirteenth floor."

"High enough."

"Your advice, it was amoral: survive, lie backward, emerge on the other end, come out on top."

"I am an immigrant. A refugee even."

He drains his martini glass and motions to the bartender to refill it.

"What does that have to do with anything?"

"We scrape."

"You told me that if I play it right, I would own something big: remorse. Your words exactly: 'You can't overdo remorse. It's infinite.' And another thing you said: 'When you stake out your claim on remorse, name your Porsche after me.'"

"Did you?"

"A Porsche named Katzenelenbogen? No. I named it Remorse. Same as the memoir. Have you read it?"

"No. What color?"

"The Porsche or the memoir?"

"Porsche."

"Yellow. You should've kept in touch. I fell from grace, sure, but I didn't die. I kept thinking about you all afternoon, since I heard about the firing: 'If Bill were a disease, which disease would he be?'"

"Is a 'fuckup' a diagnosis recognized by the American Psychiatric Association?"

"I was in the realm of the American *Medical* Association. You are diabetes, Mr. Katzenelenbogen."

"Me? Diabetes?"

"Your wounds don't heal."

"You associate me with open sores? Amputations?"

"I guess it might explain why I want to touch your hand and tell you it's okay."

They look away from each other. She was once forbidden, first as an intern, then a disgraced reporter, a falsifier of fact, a betrayer of public trust, a threat to the safety of journalistic boundaries.

He reached out to her when she was found out, when she was unmasked. He listened. He offered advice, good advice at that, it turns out. But at the time that was all he could be, an off-the-record friend, a secret well-wisher. She was radioactive, and he had no death wish.

"It's great to see you, Gwen, don't get me wrong, but why are you here?"

"To watch you drink, take you to your apartment, and tuck you in."

"To make sure I don't blow my brains out?"

"Returning the favor."

She pinches his cheek in the boundary-transgressing manner of old Jewish ladies; where did she learn that skill?

They down three rounds of TBs, soak the toxins with liver and onions, a Martin's specialty, then get a second wind.

The walk up Wisconsin Avenue to Bill's apartment takes about half an hour.

"Why did we get into the racket?" he asks as they pass the gray marble hulk of the Russian embassy.

This little strip of the USSR just happens to sit on the highest point in Washington. If the president-elect is planning on draining the swamp, this joint is as far from a swamp as you can get.

"Journalism? It was very personal, I guess. I was tired of being told that things were not as they appear," Gwen answers.

"Such as?"

"That the smell on my father's breath wasn't alcohol. That my mother wasn't kissing the next-door neighbor. That Mom and Dad weren't really fighting last night. That they love each other. That Grandma's death didn't matter because life is for the living. That my dislike of spinach was illusory. That I could discuss anything with my parents, that they accept me the way I am."

"Gwen, that's dysfunction, alcoholism. What does it have to do with career choices, the mission in life?"

"I thought that as a reporter I would be able to tell the truth as I saw it, with the emphasis on *as I saw it*. No second-guessing, no denials."

"Yes, Gwen, the world is knowable, or so we journalists want to think. We are wrong."

"It seemed knowable at first, until lies took over, yet—paradoxically—I am no worse for it. What about you?"

"I had no choice. My mother was murdered by a quack. My father is a felon."

"Convicted?"

"Which? The quack or the felon?"

"Both."

"It gets complicated—but both are guilty as fuck."

"Your father—tell me about him."

"If you cross American fraud with Russian literature, you get what?"

"I give up."

"You get Melsor Yakovlevich Katzenelenbogen, an expert in both—my beloved father."

"I can see the two of you are close. Are you even in touch?"

"We haven't talked in a while."

"A few months?"

"A few years."

"Two?"

"Ten, maybe twelve. Let me guess, you come from a line of wing nuts?"

"Not at all. Progressive as can be. Professors at the University of Michigan. Dad is in the English department, Mom is an ethicist. Why would you ask?"

"Being a reporter."

"You were judging, actually. You can't find a smidgeon of charity in your cold heart to forgive your poor old father, an asshole though he could be. Judging, judging, judging."

"That's what we do. We are judges of the benchless sort. That thing about crime, punishment, betrayal, it runs right through the gut."

"It can't be helped, I suppose."

Bill's palm brushes against her back as they walk up the stairs and enter his apartment. Her overcoat is soft, blue, cashmere, maybe camel hair.

He lives in a one-bedroom, above a restaurant on the corner of Wisconsin and Macomb.

"This place hasn't changed in a decade. Eight years, forgive me. Danish modern, Swedish functionalism, industrial this-and-that. I would never have believed that a guy like you would gravitate to this."

"I look like a Salvation Army sort?"

"Sort of. And this place is like something out of *Dwell*."

"Cognac, anyone?"

"No, I am good. I am open to one kiss—just one, half on the lips, a little longer than casual, but not by much—hear me?—and then I will go home and sleep in my bed, alone."

"Of course, it wouldn't be contextually inappropriate for you to spend the night, if you can pardon the multiple negatives."

"I disagree. You'll fuck me for the license to talk all night about the boundary between fact and fiction and right and wrong."

"Maybe."

Gwen kisses him on the cheeks and quickly pulls away.

"Spare me, Bill . . . They are porous. No hard walls—it's a continuum. Playing with them is like scratching a scab—don't, Mr. Diabetes. With that, I bid adieu, with full expectation that you will call me when you are ready to ask me out on a proper date, which you didn't do last time I was here—asshole."

2

REMORSE

If you are a reporter and you are good at it, it's not an avocation you are pursuing. It's your mission, your you.

Journalism, as Bill has always seen it, is the solid core of the universe surrounded by nebulae; feathery, cold, unexplored, a soft, vertical wilderness. As these images start to spin around him, he is coming to terms with being ejected into that realm of disconnected irrelevance, the vast kingdom of uselessness. It's a good thing Bill isn't prone to crying—he considers displays of emotion unmanly. Had this not been the case, he might have started to cry and never stopped.

Things sucked for Bill from the outset of his career, or his mission, or whatever it is, or was. His curse: when he was in his prime, Americans could accept an immigrant in almost any role—a doctor, especially in an obscure abbadaba subspecialty, an engineer, even a Web security consultant—but not as an investigative journalist. Bill could reach the top tiers, never achieving the pinnacle. Something about the ever-so-subtle remnants of his Russian tonality and his so-unpronounceable and so-unspellable name—a name he sometimes, for the sake of user-friendliness, abbreviates as KZB and WKZB—made the doorkeepers bar the entrance to the club.

Two caveats:

- That's what Bill believes, and
- The world may have changed.

It's his misfortune to be a man of acronyms. It's even less fortunate that the shorter of these acronyms—KZB—sounds as sinister as a secret police organization and the longer—WKZB—like a radio station: "You are listening to WKZB! Radio Moscow! All bullshit all the time."

The thought of waking up post-career terrifies.

"Will the sun rise?" is the first in a series of questions asked by all journalists as they imagine this separation.

"Will I have a place under it?" is the second.

It's January 7, between 4:32 and 6:07 A.M. Bill denies being awake. He is purifying his consciousness, purging thoughts as they emerge, snipping off their snake heads. It's an intracranial dialogue, Socratic masturbation:

Was I really fired?

Zap it . . .

Is this a dream?

Purge . . .

I need to get to my desk ASAP, tons of calls to make.

Away, consciousness, away, take yesterday with you, surround it in a cloud of infamy, lift it, take it to the middle of the sea, piss it out. And, please God, please, let yesterday be struck from the record, let me return. Have I not been through this separation in a dream, time and again, and yet I went on? Let this be that.

He thinks he sees his mother's face. He sees her as she would have been on her final day. He wasn't there, was precluded from getting there. Does she understand that FDA-sanctified drugs, legally administered in gonzo doses by a state-anointed physician who is sort of prominent in his field, are about to push her off the ledge, that in her case the line between therapy and execution has been erased, that her death is not from disease, but from treatment thereof, that scientific nonsense on the dawn of the twenty-first century is more lethal than the most lethal of diseases—hers?

Does any of this matter, or is meaning contained entirely in the fall?

Beset by visitations, Bill doesn't want the sun to rise. Prostrate, his shoulders plastered against the mattress, he wrestles against the sunrise, bargaining hopelessly with the God whose existence he denies.

At 6:07 A.M., a text from Gwen.

It's a link to a story: PLASTIC SURGEON PLUNGES TO HIS DEATH.

Gwen's message: "If u r reading this, ur brains r still in cranium. If not, fuck u."

Readers who have had three or more years of therapy or earned a master's of fine arts degree in creative writing will ask: How did Bill *FEEL immediately* upon learning about his friend's death? They should be encouraged to wait for this story to develop in accordance with its own rhythms or proceed to generate their own material reflecting the manner in which they were treated and/or trained.

Feelings can be emanations of our inner lives, but not always. A plot point this is not. That would be too easy.

"Fuck," Bill texts back. "He was my college roommate. Great guy. Friend."

This is what shock and grief look like in January 2017. An expletive via text. Is there time to experience the suddenness, unexpectedness of news, to dwell on the feeling of loss? Does it set in? Can it, after the original moment, the moment of discovery, slips out of reach?

"Shit," you say, adding "Fuck" for good measure, if the loss is unfathomable.

Why did she send it?

Surely she remembered Bill's appreciation for a bizarre story. He collected them once, creating a repository, a database, of four-paragraph beauties. Much of this repository involves utilization of hand tools and stuffing whole bodies or body parts into fifty-five-gallon drums. Life in four paragraphs with a perfectly chiseled AP lead is a haiku. A searchable database it is: try "fifty-five."

How could she have known that Bill and Zbig were roommates at Duke, that the two had fond nicknames for each other. Zbig's was Ye Olde Olde Sheep-Plugger of Warsaw. Bill's were less imaginative: KZB, WKZB, Mad Russian, and, for some reason, Igor. How was anyone to know that they remained close for the first two decades after graduation, that it was as unthinkable for Zbig to come to D.C. and not call Bill as it was for Bill to come to South Florida and not call Zbig?

Had they come to each other's realms more often, they would have surely remained closer friends instead of allowing their friendship to dissolve into Facebook displays of communication of useless fact that extends the genre of braggy, soulless Christmas letter into a year-long affair.

Bill follows this with another text: "I still have my wits (or at least brains) within me."

"Seriously? You know this guy?" she texts back.

"Did."

"Your next gig: write a book. Death of the Butt God."

"U r crazy."

No. Bill is not having feelings—not yet. He is texting the pesky buggers away. What about the book? Is it possible that Gwen is right? Symmetry is hard to miss. Bill had pointed Gwen toward ownership of Remorse, which she now does, in fact, own, and which generates rents that enabled the acquisition and maintenance of one yellow Porsche.

Gwen promoted her memoir exceedingly well, wisely declining to do a *Playboy* photo shoot, but letting it be widely known that one was proposed. She did undo her blouse for *GQ* and she did write a narcissistic whatnot for *Cosmopolitan*.

Remorse did well, spectacularly so. Movie rights were sold, a film was actually produced, and Gwen established Remorse Ltd., a crisis management consultancy specializing in contrition. You need Gwen when the broomstick is in, more attractive options are used up, splinters are a viable threat, and sitting a challenge.

Now Gwen is pointing him toward ownership of Grief, or the Edge, or the Fall. He might even stand poised to recapture *Vertigo* from Alfred Hitchcock. Imagine the rents on that.

Later that day, Bill clicks around on the Web, finding that a British tabloid took a less than decorous stab at the Zbig story: BUTT MAN'S SPLAT. It takes a Brit's pervy mind to speculate about Zbig having been with two women "only one of whom was his wife."

The story cites "an individual with direct knowledge of the police investigation," shorthand for a badge-carrying drunk, a cop who talks too much at bars. According to this report, the dead man wore Brunello Cucinelli, a light-colored suit. Bill looks it up: a mod jacket that's a bit short, high-water pants; probably goes with long, narrow shoes or Converse sneakers. In his final moments, Zbig was seeking—commanding—attention.

Bill can't imagine spending five thousand dollars on any suit, let alone a suit that looks like that. And why the two girls, if that was indeed the case?

The stiff is a friend. Make that "was" a friend. A stiff is was—always. Also, make that "a close friend."

You can learn a lot about a guy by analyzing his doodles. Some doodle circles, others phalluses. Bill's are rectangles, intricate amalgamations of rectangles. Call them boxes, call them grates, call them prison windows. Maybe he seeks to place things in boxes, a classifier of everything, holder of nothing.

Or maybe the boxes he is doodling are memorials to his late friend Big Zbig, a valiant rogue who fell in the midst of gallant pursuit of beauty, who had been photographed, body-bagged, and boxed. The man was a hoot, the man was larger than life, the man was an operator, the man was a magician. This was not the death—or the life—either he or Zbig ever imagined, but one doesn't get to pick.

Investigators don't require time to generate hypotheses. The process is preverbal: hypotheses flash before words form. Alas, in the case of Bill's version of his college roommate's final flight, no explanation appears at his cranium's door. A feeling forms in its stead. It's oblique, something from the nether reaches of the soul: it's a sense of flight devoid of a graphic component.

That raspy, screaming Muscovite Volodya Vysotsky, the

Russian Rimbaud, captured that feeling before his demise from booze and opiates. Vysotsky owned the genre of death that Big Zbig entered in the early morning of January 5, 2017, the sort that has you soar with the birds as the rest of us sink in the muck. "I'll water the stallions, I'll finish the song, I'll stand on the edge for a moment more!"

Before there can be grief, before emotions blow in, Bill remains suspended in the undifferentiated feeling of flight. What is this? Could be a spiritual remnant of Zbig, a lingering, transmitted final wish. I wish I could fly. I wish I could land splatlessly. What-ifs are corrosive. How different things could be if Pushkin wore body armor, if Trotsky had a Kevlar helmet, if your grandmother had wheels. The wheels bit is the sanitized American translation from the Yiddish original: What if my grandmother had balls?

The answers:

- In the Anglicized/sanitized version, she would have been a streetcar;
- In the authentic Yiddish version, she would have been my grandfather.

Vysotsky's song rings in his head, like the ISIS-sympathizing intracranial voices that ordered yesterday's shooting in Fort Lauderdale:

Чуть помедленнее, кони, чуть помедленнее!
Вы тугую не слушайте плеть!
Но что-то кони мне попались привередливые,
И дожить не успел, мне допеть не успеть!

Slow down, my stallions—slow!
Do not gallop, do not heed the whip!
But the stallions they gave me do as they wish,
If my life is cut short, then perhaps not my song!

Back in the 1980s, in a Cold War film drama called *White Nights*, Mikhail Baryshnikov performed a dance interpretation of that song.

To hold off feelings a bit longer, Bill looks it up on YouTube. He keys in three search terms—Baryshnikov, White Nights, Vysotsky—and up it pops.

Next, Bill turns to the Web to check whether Tesla makes hearses. It doesn't, which is just as well, because Zbig would have wanted the thing driven in "ludicrous mode," crazy fucking fast. Is there a finer tool for spreading ashes?

Bill's grief receptors are taking their time. He loathes the chills that signal their arrival. He focuses on the feeling of flight. He experiences height in the same way as sharpness, as in sharpness of a blade—it's a feeling of coldness. He fixates on flight in its least impeded, purest form. Not airplanes, not even gliders.

He begins by looking up BASE jumping on the Web, finding videos of bird-suited men and, occasionally, women, flying close to rock ledges, jumping out of helicopters, performing somersaults off diving boards positioned over fjords, opening the doors of ski resort gondolas, and—yes—flying off tall buildings.

This pastime overshadows grief. This is a good thing.

Bill cannot rattle off the list of events that preceded Big Zbig's final flight, but he is an expert in obtaining information and has a box of dusty plaques to show for it. We have mentioned that at another point in his career, he was a serial finalist for the biggest awards in American journalism. They can take away your job, but not the skills and passion you bring to it.

Journalism has few rules, no entrance exams, no license, no shingle, no possibility of expulsion from the ranks, if you don't count firing and being unable to land on your feet. There are a few rules of thumb, however, including not ending sentences with ", however," unless absolutely necessary.

Another rule: if you must mix your life with your craft, you can, sort of, but watch your step.

If you are—or were—with the press, you know how to obtain recordings of 911 calls. Of course, you don't need to be with the press. You can get these if you are an ordinary warped human being.

DISPATCHER: 911—Can I help you?

CALLER *(speaking rapidly with a Spanish accent)*: Somebody fell down from—I don't know what floor. He fell from— through the glass, there's glass all around—I think he is dead . . .

DISPATCHER: Uhm . . . Excuse me?

CALLER: Someone fell through the atrium, and I don't think he is okay, I think he is dead, yes. He is near the bar.

DISPATCHER: Is he breathing?

CALLER: I don't know.

DISPATCHER: Sir! Is he breathing?! Could you check?! It's very important!

CALLER: Okay.

DISPATCHER: Please . . . this is very important!

CALLER: Hold on . . . I can't tell . . . He broke a bar stool. Just stepped in some foam. Sorry.

DISPATCHER: Please . . .

CALLER: No . . . He is definitely not okay.

DISPATCHER: Sir! Is . . . He . . . Breathing?!

CALLER: No. Not. He is dead.

DISPATCHER: Thank you. We'll send a unit . . .

Bill texts the recording to Gwen.

"What an opening! Get to work," she texts back immediately, adding the emoticon of an airplane.

"Not sure I am up to this. This is my friend's skull that cracked open."

"How do u know re: skull?"

"The 'foam' in the 911 call is not foam."

"Brains?"

"Brains."

Gwen texts back immediately: "Lean into it! I'll drive u to National. xo."

"I guess I'd fly to Miami International."

"Fort Lauderdale has reopened—just checked."

"Mopped up the blood and spackled the bullet holes   "

"The American spirit, Bill. We press on."

Gwen is right. This is starting to look like at least a story, maybe even a book.

Bill devotes January 8 to reading newspapers—every newspaper he can find—and brooding.

After dispensing with his usual two, Bill stumbles out to CVS and gets two more. By 2 P.M., he has read *The Washington Post, The New York Times, The Wall Street Journal,* and *The Financial Times.* Next, he turns to the pile of old *New Yorker*s, *Atlantic*s, and *New York Review of Books* on his coffee table.

That pile sucks him deep into its vortex, prompting him to desecrate the margins of these esteemed publications with little drawings of Donald Trump and scribbles declaring that "we are so fucked."

No question about it: Bill is seeing a convergence between East and West. Authoritarian strongmen are succeeding where proletarians had failed. They didn't unite, those proletarians of the world. The United Front against Franco and fascism was not a success. The prewar clusterfuck of Stalin, Hitler, Mussolini, Hirohito, and Franco was a more formidable, more pragmatic life form. It took an incompetent like Hitler to overreach and, in a fit of narcissism, blow it all. America had the opportunity to join that alliance, but didn't. Bill predicts that in exactly ten days, after the coronation, after January 20, 2017, we will become a part of something similar, a new kind of an international criminal conspiracy.

Bill would have benefited from a drink and would surely have poured himself one had he not forgotten to do so. Such are the perils of living alone. He continues to brood through January 9 and 10, allowing his thoughts to roam as they please.

There are three Russian Baltika beers in the refrigerator; he has no idea where they came from or how long ago. Indian dinners in the freezer are of uncertain age and provenance as well. There is no vodka, no gin, no whiskey of any sort. Fortuitously, there is a half-gallon bottle of gold-colored Appleton rum. Again, no way to know how it got there and when it got there. Bill doesn't like rum—Appleton tastes like perfume—but it's here, it has been through a still, and it suffices.

His thoughts during those three days of near-seclusion invariably return to the *Post*. His dismissal is different from those of his colleagues a few years ago. At that time, the paper was heading in the direction of the graveyard. Now, dripping with Amazon money, it's expanding, hiring. And the offices are new, Google-like.

They didn't fire William M. Katzenelenbogen because they had to. They fired William M. Katzenelenbogen because they wanted to. It sucks—all of it—but Bill feels little anger toward the *Post*. Granted, had he been given the courtesy of selecting the true cause for his termination, he would not have chosen "insubordination."

Using hard, objective metrics, his performance was never anything but fine:

- Attendance—exemplary.
- Ability to grasp complicated policy concepts—observed.
- All reporting calls—made.
- Punctuation—in place, as required.
- Deadlines—met, always.

His sin, his fatal flaw, was his inability to conceal that he hadn't given a shit about anything he had written in six years. Longer, actually. The precise moment of the onset of not-a-shit-giving is rarely visible to the sufferer. The evaluee's ability to bang out a yeomanly story may be unaffected by this condition, but when you feel nothing, there is nothing. Bill had become a news-room zombie, one of the typing dead.

The only thing the *Post* had on him had nothing to do with anything.

The bozos from WRC-TV Channel 4 showed him taking a deep nap at the Fairfax County Government Center while covering a hearing of the Board of Supervisors.

This wasn't an act of hostility on the part of the WRC crew— they had the camera sweep across the room, and there he was, head tilted back, mouth open, possibly snoring. They couldn't help letting the camera linger a bit, even look into his mouth for a moment. There was some light joshing back and forth by the news team that night; the bozos never figured out that he was from the *Post,* their colleague, or they wouldn't have done this to him. Journalists have professional courtesy; it's a fact.

Bill's sleeping patterns were erratic during his marriage (more on that later), but they were normalizing after separation (more on that later as well). He has no recollection of sleeping at that meeting, but he can demonstrate that dozing off didn't detract from the quality of his coverage of that or any other story.

Mostly, he is still hoping someone will tell him how, under which laws or which country, sleeping at a boring-as-fuck hearing constitutes insubordination. Punching an editor is insubordination. Napping at the Fairfax County Government Center is innocent, healthful even.

It's Bill's fault that it's now up to untested recruits to cover the gangs of suit-clad honest crooks and alt-right ideologues of the nascent administration. They will be on their own, kindergarteners in the minefield. You need decades of experience to cover conflicts of interest—there are no shortcuts. Even assuming the confluence of good work ethic and good fortune that produces great journalism, hasn't the rise of the soon-to-be President Donald exposed the limitations of significance of truth-telling?

It hasn't been traditional to ice reporters in America, but Bill sees no reason for this tradition to endure, just like there is no reason for anyone to believe that the people will notice when these little guardians of the public trust and social justice get shot out of the Washington sky. Their demise will be taken in stride. Reporter. Shot. Execution style. In the back of the head, face turned into a crater. To be expected. Happens all the time in Putin's Russia. We are catching up.

Not being employed at fifty-two, Bill accepts the overwhelming probability of spending the rest of his life trying to land low-paying gigs.

Perhaps there is a story in Zbig. Perhaps Bill is the right man for telling Zbig's story, assuming he can still write. It would be perfect for *The New Yorker*, but he doesn't know anyone there, and they rarely take stories from outsiders, and Bill is now most definitely an outsider.

He needs a bolus of money—now. A book advance is the answer—same as it was for Gwen. It's hard to imagine that any editor would be crazy enough to turn down a book about the spectacular demise of a South Florida plastic surgeon known as the Butt God of Miami Beach, but it's possible.

This would be a sympathetic portrait, of course, insidery, done with the right mixture of responsibility, respect, and, if appropriate, restraint. Humor, if any, would be dark, dry.

Bill's previous book idea crashed and burned. It involved the role of political philosophy in the design of clinical trials of cancer drugs. The idea was brilliant, argumentation airtight, but no editor had the cojones or vision to make the acquisition. Soon after that project crashed, Bill's agent said he would no longer take nonfiction projects on drug development. Fuck him!

With this Zbig thing, there could be multiple takers, a bidding war. He'd need to find another agent quickly, but that shouldn't be difficult. This thing has the makings of a book, a play, a movie, a musical, an opera even. DEATH OF THE BUTT GOD. It would be an investment in Bill's future, and certainly an investment in his past—the safest investment of all. This is magical thinking, perhaps, but it's either that or driving an Uber.

Actually, Uber is not an option. Bill doesn't own a vehicle and his driver's license has expired.

Gwen is expecting a call, no doubt, but a smattering of texts is all he has in him.

In Bill's past life, the *Post* would have picked up his travel expenses.

Post-*Post*, Bill needs to shell out his own cash. There will be no expense account on this trip. Bill will be playing for keeps.

He uses his own $398 to buy the ticket to Fort Lauderdale. But where can he stay? The Diplomat? The Grand Dux? The Fontainebleau? He is already past the point of no return on meeting his rent for February.

Bill—swallowing whatever pride he may still possess—takes the first step toward détente with his father. At 4:37 P.M., January 10, he makes a phone call, and Melsor's current wife, whom he has yet to meet, graciously invites him for a visit. Done.

Bill grasps the rough contours of his next project.

He knows about Zbig's getup—a Brunello Cucinelli suit made of something called Wales wool; $5,000ish. (A Brioni—$8,000 or thereabouts—would be better for the book proposal, but the truth is the truth.) Bill knows that Zbig's brains had spilled. He knows roughly where it happened. Having once been a police beat reporter, Bill has seen spilled brains on several occasions. They are spongy, light colored, bloodless, slimy like the soft underside of a bolete mushroom on a misty day.

Will he be able to pinpoint the cause of the fall? Will he be able to find the exact point of impact? The glass panels of the atrium ceiling were surely replaced within days. Will he be able to stand being there? That last one is an emotional question, and in Bill's life emotions have learned to wait.

Why is he investing his bottom dollar in a story about which he has no better clue than a casual passerby? The two men weren't particularly close in their middle age. Bill and Zbig hadn't seen each other in five years.

In his quest for insight, Bill obsessively listens to the audio file of the 911 call, clicking "Play" immediately after the recording stops running.

———

January 11 is cold enough to feel better about the future of the planet. Perhaps the polar caps aren't melting. Perhaps oceans will not rise. Perhaps we will not drown. Perhaps this Trump will not be so bad. Perhaps the bullet intended for you will fly by and hit someone else.

Bill squeezes his luggage—a scratched-up ancient Halliburton bag and an electric-blue bike messenger's bag—in the back of the Porsche and sits down.

"You look *so* uncomfortable, dear," says Gwen, and revs the engine.

Dear?

The Carrera Cabriolet looks more like Mockery than Remorse.

The roar of the engine makes conversation difficult, the speed makes it unnecessary.

"Are we dating, Gwen?"

"You are off to South Florida last time I checked. You don't need a romantic entanglement, not that this is the right time and place to consummate one. Reconsummate, I should say."

He is silent.

"Say something, Bill. What's on your mind?" she shouts over the engine.

"Marx!"

"Karl?!"

"Karl! The theory of alienation! Manuscripts of 1844! Economic and Philosophic!"

"Seems random!"

"Completely nonrandom! In early Marx, division of labor alienates the worker from the product of his work, from society, some other shit, and—finally—himself!"

"What does it have to do with us?!"

"It has to do with me, pardon my navel-gazing—and us by

34

extension, probably! I am realizing that the past few years at the *Post* left me alienated from something that used to be at the core of what I was! Storytelling!"

"Storytelling?! They had you doing shit work! You were programmed for alienation!"

"And it worked! I am not sure I can do this anymore! And if I can't, what am I?"

"*This* is a story, Bill! Tell it, dammit!"

At National, she stops the car, faces him with a smile, and takes off her glasses as an invitation for him to go in for a kiss, which he does.

"You saved my life, you know," she says, pulling back for a moment.

"And you mine, maybe."

"Has anyone told you you have a scratchy beard?"

"Never."

"And, you should know, I am scheduled to pop in for a one-day conference. NFL team owners . . . very hush-hush, about players beating their wives, so you don't know."

They kiss again.

"Did I say very hush-hush . . . Middle of the week . . . But I will have to get back same night, preexisting meeting I can't change."

"But would if you could?"

"I surely would . . . So, just time for dinner . . . In Florida . . ."

"Alas . . ."

"Alas . . . Where are you staying, by the way?"

"At my father's."

"The fraudster poet? Oh my . . ."

Bill opens the door, gets out, and grabs his bags.

"Keep me in the loop!" she shouts, and in a burst of unbridled speed leaves him on the departures curb.

3

INSPECTOR LUFTMENSCH

On the morning of January 11, as the Fort Lauderdale–bound plane taxies toward takeoff, Bill has no trouble tuning out the college students who seem to form a tight ring around him.

He wears a scratchy gray herringbone sport coat (Bill Blass), a pair of thoroughly weathered Carhartt jeans purchased in New England a decade earlier, and a pair of sock-free ancient Sperry Top-Siders.

The Top-Siders look like they might emit the sweet scent of the rotting flesh of a water buffalo slaughtered on a hot day, but thanks to systematic treatments with baking soda they are utterly odor-free. His Halliburton bag subtly pushes the limits of the definition of a carry-on. His bike messenger's bag is a monument to resourcefulness. It's made by a Swiss company called Freitag out of a tarp used on a European truck. You can find one of these bags at the Museum of Modern Art in New York.

Bill looks like the sort of professor you would want to smoke pot with, the sort who knows his shit, takes pride, and grades tough.

Bill pulls out his reporter's notebook and starts to summarize his theory of the case.

"Meaning" is the first word he commits to paper.

This word is given the place of honor atop a thin, narrow page.

What is said meaning?

He can only brainstorm, free-associate, philosophize.

Meticulously, down the length of the page, Bill draws a large question mark. It's cartoony to begin with, and it becomes more so as it grows thicker. Curly doodles make a home inside it.

Bill proceeds to sketch the outlines of the Dux. It's a twin-tower affair, South and North, a lot like the nearby Diplomat, but bigger, taller.

He draws a birdlike creature beneath the top of one of the towers: a soaring BASE jumper in a flying suit. The soaring BASE jumper needs birds to keep him company, and Bill draws the birds. Why is he—William M. Katzenelenbogen—flying south? What beckons him? Where is said "meaning"? Where is its hiding place?

Consuela Ramirez-Wronska, the latest Mrs. Zbig, didn't return Bill's calls. Presumably this means that she wouldn't cooperate with his investigation, if that is what it is.

Does Bill think it possible to investigate an occurrence that left him without a clue, to launch an open-ended, directionless, hypothesis-free, Bayesian search for the hidden? When you have no beginning, you aren't entitled to an end.

Suddenly, an idea flashes in Bill's skull. It is as cartoonish as the question mark—and Bill dutifully commits it to paper:

EXISTENTIALIST INVESTIGATIONS L.L.C.
William M. Katzenelenbogen, Inspector Luftmensch

Devoid of evidence, with no mandate, lacking credentials, un-burdened by clients, without even a tinge of funding, this is to be an investigation by instinct, experience, spirit. You would go from place to place to place and *feel.*

You, Sir William, have become a sleuth of air, a marathoner of the clouds, Inspector Luftmensch.

Only one person can bring you down, Sir William, and surely you know that you are heading directly into his domain.

Even if you would rather be any place but South Florida, you may not be immune to the feeling of infinite possibility manifest in the first exposure to sunlight that pierces the cab's windshield the instant you emerge from the shadow of structured parking at Fort Lauderdale–Hollywood International Airport. Even if you would rather be any-place-other-than, how can you not take note that this flash so completely captures the absence of cultural constipation? Has any place, any culture, so fully embraced the pursuit of pleasure with such small-*d* democratic small-*c* cate-chism? If you are an asshole, be an asshole. If you want a machine gun, get a machine gun. If you want to snort coke, snort coke. If you want to defraud your neighbor, defraud your neighbor. If you want to fuck a giraffe, arrangements can be made to enable you to fuck a giraffe. If you want to vote for him whose name is too painful to utter as coronation nears, vote for him whose name is too painful to utter as coronation nears. If you want to be a machine-gun-toting, coke-snorting, giraffe-fucking, neighbor-defrauding, Trump-supporting fascist ass-hole, *be* a machine-gun-toting, coke-snorting, giraffe-fucking, neighbor-defrauding, Trump-supporting fascist asshole.

Squinting, Bill reaches into his messenger's bag and puts on a well-worn black baseball cap with a big red *W* above the visor. He acquired it for those occasions when he has to blend in. If *The Post* didn't pay for it, it should have. Next, he puts on a pair of counterfeit Ray-Ban Wayfarers. Having thus prepared himself for the scorching sun, he thinks of the cold darkness of Moscow of his childhood. If absolute opposites attracted absolutely, Florida is where he is fated to end up.

Bill is in a black Lincoln driven by an elderly Cuban gentleman. As they wait for the drawbridge on Hallandale to come down, the driver complains about being unable to make a living. The Cielo Limo Service black cars are meant to be shared, he says, but the assholes at the curb gave him just one passenger and, after arguing explosively in Spanish, ordered him to move on. Translation: he is driving Bill all the way to Hollywood for the miserable sum of eleven dollars. The tip better be good.

Bill feels intense kinship with taxi drivers. Immigrants fall into four categories: those who drive taxis; those who once drove taxis; those who aspire to drive taxis; and those who fear that one day circumstances will force them to drive taxis. Of course, there are overlaps. Bill is an unambiguous Category Four immigrant. He is so empathetic that his Uber rating—awarded by drivers—is 5, the perfect score.

Years earlier, in Boston, Bill took a cab driven by a gentleman who identified himself as a former editor at Random House. He wasn't even an immigrant.

If the book thing crashes and burns, he will need to renew

his driver's license. Uber drivers told him that the company makes it easy to acquire a car, even if your credit is for shit.

It's possible that in the architect's initial sketches the twin towers of the Grand Dux billowed like sails. Alas, implementation created challenges.

Unless you are very, very good, concrete doesn't billow; neither does glass. The towers ended up acquiring the look of tall round-top structures, twin phalluses, the Twin Dicks of Hollywood, one pointing north, toward Fort Lauderdale, the other south, toward Sunny Isles.

Who would have thought that by enslaving light and space you build a dungeon? Usurping space and gulping air and sucking light, the atrium protects from storms that uproot palm trees, making a sport for those inside to watch seabirds crash into the glass. Do birds' eyes register surprise as their necks snap?

Bill looks up immediately, hoping to spot the glass panes shattered by his friend's body, staring foolishly into the midday sun. This effort to spot a pair of panes that aren't like the others produces darkness.

"Idiot," he says to himself. To see the point of impact, he will need to go up and look down.

Stretching from South Ocean Drive to the Atlantic, the atrium of the Grand Dux is so massive that no one notices anyone; no one can.

Even the indoor pool is entirely within view, displayed through the glass behind the registration desk.

A generation earlier, Morris Lapidus, the father of Miami modernism, designed a staircase to nowhere in the lobby of the Fontainebleau Hotel, a few miles south from the spot where Bill now stands. The purpose of that staircase was to allow ladies to display the magnificence of their dresses.

It isn't a travesty but a sign of the times that at the Grand Dux the display accentuates the undress. There are columns, but no walls. The place screams of sex; not godly twosomes, but threesomes, foursomes even, which means it is first and foremost about lonesome onesomes dimly illuminated by free PornHub vignettes playing softly on the iPad. It is about money, mostly, the sort that flows without regard for either sense or the Arabic number behind the dollar sign and, Bill presumes, brings no happiness. Perhaps people live like this in their dreams or for a few days a year.

This place is not an edgy performance art project funded by the now-endangered National Endowment for the Arts. It's glass, steel, concrete, self-sustaining, corporate. It's where the mainstream culture dwells.

The elevators—glass tubes with clear, domelike ceilings—hang on the ocean side of each tower.

Other passengers—a young woman and her two children—lean against the glass, exuding a sense of invincibility as the cabin speeds past the roof of the atrium. The woman, who is probably Gwen's age, looks away. She wears a gauzy coverall over an orange bikini and gold-colored flip-flops. She is occupying the very spot where Bill needs to be if he is to spot the panels Zbig's body broke on the way down.

In his ensemble of a threadbare but still scratchy jacket and other staples of the journalistic wardrobe, Bill might as well be a space traveler. Each party pretends that the other is invisible. It's 3 P.M.; the sun has long ago incinerated the swill of mist and salty air that makes men drunk, replacing it with the burning clarity of the day.

The phone goes off. A text from Gwen:

"Respiring? Ambulating?"

Bill ignores it for now; he will respond later.

He leans in the opposite direction, gravitating toward the elevator's steel door. It's solid. This is instinctive. Being in Florida—which for Bill has always presumed business—for more than three days gave him suicidal thoughts even before his life began to suck. There is death by water, death by fire, death by wild beasts, but the flavor of death he associates with Florida involves plunging from great heights. Perhaps this primal fear is fueling his fascination with Big Zbig's death. Didn't Zbig always do the things Bill feared?

Bill doesn't know how those death thoughts, those impulses, crawled into his skull when he first experienced that feeling a quarter century earlier. Is it technically a suicidal thought? Can such things be dismissed? Should Bill seek treatment? (The answer is probably yes, but how is Bill to know this?) Is it a warning? A premonition? Is it, God forbid, fate? Bill has no such thoughts anywhere else on the globe, not even in New York, where buildings are taller and where observation platforms abound.

The young woman steps off the elevator on the thirty-seventh floor.

Bill takes a pair of shaky steps toward the elevator's glass wall. He wants to see the point of impact—two panels that don't look like the others. He spots them immediately, and a minute later he is back in the lobby, staring at the exact place where Zbig's cranium released its spongy stuffing.

The point of impact is about fifty meters from the South Tower. The North Tower is one hundred meters away. This is the heart of the atrium, the area near the bar, near the oasis of potted palm trees. Was Zbig aiming for those? Was he aiming? Was he aimed?

Back in the atrium, he sets down his bags and touches the square of white terrazzo. Has anyone not seen crosses by the roadside, presumably at the spots where someone's loved one had been killed?

Some of these are adorned with plastic flowers, teddy bears, and other Grim Reaper bric-a-brac. Perhaps the dead come out and play with children's toys. We don't stop and bow at those shrines. We drive past. Should this be different? Perhaps Bill should make a shrine of it. Turn it into a monument to gravity, put down a votive candle, get incense going, incinerate photos of Marley and Vysotsky, invite Baryshnikov to improvise a solo on the subject of the boundary separating freedom from death.

Bill rests his palm lightly on the square, hoping for a flash of insight, a message from the netherworld or the world above, some remnant of the swill of salty air, morning mist, cloud and fog, surrender to rapture, the power to deploy exaltation as a mystical tool for changing the inflection of doom. It's a prayer of sorts.

"Gimme something, asshole," Bill says to his dead friend at the exact spot of the splintering of his cranium.

Nothing . . .

"Well, fuck you, dude. I'll fucking find out, like it or not. Motherfucker."

Bill picks up his bags and heads toward the revolving door just as a security guard begins to approach.

4

SVOLOCH'

Usually, family members have good reasons for missing a dozen years of each other's lives, and Bill's reasons for avoiding his father warrant respect.

Since neither Bill nor his father—Melsor Yakovlevich Katzenelenbogen—has missed contact with the other over such a long time, it would have been feasible for them to put off the reunion for another dozen years. This would constitute the path of least resistance.

Melsor lives less than a mile away from the Grand Dux. Had this been Boston, New York, or even Washington in August, Bill would have grabbed his bags and walked. But South Florida is a different kind of hot, and a scratchy Bill Blass jacket is not the thing you wear.

As he gets into the cab, the phone rings. Gwen again; he'll call her back in a bit. It seems she gives a shit, but why? Repaying the debt?

Gwen's falsehoods didn't start a war. She didn't reveal the

names of CIA operatives. But she did jot down a series of conversations that sounded like something out of *Franny and Zooey*. This resemblance tracked word for word through a long conversation. She claimed to have recorded this conversation at a meat market of a pool party for young professionals. Upon investigation by the *Post*'s ombudsman, another story included a passage that closely tracked *The Bonfire of the Vanities*.

After the first indications of the scandal went public, a prominent Republican lobbyist whose fly Gwen once famously reported to have seen wide open at the conclusion of a black-tie affair walked into the *Post* ombudsman's office, accompanied by an attorney and a paramour. The latter swore that she had, in fact, unzipped the fly in question for the purposes of performing a sexual act at a much later time that evening. It's difficult to prove the negative, but this was as close as one can get to establishing that during the black-tie event in question the fly that Gwen had described as undone was, in fact, not.

Remorse—the book's title was Bill's idea as well—was exactly what Bill envisioned, though it was produced without his participation and he is yet to get around to reading it.

Another text: "R u at ur father's yet"

"No"

"Prodigal son. Ha!"

"Yeah . . . Ha . . ."

"Courage . . ."

Two garbage containers positioned at odd angles block the ramp leading to the entrance of the building.

Brass letters on a white wall identify the place as "Château Sedan Neuve." The positioning of containers suggests that they are being used as a barricade in the Paris Commune sense of the word rather than as receptacles for construction rubbish.

This château is well fortified. There are the aforementioned barricades, there is a tall temporary construction fence, and there is a nearly identical permanent chain-link fence that seems to be protecting the building's structured parking.

Bill hands the driver ten dollars, grabs his Halliburton and bike messenger's bags, and asks to be dropped off in the midst of traffic on South Ocean Drive.

There is screeching of brakes behind the taxi, and the driver, a tough Nigerian, deals with this outpouring of rage by opening the window and slowly displaying the middle finger of his left hand. He stays in place even after Bill gets out of the car, prompting the asshole driver behind them to continue to blow the horn, evidently choosing surrender to road rage over changing lanes.

Bill, too, considers displaying his middle finger or fingers, but reconsiders after realizing that he is staring at a white Bentley convertible piloted by a scruffy-looking young man. It's possible that the driver is the youngest senior partner in the history of Cravath, Swaine & Moore LLP, and thus was able to purchase said $225,000 vehicle with legitimately earned money. More likely, the young man used funds obtained by means more traditional for South Florida, which would also increase the likelihood of his packing heat, possibly even silencer-modified heat. The convertible would afford the young man a clear shot. Seeing no measurable upside, Bill decides that it would be prudent to refrain from expressing his contempt to the honking asshole.

The barricade situation is frustrating. The building is unmistakably present, wedged between South Ocean Drive and the ocean. It has to be around twenty stories high, its shape vaguely reminiscent of a wave. But how is he to get there?

Bill had visited South Florida several times over the previous twelve years, always avoiding visiting his father. This bypassed the mitzvah of vodka drinking and the necessity of wooden conversation at dinner. Bill is perfectly capable of shooting vodka; around his father, it's safer to sip. And, of course, he sees no need for silent reliving of old resentments.

Bill has never seen this place before. Avoiding a visit to what passes for the ancestral home and meeting the lady who is technically his current stepmother are the biggest benefits of all.

Bill walks toward the twin containers, stops for a moment, and after ascertaining that no one is watching, out of habit, climbs up the container's built-in ladder and looks in. Even when things were good, even when they were very good, Bill amused himself by Dumpster-diving for modern classic furniture. Some of his best finds came from containers, and in Florida you have to be prepared for crazy shit.

These containers are empty. Since there is no active construction in sight, they are indeed being used as roadblocks, barricades.

The ramp to the building's lobby is clearly verboten.

As Bill ascends the forbidden ramp—the grand entrance—he has no difficulty imagining the place in the 1970s, as wealthy Floridians nonchalantly dropped the keys of their coral-colored Coupes De Ville into the waiting hands of valets. Both the bearers and the receivers of the keys were immigrants—the more- and less-fortunate brothers. What is valet parking but an exercise in humiliation? It has nothing to do with the parking of a car. Servitude is the principal commodity being served. Is there a better way for an immigrant to measure his station in life than by having a fellow immigrant slavishly bow?

As he walks up the ramp, Bill becomes painfully aware of the fact that Florida is bathing the street with entirely too much light. His *W* cap isn't useful. His inner eye seeks darkness, finding it in the dozen shiny black spots by the curb. On second look, Bill realizes that the black spots are actually garbage bags lined up one by one, next to a three-legged table with a green Formica top and wooden chairs, probably hundred-year-old Thonet, painted jolly canary yellow.

He walks up to one of the bags. A gaping rip in its side exposes its contents. Bill moves it lightly with his Top-Sider. A couple of shards of porcelain fall out on the pavement.

Picking up the larger of the shards, Bill sees that it's a fragment of a saucer—about a third of one. The stamp on the bottom reads "Made in Czechoslovakia." The saucer is bright orange, with white polka dots. Probably from the interwar years, a happy, goofy design, either unsuspecting of the shit to come or denying its inevitability. Bill can sympathize with refusing to acknowledge the inevitable. This is in part due to the fact that today is January 11, and the passing of the scepter is nine days away.

Knowledge has a way of dancing into Bill's arms and staying forever trapped. He doesn't know why. You can't think about all your troubles all of the time, and one way to mitigate toxicity is to look at the stuff in front of you, grazing on words, shapes, concepts, chewing the brain cud.

What harm is there in knowing a lot about dogs, cars, horses, economic policy, and real estate? Bill knows many things entirely too well and is enthusiastic about most of them. Design is one of those things. He knows chairs especially well. Unable to walk past a construction Dumpster without peeking in, he has gathered many a roomful of remarkable furniture.

Bill's apartment—the modest place which he will be unable to afford past February 1—is indeed, as Gwen noted, worthy of a profile in *Dwell*. Running past a Dumpster a few years earlier, he spotted the lower part of what was surely a Harry Bertoia Diamond Chair, and indeed it was. The chair was wearing a pristine Knoll white cover.

On another occasion, he noticed the back of a George Nelson daybed sending an SOS from a pile of rubble. Bill came to its rescue. Then, in the alley behind his apartment, someone left a Saarinen Womb Chair, perfectly orange and in need of nothing more than cleaning. A few weeks later, an Alvar Aalto Chair 44 showed up on a curb in Cleveland Park. A Danish dining table—designed by Hans Wegner, made by Getama—was cluelessly priced at a yard sale, and a half-dozen stackable Eames fiberglass side-shell chairs in vibrant pastels awaited him in a massive garbage pile behind Duke Ellington High School of the Arts, in Georgetown. The same pile yielded three large steel bookcases and a battleship-gray steel desk.

The apartment is nice—it will hurt to lose it. What would he do with his stuff if he were to decamp for he-knows-not-where?

Last time he looked, his checking account balance was $1,219.37. His savings account was at $7.49, and when he left Washington he had exactly $200 in his pocket. (Now it's $177.) He has no credit card—just a debit card, for the ATMs, not for borrowing. His *Post* expenses went on his *Post* card. He has it still, but, well . . .

His rent, which will come due in less than a month, is $1,750. This project—the book—is his only plan.

You might ask why Bill finds himself flat-ass broke at the end of an illustrious career with one of the nation's premier newspapers. The answer is: refine the question. He is not *flat* broke. He still has $1,403.86 when you sum up his checking and savings accounts and cash on hand. It's not $14,038.60, and it's not $140,386.00, because of an episode of marital unpleasantness.

He was married once, and is technically married still, to a woman he first met at the Hillel Jewish student organization at Duke.

She was from Chicago, he from Moscow by way of Washington suburbs. In those days, Friday night services at the Duke Hillel concluded with dancing. The Jews of the New York/Miami vortex turned on the Hillel community–owned boom box and discoed into the night. Some surrendered their worldly names, becoming Disco Dave, Disco Rick, Disco Kevin, Disco Nina, Disco Deb, Disco Davia, etc.

Lena didn't disco. Bill didn't disco. She had an acerbic sense of humor, which Bill found attractive. She had a Russian name, but was American through and through—the best of both worlds. She could talk about shit that mattered, and who could possibly object to the notion that the ability to discuss shit that matters is an important element in any relationship, especially any relationship that involves Bill?

After three years at Duke, he was starved for conversation. It was fated, *bashert*—call the caterer, you might say. Yet, Bill was surprised by the what-have-I-done feeling the first time she spent the night in his room. Zbig slept in a women's dorm on the West Campus that night and on many other nights.

The lovers broke up with what sounded like a sigh of relief. After graduation, Lena went off to law school at UChicago, and Bill took a bus to Washington, to become a writer, or a fighter for justice, or something in between.

They met again a decade later, starting an on-and-off relationship, which was unambiguously in the off phase when he drunkenly fell into bed with Gwen. It flipped back to on, then—almost immediately after a low-key in-the-rabbi's-office marriage ceremony—it flipped back to off.

Their incompatibility could be explained in a geometric manner, by their relationship to the concept of injustice. Awake, Bill had just one stance: warrior. To him, many things were akin to fascism. Bring it on, the bigger the better! Onward, Comrades, fight to the last drop of blood, victory will be ours!

Lena, by contrast, collected injustices, wallowed in them, bouncing out of a law firm, relegated to a life of underpaid unhappiness in the government, which resulted in an Equal Employment Opportunity action against her former employer, the Equal Employment Opportunity Commission. After much unfairness at EEOC, Lena was driven to a nonprofit, where money was tight and battles for a place at the trough especially vicious.

A one-bedroom apartment affords few hiding places, and Lena's nightly accounts of the humiliations she had experienced at work made for mediocre foreplay. The disappearance of sex brought on many accusations, all of them leveled against Bill. "Yes, Lena," Bill wanted to say a few months into the marriage, "you are right: I don't appreciate you. I don't remember whether I ever did or why," but, being a good boy, he said nothing of the sort.

Instead, he made a wholehearted effort to get in touch with his softer side, to find it within his psyche, along with that thing called empathy. This was a quixotic quest, which required much assistance from trained professionals. During this time, Bill's savings were depleted, mostly to pay for shrinks—his and hers—and lawyers in her long-pending and ultimately unsuccessful EEO complaint against EEOC.

To divorce, he borrowed against his modest 401(k) account, paying substantial penalties, but what the fuck? You do what you have to. They did get as far as an excellently worded separation agreement. The final divorce has been pending for a year now; it was just a matter of scheduling a hearing and shelling out the final installment of a few grand.

Why is Bill here, in Florida, poking black garbage bags by the curb, grazing on another person's misfortune? Surely he understands that this is not a trash pickup. Idiot, couldn't he recognize an eviction? Has he not seen evictions before, the "packing," which involves throwing everything in trash bags, breaking whatever breaks, the removal of belongings to the curb, the slowing down of traffic as passersby seek to vulture on another's misfortune? The stopping cars, the vanishing chairs, sofa stuffing wet from rain. Does Bill not recognize that his turn will soon come? Maybe he does. Perhaps this is why he lingers over the black bags.

Were it not for the intense pain of impact on his back, thoughts of this sort would have continued racing through Bill's mind.

Bill looks over his left shoulder to see what could have hit him.

He looks up just in time to step out of the way of a tiny woman—shorter than five feet, stooped, emaciated, cachexic perhaps, wearing a white nightshirt, a pink bathrobe, and fuzzy Carolina blue slippers—aiming to whack him one more time across the back with a curved aluminum cane.

She got him once as he stood pondering the deeper meaning of her black plastic bags. *"Fashist!"* she screams as her cane lands on the black plastic bag instead of squarely across Bill's back.

The impact crushes more pieces of porcelain.

"Svoloch'!" the woman shouts even louder as the porcelain, her family's onetime treasure, absorbs the force of the blow.

She lifts the cane and hits the bag again, repeating the words in succession, reminiscent of the rhythm of a beating heart.

Fashisty, svolochi, svolochi, fashisty, fashisty, svolochi, svolochi, fashisty . . .

Now oblivious to Bill, she hits the bag, and hits, and hits it again as contents shatter and crumble.

Jesus, that word: *Svoloch'*.

At this point, dear reader, please consider yourself beseeched to learn the word *svoloch'*, which roughly, very roughly, translates as vermin, or lowlife, or scum, or maybe swine, or maybe, with stretching, a whore. A dozen years have passed since the last time Bill heard that word.

It comes from the Russian word *volok*, the making of felt, fibers condensing, pressing together, haphazard like hair that mats beneath a dog's ear, uncombed, uncombable.

Svoloch' is what we become when our lives are deprived of what makes us strand-like, individual, noble, like the pursuit of truth, beauty, justice. *Svoloch'* is the making of life into felt, the turning of individual strands into filthy uniform matter.

What can Bill do but turn around and walk away at a brisk pace, leaving the old woman alone, crushing the *svoloch*ness and fascism in her bags by the curb?

5

REFUSENIK

Retreating rapidly to South Ocean Drive, Bill follows the construction fence to its northernmost corner.

He turns right, and, indeed, encounters a gate. It looks more like a checkpoint at the gates of Fort Meade, the federal government's cyber-spying outpost in rural Maryland, than an entrance to a civilian facility. Two men sit in a booth next to the gate. One appears to be Hispanic, the other Slavic.

Bill raises two fingers of his right hand to his temple. This is a quasi-military salute he seems to have more or less spontaneously developed, a gesture he uses too often. He doesn't like giving out his name; instead, he keeps moving, daring the rent-a-cops to stop him, which they do not. He passes through the gate at 5:37 P.M.

"*Arbeit Macht Frei,*" he says out loud as the gate opens. Work will set you free. Those clever Nazis put this saying on the gates of death camps. It's a private joke between Bill and himself. He says it at many gates. When you live alone you learn to amuse yourself.

Bill turns right, stepping into the structured parking lot, where he wastes a few minutes analyzing the car population.

Using his reporter's notepad—a thin pad that fits nicely into a back pocket—he sets up a table to organize the data, entering the number of Lexuses (17), BMWs (12), Mercedes (9), Audis (1), Cadillacs (1), Porsches (0), Jaguars (1), and Range Rovers (2). Even without Porsches, the place looks like the microcosm of the parking lot of the Washington Hebrew Congregation.

Of the forty-four vehicles Bill catalogues, twenty-nine display bumper stickers declaring: "TRUMP: Make America Great Again!"

These stickers had been on the bumpers for months—perhaps for a year or more. They had to be attached at the time when the long-shot Republican presidential contender slandered Mexicans, pledged to bar the doors for Muslim immigrants, and, with great creativity and determination, searched for new ways to piss off women, people of every color, the media, veterans of foreign wars, the handicapped, the Jews.

It stands to reason, subtly, weirdly, that a high-rise almost certainly dominated by immigrants would be a bastion of Trump's brand of xenophobia. Where is it written that people must love their own kind?

It's equally noteworthy that these fine vehicles are parked next to columns that tell stories of neglect and water damage. The garage ceiling is chipping as well, exposing rusted steel armature. With concrete crumbling away from rusting rebar, this château has the look of a Soviet-style perpetual construction project, a kind of place where nothing will be completed and nothing can be. In settings like this one you smell the incineration of millions of dollars.

Who are the inhabitants of the Château? Are these Russians, people of his parents' generation?

Let's say you come to America in your midforties and retire in your midseventies. For the first few years, you scrape, and then, if you are lucky, the stream of money normalizes, but what does it take to make it gush like a busted fire hydrant?

Fraud is always the answer, and Medicare the target of choice. Medicaid, too, can be lucrative. Being litigious works. Medical malpractice and employment discrimination suits are fine. To arrive at Château Sedan Neuve by age seventy-five, you need a good angle, one that may entail consumption of large volumes of blood. These folks might have earned incomes that placed them in the top second or third percentile for all Americans, but for us immigrants they are in the 99.9999th. With February rent due, Bill is on the opposite end of this distribution: the 0.0001st—the edge.

After concluding the car survey, Bill steps into what appears to be the entrance to the building. Again, he isn't challenged. The door stands wide open. Next to the elevator, he spots a lime green chair, very '70s funk. Not exactly his sort of thing, but he likes it enough to flip it over and consider the label. No surprise: designed by Milo Baughman, working for Thayer Coggin—nice. He sets it back down by the elevator door.

Not quite ready to face the inevitability of seeing his father, Bill delays pushing the eighteenth-floor button and instead pushes "L."

His back is starting to stiffen—the old woman got him

squarely across the spine. More than that, the crook of the cane landed on his shoulder blade. Three Advils would be indicated, but Bill's curiosity triumphs over pain. He wants to see more of the Château, perhaps even figure out who designed it forty or so years ago.

Two sawhorses, police tape, a "Do Not Enter" sign in English, and a *"Vkhod Strogo Vospreshchen"* (Entrance Strictly Forbidden) sign in Russian greet him in the lobby. Bill isn't deterred.

The lobby floor is marble, three or four tones of stunning taupe-to-brown stone, as elaborate as the Moscow Metro of his memory, except the dominant design here is not hammers, sickles, and heroic workers, peasants, and soldiers, but rather oversized paisleys, six-foot paisleys in shades that cascade upward, from lighter to darker. These waves of marble are intended to be reflected in the mirrored walls.

Roughly half of the mirrors are still here. Others grew destabilized by moisture and fell to the floor. Shards of thick glass are left in place.

In the center of what had once been the suspended ceiling, a smoky-glass chandelier remains pristine despite the many streams of water that passed through it. Its arms are oblong, ominous, biomorphic, like formerly vital organs of a frozen cadaver. "Venetian glass," Bill diagnoses.

Bill wanders deeper into the belly of the Château, realizing to his surprise that he is now walking through a puddle of clear water that reaches to his ankles. It appears that water pouring into this lobby is not an anomalous event, but a fact of life. The panels of suspended ceiling are gone, as are many of the interior walls.

Subtractions add to the magnificence of this set.

Behind a partition, Bill stumbles across a stack of water-stained sections of a sofa. The sections have that certain 1970s playfulness, which is to say they are just the right kind of porny, the enduring form of porny; it's Thayer Coggin.

Milo Baughman was the inventor of the sectional sofa, and Thayer Coggin produced it. No need to flip over the pieces. There is never just one Thayer Coggin in the interior, there has to be a flock, and stirring up mold is never a good thing.

Bill snaps a few pictures with his phone and shoots three of them to Gwen.

Behind another partition, he finds stacks of chrome Thayer Coggin chairs with the same green vinyl he had seen on the chair by the elevator. There are at least eight stacks, twenty chairs each. In New York, this would have the street value of $36,000; in tight-assed Washington, maybe $18,000.

Here in Hollywood, Florida, these chairs will end up in trash containers, assuming someone gets around to clearing the rubble. Bill toys with the idea of salvaging the pieces, but (a) doesn't have the cash to ship them home, (b) has no way to sell them for what they are worth, and (c) a businessman he is not. His interest in design is pure—for its own sake—which oddly makes this find both less and more useful.

Eight square Thayer Coggin tables suffering from various levels of delamination are strewn about in no particular pattern. The ones lacking legs are either leaning at perfect forty-five-degree angles or are flipped upside down in the puddle beneath.

In a corner, Bill spots at least a dozen objects that are vaguely reminiscent of birdcages. Recognition is immediate: Warren

Platner chairs in Knoll orange fabric, white with mold. The Platner tables are in a different pile. For a serious, knowledge-able collector of modern furniture, this is the equivalent of the lost ark.

He is a witness to an epic disaster. A waterlogged, crumbling building on this stretch of the Gold Coast is as incongruous as an automobile graveyard in Midtown Manhattan. And another thing: this crumbling château is clearly a landmark of Miami Modern architecture.

"Holy shit; is there a war out there?" Gwen texts back.

"No, but this place is probably designed by Morris Lapidus."

There is silence on the other end—long enough to enable Gwen to Google Lapidus.

"THE Morris Lapidus?"

"There's but 1."

Either that or it was someone who was riffing on Lapidus so shamelessly that he might as well be Lapidus. Lapidus dilapi-dated. Lapidus dilapidized. Lapidus with a stick up his assidus. Realizing that he is becoming punchy—badly in need of a glass of vodka—is all Bill needs to know he's finally ready to ring his father's doorbell.

He wades back to the elevator, breathes in, and presses the eighteenth-floor button.

Château Sedan Neuve is not so much French as it is Frenchie. Bill has never been to France, never got around to going, didn't have the time or money, even at the apex of his career, but of course he knows that nothing in France looks anything like this.

In the elevator, Bill notices a leaflet attached with thick packing tape to the Formica wall.

No, "leaflet" is not the right word.

French is a better language to use in the setting of this building and this elevator, making the word *pasquille* particularly apt.

Paskvil', the Russian derivative of the French *pasquille*, is better still.

Make Château Great Again!
We need New Board Lidership!

On December 31 your purse and wallet becomed $28,000 liter to pay for "misselenius" projects!

Triumverat of <u>Mental Lilliputs</u> on Condo Board, which take command from notorious Evil Dwarf put millions of YOUR DOLLARS in THEIR pockets!

Evil Dwarf has two Members in his pocket!

As YOUR property become unsailable, THEY get Lexuses!

- Don't behave yourselfs like Sheeps!
- Don't behave yourselfs like Blinds!
- Don't behave yourselfs like Backless Slaves!
- Sign Petishn!
- WRITE FLORIDA GOVERNOR RIK SKOT!

Don't vote for Old Board!

Three of five Members—collect SPECIAL ASESMENTS for "misselenius" reconstruction and not doing reconstruction and instead accelerate temp of **DeSTRUCTION**!

Triumverat's Next Dimolition: North Pool Deck and balkonys, which was inspected 7 years ago and those that need be repeired were. (All statements made above can be proved by documents.)

You will find pletora of open contracts made by Board where works are not define—and not deadline! Big (multimillion!) constructions (destructions) begin as "changeoforders." They have no permits and are now on changeoforder 27rd to **DESTROY** your balkonys.

STOP THEM DESTROYING OUR PROPERTYS AND OUR LIVES!

Sencirily,
Concerned Property Owners of Château Sedan Neuve

Open Your Eyes!

Bill rolls his eyes at the grand choice of words in the *paskvil'*. *Triumverat* . . . Evil Dwarf . . . Mental Lilliputs . . .

The *paskvil'* is so ripe with venom, it dares you to place a glass bowl beneath it. The toxin can be rushed to a laboratory, compounded, tried in rats, and, finally, tested in the clinic. It can be stood on its head, turned therapeutic—and, at a price of $16,000 a dose, make someone rich, perhaps even Bill, albeit not soon enough.

Bill feels blessed not to know the facts that would have made the *paskvil'* acquire context, and, through the act of bloodsucking, come to life, lose poetry, become prosaic. That's the thing about a proper *paskvil'*: it's always better without context, as an abstraction; if you want an axiom in life, this is it.

As the elevator struggles on its heavenward climb, Bill stares at the *paskvil'*, rapidly losing hope that the cables pulling the flying jalopy would pop, trapping him in the shaft for days or weeks, thus liberating him from reaching the destination, the eighteenth floor, the penthouse apartment of his father, Melsor Yakovlevich Katzenelenbogen.

Proximity to his father is making Bill remember that America was and perhaps still is the land of opportunity.

A little more consumer math: before he paid for the tickets and left Washington, Bill had $1,420 in his checking account and in cash, a figure representing his net worth.

Imagine a scenario where Bill dies. Assuming selection of the Costco "In God's Care" casket, which costs $1,299.99, how much money can Bill spend between the time of his departure from Washington and his departure for life everlasting without his net worth going into the red? (Assume that burial plots are free and body handling and transportation expenses are zero.) The answer is brutal: less than his February rent.

This is a slow elevator.

The Château's eighteenth floor is actually its seventeenth. In a numerology win-win worthy of Henry Kissinger, the thirteenth floor is skipped, and the eighteenth—symbolic of the Hebrew letter *hay*, the thing that looks like a dog with a severed front paw looking for the left margin of the page, and which stands for life—added. This observation confirms his suspicion that, notwithstanding all the Frogginess in the world, things Hebrew matter at the Château. And missing thirteen is a bow to Christians, if any.

Bill is hoping that the hallway will last forever. He notes the horizontal, six-foot-long, paisley-shaped ornaments inserted between apartment doors. The hallway is done in vomit-inducing peach. Bill is certain that the original color of these body-bag-sized paisleys had to be purple, and that the walls on which they were mounted had to be muted green, the color you get when you cross turquoise with avocado, if such hybrids are possible.

He pulls a quarter out of his pocket, inserts its edge into a crack in the peach paint, and presses. The piece of paint that chips off is larger and more noticeable than Bill hoped for, but it does reveal that in its glory days the paisley had indeed been purple and the walls green, or something like it. Morris Lapidus, the guy Bill now believes to have been the Château's architect, was paying homage to the colors that made South Florida great.

Bill congratulates himself with a modified version of a touchdown victory, a little dance, and would anyone who had been in a situation such as his—seeing the father you haven't seen since the trial twelve years earlier and for the first time actually meeting your father's wife of eight years whom you have seen only on Facebook feel so smug as to condemn Bill for procrastinating? Of course, he needs a drink, of course, he needs three Advils, but he also realizes that getting these someplace else—anyplace else—would be a safer, more rational thing to do.

Finally, Bill reaches the castle in the sky and knocks on the door inscribed with his family name.

6

WILLIAM

"Zakhodi Ilyusha, dobro pozhalovat'," says Nella, opening the door. [Come in, Ilyusha, welcome.]

William M. Katzenelenbogen, a reporter whose byline had graced *The Washington Post* for many years and was not unfamiliar to journalism prize juries, is actually neither William nor Bill.

William is his second first name. His first first—given to him in Moscow by his parents in 1965—was Ilya. He added *W* in the front and *M* in the back after coming to the U.S. in 1975, as in W-Ilya-M, in an effort to become more American.

Deferring to Bill's preferences, we will continue to call him Bill, using variations of his first first name, Ilya or Ilyusha, only in situations where these variations are invoked by others.

If Facebook is to be believed, Nella is seventy-three, a decade younger than Bill's father. In the flesh, she is even more slight than Bill imagined, her facial features angular, her hair solid black. She wears a light blue tunic and sandals. It's a look that could be classified as beach bohemian.

Nella is the second stepmother on Bill's life journey. There was no occasion for them to have met. His mother died, and his first stepmother was a neighbor who simply moved in and moved out—eight months, presumably with nothing. What was her name? Bill knows nothing about Nella, either. The only tidbit: she and Melsor stepped off a cruise ship in the Florida Keys and signed papers at a tropical courthouse. For all Bill knows, the lovers met on the same cruise.

How is Bill to greet her? A hug? An air kiss? A handshake? Bill opts for nothing.

She glances at the Halliburton and the bike messenger's bags he sets down in the corner. She assesses his luggage in the same surreptitious sort of way in which one glances at someone else's bank statement.

Clearly, his luggage fails to meet with her approval.

"*Spasibo,*" he stammers woodenly. [Thank you.]

"*Nezachto,*" Nella responds in kind. [You are welcome.]

"You wouldn't happen to have Advil or something like it?"

"Two?"

"Three."

"Big dose. Someone hitted you?"

"I saw an eviction. An old woman, presumably with dementia, hit me across the back with her cane."

"You are guilty yourself. In Florida, you should watch out, look over your shoulders."

"What was her name?"

"Roza Kisel'. She was from Nevada."

"Did she run out of money?"

"She is too crazy to know to pay special assessments. They foreclosured her, so to say."

"What happens to her next?"

"*Dzhuyka* sends person from mental health. They come to take them away for a few days. Then they let them go almost every time."

Bill remembers the word *Dzhuyka*. It's Russian-English for Jewish organizations that provide all manner of social services. These can include the Jewish Council for the Elderly, Jewish Family Services, Jewish Community This & That. The word *Dzhuyka* comes from the word *Dzhu*. Makes sense: *Dzhuz* go to *Dzhuyki* to get help.

"Sad."

"What do you expect? This is *luxury* apartment. Only one high-rise in Hollywood is closer to beach—have you seen Aquarius? It's practically *in* water."

"She may still have money to keep living there; right?"

"Maybe. But too late, so to say. *Dzhuyka* will try to put her in crazy house. They have special wan."

"Special wan?"

"Yes, wan—microbus, with driver, like ambulette."

Will *Dzhuyka* send wan with driver for Bill, a quasi-*Dzhu*, a proto-*Dzhu*, with the blood of Armenians and Russians mixed into the cauldron, when the time comes for him to wander away from his garbage bags?

Melsor had once been a poet. Perhaps he is still. He was a refusenik, too. His photo—wearing a pair of too-large Sophia Loren glasses and a Peruvian alpaca sweater given to him by visiting Americans—was blown up to poster size and displayed at vigils across Sixteenth Street NW from the Soviet embassy in Washington. It's an icon of the Soviet Jewry movement.

If you happen to know anyone who had been involved in the Union of Councils for Soviet Jews or Student Struggle for Soviet

Jewry, ask them whether they remember Melsor Katzenelenbogen.

Some people thought there were two of them, Melsor-pre-emigration and Melsor-the-American.

The Moscow Melsor was an expert in the silver age of Russian poetry: Akhmatova, Tsvetaeva, Mandelstam, Blok, Gumilyov. He wrote poetry, too. It was derivative, but it seemed daring at the time.

For five years, as Melsor sat in refusal in Moscow, his songs of freedom were being translated into English by comparative lit majors at some of America's finest colleges. Set to music, they were performed at youth group meetings in synagogue basements. What's better than a song for covering up an awkward rhyme?

In those days, young American Jews had long hair, cared passionately about Father and Son Guthrie, and guitars were used.

In 1978, at age forty-four, Melsor busted out of the tyrannical state of his birth. His blond, Slavic-looking wife and equally blond son came with him.

Melsor-the-American first became a poet laureate of the Jewish emigration movement. He was sent on a victory tour of Jewish community centers—the *Dzhuyka* Tour—where he recited the cycle of poems he wrote in Moscow. The cycle was titled *Songs About Freedom*. Not *Songs of Freedom*, but *Songs About Freedom*. The idea was to imagine freedom prior to attaining it.

America greeted Melsor with betrayal and woe.

He thought he had a government job lined up, but he didn't interview well and the bureaucrats at the Voice of America, Radio Liberty, and *America Illustrated* magazine—the three best troughs for literary immigrants—apparently recognized in him a perpetual troublemaker, an employment discrimination lawsuit waiting to happen. All three were government agencies, so the pay and benefits were superb.

The Voice wouldn't give Melsor an interview. His Moscow acquaintance, Boris Goldfarb, a poet, was ensconced at the Voice, working as a journalist. Clearly, Goldfarb was in a position to make key introductions, but he was doing nothing of the sort. Infuriated, Melsor handwrote an open letter in which he called Goldfarb a *poeticheskoye nichtozhestvo,* a poetic non-entity.

The open letter had a title: "*Prisposoblenchestvo,*" which translates literally as adaptation to surroundings, but means sucking up to Americans. "*Prisposoblenchestvo*" was submitted to a New York–based Russian-language newspaper, *Novoye Russkoye Slovo,* which failed to publish it. Bill was strong-armed into preparing the English-language version for submission to *The Washington Post* and *The New York Times,* but these news outlets were deprived of the opportunity to consider the piece, because Bill deposited the envelopes into a garbage can instead of a U.S. Postal Service box.

As an adult, Bill met Goldfarb a few times in Washington and—just as he suspected—found him to be the sort of old guy you can drink vodka with. Mostly, Bill appreciated the depth of compassion with which Goldfarb asked, "How is your father?"

Melsor lived hand to mouth, editing, writing, adjuncting, teaching courses and workshops until there was no one left to teach. Bill escaped to college and went on to become a reporter, and his parents moved from the Washington suburbs to New York. Then a catastrophe struck: Melsor's wife, Bill's mother, Rita, was diagnosed with breast cancer. Not a small lesion you zap out and go, but an aggressive disease that needed an aggressive doctor. Melsor challenged the disease as though it was Bolshevism. Rita was fatalistic. Melsor waged war. Bill, by then living elsewhere, was unable to do more than provide information and mutter "Oh shit" when it was ignored.

Some men lose their bearings in the face of death. Not Melsor. Loss made him soar. He got into business, providing transportation for the sick, predominantly Russian-speaking Brooklynites. In a matter of months after Rita's death, he emerged as an owner of a fleet of "ambulettes," vans defined as "invalid carriages" in New York Medicaid regs. The business required maintaining ties with doctors, whom Melsor either knew or found ways to court. It was about connections, an exercise of communication skills, making reality conform to his will.

Last time Bill and Melsor saw each other, the elder Katzenelenbogen stood trial at Kings County Supreme Court, accused of Medicaid fraud.

After their falling-out, Bill didn't give his father much thought. The two men ended up on opposite sides of the law, and—perhaps more importantly—on opposite sides of the boundary between the world of real things and the territory the elder Katzenelenbogen called home. Since no words were spoken between them during that dozen years, Bill has no preconceptions of what turn their South Florida reunion might take. Perhaps his father will give him the cold shoulder, a reasonable possibility since he isn't known to possess a warm one.

Perhaps he will, again, accuse him of betrayal. Is it not to be expected that sons hold on to the suitcases their fathers stuff with fraudulently obtained cash? Is it not to be expected that sons commit obstruction of justice and money laundering to honor family ties?

———

Bill hears crackling sounds emanating from the apartment's hallway.

Of course, Melsor would need to complete watching a Fox News segment or something equally important before opening the door and greeting the son who made a reluctant first overture toward an uneasy truce.

"*Kak on?*" asks Bill in Russian. [How is he?]

"*Krutit dela, krutit,*" Nella responds with a classic Russian-woman sigh. [He is cranking business, cranking.]

Bill knows enough to fear this prospect. With the elder Katzenelenbogen focused on business, someone is sure to get fleeced, someone is sure to get indicted. The latter someone may very well be Mr. Katzenelenbogen himself.

While he knows of no deaths, given the sinister nature of the windmills his father has selected for tilting at, one of those could easily occur.

"*A kak zdorov'ye?*" [How is his health?]

"*Kak-kak, kak u byka. Kazhdoye utro po pyat'desyat raz otzhimay-etsya.*" [Like a bull. Does fifty push-ups every morning.]

"*A zdes' on?*" asks Bill. [Is he here?]

"*Zdes', zdes', ratsiyu slushayet. Seychas doslushayet i vyydet.*" [Yes, he is here, listening to a radio. He'll finish it and come out.]

Her choice of the word "*ratsiya*" strikes Bill as curious. A *ratsiya* is a two-way radio, a delicate piece of technology, the sort used by Cold War spies.

Bill follows Nella to the kitchen, then wanders out to the great room.

The view is breathtaking—he can see the contours of the South Florida coast all the way to South Beach. The brightness he takes for granted outdoors is stunning indoors. His gaze follows six pelicans flying within a few feet of the balcony.

Clearly, Melsor Yakovlevich Katzenelenbogen has found someone to hold on to the cash-filled suitcase or suitcases. He landed on his feet, and this may be something to be proud of.

"Letat' zdes' khochetsya; pravda?" says Nella. [One wants to fly here; yes?]

"Da," Bill responds. [Indeed.]

After contemplating the view, Bill notices a moving scaffolding cradle suspended on thick steel wire ropes next to the balcony. It's the sort of gizmo you see dangling from steel beams mounted from the roof.

"What is this about?" he asks Nella.

"They try to frighten him."

"Who is? With what? Over what?"

"BOD, who else?"

"What's BOD?"

"Board of directors, condo board. They hang *lyul'ka* to send him message: shut up or we knock down your balcony. He gets them angry."

"Lyul'ka" is the Russian word for a cradle, a scaffolding cradle.

"Is that legal?"

It is not lost on Bill that he has seemingly stumbled into a vaudevillian act. The speech pattern: one character naïvely asks questions; the other responds with worldly wisdom, pointing out the obvious.

"What's not legal?"

"What they are doing."

"Listen yourself to what you say. We live in Florida. Understand? Flo-ri-da."

"Was that his leaflet in the elevator? The one with the Evil Dwarf and two members in the pocket?"

"What you think?"

As his familiarity with the patterns of Russian English—call it Runglish, Englussian, or Englishish—returns, Bill takes this as a yes. He doesn't envy that condo board. He doesn't envy anyone who has at any point tangled with his father.

Nella sits down in an uncomfortable-looking, translucent chair in front of the window.

"Look at how she jumps," she says in English, pointing at the expanse of blue and a moving white stripe in its center. "How beautiful . . ."

Who is this "she"? Why is she "jumping"? What is she referring to?

Bill looks out the window. The "she" in question could be that speedboat, a massive, roaring one at that, leaping from one cresting wave to another.

"You are talking about that boat?" he asks, also in English, just to be sure. "No one else is jumping?"

Nella is absorbed in following the speedboat and its white wake. She nods.

To be sure, Bill is at the top of the list of people he doesn't envy. Were this list not limited to the living, his mother would merit the topmost position.

Bill continues to look around. A funky 1970s Sputnik lamp, like a UFO transporting little green space travelers, hangs in the foyer, looking like a lost shard of the magnificent light fixture on the ceiling of Eisenhower Theater at the Kennedy Center. The thing is so perfect for the space that it has to have been hand-picked by the architect.

The furniture, however, would have made Lapidus vomit.

Milo Baughman would slit his wrists. Warren Plattner would self-immolate. It's white and leathery—a big, shiny sectional so squeaky that you can hear it from across the room. This is not Herman Miller. This is not Knoll, definitely not the sort of thing Bill rescued from garbage containers and is now set to lose. Perhaps he should have moved the stuff to a storage locker before leaving for Florida. Maybe he still could, on return to D.C.

The sectional and other stuff in the apartment are a mixture of things emanating from China, Turkey, and, to a lesser extent, Israel, claiming to be based on European design, and catering to Russian immigrants.

The art around him seems incongruent with either the noble traces of the Lapidus design or the shiny white sectional. The walls are covered with big canvases in big frames with faux gold coating decidedly non-modernist curlicues.

He counts six seascapes and a particularly disturbing painting in which his father and Nella are superimposed on a copy of a landscape by the Russian artist Isaac Levitan, *Golden Autumn*. Melsor and Nella at the river bend in Russian countryside, marring a copy of a path-breaking early-twentieth-century painting. There are more travesties in that painting than Bill is able to count, so he stops at the first six. What's next? Will rich Russians have their portraits painted among the bears in Shishkin's *Morning in a Pine Forest*?

"*Krasivo, da?*" says Nella proudly. [Pretty; yes?]

"*Da. Krasivo. Ochen'.*" [Yes. Pretty. Very.]

It's possible that Bill would have been better off staying away from the investigative track in journalism. His sense of outrage and his obsession with science and all flavors of betrayal of the public trust made him as much a dinosaur as these pterodactyl-like creatures flying in formation outside the window.

Perhaps he should have covered design, but that, too, would have been a betrayal. His obsession with design is a personal obsession. His career was—had been—driven by pursuit of professional obsessions, his private war against those who lie, cheat, and steal. By exposing villains, Bill distinguished himself from his father.

Bill continues to stare out the window, past the cluster of high-rises that people more familiar with South Florida municipalities recognize as Sunny Isles.

As darkness sets in, the contours of South Beach are no longer visible in the hazy distance.

The door of the *kabinet* opens, and Melsor bursts into the room.

It's impossible to establish beyond the shadow of a doubt what a Jew looks like. People have tried, God knows, but this was tough even before immigration and assimilation eroded the centuries-old boundaries that separated small Jewish towns from the rest of the universe.

A literary agent, the asshole who dumped Bill over the drug approval book, once told him that Jews come in two varieties—carrots and potatoes. Carrots are narrow in the shoulders, pointy-headed. Potatoes are broad-shouldered, square-jawed. This has nothing to do with height. You can be a short carrot or a tall potato—or the other way around. A carrot can beget a potato or vice versa. A carrot can be a potato's sibling, too.

All of this is a precursor to saying something that feels uncomfortable, but must be dealt with: if you have a sense of what a Jew looks like, you may be able to detect that Melsor Yakovlevich Katzenelenbogen doesn't look *entirely* Jewish.

You might suggest that Melsor's semi-Armenianness could

be rendered visible if you spend some time staring at Arshile Gorky's portraits and then, without an interruption, cast a glance at the living, breathing Melsor Yakovlevich Katzenelenbogen. The name "Katzenelenbogen" was passed on matrilineally. His father's last name was Matevossian. The couple didn't last past his birth.

Bill's quarter Armenianness is entirely invisible, drowned out by his mother's half Russianness. Melsor is a potato; Bill a carrot. Quarter Russian, quarter Armenian, and two-quarters Jewish on two sides, Bill looks like none of the above, a human terrier, a Katzenelenbogen Pinscher.

Now, in January 2017, Melsor seems shorter, more broad-shouldered, lower to the ground, heavier on the heels. His head is shaven, but, years notwithstanding, he seems strong. He must have started working out after the trial.

Also, there is gold. Around his neck, Melsor wears a massive gold chain with a proportionally sized star of David. There is a bracelet and a pinky ring. This jewelry is not intended for self-beautification. At the top of their lungs, these tokens shout: "I am dangerous! Don't fuck with me!"

"This is the guy who taught courses on the Silver Age of Russian poetry," Bill says to himself. "Did Gumilyov wear gold chains? Did Mandelstam have a Mogen David? Did Blok sport a pinky ring?"

In their lives, lead was a metal of greater significance than gold.

Melsor was just past seventy the last time Bill saw him. It was in the Kings County courtroom. He slumped in the biggest wheelchair his lawyer could find. Clear fluid was dripping into his veins, something gaseous was being pumped from a torpedo-sized tank through a mask that fully covered his mouth. The jury found him not guilty and the judge noted his heroic past and praised him for cooperating with the Department of Justice jihad to stamp out Medicaid fraud.

The flavor of fraud of which the elder Katzenelenbogen was not guilty, but from which he was apparently able to stash away considerable proceeds, is called the "ambulette" fraud. Its details will be revealed in due course.

A dozen years after the trial, Melsor seems to be feeling better. He paces madly, blurting out obscenities, and barely nodding to the son he hasn't seen in quite some time. Should they embrace? Would a simple handshake suffice? Would it be better to wait a bit and do nothing until the need for greeting passes?

"Ilyusha, rasskazhi podrobno, kto byl v budke kogda ty syuda zashel. Eto ochen' vazhno."

Mercifully, the elder Katzenelenbogen is addressing his son from across the room, standing beneath a gold-framed painting of a ship, commanding it like a corsair, a Judeo-Armenian Captain Blood.

[Ilyusha, tell me in detail, who was in the guard booth when you walked in. This is very important.]

The pirate ship on the painting is a two-mast affair. It's listing, about to dip gently to its side and go to sleep. The sharks are circling beneath the surface, readying for a feast.

Melsor is costumed for the part of the ship's captain. He is tall, broad, boxy. Blue shorts that come down to his knees, and his blue-and-white horizontally striped T-shirt are classic maritime stuff. In Russian, a version of this shirt is called *tel'nyazhka*. It's obvious that on a hypothetical formal occasion, Melsor would wear a navy blue double-breasted jacket, preferably with the insignia of a fictional yacht club, the bigger the better, Commodore Bloodsucker.

———

Melsor is clearly a man of many questions, and every one of them is urgent.

"*Ty po-russki ni s kem ne govoril posle togo kak voshel?*" [Did you speak Russian to anyone after you walked in?]

"*Net, ni slova.*" [No, not a word.]

"*Eto yest' ochen', ochen' khorosho. Okh kak povezlo! Dazhe ne predstovlyal sebe takoy rasskladki.*" [Very, very good! Very lucky! Didn't even imagine this sequence of events.]

Melsor sounds like he has won the lottery, but Bill knows better. The winning ticket has something to do with him. He bought it, or—worse—he *is* it.

"*Nu khot' ryumku rebyonku naley. Ved' skol'ko let ne videlis'.*" [At least pour the boy a shot glass. You haven't seen each other in years.]

"*Nakryvay, nakryvay na stol. Delo yest'.*" [Set the table, set the table. We have business.]

Nella emerges with a chilled bottle of Grey Goose on a tray full of familiar salty things that Bill loves and has missed.

The bottle is full, but not sealed. Bill has the capacity to interpret this: Grey Goose, a French vodka, bespeaks prosperity and generosity. That's a good thing. Its cost is a bad thing. The solution: procure a bottle of Grey Goose, consume its contents, then keep the bottle in perpetuity and continue to fill it with something more in line with what you wish to spend.

Even among his countrymen, Bill has encountered the notion that all vodkas are created equal, that you cannot distinguish French-made Grey Goose from a vicious rotgut.

In reality, it takes little expertise to distinguish Grey Goose from an impostor. Here is how you do it:

- Chill both bottles.
- When they reach the same temperature, sniff, then take a sip.
- If the vodka gives off no odor and tastes lighter than air, if it makes you feel like you could have drunk all night and still have asked for more, you have sipped a decent vodka.
- If the vodka gives off the odor of turpentine and tastes harsh and dry, like rubbing alcohol, yet still exhibits the sweet, cloying undertones of ethylene glycol, if one sip makes you feel like you may not be there to watch the sun rise over the ocean, you are drinking a rotgut. Halt the test. You will not be able to appreciate a decent vodka for at least six hours.

Alas, Grey Goose is a canard. After it's poured and consumed without a toast, Melsor brings up a half-forgotten scandal: "There was old Jewish man who told his lover—in bed—not to sleep with black people."

This sends Bill into mental fact-checking: Donald Sterling is the gentleman's name. He happened to own an NBA franchise. And he didn't say, "Don't sleep with them." He said, "Sleep with them if you want to, just don't be seen with them at my basketball games," or something like that.

This disgrace occurred in the spring of 2014. How could it possibly be so important in January 2017 that you would bring it up as Topic One in conversation with the son you haven't seen in twelve years?

Melsor has more to say: "Everyone shouted, racist, racist. But he was, so to say, in his own bed, with his own mistress—and she taped him!"

Grey Ruse—or is it Grey Russe—is vile, but at least it's cold. The conversation is turning vile, too, but it's better than anything that actually matters. As for Grey Russe, Bill decides that the moniker is unacceptably cute. He feels ashamed for having thought of it. Grey Ruse, on the other hand, is solid, accurate, appropriate. It will stay.

Bill knows what will come next: Melsor will develop the First Amendment argument, which holds that you have the inalienable right to say whatever you want as long as the band of your Jockey shorts is below your knees and you are cooling your heels, waiting for Viagra to kick in.

Bill knows that it's best to say nothing, and he makes a valiant effort to keep his mouth shut.

"Where is freedom of press when Jewish man can't say what he wants In! His! Bed! With! His! Lover! Where is, so to say, First Amendment to Constitution?"

Melsor is energized. He is the same he had been when he railed against the Soviets. Getting into a political argument with the father you have been avoiding for twelve years is never a good thing, but Bill is in it now.

"The First Amendment is where it's always been. It gives you a broad range of protections, which fully—yes, fully—extend to the right to be a racist asshole pig. Sterling's speech is fully protected," Bill interjects, still hoping that this will be a limited involvement.

This doesn't come out right. Too much confrontation too early. He will try to complete the argument and make the whole thing drop. He is trying to stick to the facts.

"Sterling controlled a government-regulated franchise, and

his contractual obligations included clauses that precluded expression of racist views. This was a licensure issue, a franchise issue, not a First Amendment issue. You can still tell your mistress whom to sleep and whom not to sleep with."

This is not great, either. Bill looks askance at Nella, who seems unperturbed. He likes this woman, sort of. She is unflappable. Perhaps Bill will be able to complete his argument, or his point of information, and the whole thing will go away.

"The same applies to your wife, or your boyfriend, or all of the above, as long as your bed is large enough and you don't own a basketball team."

"Donal'd Tramp was only candidate talking about this."

Melsor has difficulty with the name of the president-elect. Russian speakers run into brick walls when they encounter soft English *T*s and rolling English *R*s.

For some nuance-drenched reason, on the way out of Melsor's mouth, the *T* and *R* in "Trump" form a Harley-Davidson–like T-R-R, making the *U* slip off the saddle, becoming *A*-like—TR-R-A-MP.

The Russian mouth has less trouble with "Donald." But once you have a thing like Tramp, why stop, you might as well stick a soft sign behind the *L*. Make it a soft, rolling *L*. Make it "Donal'd."

"Your Donal'd Tramp paints with a broad brush," Bill replies. "That's just one of the things that's so scary about him."

At this instant, the reader should be reminded that by unpacking this exchange further, we do not endorse Bill's interpretations of events that unfold around him—and especially not his actions. Our role is to convey these events as they occur.

Bill possesses the insight to recognize the soft sign in "Donal'd" for something much greater than a term of endearment, an effort to make Tramp your own, to embrace, to adopt. To grasp this distinction fully, we might consider Nikolai Berdyaev, a Russian mystical philosopher. Being a mystic means caring greatly about small things for their potential to hide (and reveal) big things. His wackiness notwithstanding, Berdyaev explained the Russian revolution so much better than any earthbound colleague ever could.

Per Berdyaev, a Westerner is a creature of reason, a Russian a creature of faith. A Westerner rationally accepts contradictions. A Russian lets his soul do what it craves: worship. A Westerner studies Marx, critiques him. A Russian genuflects.

That soft sign after the *L* in "Donal'd" is a big thing, and Bill knows it. It channels the hugeness of Tramp. It is the Tramp Shekinah, the part of God that—sometimes, rarely—is rendered visible, embraceable even. Some mystics contended that Shekinah was the fuckable part of God, corporeally, literally—laugh not, or do. They say Moses did it.

In any case, now you have the man of the hour: ladies and gentlemen, give it up for Donal'd—with a soft sign—Tramp. Donal'd Tramp, Russified, made more dangerous through this metamorphosis of Russification.

When Bill was a child, in kindergarten in the USSR he learned songs about "Grandfather Lenin." He failed to let that little murderer of millions into his soul. Now, circa the summit of middle age, here in Florida, Donal'd Tramp is knocking on the same door.

As the words "Donal'd Tramp" roll off his tongue, the sound is so smooth, so organic, that even Bill craves a gulp of Grey Ruse straight from the bottle.

If you name a thing, you own it. If you un-name it, you unload it like a toxic asset, trample it, Donal'd Trample it. And for this reason, Donal'd Tramp trumps Donald Trump.

"I advise you get used to Donal'd Tramp, so to say."

Bill is in a fight now, dragged in, pissed at himself, unable to turn back: he is in no mood to be disarmed, won over, convinced—certainly not on this subject. He wants out of this conversation, out of this apartment, out of fucking Florida.

To gain control, Bill tries to do what all reporters do.

He asks a question: "I've been hearing a lot about 'political correctness' lately. I have no idea what it means."

"Not believing propaganda. Instead of saying that we are brothers, recognizing that some of us work and others, so to say, lazy."

"So, you want to crank up oppression, discrimination based on race, sex, religion, country of origin, sexual orientation—that sort of thing? Is this what you mean by rejection of political correctness?"

"And what do you, liberals, so to say, propose?"

"I find this bewildering, especially with your Donal'd Tramp, especially now, ten days before coronation. I live in an international city. It's diverse—please don't try to dismiss this as political correctness. It really *is* diverse. I notice that people differ from me, but I don't give it any thought. Ever. I don't know any other way to be."

"It's gone too far. It's not only black lives which matter. All lives matter, Ilya."

Bill tries to ignore the needling use of his birth name.

"I agree. All lives matter. I covered cops for years and loved it. But what you are referring to is actually complex, and the things you try to dismiss as political correctness are fundamental, things that were firmly in place before you and I set foot in this country. With Donal'd Tramp, I see the smoke screens that existed in Germany: the murder of Horst Wessel and the

Reichstag fire. I can see why your Putin would support your Tramp, but how can you, an immigrant—a Jew? That man is, plainly, a fascist."

"Not against us. Against Muslims, Mexicans. We don't even know how many refugees that Muslim let in."

This time, Bill stops himself. He doesn't ask: "Do you remember fleeing oppression? Do you remember being welcomed by America, not just the government, but the Maryland *Dzhuyka* that paid our rent and gave us subsistence money?" He takes another drink.

"Do you remember having once been a refugee?"

Bill looks up at Nella. Is she, too, to adapt the local lingo, a "Trampist"?

As their eyes meet, Nella takes another gulp of Grey Ruse and pronounces, more or less vacantly, as though repeating an axiom:

"Americans voted for Muslim foreigner. Twice!" she chimes in. "You not only break law—you break Constitution! Where else such things possible? Only in America!"

A Jew-Nazi—definitely. Bill is surrounded. He will have to learn not to respond to provocations.

"Finally, they elect normal white person," Nella agrees. "Obama didn't want to fight Muslims. Tramp will."

Ignoring this comment, as he must, Bill glances at two books on the coffee table. Pictures of Tramp as a much younger man stare at Bill from the book jackets. One is titled *Iskusstvo Sdelki*. The other is the English-language original, *The Art of the Deal*. These are, as far as Bill can tell, the only books in the house.

"Ya chitayu perevod beglo, a v nekotorykh momentakh smotryu v original," says Melsor after noticing that Bill has been looking at

the books. [I go through the translation rapidly, and then, in some cases, I look at the original.]

Melsor gulps down another shot of Grey Ruse and addresses Nella: *"Idi, vklyuchi."* [Go turn it on.]

Nella emits a deep sigh, downs her Grey Ruse, gets up, and leaves the dining room.

"Turn on what?" asks Bill.

"That thing," says Melsor, pointing at the scaffolding cradle outside the balcony. "There is machine on roof—generator."

"What generator?"

"For electricity. She knows what she does."

"What does a generator have to do with us?"

"It's already dark. We go for ride."

They stand on the balcony, looking south, at the lights of the high-rises, past the lights of the Diplomat, past the Grand Dux.

The balcony is narrow, three feet or so, not deep enough to put in a chaise *and* get past it. It's exposed, and tiles make it slippery. With his Florida phobia, Bill feels the need to touch the building's wall at all times.

Most of the balcony's length—twenty feet or so—faces east, overlooking the ocean dead-on, but a short dogleg—ten feet—winds around the building, facing south. It takes courage to get out there when the wind howls.

Of course, the moving scaffold could have been lowered to the balcony in order to scare Melsor.

Bill can see how someone would wish to attempt such a thing. Given what the two had been through—even during their protracted periods of no contact—he is able to sympathize with people who seek to oppress Melsor Yakovlevich Katzenelenbogen.

There is, of course, another plausible reason for the cradle to be where it is. The balcony on which Bill now stands could need work, defensibly, genuinely, structurally, perhaps even urgently. Why would it not need a little help after four decades of getting battered by salt and water?

Steel rods that support balconies—rebar—need to be treated with Teflon. If they aren't, they rust, become unstable, collapse. This process can take a long time or a short time, depending on the quality of rebar, the quality of concrete, and the levels of exposure. Bill had once or twice covered building collapses, and he knows that in the 1970s, when the Château was built, Teflon wasn't widely used to coat rebar. The crumbling, bulging layer of concrete is a symptom of rust that spreads beneath. In the worst-case scenario, a balcony can fold like origami beneath your weight. In a disintegrating building full of Bill's compatriots, this would be regarded as the natural order of things.

Bill believes momentarily that he feels the balcony move, but quickly realizes that it's the cradle, not the balcony, that's shifting in the wind. While Bill is leaning toward the building, his father stands in the middle of the balcony, not holding on to anything but his glass of Grey Ruse, like a Soviet sailor on deck. There is choppiness, sure, but he has seen worse. While Bill takes wide steps, his father takes almost no steps at all.

Looking down toward the ocean, with blasting wind and the moving scaffold cradle next to it, the balcony feels even more precarious than it looks.

A sound of what can be described as something similar to a motorcycle engine comes down from the roof.

"*Poyekhali,*" says Melsor. [Let's go.]

Where? Why? Bill sees no point in asking.

"*Poyekhali*" is never a neutral word.

This was, in fact, Yuri Gagarin's last word before he became the first man to be shot into space. Sure, it's a verb of motion, but the expression "fuck it" can be within the range of meaning of its translation. It follows *"poyekhali"* like spent rocket fuel.

Melsor downs his vodka, throws the plastic cup into the cradle, and, grabbing onto the railing, steps on a plastic chair, the sort that costs seven dollars at Costco. The chair's legs strain, bowlike. Melsor throws his right leg over the balcony, aiming to jump straight into the cradle.

The cradle moves outward, half a foot into the abyss, and with his left leg still anchored on the bowing plastic chair Melsor grabs onto the cradle's side, bringing it closer to the balcony. That done, he slides over the edge and smoothly shifts his feet to the bottom of the cradle.

"Khorosha lyul'ka," he says. [A fine cradle.]

Bill's assigned function in this family, when he was in this family, when there was a family, was to accept reality no matter what it dragged in. And now here he is, clinging to the side of a building as his eighty-three-year-old father dangles in a cradle suspended from the roof by nothing but two crane-like gizmos and two taut cables.

"Davay," says Melsor. The word is usually translated as "go."

Melsor's cradle slides outward, toward the stars, but he pushes on it, like an acrobat on a Russian swing, and the thing returns, slamming hard against the building, and loosening an undeterminable amount of material—concrete and aggregate—that falls to the ground seventeen floors below.

"Yob tvoyu mat'," says Melsor with what seems like just the right mixture of wonder and confidence. [Fuck your mother.] Melsor grabs the edge of the balcony and the edge of the cradle, uniting them in a vise grip.

"*Davay,*" he repeats, and, cursing fate, Bill heeds the parental command. "*Poyekhali!*"

Suddenly, Nella appears on the balcony. In her hand, she holds a twelve-inch steel ruler, which she hands to Bill.

"For slice door," she says.

This makes sense on a preverbal, preintellectual level: if they hand you an item, you take it.

"Slice door . . . ," Bill repeats, accepting the ruler. "What *is* a slice door?"

"What is that?" Nella seems genuinely surprised by his ignorance. "Slice door? *Durak ty?*" [Are you a fool?]

She speaks with the sort of familiarity that his people acquire post-alcohol. Then she points to the sliding door of the balcony.

"This is slice door!" she announces. "It doesn't open inside or out. Understand?"

With that, she slides the door to the closed position.

"If they lock it, this will open it. You put steel ruler in where lock is and it open."

Why is Bill doing this? Does he not have a life of his own? Why does he follow this refusenik fraudster poet on what will surely be an illegal, idiotic venture that, assuming they return alive, could land both of them facing trespassing, reckless endangerment, breaking and entering, and God knows what other felony charges?

Melsor could certainly afford a lawyer, but presumably doesn't have one.

Bill already has a lawyer he can't afford.

Why do all the other geezers become normal geezers, slumping properly into their wheelchairs, slobbering, emitting random exclamations, when this, *his* geezer, is suspended in a cradle—make it a *lyul'ka,* because Russian words have a way of being better—swinging outward, toward the stars, grabbing onto the edge and beckoning—ordering—Bill to step off?

Fuck you, you corsair asshole bloodsucking prick, thinks Bill, but does as he is told, for he is, in his miserable Russian soul, a good boy.

The cradle shifts underfoot, Bill's body adjusts, and he grabs onto the sides. This is the only way to stay upright. Cradles are designed to allow a workman to reach through the sides. Being something other than balcony railings, they are almost completely open. And, yes, they shift in the wind. And let's suppose for a moment that you stumble in a *lyul'ka*. Nothing will keep you from falling through its side.

From the instant Bill sets his uncertain foot in the cradle, he feels only three things: nausea, fear, contempt. Make it four: bewilderment.

In an obscure short story, the great Mikhail Bulgakov used the designation "*krovavaya lepyoshka*," literally, a bloody flatbread, to describe the hapless souls who fall from great heights. After more than five decades, would Bill now be reduced to a bloody flatbread? Would he join Zbig?

Bill knows that cradles spin out of control, and turn over, and fall, which means that anyone who rides in one without a climber's harness clipped on to an independent rope is, by definition, insane.

Bill stands in the cradle's dead center, trying to trick himself out of nausea, suppressing vomit, grabbing the *lyul'ka*'s sides with both hands. Melsor moves around freely, cursing, bending down, opening the door of what looks like a breaker box, presumably trying to find buttons that can be pushed, recklessly, Russianly, to test things out.

Obviously confused, he shouts to Nella, who has returned inside.

"It's on thick orange cable," she says in English. "Push button and it will go. You still not understand? *Tozhe mne . . .*"

It's a dismissive expression describing someone who may think he is a big deal, but is, in reality, a nothing. Clearly, Nella knows many things Melsor doesn't have a clue about.

Melsor pushes a button and the cradle jolts downward.

"Poyekhali nakonetz!" [Let's go at last!]

"Where are we going?" Bill shouts over the blasting wind.

"You will see. Don't shout. I hear."

The cradle is now under the balcony, which allows Bill to glance at its underside. It seems fine, except for the small, freshly knocked down doughnut-sized chunk of the balcony's edge, where the Melsor-bearing *lyul'ka* made impact a few minutes earlier.

"Why couldn't we just take an elevator?"

"They will see us in elevator."

"Wouldn't they see us, the people inside these apartments?"

"No. Person here is in Canada. He will not come back."

"What about under him?"

"Under him—dead, both. For sale. It will never sell."

"And beneath the dead?"

"Also for sale. Speculant. Lost shirt, so to say. In deep *zhopa.* Didn't know he stepped on shit. Under that we have good man, so to say, *nash chelovek.*"

A *zhopa* is an ass. *Nash chelovek* is one of us. As their *lyul'ka* jerks downward past the bottom of the seventeenth-floor balcony, the father and son switch back to Russian.

"Russkiy?"

"Amerikanetz, no s nami idet." [An American, but marches with us.]

"A my kuda?" [Where are we going?]

"Etazhom nizhe Amerikantsa." [One floor below the American.]

"Trinadtsatyy?" [Thirteenth?]

"U nas net trinadtsatogo." [We don't have the thirteenth.]

Of course, how could there possibly be a thirteenth at the Château? At a lesser place, they have thirteenth. Here you speed directly from twelfth to fourteenth.

As their *lyul'ka* moves past the apartment of the hapless speculator, Bill switches on his phone's flashlight to examine the balcony's underside. It's pristine. No chips, no cracks, no bulges to suggest rusting steel and delaminating layers of concrete. These balconies are firmer than the sum of everything Bill has encountered in the course of his life.

A text from Gwen comes through.

"How is it?"

"So far, so fucked"

It feels good to hear from her. Feels like a broadcast from the Voice of America, a missive from the outside world. It feels good to see an English-language text, too. In Bill's life, English has always been the language of reason; Russian of insanity.

"Hang in there"

"Believe me, I'm hanging"

Bill resolves that if this excursion fails to produce two bloody Russian flatbreads and a story worthy of six o'clock news even in South Florida, he wouldn't worry about stepping on other people's balconies. They are, at least, an improvement over dangling in a *lyul'ka*.

He will try not to worry about being an accessory to a crime. Because, of course, a crime will be committed. Why else would Melsor Yakovlevich Katzenelenbogen be involved?

At least no state lines will be crossed.

———

Bill starts to feel more or less comfortable in the *lyul'ka*, examining the balconies as they creep by, lulled by the wind and his father's raving about the Château's criminal BOD.

His comfort is bolstered by the fact that they are at opposite sides of the *lyul'ka*, at least ten feet apart, a safe distance.

Gwen texts again, probably driving her bright yellow Remorse distractedly.

"What's your sense re: Zbig? Is it a book?"

"Dunno. Saw the spot of splat. Got nothing."

"Spot of Splat: SOS for short? How is your father?"

"Batshit. Talk later . . ."

Bill is studying the underside of the nominally fourteenth-floor balcony when he feels a cold steel object the size of a quarter press hard beneath his chin.

An old man's voice comes next: "Halt! Who goes there?"

Bill is in no position to respond as Melsor pushes the button, causing the cradle to stop with a jolt.

The elderly sentry adjusts the position of what Bill is now able to recognize as a machine gun.

"Oh, Johnny, it's I. Melsor. What are you doing with the cannon, Johnny?"

"Well, this is a pleasant surprise. Hello, Melsor. Thought someone was coming to rob my place or throw me out. No one rides these things at night."

"No, we just go past your place on way down."

"Okay, suit yourself. I still see shapes pretty good, even in the dark. There are two. If you are one of them, who is with you? Who do I have my gun on?"

"Guy on who you point your gun? He is my son."

"I thought you said you had no son."

"I sometimes don't, so to say. What have you? Kalashnikov?"

"Bushmaster XM15-E2S. The best."

"Automatic?" Melsor is in the rhythm of the conversation. Bill never knew his father had any knowledge of—let alone appreciation for—firearms. The Melsor he knew was at least somewhat interested in literature and his frauds were always nonviolent.

"Semi. Some people don't like semi. They want to spray all over the place."

"Right. You put on pants one leg first. You walk one step in a time. You fire gun one bullet in a time. Just pull trigger faster. What's the problem?"

"I know a guy who can convert it to automatic for no charge, as a favor, but I don't bother."

"Could you please get the muzzle away from my neck . . . Sir . . ."

"Certainly! Pleasure to meet you. What's your name?"

"Bill."

"Come on through, my friends."

"Not this fast. I want to hear your cannon. Shoot one round for me."

"Happy to oblige."

"Shoot into sea, Johnny, like you did when we drank vodka, one year ago."

"You aren't standing in front of me? I see okay by day, but not by night anymore."

"No. I am on right."

"And your son? Not directly in front of me?"

"No. He took step to left when you lowered gun. He ducked down right now."

"Don't want to take a chance on hitting the wrong person. My eyesight took a beating in the war, and it just keeps getting worse."

The old man points the semiautomatic in the direction of the ocean, toward the brightly lit contours of a cruise ship on the horizon.

The sound is muffled, not as loud as a shot should be. Perhaps Bill's hearing is to blame—the cumulative impact of high altitude and winds blasting into his ears.

"You killed shark."

"Yeah, funny, Melsor. Where you gentlemen heading?"

"Under you. To your friend."

"The Evil Dwarf? Help yourselves to the gun if you want. Might as well bump him off while you are at it."

"No thank you; not yet. He is not there. This is why we go."

"Oh, that's right, his sister died. He must be back in Buffalo planting her."

Melsor pushes the button and the *lyul'ka* lurches again. Bill doesn't panic. He clenches his teeth and grabs onto the *lyul'ka*'s railing. His nausea returns.

As they pass Johnny's balcony, Bill walks to the center of the *lyul'ka* to ask: *"Chto eto za muzhik?"* [Who was this?]

"That was Johnny Schwartz," Melsor shouts in response. "Good guy. He lied about his age to go to fight Hitler. He is almost ninety, has prostate cancer, is behind on special assessments. They want to throw him out to street. In Florida we have expression: 'Outlived his money.'"

"Where was he in the war?"

"He once said in Belgium. In 1944."

"The Battle of the Bulge?"

"Something in that spirit. But it wasn't bad until later. He stayed in the army till Germans surrendered."

———

The *lyul'ka* drops down to the level of the twelfth-floor balcony, slamming not-so-gently into its side, and releasing a few handfuls of concrete and aggregate.

"*Priyekhali,*" Melsor announces. [We've arrived.]

This is how it works: you say *poyekhali* when you set out. You say *priyekhali* when you arrive. Russian verbs of motion are a bridge of fools; they exist to torture students. The elder Katzenelenbogen grabs onto the balcony's railing and pulls the *lyul'ka* to its side.

"Do you have belt?"

Bill pulls off his belt and hands it to his father. The old man ties the *lyul'ka* to the balcony, then, grabbing the railing, rolls over, stepping onto a narrow iron chaise. Bill follows. His feet are now upon another man's property. He is here with no knowledge or authorization from the apartment's lawful owner. This constitutes a clear-cut case of criminal trespassing, or is it breaking and entering, a felony for sure, even in Florida. Knowing Melsor, it's not going to stop at this. What will he do next? Smash through the "slice" door? Break the windows? Douse the place with kerosene and set it on fire?

Honesty and ethical restraint were the two features that separated Bill's life from his father's. This was the order of things: the elder Katzenelenbogen defrauded the public. The younger Katzenelenbogen defended the public from people who intended to defraud it. By defending the public from his father, Bill also defended himself.

It's hard to characterize this as a win-win-win. Just as easily, it can be lose-lose-lose. What's Bill doing in this *lyul'ka*? Why is he trespassing on the balcony and why is he on the verge of breaking into an apartment of a man he doesn't know, a man who, by default, has to be more trustworthy than his father?

Is it the vodka?

He didn't have that much.

Is it the Florida sunshine?

He stayed in the shade, took cabs, wore his *W* baseball cap.

The profit motive?

He has nothing at stake, nothing to gain.

Boredom?

He has an investigation to conduct, and this, clearly, has nothing to do with that.

Not a single explanation holds water, leaving only one—maybe. One he isn't ready to admit.

Melsor slides the slice door open. It's unlocked. Why would it not be? There are no adjacent balconies. Who would possibly enter the twelfth-floor apartment from the outside? Under normally foreseeable circumstances, people don't dangle in *lyul'ki* with twelve-inch rulers in their pockets. This likely holds true even in buildings with substantial Russian populations.

The curtains in the apartment are thick and tightly drawn. While Melsor goes straight after the computers and the telephones, Bill—who has no agenda—looks around the apartment. It's indeed worth examining. A massive hutch decorated with large painted hearts exudes great greenness, a relic of Mitteleuropa by the Florida seaside. Usually these things are filled with small trinkets—thimbles, steins, boot-shaped cups painted in an array of nauseating colors.

The contents of this hutch are surprisingly restrained. There are three sets of finials one usually sees on Torah scrolls; six finials altogether, ranging in height from five to eight inches. Each is decorated with small silver bells.

Torah breastplates are leaning against the back of the hutch on the shelf below. There are five altogether.

Bill opens the door of the hutch to run his fingers over one of the breastplates. A chain is attached to it, waiting to be hung on a scroll that appears to have gone missing. An index finger is all you need to distinguish a genuine object from a fake. Bill doesn't know enough to determine the age, but his gut says mid-nineteenth century, maybe a bit older. You make these determinations by instinct, by touch. You run your finger over the breastplate's surface. He touches one of the breastplates—it is what it looks like. He couldn't prove it, but he is certain.

Behind one of the breastplates, he finds five small velvet bags. These are usually used to store tefillin, the phylacteries, basically two leather boxes containing small scrolls, with narrow belts attached. Bill picks up one of the bags. It feels a bit heavy. He stands in front of the breakfront, mesmerized. Opening the drawer, he finds kiddush cups, all of them in silver, all showing wear and oxidation. The drawer is deep. He sticks in his hand, making the cups part, and causing two to be displaced and fall overboard. There have to be at least a hundred.

In the other room, Melsor is cursing. He is done with whatever it is he set out to do.

Bill is half in shock when he and Melsor pile back into the cradle. Beyond apprehension, beyond fear, he can think of nothing other than the objects he has just touched, objects that spoke to him in a way that Zbig did not when he touched the Spot of Splat.

"Who lives there?"

"*Svoloch'*."

That word again, wafting in Florida air, becoming one with the ecosystem, like filthy felt, like sewage pumping into Biscayne Bay.

"Is he a Judaica dealer?"

"No. Lawyer. He was, what's that word? Means *vypizzhen*."

"Disbarred. Sort of."

"Disbarred. *Spasibo*. Now he steals from us."

"How did he happen to acquire this collection?"

"His wife got it from her father."

"Was he a rabbi?"

"No—Nazi. Did you take anything?"

"Of course not! How can this dwarf you describe . . . What's his name?"

"Greenstein."

"*Greenstein?* He's a Jew!"

"So? Fascists can be Jews. Why not?"

Bill considers his father's words.

"I suppose that's true. And it's becoming increasingly true by the day."

"After war, her father worked for Ford in Detroit. He had box of gold teeth under bed whole time after war. When he died, his daughter took teeth from box and melted them, sold broth, and bought this apartment."

"Broth?"

"Gold broth."

"You mean bullion?"

"Yes, bullion. Gold bullion. Not broth. This was in one of the times when oil was high, dollar low, and gold very, very high. Next they will melt silver, I guess."

The *lyul'ka* reaches Melsor's apartment balcony.

"*Priyekhali*," Melsor announces. [We have arrived.]

Nella is still on the balcony, still smoking.

"*Nu, postavili zhuchka vashego?*" [Have you planted that bug of yours?]

"*Da, batareyki na nedelyu khvatit.*" [There is enough battery for a week.]

"*Nu tak bol'she i ne nado.*" [You don't need more than a week.]

"Why not?" asks Bill.

Would they need to perform this trick again? If he were honest with himself, Bill would have admitted to mixed feelings about that experiment in felonious conduct.

"In one week, we have election. Now we must know what he thinks, what he plans. Next week, it will not matter—unless you are federal prosecutor."

Bill goes into the kitchen and emerges with the bottle of Grey Ruse.

"Good idea," declares Nella, raising a glass. "You think correctly. Well brought up child."

"*Za nas s vami i khuy s nimi,*" says Bill, raising his glass. [To all of us and fuck them.]

It's a traditional Soviet toast, which Bill appears to have missed more than he realized. He knows that the toast applies to the situation in which he now finds himself. He just doesn't yet know how.

After a long, drunken evening where not much of substance is discussed, Bill is told that he would be staying in the "other apartment," one that belongs to Nella and is used mostly as storage for her art business.

"You will take freight elevator, and if you run into anyone, which you will not, because they are all sleeping, you will not say a word in Russian."

"Do you think they are also bugging *you*?"

"No."

"How would you know?"

"They are soft. And also . . . you will not say to anyone that I am your father. Johnny Schwartz is okay—no one else! Don't answer questions. Tomorrow I will tell you more. We will meet at Broadwalk and talk in fundamentals."

Melsor's English seems to have improved since their conversation at the Kings County Supreme Court. You could sense that Katzenelenbogen the Elder is on the verge of experimenting with articles, sometimes definite, sometimes indefinite.

"The English word is 'boardwalk.'"

"We say 'Broadwalk.' It has no boards and is broad. *Shirokiy.*"

"Well then . . ."

"You will walk out of Château at five forty-five A.M. Don't talk to anyone, and—this is very, very important—don't speak Russian. Give guards in booth angry look. You will pass Aquarius, Trump Tower Hollywood, and Wave. Turn right, and you will see Magnolia Terrace street. Five blocks from here exactly-exactly. Wait for me. I leave Château at six A.M., and we rendezvous at six ten. We will be on Broadwalk before these soft-bellied *shtetl gonifs* wake up."

Bill considers correcting his father's Yiddish—plural of *gonif* (crook) is *ganovim*, not *gonifs*—but thinks better of it. You could ask him how and why he knows this, but this will not be useful. Bill knows many things; usually, he has no idea how or why.

Perhaps the father and son Katzenelenbogen are still in competition. There is no fathomable reason to acknowledge it.

Isn't it better to just win?

7

AMBULETTE

Nella's one-bedroom apartment, located on the thirteenth floor passing for the fourteenth, is filled with canvases, all of them couch-sized, all of them stacked on the floor.

There are obligatory paintings of Paris cafés, of two-mast ships in the storm, multiple nauseating paintings of angels, paintings that blasphemously combine portraits of rich, or rich-enough, formerly Soviet Jews with works that—deservedly—hang at the Tretyakov Gallery in Moscow and the Hermitage in Saint Petersburg. You could see that this is the part of the business that moves. The canvases are all waiting to be packed and shipped.

In the bedroom, Bill finds a stack of paintings he actually considers intriguing. These are based on the erotic eighteenth-century poem *"Luka Mudischev,"* whose hero is endowed with a penis so large that it's lethal. This series of paintings is done with a straight face, with text reproduced on the canvases. Clearly, several artists were involved in painting this series, each of them bringing his own brand of naughtiness.

This was actually more than a mere wall hanging—it fits into Bill's definition of art. Drinking vodka with these painters would likely be as pleasurable as it would be suicidal.

After a self-guided tour of Gallery Nella, he spots a bottle of vodka on the kitchen counter—it's a super-cheap brand, in a plastic half-gallon bottle with a handle. This type of bottle is called a "handle," perhaps because it features a literal, physical handle, or perhaps to suggest that its consumer may be losing his grip. There is a dancing Cossack on the label. The stuff is called Kozachok, but it's made in Philadelphia.

Bill takes a sip from the bottle. In Russian, this manner of drinking is called "*iz gorla*," from the neck.

The plastic bottleneck feels warm. Vodka at this point in the evening stops being about pleasure. It's an obligation, a compulsion, a *mitzvah* even.

He has no assignment, no deadline, no editor—just emptiness. If there is mystery in its infinity, it eludes him. This flavor of infinity is devoid of wonder. His hands long for purpose and a keyboard. He picks up a television clicker. There were screens in the newsroom, but someone else tended them. At home, he had no functional television set, having forsaken recreational use of the medium circa 1995.

The technology—or at least the number of buttons—now present in the clicker mystifies him. The thing is busier than his smartphone. Experimenting, Bill pushes a button near what looks like the front of the thing, causing the screen on the wall to light up. Good guess. The screen is split into sections, and the largest of these sections, on the left side, is displaying what seems to be a fragment of a television show.

It seems to be completely idiotic. It displays a coffin draped in black cloth. On top of it sits a pair of red, ultra-tall pumps, the kind that scream porn, or at least the kind that used to scream porn. He doesn't know any women who wear that sort of thing. Maybe Gwen would have, in her gonzo days, at Style. Or now, perhaps. He has no idea.

The show is called *Merry Widows*. Reality television, it's called, complete with "contestants" matching the dearth of shame and brains in pursuit of valuable prizes. He keeps track of that sort of thing when it gets filtered through *The New York Times* and *The New Yorker*. The show is a work in progress—coming soon. What could the prize be? A contract on the husband? Can't be. He is already dead. He had it coming.

He turns off the television set, steps out onto the balcony, walks up to its edge, and takes another gulp of Kozachok. It's room temperature, a solvent.

He looks at the lights of the South Florida coast. He owes Gwen a call. What's he to do, ask her how her day went? Pretend that they are a couple? They were together once, a decade ago, before her fraud. Does he have to confront her? Does she get to confront him back? Does everyone need to confront everyone else? Give it a break . . .

He did not come to South Florida to make peace with his father. No need for that. He had been to Miami before, reporting stories, speaking at a conference—two of them, actually— and never did he consider calling Melsor.

Neither of them is gravely ill. Melsor has the powerful look of a geezer who will one day crumble like a mighty oak, obviating the need for peacemaking. It will be unforeseen, unless the statement above could be classified as foresight. Peace is overrated.

Bill peers over the railing.

"Jump," the impulse screams.

"Fuck you," he responds out loud.

A deep gulp of Kozachok from the plastic bottle . . .

This is nothing like hammering TBs at Martin's. He imagines the fall. He has seen the videos, watched obsessively for days, felt them beckon. How long is the fall? He grabs onto the railing, grasping, squeezing till pain sets in, till knuckles whiten. Is the free fall the point? Not yet, not to him. The edge is a state of consciousness, a state of being.

Will Kozachok give him the courage he lacks—the courage Zbig seems to have had, unless it was an accident? Is determination of the truth among the goals of an existential investigation? Is negation of the truth—exaltation—an even higher goal?

You can calculate the seconds, the fractions of seconds the drop takes—it's a simple formula; sixth-grade physics—but what of the feeling, Zbig's feeling? What secret of the universe did he come to grasp? Can words express his final knowledge?

The phone rings. It's Gwen. He lets it ring.

Bill sets up the cot near the stack of Luka Mudischev paintings. Stretched out fully dressed, he pops open his laptop, sets it on his chest, and searches for "BASE." Before, he looked at BASE jumping videos as he tried to fathom the idea of unencumbered flight. It was art, really. Now, he is considering chutes as something real, as equipment, as something that can be acquired and—yes—used.

Jumping with a parachute somehow seems easier than using a flight suit, but even jumps with chutes aren't recommended for people who haven't completed hundreds of skydiving jumps. Bill's number of jumps is zero, plus he has a complicated relationship with heights.

Stories he reads warn about extreme dangers and illegality (you have to trespass), which only eggs Bill on. Some say that even experienced skydivers need to work with mentors when they move on to BASE. Drunk and getting drunker, he is amassing information with the zeal of a science writer—his zeal.

He finds an info-graphic summarizing the causes of death of BASE jumpers, and he finds a cool epidemiology study of injuries, nice work by a Dr. Omer Mei Dan, an Israeli-born orthopedic surgeon who practices at the University of Colorado and BASE jumps a lot.

Of course, it makes sense that as a BASE jumper you face double jeopardy: slamming into the ground and slamming into the object you are jumping off. This is why a round chute used by skydivers isn't the thing you need. You need something called a "ram-air chute," a rectangular canopy that lets you maneuver.

Bill couldn't have done a better job of gathering information if he were sober, though if he were sober, he would have stopped short of pricing the chutes. New ones cost $3,000, give or take, but a used one can be picked up for $1,700, still way the fuck too much, considering Bill's financial handicap.

Also, sober, he wouldn't have called the seller in California, telling him that the chute should be packed and ready to use, and he wouldn't have used his *Washington Post* credit card or put down the Château as his mailing address.

It was a self-correcting problem though. Surely the card has been canceled and the charge will be declined.

A call comes in: it's Gwen.

Bill picks up.

"I've been thinking about you, worrying a little," she says.

"Good to hear your voice."

"How many years have we known each other?"

"Fifteen? A bit more, actually."

"I never thought of this before. All the Russians I know are named Alex. You are not really William, are you?"

"No. It's Ilya. I slapped on the *W* and the *M* when I was young and stupid."

"May I call you that?"

"I'll answer to anything."

"Nice name: Ilya. What does your father call you?"

"Nothing. He just says 'You,' and I respond. His wife is a 'you' when spoken to and a 'she' when spoken of. We don't use names in my family."

"Is this something Russian?"

"No, just something warped."

"Now, Ilya—this sounds good—your father, I imagine him as a tough gangster sort, muscular, lots of gold—Miami."

"You're closer than you know."

"What's his name—is it Alex?"

"Melsor, actually. Melsor Yakovlevich Katzenelenbogen."

"Which means . . ."

"Katzenelenbogen means 'cat's elbow' in German. There is a ton of spelling variations outside the Fatherland. No idea how the name became Jewish and why a cat's elbow and not, for example, a dog's."

"And his first name . . . Melsor?"

"It's an acronym: Marx, Engels, Lenin, Stalin, and the October Revolution. Children used to be slapped with ultra-patriotic names in the 1930s."

"Melsor . . ."

"He could just as easily have been named Elrad, as in electricity and radio, or Tractor, as in tractor. It's a remnant of his father's extreme Bolshevism."

"Why didn't he change his name here, like you did? A name like Mel would be less fraught. Or Alex."

"I asked him that years ago. He said the name Melsor makes him a monument. All Russian poets dream of monuments—Pushkin, Akhmatova, Vysotsky even. But Melsor is already a monument, many monuments, in fact. To totalitarianism, true, but they are monuments nonetheless."

"I look forward to meeting him in a few days. Will I?"

"Careful what you wish for, Gwen. There could be remorse involved."

They hang up eventually, and as Bill tosses on the cot, sweating, memories, dreams, reflections visit him. The most important of these stems from the Kings County Supreme Court.

Properly used, ambulettes are as benign as any other van with a driver. The fraud involving them is so simple that it might as well have been invented by Gogol:

You find a doctor to determine that a Mrs. Cohen is not well enough to take a regular taxi when she goes to her physical therapy appointments. Instead, she needs an ambulette. A bus costs two dollars; standard car service costs twenty dollars; an ambulette charges Medicaid sixty dollars or more.

The scheme works optimally when no one goes anywhere:

- Mrs. Cohen, the patient, gets ten dollars in cash from the ambulette service to stay at home, which she prefers to do anyway.

- The doctor gets ten dollars for prescribing the ride, and
- The ambulette fleet owner keeps forty dollars, which goes even further, because he doesn't own an ambulette and employs no driver.

Some foolhardy operators own physical ambulettes, which invites trouble, because a physical ambulette can be followed by undercover investigators, even reporters.

Melsor's metaphysical—nonextant—flock of ambulettes was not vulnerable to such primitive surveillance. Alas, when his reckless competitors were caught, they ratted out Melsor.

He was indicted on May 1, 2001, the day he subsequently called "My Personal Holocaust."

During a court hearing, the situation was compounded by the fact that the lead prosecutor was Bill's former colleague from *The Duke Chronicle,* the student newspaper. The dude's name was Jon Abramowitz.

This connection came to light in the hallway, when the prosecutor greeted the son of the accused with a friendly shout, "Hey, Bill, dude, what the fuck?"

Recognition caused Bill to roll his eyes and the prosecutor to chuckle.

"I didn't know you were Russian," he said, and Bill chose not to respond.

The elder Katzenelenbogen observed this exchange from his wheelchair. Things moved beyond awful when Melsor demanded that Bill do two things in the name of the family ties. Bill was expected to:

- Explain some key points to the prosecutor as part of an off-the-record "gentlemen's conversation," and

- Hang on to a suitcase stuffed with hundred-dollar bills until the matter blows over.

Bill said no and no.

How could Melsor even consider dragging his son—a man whose career is grounded in honesty—into the sewer that he inhabited?

"Predatel'!" Melsor shouted in Russian from the wheelchair pushed by his second wife, the one who stayed a few months and whom Bill didn't get to know. [Traitor!]

"Sorry you feel this way," said Bill in English, and left for Washington before the trial concluded.

This was a distasteful event. Even without obstruction of justice, prosecution was halfhearted, and most of the already reduced charges were tossed out by the judge, who cited the defendant's courage and past contribution to the struggle for human rights. In addition to being wheelchair-bound, Melsor claimed—through his attorney, of course—that he engaged in the ambulette fraud in order to pay off the medical bills incurred when his wife was dying of breast cancer. This was technically correct.

The penalty was irrelevant. Melsor Yakovlevich Katzenelenbogen had to promise to refrain from conducting unsupervised business with Medicaid for five years. Prosecution must have realized that Melsor's stash was so well hidden that they saw no point in looking for it. Does anyone care about fraud perpetrated by an immigrant who ambulates in a wheelchair and respires with the help of an oxygen tank the size of a small WWI torpedo?

Melsor wasn't "disgorged."

The day after the verdict, Melsor's health improved. He

junked the wheelchair, returned the rented oxygen tank, and bought a condo in Florida.

Since Melsor gave up his crooked-doctor accomplices—including the asshole whom Bill blamed for killing his mother—the government pressed the sexier charge of conspiracy against the docs who prescribed the ambulette rides in exchange for kickbacks.

The doctors were disgorged, lost their licenses, and the most obnoxious member of what was described as a "ring" may still be a guest of the federal government.

The *New York Times* reporter who broke the story about the ambulette fraud—Gardiner Harris—was actually a friend of Bill's, or so Bill thought.

Though the two spoke often, Gardiner disappeared for a few months, but on the day the story on the ambulette caper ran, Gardiner sent Bill a two-word e-mail: "Sorry dude."

Bill responded with a one-word e-mail: "fucker."

Gardiner wrote the story with the flourishes intended to get you on the front page. His tone sucked, too. He was taking an elitist, detached posture, gently ridiculing immigrants as they fight for survival.

Fortunately, the initial story ended up on page eighteen. The final story—the trial—was buried even deeper.

Bill gets up from the cot, undresses, and, stretching out, utters a phrase his father will neither hear nor comprehend:

"I am fine, Dad. My career, which meant everything to me,

is completely, irrevocably over. I am fifty-two years old. I have no personal life to speak of, and I am oh-so-close to the edge."

At this point, Bill switches to Russian: *"Plokho mne, okh khudo."* [It's tough, very much so.]

In English, he adds:

"Thank you for asking, you narcissistic prick."

8

ART OF DEAL

It would be incorrect to describe Bill's morning-after condition as chipper. On the morning of January 12, his eyes are puffy and, should he look in the mirror, he would notice that they are bloodshot as well.

The back pain is intense, a reminder of his encounter with a crooked cane.

At dawn, Bill struggles to power through these challenges and climb out of bed.

His fashion choices that morning: a pair of cargo shorts and a bike jersey. He doesn't own a bike anymore, but he likes having three massive pockets at the small of his back.

Stumbling over paintings, he makes his way out the door, taking a freight elevator. Bill is never late. Usually, he is a little early.

He exits through the valet parking area, the place closed off with the Dumpsters.

Florida is bathing the street with entirely too much light for his hung-over, uncaffeinated comfort. The rounded curb is so white that the rays it reflects are wreaking havoc directly in the center of his cranium. Mrs. Kisel' is, of course, gone from the curb, as are her bags and her furniture. The *Dzhuyka* wan with the driver from mental health must have made a curbside pickup.

Surely her stuff is resting in the Dumpsters. Bill is so certain that he resists his natural urge to climb up and check.

At the guard's booth on the corner of the building, Bill sees the same Slavic-looking man he saw the day before. He looks up as Bill gives him his quasi-military salute.

"Poor, pathetic fucker," Bill says to himself.

Turning right on Ocean Drive, Bill heads toward the "Broadwalk."

His back pain is persistent, dull. Why is he getting himself sucked into someone else's intrigue? Is he so desperate for parental approval? Is he, at age fifty-two, a good boy? As a reporter, Bill knew where to draw the line, even when family members were involved. But now, as a God-knows-what, he is God-knows-where, and this state of affairs somehow seems appropriate. He has what he deserves.

Bill stands on the appointed street corner, checking his e-mail. Nothing even remotely interesting. Flacks pitching stories.

He returns the phone to the back pocket of his bike jersey. His right arm lingers atop the bruises on the impacted spinal disk and beneath his shoulder blade.

Ocean Drive is coming alive with buses and taxis. Flowers he doesn't know the names of are in bloom. Bill looks up, marveling at the rapidly approaching object on the horizon. This is

Melsor. He remembers that the man always hopped up slightly when he stepped on his left foot. It's the signature Melsor hop. A thousand years earlier, when they were a family, before emigration, before things went completely, spectacularly to shit, Bill's mother teased Melsor over that hop and even tried to reeducate him.

He never learned to walk like a human, and, if anything, at eighty-three, his hop is more pronounced, faster, higher, arthritically automatic.

"Fucker," says Bill, watching his father approach.

Again, no handshake, just a nod.

"I walk fastly. If you can't keep up, we talk later."

"Good morning."

"Speak English. I don't have practice here, except reading. I need English for, so to say, *paskvils*. I don't want to slow. You can wait in café, I don't know where there is one."

"No problem keeping up."

It's a lie. He is keeping up, but this pace is unnatural, startling, faster than a walk, slower than a run, a geriatric marathon.

"Nella says Roza Kisel' hit you across back yesterday?"

"I am told it's my own fault."

"In Florida, you don't slow down and yawn. In Florida, you have to be assertive, because if you are not, someone will hit you across back."

"That's what I hear."

"You are guilty yourself."

Melsor didn't always require the underpinnings of reality, but there were times when said underpinnings found him.

His campaign against the Soviets—which resulted in the family's emigration—was, without doubt, based on a solid ethical foundation. And the ambulette scam, criminal though it was, produced results. Ill-gotten, but tangible, quantifiable, concealable, probably not bankable, but obviously undisgorgeable.

The previous night's journey on the moving scaffold, though unsafe and criminal, didn't result in deaths or arrests. Melsor Yakovlevich Katzenelenbogen was easily underestimated, and from this his power stemmed.

Bill had never misrepresented himself to a source, never broken into an apartment in search of clues, never hacked into anyone's computer system. But that was Bill on his own turf—the solid matter of his own creation. Now the turf is his father's, and on Planet Melsor the laws of physics are not the same. The laws of economics and especially ethics aren't the same, either.

They walk past a cluster of motels, past a parking lot, toward what appears to be the promised Broadwalk.

"Are you still writing poetry?" Bill asks, trying to be civil.

"Yes, but only for political purpose."

"About your Donal'd Tramp?"

"About *svolochi* on condo board. For now."

"Poetry about the condo board?"

"Why not? I wrote about Communists . . ."

"Are you publishing?"

"Yes, on Web site, stihi.ru, and in *Machta*."

Stihi is poetry. Has to be a Web site for poets, amateur and professional. *Machta* is a mast, the thing on a sailboat.

"*Machta* is a local Russian newspaper, I presume?"

"Shopper. They have ads for Russian stores, doctors, lawyers.

They don't pay anything, but they publish everything, and everyone reads it."

"It's okay. The First Amendment applies, you are fully protected."

Bill looks up at a cluster of aging high-rises. Scaffolding cradles hang on two of them. Bill considers them with a quiet sense of achievement.

"I will give you poem to translate. I brought it. You can translate on back of same page when I go to bathroom."

"Sounds reasonable."

"I have to put it on leaflet today."

There is a dune to their right. It's 7 A.M.—too early for bathers and even some runners.

The sidewalk shifts to the left, and the father and son walk past a rack of rental bikes and encounter a low fence on the ocean side.

"I walk from mezuzah to mezuzah."

There is a presumption—an erroneous one—that Bill grasps the meaning of walking from mezuzah to mezuzah.

Melsor walks up to a wire-mesh fence, touching the back of a rotting fence post and proceeding to kiss his middle and index fingers. The act of touching and finger-kissing has the look of a cultist sex act, a mechanistic, ritualistic observance, as far from passion as you can get.

"From mezuzah to mezuzah, two and half miles, what I have walked is one mile, so it's seven there and back."

Bill doesn't know what to make of this, other than that someone—probably a black hat—had secretly attached the mezuzah, a small tube containing a Hebrew scroll, to the back of a fence post.

Why anyone would do that is beyond Bill's ability to comprehend. A two-quarters Jew, he isn't observant. But in places where he often found himself—Northwest D.C., Bethesda, Maryland—a mezuzah is standard equipment.

Bill can see how one would nail the thing to the doorpost. He can even see the rationale for nailing it to a gate leading to a Jewish home. But the idea of affixing a mezuzah surreptitiously to the entryway of a public park constitutes a secret, even mystical, incursion on a secular public space, an act of kabbalistic expansionism. What happened to separation of church and state? What happened to the distinction between yours and mine? Fuck that, what about the distinction between you and me? Why would someone like Melsor—a man who owns no indoor mezuzah and has no idea what is written on the scroll that goes inside it—(a) be cognizant of the secret outdoor mezuzah and (b) feel the need to touch said mezuzah?

Observing Melsor kiss his own hand doesn't surprise Bill. Poets are prone to such conduct. Bill is gathering the courage to ask his father the questions he intended to ask him for decades— at least three, perhaps as many as five.

"I think of poets as people who suffer—a lot. But you don't suffer at all."

He is making a path for his ultimate question: Hey, Dad, how do you reconcile being a poet with committing fraud? This is rich in subtext: just because New York State and the feds didn't have the *beytsim* to go after you all the way makes you an unconvicted felon, guilty as sin, but, for some absurd reason—i.e., unjustly— free and insulated from consequences of your felonious actions.

Does Bill want to see his father behind bars? What kind of idiotic question is that? Yes, of course, he does—yes!

"Ya sebe ne vrag." [I am not an enemy to myself.]

Then in English:

"I make enemies to suffer."

"What about the things you did that were of, shall we say, disputed legality?"

"After your mother died, I had no choice. I had debt, and that doctor gave me excellent opportunity. I took it."

"Did you like doing what you did?"

"I did it well—and money was the best."

"I can see that."

"Are you specialist in insurance?"

Bill responds with a nod. Insurance is gambling and gambling can be a crime. The rest is regulation, law, procedure. A reporter who doesn't understand insurance well enough to love it is not truly a reporter.

"Imagine you buy insurance for apartment. Then you walk out and don't lock your front door, and thief comes in and takes your new Samsung television. Will insurance give you money back for it?"

"I think it will. You insure against stupid shit like forgetting to lock the door."

"Okay, maybe, but it absolutely shouldn't pay in this situation!"

"Why not?"

"Because you commit—tributary negligence."

"Contributory negligence."

"Yes. If you don't protect valuables and someone takes them, is that stealing?"

"Yes."

"Taking Samsung from unlocked apartment is same as taking garbage from trash can."

"Are you arguing that Medicare and Medicaid assets are, in effect, abandoned property?"

"Yes. Government commit tributary negligence."

People are starting to come out on the Broadwalk.

They walk in groups of three or four, with the majority of groups speaking Russian and a few speaking English. All the solitary walkers speak loudly into their cell phones. Bill looks into their faces. Regardless of the language they speak, all the passersby exhibit a similar range of scowls. Some are glum, others angry. A few appear to be only mildly disaffected. Bill keeps looking for smiles, but sees none. Perhaps happy idiots are destined to stay in cold climes, in subsidized housing. This form of retirement, these modes of alienation are the provenance of the chosen few—the best of the best.

"I stop at Margarita Will. They have bathroom."

"Margaritaville?"

"Yes. You need to go?"

"No, but thanks for asking."

Melsor reaches into his pocket, produces a crumpled piece of paper, and hands it to Bill.

"Here. Translate. I will be long time. You have pen?"

"Always."

Though not a poet, Bill cares deeply about poetry, especially Russian poetry. Alas, Melsor's poem has a certain slapped-together propaganda look, a bubbling brew of threats and innuendo. Does he actually expect Bill to *translate* it? Does it need to exist in English? Had that thing been actually good, Bill would have been honored to spend the time, deciding whether to preserve the meter, the rhyme, or the meaning.

As a teenager in America, he was once forced to hand-print his father's CV. The Katzenelenbogens didn't yet own a Latin-script typewriter. He remembers being strong-armed to translate court filings, business letters, film scripts—Melsor called them "scenaries," from the Russian word *scenarii*. There was a time when Melsor penned television commercials, and Bill's attempts to convince him that no one anywhere would have any use for this work were met with commands to shut up and write.

"Yaytsa kuritsu ne uchat," Melsor said at that time. [Eggs do not teach a chicken.]

Sometimes Bill executed translations while holding his nose. This was expected of him, ordered really. He had no choice. Is it any surprise that being relegated to service as his father's writing tool made Bill's Inner Child exceedingly angry?

Perhaps it was this upbringing that made Bill the reporter he was. He was not an obsessive broomstick-armed pursuer of *the truth*. He was an obsessive broomstick-armed pursuer of *reality*, which, of course, constitutes a target even more fundamental.

If you want to fill the world with guys like Bill, make more guys like Melsor.

Melsor's propaganda screed could be given its due in the exact time it took Melsor to work his eighty-three-year-old prostate. He sends a copy to Melsor, and, for the hell of it, a blind copy to Gwen.

"You finished?"

"It's in your e-mail."

"Give me original."

Melsor takes the paper and stuffs it in the pocket of his shorts. Taking the translation as his due, he sees no reason to say thank you.

"Tell me about the demographics of your Château."

"Half Russian. Half American."

"All Jews?"

"About ninety-five percents."

"Okay. They, I mean, you, hate each other?"

"*We* don't hate Americans. They hate *us*—zoologically."

"Why would anyone hate us? We are such nice, trusting, honest, sincere, easygoing people . . ."

"We are completely different people. We go on Broadwalk in early morning, they sit in their units and read newspaper. In afternoon, we swim in ocean, they don't swim at all. They sit near swimming pool under umbrella, smeared with lotions. We are brown. They are completely white."

"You stay away from the pool completely?"

"Usually, but when we use pool we jump in."

"Different esthetics, too?"

"They say we want things done cheap."

Melsor deliberately stretches out the word "cheap," making it sound more like "che-e-e-ep," with an upward inflection.

"They say Russians want things chip-chip-chip. They shout at us when we speak at North Pool: 'This is public space—speak Russian in your unit.'"

"What about this Johnny Schwartz, of the Battle of the Bulge, the one who almost blew me away with his Bushmaster? He is American."

"Yes, he is with Russians. He has no money. His unit is almost in foreclosure."

"It's a porous divide then."

"He is exception. Everything else is rule."

"Do the Americans have more money than the Russians?"

"No. We have about same. Look at foreclosures list: half Russians, half Americans."

"Interesting."

Lists of foreclosures are the sort of thing Bill would seek out as well. His geezer is many things, but stupid he is not.

"In a week, we have election. Future of Château will be decided."

"Seems fitting. We just decided our country's future."

"That was good, with Donal'd Tramp. Except our situation is completely different."

"Hmmm. What's the problem here?"

"Special assessments. BOD want to spend nineteen millions more to knock down balconies. Our balconies are excellent!"

"So why knock them down?"

"Because of *otkat*. What's English word?"

"Kickback."

"If you are on BOD and support them, ICII give you three-year lease on Lexus."

"What's ICII?"

"I call them ISIS. They are construction contractor."

"How does it work?"

"BOD has five people. You need three members to win."

"I saw that in the *paskvil'*: something about having two members in one's pocket."

"Our ruling block is led Greenstein, whose apartment you saw yesterday."

"Greenstein is the board president?"

"No! Greenstein is *vice* president. He is too smart to be president. Nobody wants to be president. President signs all papers. If there is forensic audit, he goes to prison. You take biggest idiot you have and make him president. If he is crazy, they can't persecute him, they can't disgorge him. Woman who hitted you on back was for two terms president."

"So whom does Greenstein have in his pocket?"

"Two Russian guys. Roytman and Kushman."

"Greenstein is American, and Roytman and Kushman Russians?"

"Yes."

"So it's not exactly broken along Russian-American lines?"

"It's more about kickbacks, and Americans like *otkaty* as much as we. They vote: start to break parking lot. They break parking lot, then they don't finish, and go on to break South Pool, then, after that's broken, they will break North Pool."

"Don't they get permits?"

"No."

"Are there deadlines specified in the contracts?"

"Clever boy. They have deadline, but contracts are given as change-orders to ISIS. In this way, there are no competition bids."

"I see . . ."

"You add one year and one year and one year, and it becomes accumulative."

"You could sue, I suppose. You've sued people before, God knows, you know how."

"I sue only on contengincy."

"Contingency?"

"First meeting is always free. One lawyer, old Jewish man, explained to me: 'You could sue. You could get lawyer, not on contengincy, to argue that it is violation of Florida law and Declaration of Condominium.'"

"Okay."

"Yes, and if I lose, I will have to pay for my lawyer *and* condo board lawyer. And if I win, it's even worse. If I win, judge will say: 'Yes, I agree, condo board violate Florida statue, shame on you, break up what you built and make it the way it was. What condo board did is very, very bad, but penalty is nothing.' So, it cost us to build, then it cost us to destroy, then it cost us to build again. Judge will not tell you to fire contractor. So, if I win once and ISIS win three times: they build, they demolition, they build again!"

"Does anyone actually *like* your BOD?"

"Widows."

"Why widows?"

"Their husbands left them more money than they have brains to know what to do with."

"Is there anything you can do?"

"I run for BOD right now."

"Do you stand a chance?"

"I think I may . . . It will take miracle, but I, so to say, believe in miracles."

They walk in silence for a few minutes, passing a mixture of eateries and motels.

They pass a building that looks mildly Italianate in that Las Vegas sort of way, then they enter what looks like a park, complete with low trees.

"They have two mezuzahs here," says Melsor, stepping off the path and transferring kisses to both.

Bill toys with the idea of reminding the old man that he is half Armenian, but thinks better of it. If Melsor self-identifies as a Jew, a Jew he is. Bill self-identifies as (a) a Homo sapiens,

(b) a small-d democrat, and only then (c) culturally a Jew. You don't have to be born Jewish to be the kind of Jew Bill is.

"I read Donal'd Tramp's memoirs, *Art of Deal*. He is philosopher—people don't understand. I want you to see what he writes."

He pulls out a phone and hands it to Bill.

"Make it bigger. I took picture for you."

Bill pushes apart the words on a photo of page sixty-three of *The Art of the Deal*:

"Money was never a big motivation for me, except as a way to keep score. The real excitement is playing the game . . . If you ask me exactly what the deals I am about to describe all add up to in the end, I am not sure I have a very good answer. Except that I've had a very good time making them."

"I am happy for him, less so for this country . . ."

"They don't like him in Washington—or Hollywood. Not this Hollywood; other Hollywood."

"But they like him in Moscow well enough. I am afraid we've just elected a Russian agent to the White House."

"In White House, he replaces agent of International Islam! Putin did right thing. He helped Tramp—yes, but he didn't make up anything. He didn't forger letters from our fool Debbie Wasserman Schultz, my congresswoman, so to say. He knows how to do business."

"True, he wants Crimea, he takes Crimea. He wants Washington, he takes Washington."

"You are probably one of people who call him tug."

"True, I have, on occasion, called him a thug."

"You can say Tramp is tug, Tramp is crazy, Tramp is stupid, Tramp is narcissist, Tramp is fascist, but if you read him with open mind, he is like Albert Camus. If you want to understand me someday, you should read Tramp."

"I didn't cover this election. I haven't met any Trump supporters—until now. No one I know voted for him, of course. Most of us are in mourning for our country."

"All your friends have been to college in America. All professors are leftists. In November, this country was saved by people who didn't have this, so to say, education. They didn't learn political correctness."

"I am grateful."

"Common sense must always beat political correctness."

"You were once a leftist professor; remember?"

"That was in Moscow."

"Yes."

"In Moscow I was for capitalism. Communists were on right. That put me on left."

"The world turned around for you?"

"Tramp reminds me of me. I didn't believe it was impossible to leave Soviet Union, and we left Soviet Union. He didn't believe it was impossible to become president, and he became president."

The walk ends with Bill doing something he hasn't done before, even as a teenager: he asks Melsor for the car keys. (When he was young, the family didn't own a car.)

As Melsor hands him a fat key to a Toyota Prius, Bill reminds himself that upon return to D.C. he really should obtain a valid driver's license.

9

GUCCI

The stroll on the Broadwalk is refreshing: seven miles at a brisk pace is more than Bill would do at home.

Upon reaching the Château (they return separately, as per his father's instructions), Bill needs to remind himself why he came to Florida in the first place.

At the apartment, he clicks on the 911 recording describing Zbig's hard landing at the Grand Dux. He tries to focus, which first and foremost entails recapturing the emotional component of focus. Bill does have emotions. They are slow, granted, but they are present.

He looks through the list of contacts on the iPhone, only to realize that he doesn't have Zbig's home number. He calls the cell phone, feeling odd, knowing that he is calling a dead man.

What is that Hindu custom of wives killing themselves to be cremated with their husbands? The Brits didn't appreciate that custom when they ruled India. Was he expecting that Pani Consuela Ramirez-Wronska would kill herself to be cremated alongside Zbig? He is building up to another absurdist concept: Should cell phones be cremated with their owners?

He dials and gets a recording. Not Zbig's voice, but standard-ized call-has-been-forwarded shit from the phone company. He calls Zbig's office, but also gets the-number-you-have-dialed-has-been-disconnected.

The White Pages offer nothing of value. Bill decides to find the house by memory. He hasn't been there for seven years, but he remembers the style as Bauhaus-on-Acid. The place was white. There seemed to be a hot tub on the terrace, and a view of Miami.

The Prius prances silently southward on Ocean Drive, Bill takes in the peninsularity of the place. It's predominantly north/south; no east/westness of any significance. If you are unable to find a house on so thin a grid, you are, as Mr. Trump might say, a loser.

Bill turns left, then, through the windshield, silently takes stock of new construction, the old placeholder buildings, the di-lapidated motels, the ultra-tall high-rises for the ultra-rich.

He has difficulty recognizing Lapidus's Fontainebleau Hotel, the landmark of landmarks. There is a tower next to it. Why? The place looks expanded, bifurcated. Has the stairway to nowhere survived this desecration? Bill has never been inside; never got around to it. Too late now.

Continuing his southward trek, he starts to encounter the beautiful, more modest Art Deco structures, a Bauhaus haven, painted in shades of coral and chartreuse green. The Prius seems to know what to do, drifting silently past the base of the viaduct to Miami, then on to the roads that hug the eastern shore of Bis-cayne Bay.

The place is in a gated community, because of course.

Bill shows his D.C. press pass, and the guard surprises him by waving him through.

Inside, he notes a cacophony of architectural styles, from genuine Spanish Colonial mansions, to Disneyized Spanish Colonial, to porno-Italianate, to Narco Deco, to Deco Proper, to Last Wednesday's Mish-Mosh with an Obscene Fucking Roofline. Bill is looking for Bauhaus-on-Acid.

He follows his instincts as impressionistically as he can, but this gets him nowhere. The only house that seems vaguely familiar is painted a light shade of green. It has to be the wrong place, because Zbig's house was definitely, aggressively white.

A text announces itself. It's from Lena, the ex-wife, who is technically his current wife:

"A REMINDER: The separation agreement unambiguously stipulates that you are responsible for paying all the fees associated with the final divorce proceedings. I know you don't like your lawyer, but my lawyer agreed to complete this for $2,500—flat fee. If this is agreeable, please make a wire transfer to me ASAP and I will disburse it downstream."

Lena hasn't bothered Bill for some weeks. Lots of people stay separated for years, decades even, not because they hope to reunite, but because they can't get around to spreading the ashes. Why is she bothering him now? What changed? Maybe she heard about his firing and wants to make sure that she gets the last—albeit nonexistent—$2,500? What should he tell her?

He will deal with this later.

He looks for phone company trucks—with the right story those guys might give you the address—but none can be found. Finally, he decides to find a house—any house in the approximate neighborhood—knock on the door, and act lost. This trick works only with houses that don't have servants who open doors. If you chance upon a friendly, ditzy busybody, you will get the help you need.

Now, Bill is looking for cars and license plates. Not New York. Not New Jersey. Not Maryland. Maybe Virginia, people are friendlier in Virginia. He spots Kansas—perfect! A Cadillac Escalade, big enough for grandchildren. Beige.

The house is new. It displays no identifiable architectural style other than rich. The place is a little smaller than the neighborhood average—not large enough to employ a butler. It's still worth something in the millions, of course; Bill has no way of telling how many. The door is painted turquoise—not a Florida shade, but friendly to a fault. Bill spots an oversized mezuzah. Colorful, Israeli.

A trim, petite woman in her seventies opens the door.

"I am looking for . . . ," Bill begins, but the woman interrupts.

"Ya ne govoryu po-angliyski," she responds in Russian.

Even better. Switching to Russian, Bill tells a version of the truth: he is lost, looking for the house of his friend Zbig Wronski.

"Tot chto razbilsya?" asks the woman. [The one who fell to his death?]

Again, Bill tells the truth, and the woman points him to the greenish house he remembered as white.

He doesn't need to wonder what a Russian-speaking older woman is doing at a Miami Beach mansion with an Escalade with Kansas plates. In twenty-first-century America this question is absurd. Is it not possible that her son—or daughter—had purchased green cards for the entire family by investing $500,000 or more in a U.S. company and creating jobs? Can anyone suggest a better method for laundering money than, say, buying into production of alternative fuels in America's heartland, or building high-rises in Hollywood? And if you have a few gold bars to spare after that, why not buy a mansion?

There is no answer at Zbig's house. Perhaps Consuela Ramirez-Wronska has decamped for Rio or moved in with a lover or lovers. Consuela is Brazilian, a former model who posed in and out of swimsuits. Bill met her only once, the last time he saw Zbig. While he tried to strike a conversation, she sat silently staring into her drink and her salad, running out the clock.

As he returns to what he now knows is the right house, Bill vows never to doubt his wondrous combination of memory and instinct. Has he not become a sleuth of air, a marathoner of clouds? Inspector Luftmensch!

After ringing the bell repeatedly, Bill looks in the window, seeing a lot of modern white Italian stuff. No trace of humans. Heading back to the car, in front of the garage, he spots a large box with the words "Salvation A." written with a black marker on its side. The box is hard-sided cardboard, probably from a light fixture.

Bill opens a flap to realize that he is staring at the sole of a loafer. The rest of the box is filled with men's clothes. He places the box in the back of his father's Prius and drives off.

Under normal circumstances, he would take Collins Avenue, also known as US-1, and keep going till the Château shows up on his right.

This time, he feels the urgency to get the hell out of there and takes I-195—the viaduct—to I-95.

As he heads back, Bill glances at a billboard in the vicinity of the I-95 North ramp.

A billboard-sized doctor in a white coat, looks handsome, professional. A stethoscope around his neck attests to his goodness, or at least legitimacy. The doctor is on the corner, superimposed on a photo of a beautiful bikini-bottom-clad woman on white Florida sand. She looks up, smiling, exposing her white teeth and, to a lesser extent, her breasts. But the focus of the photo is the woman's behind.

The question, posed in massive block letters: "ARE YOU PERFECT THERE?"

A red starlike shape provides an addendum: "Make No Payment till August!"

The doctor is broad-shouldered, handsome. His facial features are broad, Slavic, familiar. His name is Zbignew Wronski, MD. The woman looks familiar, too. Her name is Consuela Ramirez-Wronska.

Meanwhile, at the Château, all three elevators display a new *paskvil'*, titled "Ode to Condo Board on the Occasion of Upcoming Election."

In this *paskvil'*, the English and Russian texts are displayed side by side:

Губернатор Вам не страшен,
Президент Вам нипочем,
Здесь миллионные расстраты
Поощряют Лексусом.

Во Флоридском нашем кондо
Невозможно стало жить.

Наводнение в Мейн Лобби,
Исколеченный Сауф Пул.

Но проделкам Вашим наглым,
Верьте мне, пришел конец!
Да, приехал гость желанный—
Федеральный прокурор!

Будет здесь 'фарензик одит,'
Мы вернем свое добро.
Не забудьте Вазелинчик
Захватить с собой в тюрьму.

You don't fear Florida Governor,
And the President, to boot.
Squander millions, and as kickback,
Get a prepaid Lexus lease.

There's no room for joy and laughter
In our beautiful Château.
See the flooding in Main Lobby!
Behold the crippling of South Pool!

But your profligacy's over,
Yes, I know of what I speak!
Yes, a welcomed guest is here:
An inspector with a badge!

Upon a forensic audit,
We'll reveal your foul crimes.
Wearing stripe, in federal prison,
You will take it in the ass.

Publication of this poem on these pages should not be construed as an endorsement of either artistic value of the original or faithfulness of translation.

The *paskvil'* is cited in full to demonstrate that Bill made some telling choices in his translation. In the original, we do not see "an inspector." Instead, we encounter a "*federalnyy prokuror*," a federal prosecutor.

Bill takes the liberty to translate this as "inspector," as in *The Inspector General*, a comedy by Nikolai Gogol. Bill rereads it every few years. It's a classic comedy of mistaken identity: a young man arrives in a small provincial town, where corrupt officials mistake him for an inspector general from Saint Petersburg, traveling incognito with secret orders.

The two closing lines are noteworthy, because the author of the Russian text employs the word "*vazelinchik*," a diminutive for the word "Vaseline," a lubricant sometimes used in sexual encounters.

The translator, in contrast, goes straight to the point, which in this case also constitutes a threat: upon a forensic audit and prosecution, the once-pampered, esteemed members of the Château's BOD will have to face the harsh reality of prison life.

At the apartment, Bill reaches into the box of Zbig's clothes, pulls out the loafer, and slips it on his foot.

It's dark blue. It's suede. It has a gold buckle—a horse-bit-like buckle in the spot where Bill is used to seeing worn leather laces, or, on more formal occasions, pennies. It's Gucci. It fits perfectly.

He and Zbig borrowed each other's stuff all the time when they were at Duke. It feels good in a strange way to know that they still can.

A text from Gwen:

"That poem—WTF?"

"A faithful translation of my father's work"

"Seriously?"

"I let him rave"

"Non-confrontation?"

"I don't care anymore. He is not I"

Bill reaches deeper into the box to find the loafer's brother. He slips it on as well. He rolls his feet. The feeling is akin to standing barefoot on a yoga mat. He takes a step, observing his feet, which no longer feel like his own. Is that not a burst of Zbigness radiating upward, toward his consciousness, something that was absent when he pressed his palms against the marble floor at the Grand Dux?

Is this box not a treasure trove of clues that would have eluded an investigator more earthbound than our Inspector Luftmensch?

Returning to the box, Bill spots a bit of blue, tufted silk. He pulls on it. This produces an odd-looking sport coat. Burberry.

He is aware of the look: sockless Gucci loafers, a Burberry sport coat over a T-shirt, a prickly, unshaven face. Now that look is his, seamlessly so.

Surely there would be jeans in the box—black.

With these finds, Bill feels ready for Art Basel.

He is about to rifle through the pockets of the remaining clothes when he receives a text from his father.

"MIT MI HIR IMEDIAT!" Melsor commands in all caps. "URGEND!!!!"

10

THE INSPECTOR GENERAL

While Bill is proudly a Luddite, Melsor is not. His *kabinet* is filled with gadgets, most of which have the bulky look of obsolete recording devices that cost a fortune in their day.

The computer is new—a massive aluminum-clad Apple desktop.

"Slushay, vot . . . Eto o tebe," says Melsor. [Listen. This is about you.]

He clicks on the "Play" arrow, and a crackling recording of a conversation between two men fills the room. The bug Melsor and Bill had planted the previous night is cranking out intelligence.

One of the people on the recording is young and Russian, clearly the guard Bill encountered at the gate the day before.

The other is Greenstein, "the Evil Dwarf," the chief Jew-Nazi of the Château, the *obersturmbannführer* of bloodsuckers, the *crème de la svoloch'*, the sort of Jew who has no problem living in an apartment purchased with gold bars obtained by means of melting the teeth of Holocaust victims, some of whom could very well have been his cousins.

How many teeth per square foot does it take to get to South Ocean Drive? Should the previous owners of those teeth reconstitute from ashes, arise from the golden sands, and, with guns in hands, seek restitution? And what of those Torah breastplates Bill saw in the Greenstein apartment? Where did the scrolls go? That's the problem with fascism: it's messy, it leaves traces even after the last tooth has been melted. Has Inspector Luftmensch acquired a client? Has he become an agent of the dead? Should he jump back into that *lyul'ka*, liberate the Nazi loot, and, under cover of darkness, drop it off on the doorsteps of the closest Holocaust museum? There must be one in Miami . . .

The security guard's name is Stepan.

STEPAN: Mr. Greenstein, someone I haven't seen before just went in here, into complex when you weren't here.

GREENSTEIN: Who?

STEPAN: Looks like someone in official capacity.

GREENSTEIN: Young?

STEPAN: Comparatively.

GREENSTEIN: Meaning?

STEPAN: I estimated him at fifty, but still hardboiled, thin. Had Halliburton bag.

GREENSTEIN: Where did he go?

STEPAN: That's worst part. To Katzenelenbogen.

GREENSTEIN: Maybe his son?

STEPAN: I thought he always said his son was dead. And they don't look alike.

GREENSTEIN: This indeed doesn't smell good, Stepan. Think it's FBI? Or is he one of the Florida agencies? DBPR?

STEPAN: I don't know, but I feel something wrong. He's not one of us. Clearly doesn't speak Russian.

GREENSTEIN: Did you try to speak with him?

STEPAN: No, we didn't speak. Later, he walked around lobby, looking at damage in details.

GREENSTEIN: So, you looked through the camera as he splashed around in the lobby. You should have come up, asked him to show documents.

STEPAN: I could, of course, but got scared. I don't have document myself, no work visa, no Green Card.

GREENSTEIN: You are a loser and a slave, Stepan. I should have driven you out a long time ago. You don't have a visa and a Green Card because people like you don't deserve Green Cards. Take my word for it, Stepan, when Trump sends visas and the National Guard to get you, I will not stand in their way.

This is followed by another call, several hours later, in which Stepan reports the contents of the tasteless poem affixed to the elevators' walls.

The poem contains the following lines:

Но проделкам Вашим наглым,
Верьте мне, пришел конец!
Да, приехал гость желанный—
Федеральный прокурор!

"Read it in English," orders Greenstein.

But your profligacy's over,
Yes, I know of what I speak!

Yes, a welcomed guest is here:
An inspector with a badge!

Greenstein thanks Stepan for the report and hangs up. Melsor looks away, pours himself a glass of Grey Ruse, and downs it. Bill pours himself a glass as well.

"I don't like that poem," says Melsor, looking out at the ocean.

Father and son Katzenelenbogen are sitting on the bright white leather sofa. Bill is staring at the horse bits on his Gucci loafers. Amazing things happen when blue suede catches Florida sunshine. It's entirely too early to start drinking vodka, but what's done is done.

"I couldn't do that poem justice in the time allotted."

"No, it not you. It was too long. Americans don't like long things. Tramp uses Twitter—one hundred forty characters—and he is in White House! I need new format. I wrote something Americans will like. *Chastushki*. I will write them, you translate, and we find singers to perform them at political rally. I will publish them in *Machta* without pseudonym after that."

Here we go again, the same mechanism: just as Bill starts to feel more or less safe, just as he thinks it might be okay to talk about the loss of his mother, the fucker pulls his next insane stunt.

Chastushki are four-line Russian folk poems, sort of rhyming, limerick-like, usually obscene, often sung by women in traditional costumes. They have been used for political purposes, too.

"I wrote the first in the cycle—here," says Melsor, handing Bill three pieces of paper with an old man's shaky-handed scribbles.

"Holy fuck," Bill says to himself after looking at the first rhyme. It's—fuckfuckfuck—about him, sort of:

К нам приехал ревизор—
Сволочная гадина.
Ни хрена он не найдет!
Всё уже украдено.

An inspector has arrived,
Poisonous and bastardly.
He won't find a single thing,
All was stolen long ago!

Imagine this performed in English by Russian women in native garb. Holy Mother of God! Even whatshisname, Donal'd Tramp, as he is known around these parts, might have a better grasp on reality.

Bill has three serious questions for God, and he is starting to believe that he is entitled to some answers:

- Why is it that all narcissists in your Creation ultimately get their due, while this narcissist—mine—continues to exist, indeed thrive, in blissful isolation from the world you created?
- Are you perchance sending your angels to hold back sword-wielding hands that so appropriately and deservedly aim for Melsor's back?
- Why, my Lord, have you not done the same for me, your sometimes-faithful servant who until recently lived strictly by your laws as reflected in journalistic ethics?

The remainder of this cry of Bill's Russian soul consists of extreme obscenities that can be easily imagined by the reader and thus need not be reproduced. The old man is just getting going with his *chastushki*. With luck, he will get distracted.

After this silent meditation, Bill asks his father for more information about Greenstein.

He got a law degree in night school. He represented manufacturers of dietary supplements, but ultimately was disbarred in a sting operation when, on behalf of a client selling amazing cancer cures, he handed an envelope stuffed with hundred-dollar bills to an FDA inspector. Through bungling on the part of the DOJ, Greenstein escaped conviction, but was disbarred. Now he serves on the BOD of the Château's condo association and drives a 2017 white Lexus GS, one of the cars Bill catalogued in the parking garage.

Not much needs to be said about Stepan; he is obviously a run-of-the-mill thug, except he is a thug with an endearing quality: his sense of self-preservation.

"I need you to help me. I need you to walk around complex and say nothing. When they speak to you in Russian, say you don't understand."

"What the fuck for?"

"I will explain. They think you are from FBI. They think you could also be from DBPR, undercover. They think I am working with you."

"What's DBPR, by the way?"

"Florida Department of Bribery and Profitable Relations I call it. They think you are inspector."

"What is it really?"

"Department of Business and Professional Regulation."

"Not a bad plan, actually."

"They will come to you. They will come and be your best friend and you will get what we need—*kompromat*."

"*Kompromat.*"

"Yes."

"Meaning what?"

"*Kompromentiruyuschiy material.* Must be English word for it."

"Compromising material."

"Sounds right. They give it to you, and you will turn it to me."

"Why would they give me anything?"

"To make deal with persecutors, you do it early, get on ground floor, prevent unpleasantness. I did it in Brooklyn, which is how I kept all this!"

"You were charged. Remember? Felonies?"

"Details . . ."

"And what do I get for taking part in this demented charade?"

Melsor doesn't respond. Likely, he sees no need to.

PART II

|||||||||||||||||||||||||||||||||||||||||||||||||||||||||||||||||||||||||||||||||||||||||||||||||||

*There are people—I categorize them as life's losers—
who get their sense of accomplishment and achievement
from trying to stop others. As far as I am concerned, if
they had any real ability, they wouldn't be fighting me,
they'd be doing something constructive themselves.*

—DONALD TRUMP
The Art of the Deal

|||||||||||||||||||||||||||||||||||||||||||||||||||||||||||||||||||||||||||||||||||||||||||||||||||

11

THE WATERS OF THE CHÂTEAU

A hardened, yellowed, fat-stained strip of paper is attached with thick, clear packing tape to the elevator wall.

The paper is decades old. It's yellow, crumpled—about a quarter of a standard page, cut unevenly with scissors, a corner ripped off by hand.

It's a warning scribbled with a ballpoint pen in an old person's shaky handwriting:

Stop throwing Orange Peels Over Balcony.

There is a dichotomy out there, in the world: people are divided into those who throw orange peels and those who rage about this practice.

Maybe it's not strictly a dichotomy. There are also bystanders, wallflowers. Bill has not thrown a single orange peel over a balcony railing since getting to Florida. In fact, he has no recollection of having thrown orange peels over balcony railings at any point during his life. But neither has he ever felt outraged by peel-throwing on the part of others, and he has never attempted to threaten or hunt down the peel-throwers.

A question: How can you be certain that the object dropping past your balcony is, in fact, *orange* peel thrown by someone above you? Do you extend your hand and catch it?

Bill briefly considers detaching the note from the Formica wall of the elevator and saving it as a document of the time and place, but ultimately leaves it undisturbed.

Rows of white concrete planters create the feel of a grand white alley leading to an intensely blue speck of water. Amid the oversized paisley theme of the Château, this pool is a basic rectangle, decidedly non-Lapidus; post-Lapidus, anti-Lapidus even. It's "other," like a cold, tempered steel blade in your side.

The designers of the obviously renovated South Pool appear to have made a miscalculation. The planters are too small to sustain vegetation. Vegetation exposed to direct sunlight and imprisoned in small containers has to be watered continuously. In Florida, even that may not be enough. Grand as this alley was intended to look, every palm tree and fern lining it has withered. On a scorcher of a day—and January 13 is very much that, even at 10 A.M.—you can hear the crackling and hissing as the leaves of the palm trees take on brittle rigidity, transitioning from green to brown, from succulence to death.

In this temple of defoliation, the pool conjures the archetypal memory of oases Israelites encountered during their forty years in the desert. Discomfort of that memory may explain why there is only one person in the vicinity of the South Pool. Dressed in International Janitorial Blue, he is fishing a large brown palm leaf out of the pool's dead center. Bill mutters a greeting, but, avoiding eye contact, the workman lowers the dead, soggy leaf into a yellow caddy and proceeds to wheel it toward the building.

An architect like Lapidus would have sought mercy killing had he seen this pile of architectural horseshit dropped on what was once his project, but a client like Benito Mussolini would have found this alley esthetically pleasing, even soothing.

Exposed in the middle of a plaza, Bill looks up, forming a visor of his right hand to block out the sun (he forgot the fucking hat), scanning the balconies of the towering Château. He doesn't suspect that someone is staring; he knows someone is. Several people, in fact. Seeking color, his eyes home in on American flags—there are four of them fluttering above, like kites in the wind. On a ninth-floor balcony, he spots a shirtless, rotund man in enormous bright red swim trunks, a septuagenarian surfer. In their endless summers, the Russian people—men and women—gravitate toward loosely fitting Hawaii- and California-themed surfer garments.

As Bill looks up, the man lowers what looks like a pair of black military-style binoculars.

Bill tries to guess this observer's backstory. He could be a re-fusenik who wouldn't be denied, another ambulette fraudster from Brooklyn, a gasoline-tax scammer from Jersey City, a lucky winner of a medical malpractice or employment discrimination suit anywhere in America, a Donal'd Tramp supporter, a Josef Mengele son-in-law. Those gold teeth can buy a lot of Florida real estate.

On the top floor, three balconies away from Melsor's, Bill spots a woman and a man. Both continue to stare even as he re-turns the gaze. They, too, are dressed for water recreation. The man wears massive sky blue trunks. The woman's Zeppelinesque figure is jammed into a leopard-print one-piece bathing suit. Her hair is out-of-the-bottle red. Do they believe they had made themselves invisible and thus can stare in an unimpeded fashion? Or do they simply not give a shit?

Bill is far from sure about what his father wants from him and how firmly that task is based in reality, but if he is to gauge the attitudes of the natives, he has to accept that (1) he will stand out and (2) the barren, scorched white plaza framing the South Pool is not the place to start.

The North Pool, a larger body of water, is nevertheless a more intimate affair. Real estate ladies might call it "dated." Translation: untouched by the dehumanizing bulldozer of renovation that makes all things the same.

Bill is pleasantly surprised to see that the mosaic on the deck sports Lapidus's oversized paisleys, coral and chartreuse. The pool, too, is in the shape of a very large paisley. It's deeper than you would expect from an apartment building or hotel pool. A large, upright, paisley-shaped tower at the deep end suggests that the pool was at one point used for diving.

Though some folks sprawled out to broil atop plastic lounges might self-identify as swimmers and divers, from the liability point of view, it is generally considered imprudent to enable 280-plus-pound objects to drop from great heights into deep water. In a wise move, the diving board has been removed, neutralized, and the entrance to the whimsical diving tower barred.

Bill first considers the chaises. These are mostly plastic, Costco-bought, with older aluminum-frame pieces mixed in. In the corner of the deck, he spots a pile of broken-down outdoor furniture. These pieces are of a different sort. This is Richard Schultz, the original stuff. Not a surprise. You expect to see a pile of crippled Schultz chaises on the deck of a château where Plattner and Baughman pieces rot, rust, and mold in the dungeons.

Schultz's "contour chaises" offer few sitting positions. A contour chaise doesn't recline, because why should it? Bill had seen those things in photos, but had never experienced one.

The chaises around the North Pool are replaced with more democratic models, but the tables are still Schultz. Alas, some barbarian—surely a *Homo Sovieticus*—had painted them with a rough brush, cheaply, viciously, in accordance with the traditions of the Gulag. This was done repeatedly, year after year. Bill snaps a picture of the pile of Schultz lounges and texts it to Gwen.

"OMfuckingGodJesus!!!" Gwen shoots back.

In this case, "OMfuckingGodJesus!!!" is an exclamation pregnant with meaning, teetering on the edge of bittersweetness.

Schultz's furniture surrounded the swinging-singles swimming pool where, in another lifetime, pre-Remorse Gwen purported to have overheard the conversations that ended up in her ill-fated Style piece.

You'd think people know when they are plagiarizing *Franny and Zooey*.

Two dozen Châteauites of different ages are assembled in three distinct groups.

Bill walks up to the pile of Schultz lounges, picks one that looks more or less stable, and sets it down between two of these clusters. Even beat up, at the North Pool of Château Sedan

Neuve, a Schultz lounge looks like a sleek Concorde supersonic airliner surrounded by a fleet of B-52 clunkers.

One of the groups—the English-speakers—immediately switches to a whisper. The other—the Russians of Jewish variety—continues to communicate at high volume, shielded by the secrecy of their language. These are people of Melsor's generation, those who fought their way to freedom and prospered rapidly. In some cases, even legally. Bill believes he recognizes the man in red trunks who was studying him through binoculars earlier that morning.

The third group consists of four very pregnant women whose high cheekbones and demeanor of quiet aloofness scream of their tribes of origin—Slavic beauties, who, were they not very pregnant, would be Trump's type, the Trumpettes, presumably the type he has bragged about grabbing by the whatchums. They are wives and girlfriends of the so-called "New Russians," men with enough money to send their pregnant wives to the U.S. Children born in the U.S. automatically qualify for U.S. citizenship, which gives them the option to escape when things go bad.

Schultz could well have designed the Contour Chaise with Bill's contours in mind.

Another text from Gwen: a link to a catalog where a Schultz's Contour Chaise can be had for $2,164, quite a bit more than Bill's net worth.

The rest of her text: "I think I need 1 for my terrace! Shd I get 2?"

"Hmmm . . ." Bill writes, then reconsiders pushing "Send."

He reaches into his bike messenger's bag and produces Melsor's dog-eared copy of *The Art of the Deal*.

———

Bill limits his exposure by going through the lines his father has underlined.

For starters, there is this insight: "I believe in spending what you have to. But I also believe in not spending more than you should."

Abstracted, this looks almost okay, and it gains in the Russian translation, which is penciled in on the margins. Leafing through, Bill spots another highlighted pearl: "I like thinking big . . . To me it's very simple: if you're going to be thinking anyway, you might as well think big"—an idiot's riff on Goethe's "Dream no small dreams for they have no power to move the hearts of men."

To his credit, Melsor scribbled "Goethe?" on the margin, in Russian.

Another passage, marked and translated with reverence:

"One thing I've learned about the press is that they're always hungry for a good story, and the more sensational the better . . . The point is that if you are a little different, a little outrageous, or if you do things that are bold or controversial, the press is going to write about you."

And this: "You can't con people, at least not for long. You can create excitement, you can do wonderful promotion and get all kinds of press, and you can throw in a little hyperbole. But if you don't deliver the goods, people will eventually catch on."

This selection and underlining tell a story, and it's not the story of Donal'd Tramp, but the paradox of the intense appeal of authoritarianism to a man like Melsor, the boy whose very name says Stalin, but who nonetheless grew up to despise Stalin and Stalin's heirs.

Unlike self-described progressives like Bill, Melsor actually fought against authoritarianism—fearlessly at that. What does Melsor Katzenelenbogen see in this Donald Trump? Wouldn't a quote from Stalin, radiating surefooted certainty of a shiny-booted barbarian, feel at home in a book by Donald?

If Trump's meaning can be stretched into a philosophy, Stalin's is more in the realm of stand-up comedy. His stakes are high, shades dark, phrasing blunt. History is on his side, too. His lines always get a laugh, or at least a smirk: "The death of one man is a tragedy. The death of millions is a statistic." Also: "Ideas are more powerful than guns. We would not let our enemies have guns, why should we let them have ideas?" And there is this: "Death is the solution to all problems. No man—no problem."

There is a reason Bill remembers all this. Decades ago, in Moscow, Melsor was famous for quoting Stalin's pronouncements. He did this with a faux Georgian accent. This was a parlor trick of sorts. And now Melsor is adoringly underlining, translating, embracing the latter-day dime-store version of the dictator he once despised.

Hearing the stomping of feet followed by a thunderous splash, Bill looks up in time to see a broad figure submerge in what can best be described as a modified belly flop. The sight is reminiscent of the dive of a Typhoon-class submarine.

The four pregnant Russian girls look up. They are sitting on the side of the pool, soaking their feet, drinking water out of large plastic cups. They are young, beautiful, and their pregnancies make Bill hold his gaze longer. All four appear to have gone to the same stylist. Their hair is shoulder-length, completely straight. One might jump to the conclusion that Bill's attention to them bespeaks his primal wish to procreate, because at this stage it's increasingly unlikely that he ever will. Perhaps he is drawn by the look of detachment on their faces and the electricity of their aloofness that is surely generated by friction with their beauty.

Red Trunks executes a lap in a powerful, splashy butterfly style, and, still grunting rhythmically, pulls himself up on the edge of the pool, rubs his belly in a rounded, spontaneous, Buddha-like gesture, and starts humming an unrecognizable Soviet march.

This has to be the man who was studying Bill through binoculars earlier that morning.

Red Trunks walks past Bill, returning to the chaise. The flat sheet of plastic visibly gives beneath his weight, straining heroically, bowing a bit, resisting, but in the end it remains structurally sound, upright, true to itself.

Red Trunks stops humming the instant he settles into the plastic chaise.

"*Revizora nashego videli? Polyubuytes'*," he announces loudly to the group of Russians around him. [Have you seen our inspector general? Behold!]

Men like him have only one volume level—all the way up. No dial is provided. With the volume being the message, this determines the character of the conversation that follows.

Bill is six feet away, his face stuck in a book so moronic that it would benefit from being held upside down.

"*Eto Melsor Yakovlevich yego vyzval?*" asks a woman in a zebra-print bathing suit, presumably the same one Bill spotted on the eighteenth-floor balcony a few minutes earlier. [Did Melsor Yakovlevich summon him?]

"*A chto eto za mudak? FBR?*" asks a woman in a black bathing suit. [Who is this fuckup? FBI?]

"Kak znat'? A po proiskhozhdeniyu on kto?" asks a man in blue trunks. [What do you think his ethnicity is?]

RED TRUNKS: *Irlandets, Anglo-Sakson khuyev. Oni vse v FBR takiye. VOSPY. Ni khera v nas ne razbirayutsya—on ni khera i ne poymet.* [Irish, some fucking Anglo-Saxon. They all are at FBI. WASPS. They don't understand a fucking thing about us.]

Who are these people?

Bill understands their language, but they are nothing like him. Their speech is deeply uncouth, not because of its vulgarity (vulgarity can be a positive), but because of complete absence of intonation. Properly spoken, Russian is operatic, its song soaring and dropping like an aria well performed. Here, there is no up, no down. Bill understands all the words, all the grammatical structures, but he has to struggle with the sense.

ZEBRA-PRINT BATHING SUIT: *On tyt, govoryat, inkognito.* [He is traveling incognito, they say.]

BLACK BATHING SUIT: *Da esche s sekretnym predpisaniem.* [With secret orders.]

At least these people are able to quote from the opening scene of *The Inspector General.* This is not necessarily a sign of great erudition: most people of their generation are able to remember parts of that play.

Gogol was skewering provincial officials and the culture of corruption in nineteenth-century Russia. These people appear to be skewering the investigator taking on latter-day corruption.

The play Bill finds himself in appears far more sinister than *The Inspector General.* This is more than a case of mistaken identity. These people are dismissing any efforts to stem corruption, challenging him to teach them a lesson, to defend the honor of the Federal Bureau of Investigation.

BLUE TRUNKS: *Trampa chitayet.* Art of Deal. [Reading Trump. *Art of Deal.*]

BLACK BATHING SUIT: *Oni yego boyatsya. On priydet, i ikh v sheyu pogonit, chtob bisnesu ne meshali.* [He will come in and throw them out, to keep them from getting in the way of business.]

ZEBRA-PRINT BATHING SUIT: *Chto oni, eti FeBeRovtsy ne ponimayit chto etot Katzenelenbogen avantyurist, moshennik prostoy?* [Don't they, the FBIniks, understand that Katzenelenbogen is a simple crook?]

BLUE TRUNKS: *Professional'nyy dissident. Chego s nego voz'mesh?* [A professional dissident. What do you expect from him?]

BLACK BATHING SUIT: *A im to chto? Im by tol'ke den'gi v settlementakh kachat' da disgorjmenty delat'.* [What do they care? They just want to get their settlements and disgorgements.]

Bill has never heard any Russian émigré describe dissidents as cranks who should be disregarded, avoided.

True, his people migrate to the right, but in the past, Republicans, even Republican wing nuts, have always sided with the dissidents. This was somewhat incongruent, to be sure: the very people who oppose civil liberties at home wanted to export them behind the Iron Curtain. And now they simply don't give a shit. Is this what convergence looks like? Has the world become a big crooked condo board?

Bill is generally inclined to sympathize with anti-Melsor sentiments. But Melsor's dissident past is actually something he admires; it's the reason, the only reason perhaps, to give him the benefit of the doubt.

That's what the judge did, and for the first time, Bill starts to think that—maybe—the judge was right to let the old man walk and keep his stash.

ZEBRA-PRINT BATHING SUIT: *On v vodu ne idet. Yego Roza Kisel' po spine svoeyy palkoy yobnula. Sinyachische gromadnyy navernyaka sozrel.* [He is not going in the water. Roza Kisel' whacked him on the back with her crooked cane. A big bruise is ripening, for sure.]

BLACK BATHING SUIT: *Pizda staraya.* [Old cunt.]

ZEBRA-PRINT BATHING SUIT: *Federal'noye prestupleniye FBRoshnikov po zhope khuyakat'.* [It's a federal crime to whack FBI agents on the ass.]

BLACK BATHING SUIT: *Yebanatikam vsyo mozhno.* [Crackpots may do as they please.]

BLUE TRUNKS: *Ladno, a chto vy dumayete oni zdes' naydut?* [Enough on that. What do you think they can find here?]

RED TRUNKS: *Obychnoye delo, sami znayete. Otkaty, da ne to chtob ochen' bol'shiye, v meru.* [Nothing unusual, you know yourself. Some kickback, but not too much, well measured.]

BLUE TRUNKS: *Kak umnomy cheloveku ne vzyat'—ny kak u Gogolya skazanno—kogna samo v ruki plyvet.* [How can a smart man not accept things that—like Gogol had it—swim into your hands.]

RED TRUNKS: *Kak v* Revizore, *u Gogolya, khmyr' govoril, "Ya beru vzyatki, no tol'ko Borzymi schenkami. A eto sovsem inoye."* [Remember in Gogol, *The Inspector General,* one of the men says, "I take bribes, but I only accept Borzoi puppies. And that's a completely different thing."]

ZEBRA-PRINT BATHING SUIT: *A Lexus to u tebya kak?* [How's the Lexus running?]

RED TRUNKS: *Normal'no, chego tam, kak i tvoy.* [Normal, just like yours.]

BLACK BATHING SUIT: *Slushayte, muzhchiny, vy-b k nemu*

podoshli, potolkovali, mozhet vy s nim snachala dogovorites' kak obychno, chtob nam bez disgorjmenta kak-to, poka Tramp ne priydet. [Listen, gentlemen, what if you were to come up to him, had a man-to-man conversation, as it's always done, so there'd be no disgorgement, until Trump comes.]

RED TRUNKS: *Nu my sobstvenno tak i sobiralis', tol'ko davayte prismotrimsya.* [That was the plan. Just let it play out a bit while we take a look.]

Bill shifts his attention to the Americans.

They seem to be roughly the same age as the Russians. They spring from the same *shtetlekh*, have the same ancestors, snooze in the same synagogues.

They can easily be each other's first cousins, but if that's the case, they are cousins separated by history, cousins who hate each other's guts, squabbling over inheritance, holding eternal grudges. Some years ago, in the 1970s and '80s, these very Americans displayed "Free Soviet Jewry" signs in front of their houses of worship. They did this because that's what the rabbi wanted, so who gives a shit. Now, they would happily display a big neon-lit "Take Them Back" sign in front of the Château.

An older woman and a grandchild walk through the doors and settle down in the American group. The woman is petite, her hair permed, painted a shade of beige.

The Russian women don't seem to be impressed by the strategy she's employed in the preservation of youth and pursuit of beauty.

"*Obezyana,*" mutters the redheaded woman in the leopard-print bathing suit. [A monkey.]

Her comrade in the black bathing suit is equally unimpressed. *"Smotri kak morda natyanuta. Spit s otkrytymi glazami."* [Look at how tight her face is. She sleeps with her eyes open.]

Meanwhile, the child, who seems to be around two, takes off in the direction of the cluster of Russians, heading straight toward a large bag, and grabbing onto it. Surely he thinks the bag contains toys, buckets and such.

Red Trunks lazily grabs the child by the arm, pronouncing him arbitrarily an *"ublyudok"*—the product of indiscriminate sexual activity—and waiting for the monkey to pick up the now-screaming child.

As the grandmother comes up, Russian conversation grows louder, to drown out the screaming, physically restrained child.

The woman's name, Bill overhears, is Martha.

In conversation, she is described as a "Chicago cunt." [*Pizda Chikagskaya.*] Conversation related to Martha now focuses on Botox, sundry other cosmetic interventions, even a suggestion that the child's grandmother purchases sexual services of young men on Craigslist.

Walking slowly to pick up the child, Martha throws an angry glance at each of the Russians individually.

"This is a public place!" she declares. "This is America! We speak English here! Speak Russian in your units."

The woman in the zebra-print bathing suit responds for the entire group: "We don't afraid you. We speak what we want!"

"Svoloch'," interjects one of her comrades.

At the beach, the waves make swimming a challenge.

Bill looks around. There are six groups milling here, elderly men and women standing in circles of five or six, speaking in an agitated manner. He walks slowly past two of the groups, long enough to determine whether they are speaking Russian or English. The English-speakers immediately switch to a whisper or complete silence. The Russians—all of them old Jews—continue to converse loudly.

Bill places his towel on the sand. He is now positioned between two circles—Americans and Russians. From here he can focus on whatever shreds of conversation come his way.

At the beach, all conversations revolve around the pending $19 million special assessment that the BOD is about to impose on the Château's 360 unit owners. There is also some discussion of Melsor—nicknamed *"Dissident"*—running for a seat on the board.

One shred of conversation, in translation: "Some say he is insane, but it's not that simple. He becomes agitated when the world fails to operate in accordance with the rules he believes must apply."

Bill regards this as an astute analysis, but says nothing.

One of the Russians, a short man with a goatee, breaks away from the group and approaches Bill. He is dressed for extreme leisure—light-blue plaid shorts and a faded yellow T-shirt that reads "Glasnost," a long-abandoned Gorbachev-era slogan.

The man looks remarkably like Lenin, not the heroic Lenin of Soviet posters and paintings, but a real-life Lenin, the little guy you see in photographs.

"We have proverb in Florida," he says with a thick accent that seems vaguely French. Bill has seen this before: for reasons that he is unable to fathom, some Russians affect a version of a French accent, which grows in both Frenchness and fauxness as they drink.

"You know why it's good to be on beach?"

Bill smiles, but says nothing. He wants the guy to keep talking.

"Because on beach you are surrounded by idiots on only three sides."

"And on the remaining side you have what?" asks Bill.

"Sharks," says the man, pointing to a small figure bobbing in the waves. "This is Herr Doktor of Jurisprudence Greenstein, king of . . . How you say *otkaty*?" he shouts to his group.

"Kickbacks!" shouts the woman from his group.

"*Dura, eto-zh ty po-angliyski yemu vykriknula,*" says her friend. [Idiot, you just shouted it in English.]

"*Nichego, puskay ponimayet,*" she said. [It's okay, this way he will understand.]

Bill looks up to the top floor and sees his father, presumably holding binoculars.

His plan is to get out into the waves, toward the small bobbing figure. Alas, the man who ensnared him is not ready to let go.

"Call me Alex," the man offers.

"Bill . . ."

"My nephew works at Department of Justice—Antitrust Division? Have you heard? Washington? He is Ilya Vilner; my sister's stepson; she raised him. You know him?"

"It's a big place."

"The world is *shtetl*; everyone knows everyone; always good to ask. He is investigator also."

"Okay."

"Lives on Connecticut Avenue, near famous bookstore, Politics and Prose, but closer to Calvert Woodley, liquor store; both on same side of street."

"Sounds good."

"Russian Standard was almost seventeen dollars for seven-hundred-fifty-milliliter bottle at Calvert Woodley when I visited."

"Hmm."

"I am used to less. I keep track of such things. I finished Historico-Archival Institute . . . in Moscow. They teach you that history is under your nose. History in Kremlin and White House is same history in your flat, which is same as history in your street, and your condo, in this situation. You understand concept? You want to know anything about Château, come to me. I have original sales brochures. You play chess?"

"Badly."

"Better badly than not. Means I will win. Chess died because of computer. My grandson shoots at tanks all day."

"It's a skill. May become necessary."

"I even have elevations signed by main architect, Lapidus himself! It's always same thing: they throw away history to keep control—I rescue it. It's war, people's war—eternal. When it will end, everyone will die. Or it will end after everyone dies. I don't know yet. Erosion of truth is same as erosion of sand on beach. You don't win, but you fight."

"Historico-Archival?"

"They destroy records—I save records. It's like game: cats-mice, *koshki-myshki*. I *am* history in exactly same way that you are history. Not like their Tramp—he is narcissist—everything rotates around his belly button, he is whole world."

"Does that mean Trump is history?"

"No. He think he is history, but he is not history. We saw this before."

"Well put."

"We are different: what we do it's not for us. It's for truth, it's for mankind, to establish record, to preserve. Truth is best weapon against fascism."

"Hard to disagree."

"The guy who they say helps you, Melsor Yakovlevich, they say he is crazy, but I say no. He is potentially most effective person here, who is not completely crooked. I repeat so you will understand subtle point: he is not *completely* crooked, only *partially* crooked, which in our situation creates hope. Sometimes he is one of them, sometimes he is one of us. Problem is, crooked people are effective, and we need help."

"Everyone does."

"Melsor Yakovlevich is offended at me. He and I were almost friends when I come here. But then he showed me his poems and I said—not to him, but to common friend—that I used to have dogs in Moscow, Scottish terriers, and when they took shits, their shits were better than poems by Melsor Katzenelenbogen. I called him a *grafoman*. How do you say that?"

"The condition is called graphomania, compulsion to write."

"So, he, so to say, learned that I said it, became very offended, and he doesn't say hello to me when he sees me. If you talk with him, tell him Alex Bogomolov didn't say any of it, about graphomania and dog shit."

"I'll try to remember, should I talk with him. But you did say it?"

"Afraid so. Guilty. There are big lies in world. This is little lie. Innocent lie. Thank you for being here. You know, their next special assessment—nineteen million dollars—means I lose my daughter's apartment."

"Sorry to hear that."

"But it's not me. Individual is besides a point. It's about place. This place is like nothing else. They should make it historical monument instead of fucking it up more and more and getting rich on *otkaty* . . . kickbacks. Architect, whom I already spoke about, was very famous. Morris Lapidus! You know about him?"

"Yes, I actually do."

"Lapidus is father of Miami Modernism current. Developer fired him from this building halfway through design. He wasn't making it French enough, they say, I have letters. It says: put in more French symbols, the lilies, but he says—no—paisleys. They say paisleys are from India, but he says, no, no, and no. You know how this ends. Swimming pools; you've seen? They destroy South Pool already; it's nothing to see—dead. North Pool will be destroyed next. It will be crime. You were there?"

"Yes."

"You know why it's deep?"

"No."

"Ah, this is fascinating. It's deep, because water was used to work as air conditioner for whole building. It was quietest air conditioner in the world. It was separate utility, you paid for it every month. It was candidate for inclusion in American Pavilion in World's Fair in Montreal. It was nominated; I have letters. They were going to make a to-scale working model of it to put on truck to Canada for exhibition! Even now we have kilometers of pipes in walls, they don't know anymore where it leads or what to do with it. If you have questions, run fast to me, I am in unit 215, like Philadelphia. Easy to remember: 215; 215—Alex. Alex—Alex Bogomolov."

"Thank you."

"Don't go in water—there is shark there."

———

Alex points again at the small figure bobbing in the waves fifty meters offshore: the esteemed Herr Greenstein, vice president of the BOD of the Condominium Owners Association of Château Sedan Neuve, the man whose apartment Bill and Melsor had surreptitiously visited via *lyul'ka*.

When he reaches Greenstein, Bill is up to his rib cage in water, jumping up in the waves.

He has no plans to initiate a conversation, only to give Greenstein the opportunity to do so. He knows what Greenstein looks like, a short, beefy man with broad shoulders, dwarfed by his wife, a woman who maintains herself aggressively fed, permed, and dyed.

The picture Bill saw showed Herr and Frau Greenstein at a formal event of some sort, with him in a plain black tux, and her in what looked like a shining blue tarp, balancing her mass on remarkably high heels. In that picture, they seemed to be held together by an unbreakable bond. She had the height, the mass, the territory. His body was proportional enough to rule out dwarfism, but while he was corporeally minimal, he was projecting inner power, looking like someone who will not be moved, someone feared by lesser men.

Did Frau Greenstein's father approve of his daughter's choice of husbands? Was he a true believer in racial hygiene? Was he a simple soldier who followed orders, or a bureaucrat embracing the technical challenge of making Europe *Judenfrei*?

As an amateur shrink, Bill is far from good enough to hypothesize.

Greenstein comes out at Bill from up high, his big face emerging through the middle of an oncoming wave, but as the wave moves toward breaking, Greenstein hangs back, paddling backward, his intense gaze focused on Bill.

That face makes up for what he lacks in body size: it's meaty, with a unibrow, which becomes all the more prominent because his head is completely shaven.

Bill's Yiddish-speaking grandfather—he had only one Jewish grandfather—had an expression: *a yam potz*. A sea prick. It's used to denote men so peerlessly awful that two of them haven't been known to exist. We know of sea horses, sea urchins, sea birds, but no sea pricks. Yet Greenstein is a *yam potz*, emerging from the waves, unifying the literal with the figurative.

"I think I can save both of us some time," says Greenstein, accidentally gulping and spitting out seawater. "There is no shortage of stories here."

Bill doesn't respond.

"It's terribly entertaining, but they are all unsubstantiated rumors," Greenstein continues.

"Rumors?"

"Malicious, delusional—ubiquitous, unfortunately."

"Ubiquitous?"

"Some of it is actionable, assuming you are desperate for something to do. Not the sort of thing you build a case out of. I am an attorney—I can assure you. This is a waste of time. Nobody wants a goat parade."

Bill is out of uninformative responses. "Hmmm" is genuinely the best he can do.

"I would be happy to go through it point by point. The rumor about the contractor being hired based on willingness to pay kickbacks is completely false. Murthy is a brilliant engineer, whose bids always come in lower than those of any two competitors.

"The people spreading rumors want to do business the Florida way. You know how it's done: three contractors gather on a yacht twelve miles offshore, determine their bids, and decide who gets which job. So they decide a priori.

"So, let's say, you get the Neptune contract, your associate gets the Mermaid, and his girlfriend's company gets the Wave. I am not talking about specific places. I am just using these names to illustrate the point. You know the drill, but it's all collusion outside territorial waters, so there's nothing you can do.

"This contract is not like that at all. It's all completely aboveboard, completely transparent. I can justify every little piece of it.

"And the urban legend about Lexus leases. That's just insane. I will not dignify it with a comment. I know you've been listening to that dissident, Katzenelenbogen. He is completely unreliable, a disturbed individual, completely out of touch.

"Can you imagine him in court? Even in his fraud case in Brooklyn, the ambulettes, with his life on the line, his lawyer didn't dare let him take the stand. They made it look like he was about to die, I am told, and the judge used to be a Soviet Jewry activist. He is viewed as a hero, though God knows . . .

"Pathetic—it had to be like hauling in Sharansky for shoplifting."

Bill throws in a "Hard to imagine," and indeed it stokes the flow.

"Look, I am just trying to save you the embarrassment. You are free to dismiss anything I say when you write your . . ."

"I don't know what you mean."

"Of course, I am sorry. It's not Americans versus Russians. Two of my most steadfast allies on the BOD are of Russian Jewish descent.

"When Wilfreda and I moved here, this was a friendly building. People said hello to each other, people invited each other for drinks, people went to dinners with each other. Now, it's just name-calling.

"The vice president has two members in his pocket . . . Ridiculous. I don't care what race you are, what country you are from. I just care whether you are a nice person."

With this, Herr Greenstein, JD, wades in to shore.

Bill is done here.

He shoots a text to Gwen: "Can someone in your crisis mngmnt firm run license plates? I may need several."

"Easy-peasy," Gwen responds.

12

COMRADE KOZACHOK

Sometimes in life there are moments when we wake up struggling to reconstruct the series of events that led another individual to appear on the adjacent pillow. This moment of uncertainty can occur after a night of unbridled revelry, or—just as easily—after a quarter century of production of offspring and acquisition of property.

One morning, more than a decade earlier, after an office party that went longer than planned, he woke up staring at a bare shoulder he recognized as possibly belonging to a woman younger than himself—presumably Gwen. Not a good thing. She wasn't out of her twenties at the time. He was in his early forties. She had once been an intern he worked with; a student, basically. Yes, she is an adult now, a journeyman reporter, the princess of Style.

The rule he broke that night was more the stuff of the unspoken code of conduct than the stuff of the employee handbook.

Bill's left hand spent the night—or at least a portion thereof—between small breasts that he would have estimated to be consistent with Gwen's. As his fingers brushed past her breast, the woman turned toward him, revealing, at last, that he had guessed correctly.

"I don't sleep with guys in the newsroom," said Gwen. There was a smile on her face.

"Of course not."

"Did we fuck?"

"Tried to, probably."

"I want us to try again."

That night is a memory now, left behind with nothing but a smile and pleasantness of a shared history.

Bill's night of guzzling room-temperature Kozachok out of a large plastic bottle and contemplation of falling from great heights seems to be different. It seems to have produced a tangible reminder—a large box addressed to "Bill c/o Melsor Katzenelenbogen." The box hails from someplace in California. If the sender's compounded neologism of a name is an indication, it's something techy.

It seemed possible that a plastered Bill had ordered an industrial-strength router. He could have bought toy cars, buses, and Caterpillar tractors for his Inner Child to play with. It wouldn't take a big shopping spree for his net worth to dip into negative numbers. How much did he spend?

Melsor is unavailable. Nella explains that he is preparing for a colonoscopy. In the old days, before he decided to insulate himself from the consequences of his father's decisions, Bill would have inquired about symptoms that would classify the procedure as diagnostic. If no symptoms were present, Bill would have pointed out that, as per recommendations of the U.S. Preventive Services Task Force, men of Melsor's age—over eighty—shouldn't get screening colonoscopies if they are at average risk of developing colon cancer. Today, he chooses not to go there; too much complexity.

"I was expecting this," Bill lies to Nella, lifts the box—it's surprisingly light—and takes the thing downstairs to find out what it might be.

At the apartment, he makes a quick incision on top of the box, finding a packing slip and a handwritten note. A document indicates that Bill's American Express card ending in *2002 was charged $1,850 for a "Canopy" and a "Container," whatever those may be. Expedited next-day shipping, at least, was free.

What American Express? He no longer has an American Express card. He had one when he was at the *Post*. Did Comrade Kozachok cloud his consciousness so profoundly that he charged nearly $2,000 to the fuckers who had just fired him?

The handwritten note, scribbled on a thick piece of paper and ripped out of a spiral sketchbook, reads:

> *Hey Bill,*
>
> *It was a pleasure to speak with you. Here, as discussed, is a Canopy and Container that belonged to a good friend of mine. He never used it, so it's not technically "used," though I priced it that way—happy to provide a "good deal" for you.*
>
> *My friend is in a "Better Place" now, and his wife sold his unused equipment back to me. Tell me if you need anything else, Knee Pads and a Helmet for example. His fly suit is the only thing I can't offer. (You understand.) This is not a "safe sport," like golf, as you well know.*

*As I said, I am passing this one "at cost." I packed the Canopy
into the Container, as per your instructions, so it's "jump-ready."*

*From what you told me, sounds like you're an experienced
jumper. Surprised our paths haven't crossed before.*

Fly safe!!!

Your friend,

Jason

You might surmise that Bill would immediately recognize the
magnitude of his transgression. You might think he would stop
right there, seal the box, ship the canopy and container back to
Jason, his new best friend. You might also expect that he would
call American Express and the *Post* and apologize: there was a
misunderstanding, it's dealt with, please cancel the card.

Inspector Luftmensch does nothing of the sort. With entirely
too much excitement, he opens the box and pulls out the canopy-
bearing, "jump-ready" container—it's a backpack, really—and
slips it on.

It feels good, like a well-tailored sport coat. He walks out
onto the balcony and, adjusting the buckles of a dead man's
chute, takes in the expanse of the ocean, the low clouds. Bill
doesn't actually know this, but he surmises that the world is a
different place if you carry a gun. In presumably the same way,
a man with a chute experiences heights differently than a man
without one.

The clouds suddenly feel within his grasp, and as he con-
quers the clouds, one more mystery of the universe will have
been eroded.

Achtung! William Melsorovich Katzenelenbogen, Inspector
Luftmensch, is in the midst of an existential investigation, perhaps the first of its kind, perhaps the last.

———

Now there are two big boxes in the apartment.

One, hailing from California, has provided Bill with the container and canopy that are now on his back. The other, a larger one, is filled with clothes that once belonged to Bill's friend Zbig, the Butt God who fell from the sky.

Bill dumps out the clothes. The pile is big. He has gone through it in a cursory manner a bit earlier. Now he is on the lookout for the usual dross people generate in the course of a normal day: receipts, keys, key cards, business cards, hand-scribbled notes, phone numbers.

There is nothing in the Burberry sport coat, nothing in the black jeans of a variety he has never seen: Ermenegildo Zegna (he thought Zegna only made yellow ties that famously appealed to Bill Clinton's paramour Monica Lewinsky). The jeans feel less comfortable than Bill's proletarian Carhartts. But with Gucci loafers and a black T-shirt, the ensemble clicks. The pockets, alas, are empty.

In the box, Bill finds two more pairs of Gucci loafers, which he admits he no longer holds in contempt, as well as a pair of Ferragamo loafers, which to him look like bedroom slippers. A Moschino shirt looks Hawaiian and thus is not his thing. Also, there are two black and vaguely silky Versace T-shirts (not manly, he determines), a light blue Brioni suit (maybe okay, if suits are your style), a Brunello Cucinelli leather jacket with wide lapels and a profusion of zippers, a pair of Tom Ford dark indigo jeans, two pairs of Dolce & Gabbana blue jeans, and a bottle of cologne (also by Dolce & Gabbana).

Bill goes through every pocket, finding nothing. Some items—the jeans and the Brunello Cucinelli thing—still have price tags. Nobody has just one Brioni suit, Moschino shirt, etc. Where there is one there are a dozen, where there are a dozen there are fifty. This box is just one of many that are now making their way to the Salvation Army donation pile, and—unless, of course, it's the last box to depart—there will be more.

There is nothing in any of the pockets. Zbig is guarding his secrets. He didn't yield a single clue as Bill's hand touched the exact spot where Zbig's cranium popped, spilling its jelly-like stuffing onto the white terrazzo tile. This was the spot of the meeting of the spheres, Zbig's cosmic opportunity to communicate with Inspector Luftmensch.

On the bottom of the box, Bill finds two items that seem out of place. One is a pair of well-worn Levis. In the front pocket, he finds a package of terazosin, an alpha-blocker used to control high blood pressure. Two condoms, in packages, cling to it.

Beneath the jeans, he finds an old rucksack. It looks like something from World War II. The memory of that bag returns suddenly: it was bought at a military surplus store in Georgetown, near Key Bridge.

The bag was of unknown military provenance, but it was solid. It seemed some idiot took a ballpoint pen and gave it a new past, writing in block letters across the back pocket: RAF No. 303 Polish Fighter Squadron. This was not a disingenuous act by a ruthless militaria dealer. The forgery was too obvious for that: there were no ballpoint pens during World War II. The idiot who bought this bag at Sunny's Surplus for (he still remembers) $12.99 was none other than Ilya "William" Melsorovich Katzenelenbogen. This was a birthday present for Zbig. The year was 1985.

Something about Zbig reminded Bill of the brave men of the RAF Polish Fighter Squadron. Sure, they were Catholics—probably just about all of them—but spiritually, they were the brothers of people Bill identified with—the fighters of the Jewish ghettos.

This is the bond—the polarity—that unites Bill and Zbig even now, death notwithstanding.

See it meander through history, watch it boil down to a hard, solid sediment—an existential fundamental, if such a thing is more possible than firmament of the clouds.

Zbig's family was not in London during the war. His grandfather was a fighter in Ludowe Wojsko Polskie, the Polish regiment of the Red Army. (Bill's grandfather was fighting nearby, as part of the regular Red Army.) Zbig's father, a doctor, had three families—serially—and Zbig was the sixth and final child.

The family's move to London, and later to White River Junction, Vermont, had little to do with politics. The elder Wronski wanted to become the best cardiologist he could be. They are dead now: Dr. Janusz Wronski of old age; Mrs. Carol Wronska, a Vermont potter, of pancreatic cancer; Dr. Zbigniew Wronski of a fall from the forty-third floor of Hotel Grand Dux on South Ocean Drive, here in Hollywood, Florida. A woman named Consuela Ramirez-Wronska is, by default, the guardian of a rich heritage, which she is now packing into large boxes and shipping off to Salvation Army.

And here is Bill, reclaiming it, getting his gag gift back. Zbig used that bag through Duke and presumably through medical school (Dartmouth) and residency (University of Miami). At Duke, it seemed Bill would become a reporter, one of the best. With his passion for bringing out the truth, was there even a possibility of a second best? Zbig would probably join Doctors Without Borders. It seemed possible that they would meet up at some tent hospital in Africa and spend the night drinking vodka, Polish, of course, and talking about shit that matters.

Bill's career is over, ended in dismissal, and here he is, in Florida, camping out on his stepmother's cot, surrounded by juvenile paintings. Zbig's path is a mystery, too. Instead of joining Doctors Without Borders and saving mankind, Dr. Zbignew Wronski devoted his life to serving the cash-on-the-barrel–paying rich and insecure. It's possible that rumors of patient fucking were true—usually they are. This is as far as you can get from Doctors Without Borders. Zbig joined the ranks of Doctors Without Boundaries.

Bill reaches into the bag. Nothing in the big cargo bay—the place where medical books once lived. Again, no clues. But in one of the smaller pockets he finds a crumpled piece of paper with the words of Volodya Vysotsky:

I'll water the stallions,
I'll finish the song,
I'll stand on the edge for a moment more!

The handwriting is, of course, Bill's, a package of chills from another time. Bill now is not Bill then; Zbig is no more; but the edge, it never changes.

Bill unstraps the container, sets it carefully on the nearby armchair, and, unparachuted, stares out the window at the rushing waves below.

Can a terrestrial investigation (the Château) mix with the existential (Zbig)?

Is the realm of Inspector Luftmensch contaminating the realm of the inspector general or vice versa? On the Château matter, the terrestrial front, Bill needs to talk to Melsor, if only for a few minutes while Katzenelenbogen the Elder is devoting his day to drinking chalky milkshakes and dealing with their consequences.

He imagines that the Zbig book would be a lot like a news story, only longer.

The Zbig story—the Zbig book—is the reason he is in Florida.

However, something at the Château emits that unmistakable smell of wrongdoing. The Château investigation looks like it may actually pay the bills—somehow, maybe. At the very least, it's undeniably his path to free rent while he pursues the Zbig quest. There is no problem with any of this. Bill is not the first investigator to use one job to finance another. All he needs to do is keep his methodology sound, and keep his facts in isolation from his obsessions. If anyone in God's creation has the capacity to keep these tasks—these universes—bifurcated in a manner consistent with recognized and accepted best practices in the field of mental hygiene, that man would be none other than William Melsorovich Katzenelenbogen.

Nearly two days have elapsed since Bill's landing in Florida. On past visits, three days in Florida produced specific suicidal ideation. This time, possibly thanks to Comrade Kozachok, those buggers visited him on Night One. If you accept the notion that nothing in life is accidental, you may see deeper symbolism in Bill's ownership of the container and the canopy. You might think of them as his shield from suicidal thoughts, his protection from height, his flying blankie.

Bill is on the twelfth floor. He has no idea whether that's

enough height for the chute to open. The trick is to avoid slamming into the side of the building.

"Gucci-*shmucci*-Versace," Nella comments on his getup.

Melsor is in the kitchen, eating green Jell-O out of a cup.

"*Ty chto, gomikom stal?*" he asks. Rough translation: Have you gone gay?

The wide lapels of the Brunello Cucinelli jacket, combined with the hyper-tropical Moschino shirt, slinky dark indigo jeans, and slipper-like Ferragamos (Ferragami?), represent a significant departure from Bill's Washington journalist's wardrobe.

"*Yesli-b stal, ya by tebe nepremenno soobschil,*" he responds. Rough translation: Had I gone gay, you'd absolutely have been the first to know.

"This is all they let me eat before procedure. Chemicals. She bought twelve, one for each apostle."

"And you are Christ, no doubt. Can you get away for a few minutes?"

"I took drug. Must stay close to toilet."

"Do you think you have twenty minutes before you have to go?"

"Not possible to know. I don't want to take risk."

"Fifteen minutes?"

"What's urgent?"

"I want you to go to the parking lot and point out the cars of the BOD members."

"How does it help me?"

"You could trust my judgment, perhaps."

"If they say trust me, it means don't. Read Donal'd Tramp! He says it better than anyone."

"Let's go."

"I will go, but you will go to Klub Susanna—put it in GPS—and find their singer to sing my *chastushki*. Offer her eighty dollars in beginning, but go as high as one hundred twenty. You will translate them to English."

"What is Klub Susanna?"

"Restaurant. Near here. Everyone goes there, my eightieth birthday was there. You don't remember."

"I wasn't invited."

"Yes."

"Is there a specific singer you know there?"

"They are all same. Long legs. No voice. Tragic stories."

"Just want to make sure. You want them to sing *chastushki* in English? How does that work?"

"The way you sing anything. Anything is song if you sing it."

"Fine. Give your damned *chastushki* to me."

"I need to put on different clothes. Wait."

Bill glances at the *chastushki*. He recognizes immediately that even for his father, these little songs represent a new level of contempt for the world as it is.

Also, he recognizes that being in Florida is making him grumpy. He has to get out—soon.

Sitting on the porny white sofa while his father changes costumes in his *kabinet,* Bill recognizes that these are not ordinary *chastushki*. (The poetic form is especially well suited for description of genitalia, sexual acts, often al fresco, often while intoxicated.) These *chastushki* are about Florida, about the Florida condominium laws, practices, and traditions, and about specific individuals involved in governance of Château Sedan Neuve, i.e., specific members of its BOD.

In the old days, Bill would have protested. Sure, he would have said, the Russians would understand this poetic form. But even in Russian, what political purpose would that accomplish? Congratulations, you've just ridiculed the BOD Château Sedan Neuve Condominium Association. So what?

Does Melsor believe that the scoundrels who sit on the BOD of CSNCA would feel intense shame, recognize the errors of their ways, and step down one by one? Has he not heard poolside conversations? These people have no conscience. Is he applying his old methods—ridicule of the Soviets—as a way to demonstrate that he doesn't fear them, that their secret police is powerless before him, that Melsor Yakovlevich Katzenelenbogen is bigger than Gulag?

The idea of translating this and singing it in English lies beyond the boundaries of this universe.

Как во нашем да во борде
Разгулялись АЙСИСы.
Разломали наш Шато
Сели суки в Лексусы!

How would Americans, especially those Bill saw at the Château, even begin to fathom it? They would require an hour-long lecture on *chastushki* as a poetic form as well as a brief history of *chastushki* and their use for political purposes today. (Putin uses them, for example.)

It would be the sort of lecture you could get away with at a place like Middlebury, but probably not Duke. How does Melsor expect the cranially calcified, recto-cranially inverted, Lexus-driving, entitled geezers to want to get any of this? Don't they already know everything worth knowing? Have they not eased into lives of applying their vast knowledge to new circumstances? Has Bill not heard one of them admonish those loud Russians for speaking their language in public?

Even assuming the unassumable—i.e., that anyone sits still for a long lecture—the rhymes Melsor has concocted would remain untranslatable. You might get the sense of what he is after, but getting pleasure out of it is beyond feasibility.

In English, this *chastushka* would have to be something like this:

On the board of our condo,
We've elected ISISes,
They have wrecked our Château
And got their Lexuses.

When he was young, Bill made great efforts to explain the world to his father. His failure rate was so high that he started to feel like he had no place to go, no place to put himself.

On one occasion, in the mid-1980s, when Melsor believed that he was entitled to a job at a Russian-language journal called *America Illustrated*, published by the United States Information Agency, he composed a fifty-page legal brief that he wanted to bypass the lower courts and be presented directly to the U.S. Supreme Court. Melsor felt entitled to a job. He wanted justice, he wanted it to be big, resounding, and what's a bigger place to get justice than the U.S. Supreme Court?

Bill, who by that time had taken eleventh-grade civics and was eyeing a career in law, attempted to explain to his father how the courts work. Melsor's brief, no matter how well argued and translated—even if it began with a quote from Thomas Jefferson (which was the case)—would not be considered by the U.S. Supreme Court. It would have to begin as an actual lawsuit, it would have to go through lower courts, and even if questions remain unresolved, the Supreme Court gets to decide which cases end up on its docket. What if the justices don't give a rip about Melsor's fate? Imagine that . . .

Besides, Bill had homework, and a fifty-page translation would interfere with his efforts to practice writing essays for college applications.

Melsor called his son a traitor—*predatel'*. Melsor called him *svoloch'*. Melsor used his favorite Russian proverb: "Eggs do not teach a chicken." After an hour, their standoff was not showing signs of running out of energy.

Bill stood up, and, shouting *"Muduk!"*—a word that falls into the range between a loser and a clueless motherfucker, but stems from a folk word for testicles—bolted in the direction of the closest wall. It was a strong, fully committed headfirst dive. Impact brought relief, the wall parted, drywall crumbled, wiring moved, a two-by-four stud was next to his ear, and there was light. Bill's head was now in a neighbor's apartment.

"I am sorry," he said to the neighbors.

The January 13, 2007, issue of *Machta* features the original Russian text of Melsor's *chastushki*, which appear side-by-side with a quarter-page Russian-language advertisement of a range of delicate procedures that can be performed by Regina Y.

Karasik, MD. The name of one procedure—**Vaginal Rejuvenation**—is set in large font, boldfaced, and underlined, which would suggest that it's a specialty of the house.

Below Melsor's *chastushki*, in another quarter-page ad, a puffy, bespectacled, bearded gentleman named Viktor A. Vinokur, JD, is offering a broad range of legal services: criminal defense, accidental falls, wrongful death, real estate transactions, wills, and immigration. A one-sentence testimonial describes Mr. Vinokur as—large font, underlined, boldface—**The King of Green Cards**.

Clearly, *Machta* is a shopper with a mission: it is entertaining its readers with faux *chastushki* while helping them become permanent resident aliens with sturdy vaginas.

13

FUCK THEIR MOTHER

"Okay, you will walk me through the parking lot, and I will write down the license plate of every car belonging to a BOD member or a former BOD member."

Bill's reporter's notebook is ready.

"I don't have time."

"Do you want me to help you?"

"What will you do with this?"

"This is Investigations 101."

"What is that?"

"Sorry. You didn't go to college here. It's how college courses are designated, or were: Economics 101, elementary econ, or English 101, introductory English."

"I went to better university than that. Moscow University is like Princeton. And I was adjunct professor here. What did your Duke get you except debt?"

"We can have this conversation later."

"You could have gone to University of Maryland and gone

to officers' program that pays for everything. It's same degree, there was no war, and they would have paid for law school. You could be lawyer."

"I could be lawyer, sure, unhappy one at that, but we are past that. I am fifty-two. Is that why you didn't give me a dime for my college education?"

"You had other possibilities."

"True, you didn't have money then. But a few hundred dollars, even symbolically, would have been nice."

"I brought you to America. You should be full of gratefulness for that."

"I didn't start this conversation. I need you to identify the spots where BOD members keep their cars."

"The cars you want are in spots 394, 302, 249, 173, and 117. I have to go to crapper."

"Thank you, Father."

Aside, he whispers: "Fucker."

Why is it that the Old Bill never called his father Father? He didn't call him anything but "*ty*," "you." He would have preferred to call Melsor "*vy*," the formal version, because the formal address would push the bastard further away.

In Moscow, Bill was proud of his father, the man who stood up to the Bolsheviks, who didn't fear being in contact with the American press, who appeared at demonstrations in front of the Moscow synagogue, who didn't give a rip about getting arrested. When his father's poetry was read by announcers at the Voice of America, Radio Liberty, and the Voice of Israel, Bill was a proud boy.

In America, he came to fear that his father would one day appear at the private school that gave him a scholarship and provoke a fight with the headmaster.

———

In the midafternoon of January 14, the Wronski residence looks as uninhabited as it did two days earlier.

This time, Bill doesn't ring the doorbell.

Instead, he heads straight to the garage, the spot where he had earlier picked up the box of clothes intended for the Salvation Army.

The garage door is partly open; perhaps off its track.

It's heavy, but it lifts, and as it reaches Bill's shoulder, he realizes that he has made a mistake, a bad one.

He sees blinding lights, and with them a camera crew, a rolling camera, and in front of it all, Consuela.

She runs toward him, shouting questions he doesn't wish to answer:

"Why are you here?"

"Why are you wearing my husband's clothes?"

"Who sent you?"

"When will you stop bothering me?"

He is caught, he has no legitimate business in that garage, he is trespassing, wearing a dead man's clothes, and now whatever he says, whatever movement he makes, will be captured on camera.

Bill begins to stammer.

"I am your husband's friend . . ."

"You are a reporter. I know you! He is dead! When will you stop bothering us?"

Bill turns around, and, moving slowly, with a camera following, gets in the Prius and drives off.

———

Bill looks up at the familiar billboard at the I-95 North ramp. Zbig is still there, larger than life, holding forth about beauty, looking down at the motorists as his wife displays her buttocks.

"Dude . . ." Bill says to his dead friend.

Zbig is still there all right, as is Consuela, but the billboard has changed. Zbig's presence is now rendered nebulous, see-through, ghostlike. Consuela, by contrast, is unchanged, except a large orange-colored arrow is now pointing at her exposed buttocks.

The purpose of the billboard has changed, too.

The original question is still posed in massive block letters: "ARE YOU PERFECT THERE?" Yet someone has painted over it in fat, lime green brush strokes: "MERRY WIDOWS—Watch it on VIVA!"

This is not a defacing of the old, cheesy billboard—it's a relaunch, an upcycling.

So that's what the camera crew, and the confrontation. That's why Consuela didn't want to part with any information about Zbig's life and his death. She got a part—a big part—on reality TV.

You might say she is feasting on Zbig's carcass, and if you are especially devoid of charity, you might add that Bill has been outmaneuvered.

Bill's hands shake a little as he drives up to Klub Susanna. Getting busted does that.

He attempts to put his situation with Melsor in perspective. Though financial details of their arrangement haven't been worked out, Melsor is, in effect, Bill's client. A professional is defined as a person who puts client interests above his own.

Same might hold for acting as a member of a loving family, but Bill wouldn't know much about that.

As a reporter, as an investigator, Bill always believed that his client relationship was with the public. Now, all he has to do is drop in his father's full name—Melsor Yakovlevich Katzenelenbogen—in place of the public.

A psychiatrist is trained not to take it personally when her delusional patient calls her a whore. Similarly, an attorney representing a difficult client doesn't necessarily resign when said client is resistant to taking considered advice. Sometimes a professional has to allow events to play out, which is what Bill is going to do on his father's behalf right now.

Of course, these *chastushki* are not Bill's idea of what it takes to bring about change at the Château or, for that matter, anyplace else. Bill would no sooner write a *chastushka* than he would attempt to submit a grievance directly to the U.S. Supreme Court. It should be noted that after the blowup and the wallramming incident, Bill did translate that thing, and after it was mailed out, Melsor forced him to make multiple telephone inquiries to the clerk's office. After forty years, the matter is still pending, it seems.

Klub Susanna is located in a strip mall a few miles inland from Collins. At one point, the space might have been a Costco, a Petco, or a BJ's. Judging by the fact that the front doors are still locked at 4:30 P.M., Klub Susanna does its business late at night. Bill looks in through the glass front doors, sees no one, gets back in the car, and drives around to the back of the mall, where the loading docks should be. He gets around several trucks as their cargo is being unloaded at the adjacent food store, and as he approaches the dock of Klub Susanna, he sees a large white Mercedes 500 and an even whiter Bentley convertible.

Bill parks Melsor's dirty white Prius next to them.

He knocks on the heavy steel door.

"Eto kto?" asks a woman's voice. [Who is it?]

Never in his life has this question given Bill pause.

In the old days—which ended less than a week ago—he could identify himself as a reporter with *The Washington Post* and take it from there. On most occasions, the doors would open.

What should he do now? How should Bill identify himself and the matter that brings him to the loading dock of Klub Susanna?

He could say that he is looking for someone to perform two pages of satirical *chastushki*—a couple dozen stanzas altogether—first in Russian, then in English. He could say that he has prepared a translation. (He was, indeed, getting started on a translation.) This being a Russian establishment, the person or persons inside will not ask what *chastushki* are.

This project goes against his better judgment, Bill could add, lest they think badly of him. These *chastushki* are about the goings-on of a particular condo board, and, no—said BOD will not be paying for this performance. In fact, the crooks who run the BOD aren't expecting this. They are the target of satire here. They will hate it, or should.

It's really guerilla theater: the singer or singers will be escorted in past the guard desk, but they should be prepared to be bodily removed sometime during the performance. They will be paid, of course, admittedly not very much: $80. However, the honorarium could go as high as $120. (He is instructed to try to get it done for $80, and wouldn't mention $120 unless he finds himself being laughed at.)

When *chastushki* are performed, it's better to have at least two singers taking turns. It's conceivable that if multiple singers are involved, they would have to split this modest fee. Bill would have to check on that. He could also acknowledge that he is not sure that everyone in the audience will understand what's happening. Some of these folks are Americans.

Again, Bill could reemphasize that he doesn't believe in this project. He is acting on behalf of his father, being professional about the whole thing.

"*Ya ischu pevitsu,*" he says instead. [I am looking for a singer.]

Inside, someone starts working the locks—there are three.

The steel door opens and an unusually tall, painfully thin woman steps out onto the loading dock. As Bill walks in, she walks out and looks cautiously to the left, then to the right.

At six feet, Bill doesn't expect women to tower over him. She does. They are of the same height, but her pumps, which are strikingly tall for something worn in midafternoon, make her taller.

Her hair is jet black, her getup remarkably patriotic: a short, gauzy, red-white-and-blue dress paired with white fishnet stockings. She is in her midthirties, not the gym-toned midthirties of Gwen, but hardscrabble immigrant Russian midthirties. Hers is not the Russia of Champagne and caviar; it's solvent-grade vodka and Salems. Her God-given beauty is crashing tragically, visibly, rapidly, loudly, leaving a crater.

Does he introduce himself now? Does he shake her hand? Kissing her hand would be bizarre, but it might be what she expects—fuck if Bill knows. Should he speak English, which to her is the language of power, or should he speak Russian, their common tongue?

"*Mogut v lyuboy moment voyti,*" she says, slamming the heavy door and sliding in one of the deadbolts. [They can come in at any moment.]

"*Menya zovut Ilya,*" he says. [My name is Ilya.]

He hasn't used that name for four decades, but in this situation, pursuing someone else's agenda, the name Ilya became his nom de guerre, protecting his real persona and his professional standing from this thing he now finds himself in the midst of.

"*Znayu, zhayu . . . Marina,*" she says, not looking back. [I know, I know . . . Marina.]

"*Ochen' priyatno.*" [Nice to meet you. (Literally: very pleasant.)]

Ilya follows Marina to the corner of a massive room—it's clearly backstage, a place for dumping props.

He notes two halves of an oversized Fabergé-style egg, both studded with pieces of colored glass. Presumably you can use these to lower performers onstage. Each half comes up to Bill's waist. Next to the eggs stands a similarly oversized *matryoshka* doll—it's taller than Marina on heels, he notes. Next to that, there is a cage large enough for a lion, or perhaps for a stripper or two.

Two plastic palm trees stand next to the cage. A bright circle—symbolizing Florida sunshine; what else?—hangs above them, as does a three-headed dragon, probably from a fairy tale–themed number. He could imagine that number, a version of Ballet Russe, *Daghiev Does Vegas.* The small hut perched on chicken legs, which stands next to the cage, beneath the dragon, is the oddest bit of all.

As they near the cage, Marina abruptly turns around and kisses him. Her tongue reaches deeply, aggressively into his mouth. Surprised by this turn of events, Bill doesn't reciprocate. He is letting his mind run through the moral and ethical implications of the situation. Gwen . . . Are they in a relationship? Not yet, and who is to say that they will ever be? They haven't slept together in a decade, and while that relationship is "reheating," the only conversation the two of them have had on the subject of exclusivity ended with Gwen saying that, as he departs for South Florida, a hometown girlfriend is the last thing he needs. It was said in jest, sure, but it was said.

As Marina's hands reach down to grab his penis, Bill—or is it Ilya?—reminds himself that he is at Klub Susanna for a reason, a business reason, you might say, if you stretch the definitions of "business" and "reason." Nonetheless, his lips begin to move, perhaps out of respect for the young lady.

Every sexual encounter Bill has ever had was grounded in a relationship of some sort—at least one drink, at least one conversation, sometimes even a movie. An e-mail, too, is better than nothing. It had been several months—five—since his last encounter, two years since his last relationship.

Had you asked Bill whether he has any interest in out-of-context sex, his answer would be "probably not," but here, at Klub Susanna, with Marina's hand in his Ermenegildo Zegnas, his body is starting to disagree.

Bill likes women—a lot. But Russian women are a mystery. He has never dated in Russian, never made love in Russian, never even thought of it in Russian. He knows all the words that pertain to sex acts and all the body parts that can possibly be engaged—he would do fine at an anatomy lecture, at an autopsy, or in the streets, but in bed he would be lost.

Out of the corner of his eye, he notices the colored glass in the Fabergé egg catching the light of the dim light bulb at the door to the loading dock.

Marina breaks away for an instant, and, taking him by the

hand, leads him toward the egg. There, she turns around, pulls off her Russian flag dress, and faces him head on, wearing a thong that, Bill notices, is decorated with gold embroidery of a two-headed eagle.

Her breasts are small, nipples pink. After turning a little to the right and a bit to the left, thus providing Bill with the opportunity to appreciate the two-headed eagle, Marina pulls down the thong and, stepping out of it, bends over, grabbing onto the edge of the oversized Fabergé. The pumps and white fishnets stay on, held up by a garter belt, which, Bill now notices, is similarly patriotic Russian red-white-and-blue. There is a tattoo on the small of her back—again, a Russian flag and a two-headed eagle.

He is behind her now, inside her. An observer—should there have been one—might have concluded that, judging by the sound of it, Marina is experiencing the most electrifying, most fulfilling sexual encounter of her life. Bill is more dutiful. He moves in silence, biting his lower lip.

She slows down, casting a glance over her right shoulder.

"*Ilya, mne chto, podruzhek pozvat'?*" [Do you want me to call my girlfriends, Ilya?]

Bill says nothing. Her friends wouldn't assuage his hesitation, it being rooted in deep-seated preference to keep sex a behind-closed-doors activity. She senses his hesitation.

"*Esche za tysyachu baksov mozhem tebe zolotoy dush ustroit'* . . ." [For just a thousand dollars more they can offer you a golden shower.]

A thousand bucks more? More than what? Bill wonders, but says nothing. What could that possibly mean? Her girlfriends? Are they here?

The space is massive. They are wide open, in full view of anyone who might walk in. Is someone watching, God forbid? Is a film being made?

*"Govoryat vash Donal'd Tramp za etim syuda khodit . . . Teper'
pochemu-to vse zakhoteli . . ."* [They say your Donal'd Tramp comes
here for that. For some reason, everyone wants it now.]

She is still on the golden showers bit. This is not helpful.
Bill didn't ask for any of this, and the prospect of involvement of
third, fourth, or fifth parties doesn't help. Marina's kind offer
of having her colleagues piss on each other, or—worse—on
him, and, of course, the very idea of Donal'd Tramp is even less
appealing. To chase away these thoughts and images, Bill wills
his mind to turn to Gwen.

This is more a meditation than a remembrance, oblique,
stripped of graphic content, yet generating far more heat than
the situation in which Bill currently finds himself. He closes his
eyes, imagining, and if the sounds emanating from Marina are
to be believed, the thoughts revive him.

"Davay konchim v tvoyem Bentli. Ya vsegda khotela," she says,
meeting his thrusts. [Let's finish in your Bentley. I've always
wanted to.]

"Net u menya nikakogo Bentli." [I have no Bentley.]

"Kak?" [How is that?]

"Vot tak." [Just like that.]

"Etot Mercedes tozhe ne tvoy? A kto ty takoy?" [Is the Mercedes
not yours also? Who are you?]

She slows down, moving her hips forward to make him slip out.

"Menya zovut Ilya. Ya na Priuse priyekhal." [My name is Ilya. I
arrived in a Prius.]

Quickly, she leans down to pick up her thong, stretching it
over her pumps, then pulling it up her long legs.

"Ty ne tot Ilya?" [You are the wrong Ilya?] She grabs her
dress and slips it on.

"Eto zavisit ot opredeleniy." [This depends on definitions.]

"Ty nikto?" [You are a nobody?]

"Tozhe zavisit ot opredeleniy." [This, too, depends on definitions.]

"Chto ty tut . . . zachem ty syuda?" [Why did you come here?]

"I was looking for someone to sing my father's songs," Bill responds in English while trying to make himself decent.

"A ya zhdala nastoyaschego klienta." [And I was waiting for a real client.]

"Tozhe Ilya?" [Also Ilya?]

"Tozhe." [Also.]

"I will pay you. What was your rate?"

"Pyat'sot baksov?" [Five hundred bucks.]

"Let me see what's in my wallet . . . I have a hundred . . ."

Indeed, he has five crisp, fresh-from-the-ATM twenties, which he hands to Marina. She takes the money, and as Bill heads toward the door, he hears the familiar sounds of a Russian woman bawling.

As the Château gates open to receive the white Prius, Bill realizes that he is not mentally or spiritually prepared to either see his father or be alone with Comrade Kozachok, another half-gallon bottle of which he has located.

In the elevator, he presses the second-floor button and knocks on the door of Apartment 215—like Philadelphia.

"Ah, my friend!" says Alex, extending his right hand and thoughtfully stroking his goatee with his left.

The Frenchiness of his "ah" suggests that he has been drinking. It's past 3 P.M.

Bill is delighted to note that Alex is playing a recording of Aleksandr Galich. Bill grew up listening to his poetry, his cries of moral indignation done to guitar.

Galich's heyday—like Alex's and Melsor's—was in the 1960s and 1970s. Galich was then a middle-aged man reciting tales of prison camps and the utter absurdity—criminality—of life in the USSR. Those were glorious days. The truth was as easy to spot as it was when we shot at Nazis and they at us, or at least this is how Bill sees this.

During his Moscow childhood, Bill learned a lot of Galich.

While Alex looks rather like Lenin, the apartment décor is decidedly bourgeois, vaguely pre-revolutionary. The massive Europeanish breakfront—representing a fantasy of what a nineteenth-century antique would have looked like when it was new—is filled with the detritus of a prosperous life.

Yet, some of its veneer has popped off and the doors have warped enough that they remain only partly closed. The sofa, too, looks like it's from someplace else. Its wooden frame and size are reminiscent of a Venetian gondola, and its fabric features young shepherds and shepherdesses frolicking blissfully through the Renaissance. The painting on the wall depicts a hilltop castle in the distance. All of this was intended to engender respect, and in another setting—a suburb built up with McMansions—it would have.

Alex is playing Galich's "Kaddish," a musical selection that fits Bill's mood entirely too well. Back in the USSR, Galich was not officially recorded or published. He sang at "apartment concerts," and in the end, people gathered donations that enabled him to continue—and continue he did.

His "Kaddish" is a massive composition about the Polish doctor and educator Janusz Korczak, who operated an orphanage in the Warsaw ghetto, first trying to save his charges from starvation, and later preparing them for death. The song goes on for over forty minutes. Its length, its complexity, illustrate why most of the Galich songs could not be performed after his death in 1977. No one else seems to have the capacity to handle his material. If you want to listen to Galich songs, you have to listen to Galich on old recordings.

"This is very special song," explains Alex, pouring Bill a glass of Russian Standard.

This is exactly what Bill craved: a Lenin look-alike playing Galich, while speaking with a faux French accent in a faux European apartment, pouring Russian Standard as the waves of the Atlantic break on the shoreline beneath.

"It sounds pained," says Bill, faking a lack of familiarity with Galich. He is, after all, with the FBI, or DBPR, or some such.

At this moment, Galich is at the point of the orphanage's departure for Treblinka.

И дождаться доложить не может сволочь
Что сегодня Польша Юденфрай.

And the *svoloch'* cannot wait to report
That Poland is *Judenfrei.*

"This is by Aleksandr Galich; very obscure. My generation."

"Not to me," Bill would have said in an aside had such things been possible. He does his best to look clueless.

"I once heard him in Moscow, at apartment concert. That was 1970. Hostess was nice woman, I think it was Inna Semyonovna Baser."

"I hear the word '*Judenfrei.*'"

"You hear correctly. His point—when he is at his best—is there is no difference between bolshevism and fascism. He—I love this Orwellian English word—'conflates' Hitler's Auschwitz and Stalin's Kolyma."

"On purpose?"

"On purpose, on purpose. Galich is dead forty years almost. Never needed him more than today. Their Putin and our Tramp is same person. It's all same. And main question of Russian literature never changes: '*Chto cheloveku delat?*' What's man to do?"

As Russian Standard finds his soul, Bill concludes that it beats Kozachok every time.

Alex continues:

"This is not conspiracy. Conspiracy unites finite groups of individuals. It's limited, it can be exposed, stopped, its members convicted, executed, so to say. This thing is big stinking swamp of criminality that threatens to engulf all that was ever decent and noble. Polarity is much, much, much more bad than conspiracy. From polarity there is no escaping. There is no East, there is no West. No up, no down, and this is how it always was—illumination of this point is just starting to, so to say, penetrate the lead shield of our skulls. Donal'd Tramp is not external. Donal'd Tramp is internal. He lives in your closet, he lives in your head, he lives in your soul, and there—in those places—he always lived. It doesn't matter which part of approaching darkness you confront. In Spain, fascism could be stopped. Now, victory—cure, so to say—cannot be goal. Palliation is only treatment possible. You fight to defend capacity to look at yourself in mirror, to defend human attributes, so to say, when others around you surrender theirs! They cheer as they surrender, by the way. They always do. Surrender and cheer. We would be happier if we join them."

"What's that toast? *Na zdorovye?*"

"Yes, famous Russian toast. We have better toast: *Chtob oni sdokhli!* Translation is 'They should drop dead.'"

Shouting *"Chtob oni sdokhli,"* Bill and Alex drain their glasses.

"One more time, with feelings!" shouts Alex, wiping his mouth with his fist.

"Chtob oni sdokhli!"

"They don't hear us!" says Alex with feigned disappointment.

"Fuck their mother! Is that another expression you have?"

"We say, *'Yob vashu mat'.'* Should really be *'Yob ikhnyuyu mat'* Fuck their mother."

"Yob ikhnyuyu mat'!"

With this they drink again.

Alex has no playlist on his computer. He goes to YouTube and runs searches in Russian.

After "Kaddish" grinds to its ending (Dr. Korczak and the orphans die, and there is much discussion of Communist Poland being a for-shit place), Alex fishes out another perennial favorite of the Moscow intelligentsia, the song about Solomon Mikhoels, the actor and artistic director of the Moscow State Jewish Theater, who was murdered on Stalin's orders.

The ending of this *chanson*:

Наш поезд уходит в Освенцим—
Сегодня и ежедневно.

Our train is leaving for Auschwitz—
Today and daily.

As much as he agrees with the message, Bill congratulates himself on reserving just enough sobriety to enable refraining from singing along. (Bill's Englishing sometimes suffers upon blottorization, he might say. Actually, it becomes funnier, less gravity-bound—more improved.)

An evening with Alex boosts Bill's resolve to fight the good fight, but falls short of lifting his spirits. Somewhere along the way, the two reach consensus that communism has adapted, mutated, recurred, shedding some of the collectivist ideas that once wrapped it, providing an excellent cover for criminality, naked authoritarianism, xenophobia, imperialism, and if that's not fascism, what is? This kind of communism stands poised to unite seamlessly with right-wing movements worldwide.

Fascism has adapted, too. No matter what happens, the fact that "Donal'd Tramp" was not laughed out of the Republican primaries on Day One and continued to gather strength, finally overcoming a better-financed, albeit uninspired, adversary, means that the range of socially acceptable discourse has broadened sufficiently to enable convergence.

"We have Russian word: *konvergentsiya*," says Alex.

"Sounds like our word 'convergence.'"

"What is infinitive form of verb? Convergate?"

"Converge."

"I have slogan then: 'Criminals of all countries convergate! Proletarians fucked up!' It's good slogan I composed; no?"

"Criminals of the world converge!" Bill responds, topping off his shot glass.

"No, drink to entire slogan: Proletarians fucked up!"

"Proletarians fucked up!" Bill repeats slowly. "I think we should make it 'Kleptocrats of the world converge. Proletarians fucked up.' Let's do that one now."

They shout in unison, a roaring crowd of two:

"Kleptocrats of the world converge! Proletarians fucked up!"

"Powerful," says Alex. "We should make banners of this slogan, hang it on buildings."

"Let's start with the Château."

"Start with Château. You are right. Sorry there is no herring, no pickles."

"Who needs that . . . Okay, Alex, you finished Historico-Archival Institute, as you say. Until now, we were talking about historical fascism, historical communism, as you say. What do you make of Trump?"

"There is no Tramp. There is Putin."

"Concurred. What about your local fascism, at your Château Sedan Neuve? How do you see it?"

"From inside; how else?"

"From inside?"

"I am BOD member; president, actually. You didn't know? What's your question?"

"You? A board member? President even?"

"Absurd; yes? They urged me to ballotate. Doesn't sound right. What's right word?"

"Run."

"Run. I am in perpetual opposition on BOD. I am president, was chosen last year. Greenstein is vice president. He has two members in his pocket. I have nothing. President job traditionally goes to member who knows least."

"Whom does the vice president have in his pocket?"

"You saw them at North Pool, when you were sitting on chaise in front of them, I saw you when I walked by. You are big celebrity here, you should know."

"Hmmm."

"On BOD, you always need three. Nobody cares what remaining two members think. I am one of the ones no one cares about. Russians mostly hate me."

"But they voted for you?"

"No one knows how anyone votes. Greenstein's wife cooks election results. They want me because I am ineffective."

"What about the effective ones, the pocket members?"

"Their names are Igor Roytman—the big one who was in red swimming suit—and Sergei Kushman, the one in blue swimming suit. They and Greenstein do everything together. He gives orders, they stretch out and salute!"

"Who is the fifth member?"

"Old American guy Johnny Schwartz, who gets drunk every night and shoots at ocean from machine gun. He can't see at all, so he wrecked his Lexus even! He is perfect BOD member, shows up once for first meeting, talks about Battle of Bulge, then doesn't come to single BOD meeting in eleven months."

"Why should he, if all decisions are made by triumvirate? Greenstein and the members in his pocket, as you say?"

"Not all decisions. Main decisions are made by Greenstein and people he meets once a year on yacht twelve miles away in ocean.

"It's where everything is decided. They say, 'Break balconies,' and he breaks balconies. They say, 'Destroy South Pool,' and he destroys South Pool. They say, 'Give me nineteen millions,' and we announce special assessment and take loan from bank—and people lose apartments and take loan on, so to say, subprime rate, because president of bank is on yacht also."

"And you really know this, about the yacht?"

"Yes, I know about yacht."

"Have you been on that yacht, seen it?"

"No. But I know."

Bill tops off the vodka in his glass: "To Historico-Archival . . ."

"Fuck your mother!" Alex responds joyfully.

At this point in the deliberations, Bill bids adieu and departs to continue to meditate on these and other weighty matters in seclusion.

"This place is a fucking ashram," he says as he pushes the elevator button and the contraption commences verticulation, toward the twelfth floor. "An ashram with vodka."

People shouldn't laugh when they are alone, but if something strikes you as this outrageously funny when you happen to be in solitude—let's suppose you find yourself in an elevator—does anyone have the moral authority to judge you for laughing?

Bill breaks the seal on another half gallon of Kozachok and, handle in hand, takes a deep, soul-targeting gulp.

Maintaining your capacity to look at yourself in the mirror is, indisputably, Step One. But shouldn't Step One be followed by Step Two? What is Bill's role in this struggle? Has Bill's father become one of them? If so, this betrayal is bigger than the biggest, most brazen ambulette fraud on earth. Or could it be that Melsor has taken an evolutionary leap ahead of his son, adapting, surviving?

Finally, Bill's mind turns to the subject he has been struggling to avoid: the sexual encounter at Klub Susanna. That act, if you could call it that—which you could and should if you are to be honest—brought on a separate cascade of bad memories.

Bill takes another gulp.

A woman has just parted his borrowed robes and fucked him, albeit inconclusively, so to say, pardon his English, entirely by mistake. And what was that about the Bentley? It's too easy to dismiss this as a case of mistaken identity and wash your hands of the whole thing. Did he have an obligation to avoid this misidentification by stating more clearly who he was and spelling out the nature of his business, convoluted though it was? Should he have left without offering to compensate her financially instead of leaving her bawling in dark seclusion? Further, does he owe Gwen a disclosure?

How would life be different if his mother were alive? Maybe he wouldn't have drunk so much tonight, would be ashamed to. This is not the drinking he was indulging in at home in the not so distant past—less than a week earlier, much less.

That form of drinking involved a bartender, a liquid he could taste. Adverse sequelae weren't lurking around the corner. He was in no physical danger—at least no more than the next guy.

When your hands hold on to the plastic handle and your lips close around the twist-off spiral of the bottleneck, you enter a different universe, and if this isn't your cue to run home, nothing is.

Falling asleep after all that is not among Bill's problems. The ceiling above him spins insistently. The room spins, too, albeit in a different direction.

Bill wakes up at 3:20 A.M. He remembers to text four license plate numbers to Gwen. The fifth car, the one belonging to Johnny Schwartz of the Battle of the Bulge fame, turned out to be unsuitable for blind driving, and therefore was totaled.

Gwen, at her crisis management firm, has access to all the right databases and can run that check easily.

He thinks about his obligations again. Should he disclose the events at Klub Susanna?

Even in his drunkenness at 3:24 A.M., he recognizes that the prudent answer is no.

After Bill falls asleep again, he dreams of being upright, walking past a stack of paintings, bumping into them, watching them fall to the floor, being vaguely amused by this mishap. He is aware of Luka Mudischev staring at him from below. It is a dream, something about the fucking penis; isn't everything always? He steps on one of the paintings angrily, breaks through the canvas, but presses on. He is past the kitchen now, wishing he had coffee; something drops to the floor, something breaks, and he is careful not to step on the shards. He thinks he feels sharp pain in the arch of his left foot, but no matter, he will press on, he will not be delayed.

He needs air, urgently, to fight off this suffocation. Is this how Dr. Korczak and his orphans felt in their Treblinka-bound cattle car? Except they didn't get air. They got Zyklon-B, or some such. Well, not in that exact moment, not in that cattle car, but soon thereafter. After a brief struggle with what in these parts is known as the "slice door," Bill forces it to slice out of the way, letting the air pour in.

What is it about the Nazis? What makes them so relevant to this place, to his dream here? He is outside, walking. But there is a fence. He must . . . get . . . over . . . this . . . fucking . . . fence. He must get to its outer side, where there is more air, where the air is fresher, freer, and maybe his mother is there, who knows? What is she doing there? Dancing with Dr. Korczak? Teaching

English to the orphans? English; a lot of good it will do them in Treblinka.

He must get there, and he would, if it weren't for his right leg. His left leg is on the fence; perhaps if he could use his body as a counterweight, he could roll over, like a pole vaulter, sort of, just roll, it takes a single push. It would be easier if only the fence weren't so cold. Why does it feel so hard, so—aluminum? And why is his face wet? Why is the wind gust so un-dreamlike, so this-worldly?

"Fuck," he says as he wakes up atop a balcony railing, staring at the ocean thirteen floors beneath. This is unmistakably real. He is one very real jolt away from falling. Were it not for the wind driving sheets of rain toward him, he would have taken that final unwitting, sleepwalking jolt.

It's possible that the driving rain brings him back sooner. It is certain that it saved his life.

Sometime later, inside the apartment, Bill pulls a piece of porcelain out of the arch of his left foot, cleans up the shards of the broken teapot, and restacks the Luka Mudischev paintings, carefully hiding the one he destroyed while sleepwalking.

As he closes the slice door, Bill briefly considers wearing the canopy and container to bed. This would require him to sleep on his stomach. The idea strikes him as mildly amusing.

Bill's list of injuries now includes bruising from the crooked cane, the punctured, bleeding arch, plus whatever damage he has done to his liver.

The call from Gwen, which comes in at 6:29 A.M., January 15, feels almost like another in a series of jammed transmissions of a Voice of America broadcast to a Soviet citizen during the Cold

War. A missive from the outer world, an indication that someone out there gives a rip.

"Glad you picked up. Having a bad feeling about all this; you know it?"

"Would love to see you."

"I'm just dropping in for a conference with NFL folks."

"But you have time for dinner?"

"That and you can drive me to the airport—yes. I had someone run the license plates. Are you sure all these cars are in possession of condo board members?"

"What do you mean by 'in possession'?"

"The cars are leased by a third party—all of them."

"All of them?"

"Every single one. Leased by International Construction and Implementation, Inc."

"ICII. My father calls them ISIS."

"Yes. That's what I hate about this: every car you gave me is a Lexus, and they are all leased by this ISIS, and, based on what you tell me, given to members of this Château Blahblah Neuve. They give you a car for being on the board of directors. And other things, too, presumably."

"It's careless—yes. How do you get from fuckup to sinister?"

"They don't give a shit—that's what's sinister. People don't behave like this, flagrantly violating every rule, unless they're certain the entire game is rigged. Everything! This is flagrant. The cartels behave like this, Putin behaves like this—that's about it."

"Trump behaves like this."

"He'd like to, but it won't fly."

"You are so Washington. Here in Florida every man is a cartel unto himself."

"I pushed you out of Washington, to write the Butt God book. Have you done anything on that book?"

"Yes, just getting going . . ."

"I feel responsible for you. I don't want you to come back in a box."

"I'll try not to."

"Can you handle the truth?"

"Try me."

"I liked that kiss. It felt right. I want another—tomorrow. I get the feeling you are in real, physical danger. Take nothing on faith. Trust no one."

"Sure."

"Bill, acknowledge what I just said!"

"Yes, yes . . . yes, I understand."

14

ISIS

Later in the morning—it's January 15—Bill receives an e-mail from his father. The subject line: CURIOS CONVER-SAISHON—ABOUT YOU. Bill clicks on the attached audio file.

"He just left," says a man with a Russian accent.

The previous evening of vodka and Galich had left Bill with the feeling of longing for home.

America is fully his home, too. Alas, America (1) has nothing that could be regarded as equivalent to Galich and (2) has a fundamentally flawed attitude to vodka. Vodka is not a libation! It is not a moral and ethical equivalent of gin! It is not on the same continuum as whiskey! Vodka is a Platonic ideal. Vodka is—vodka!

The second man in the conversation takes a deep breath, the sort one takes when a problematic friend or, worse, a problematic parent, calls in the middle of the night with urgent shit to report.

"Remind me . . ." It's Greenstein.

It's not entirely clear why this conversation hits Bill like betrayal. The two men are on the condo BOD together. Of course, they have official business, they have their own agendas.

ALEX: Are you familiar with *Inspector General,* Mr. Greenstein?

GREENSTEIN: Federal agencies have them, HHS, DOD, but that's high ranking. This guy is low on the totem pole.

ALEX: No, no, not federal agencies—the play! By Gogol.

GREENSTEIN: No. But I am busy now, please state your business, Alex.

ALEX: Inspector general, traveling incognito, with secret orders. I am quoting, almost. Except, of course, he is not inspector general. Corrupted officials believe that he is.

GREENSTEIN: Would you like to talk tomorrow, when you are sober?

ALEX: I am fine now! I am here to tell you that this inspector, he speaks Russian—and, worse, understands Russian culture—deeply!

GREENSTEIN: I find this hard to believe. He looks like a simple flunky investigator, trying to blend in, pretending to be a friend of the lunatic poet.

ALEX: I tested him. I played music only certain people, from certain stratums, would know, and I can tell you—definitely— he knew it! There is also good language training for FBI, I am told. He was drunk, and when lines came up, his lips moved in all right ways. He understands our culture! *Really* understands. In all nuances! Also, can you say *ikhnyuyu*? Like in "fuck *their* mother"? It's toast we drank. I said it first, but he said it with me—no problem. You try to say *ikhnyuyu. Ikhnyuyu.* Even I have hard time sometimes, even now . . .

GREENSTEIN: No, thank you, Alex. What does it matter that a drunk's lips move correctly? I really must go . . .

ALEX: You know, we have expression: fisherman sees other fisherman from far. I tell you, he knows us and is pretending not to! When FBI sends agent who speaks Russian and understands Russia . . . This is complicated situation.

GREENSTEIN: What does that change?

ALEX: He clearly sang the lines from song: *"Nash poyezd ukhodit v Oswentcim / Segodnya i yezhednevno."* Which means "Our train is leaving for Auschwitz / Today and daily."

GREENSTEIN: Auschwitz . . .

ALEX: I didn't mean it as insult. Sorry.

GREENSTEIN: No offense taken.

ALEX: He also knew what "graphomania" means. It means he understands literature.

GREENSTEIN: So?

ALEX: So? It's high-level investigation, with big geopolitical implications! For them to send Russian expert . . .

GREENSTEIN: Of course, if I were to accept the premise that they did. He doesn't look like an anything expert to me.

ALEX: Yes, expert is relative term.

GREENSTEIN: A dim bulb is a dim bulb.

ALEX: This information, about the investigation, is valuable to you?

GREENSTEIN: Not at all.

ALEX: Does it mean expulsion is still going? Even though I bring you this . . .

GREENSTEIN: Yes. This changes nothing.

ALEX: I have nothing left. How am I to pay? You sucked it all out with your special assessments. Can I at least keep Lexus till lease ends?

GREENSTEIN: I will inquire with the sponsor. You have my promise on that, but it's conditional on your behavior. Goodnight, I am hanging up now.

ALEX: Goodnight.

Were it not for the previous night's near-fatal encounter with the balcony railing and the equally sobering conversation with Gwen, Bill would have reached for a bottle, early hours notwithstanding.

How can a man who plays Galich's songs while cheerfully serving his guests drinkable vodka turn out to be a two-bit *suka*? (The word translates as "bitch," but means "snitch.")

Was Alex a *suka* in the former USSR?

Probably not.

How can anyone speak of maintaining dignity, honor, and the ability to look at oneself in the mirror, and then, a few minutes later, beg Herr Obersturmführer Greenstein to delay eviction, or is it deportation, and—please, please, please—allow him to keep that ill-gotten Lexus till the lease runs out?

Is this what it takes to survive? Is evolution pushing us into becoming a lower life form, devoid of ethics, esthetics, dignity? Has Alex—like Melsor—adapted to this Pax Mediocritatem? Or is it a Bellum?

The malaise that hits Bill next is not of the existential sort, nor is it of the variety that can be found in the Diagnostic and Statistical Manual of Mental Disorders. It's questionable whether it's a disorder at all: after a rough day and a rougher night, he simply has nothing to do.

For the first time since he got to Nella's unused apartment, Bill opens the refrigerator. It's full, in a way.

There are usual staples of the Russian émigré diet—Georgian sauces, marinated vegetables. The iconic eggplant caviar in an equally iconic Soviet-era five-hundred-milliliter jar has grown a thick layer of white mold.

Bill looks in the freezer. There, he finds a loaf of Borodinski bread, an intense pumpernickel, probably several years old. He hasn't had it in at least fifteen years, long enough to work up a craving. Though the bread is chocolate brown, its outside is white, frost-bitten.

His phone emits a ding. It's a text:

"SECOND REMINDER: My lawyer needs a payment to finalize this. Your behavior is irresponsible. You should consider yourself fortunate that I didn't make a support claim."

"Sure, go ahead," he mutters. "Make a fucking support claim."

He takes the brick-shaped loaf, raises it high, hitting the kitchen's low ceiling, then swiftly slams it against the counter. This breaks apart the frozen slices.

As the smell of toasting Borodinski bread wafts through the apartment, Bill goes through other frozen foods—all Costco, stuffed this-and-that. No, thank you. However, he also finds a garland of thick wurst, stuck in a sealed plastic bag. He opens the bag, and with a deft pull, breaks off two thick links. In Moscow of his childhood, these were called *sardel'ki*. It's a superfood that can go directly from your freezer to a pot of boiling water. Bill gets the water going, and, while waiting, runs a Google search for ICII.

Investigations have rhythms of their own, and sometimes they need to slow down, even sleep. At those moments there is only one thing to do: look for an angle you haven't explored— get your ass out there—and shake it up.

He returns to the refrigerator. Mustard would be good. Alas, there is no mustard. He will have to settle for the Georgian plum sauce called Tkemali. The thing is contained in a ketchup-like bottle, but ketchup it's not.

A text from Melsor comes in as the water starts to boil: "ISIS takes battle position. Look across street."

Funny, he was just looking up ICII—a sign from the gods! Based on what he sees, ICII looks like any other construction company. It's registered as a Florida corporation. Obviously, it has a corporate fleet of Lexuses, as he has learned elsewhere. Would be interesting to find out whether the BOD members declare them as income . . . On the other hand, fuck that, let the U.S. government worry about tax revenue—Bill has enough problems, thank you very much.

He walks out onto the balcony, only to realize that he can see but a small corner of the across-the-street parking lot owned by the Château condo association. He returns to the kitchen as the water starts to boil. Bill drops the frozen links in, turns off the stove, and leaves. They will have to cook in his absence.

Overnight, while the Château slept, ISIS had installed two office trailers and perimeter fencing at the Château's unused parking lot across Ocean Drive.

Guys in hard hats are scurrying about in the dust, punishing sun, and exhaust fumes. Their movements are economical, soldierlike. They are dressed like an army—black polo shirts with ICII embroidered in yellow over the heart, on the left. The yellow lettering matches the hard hats.

Three tractor trailers are dropping off their loads. One is carrying a massive generator. Another bears a half a dozen front-end loaders. A third is laden with scaffolding. The gates are locked, the fence topped with razor wire.

A group of residents gathers at the gate, looking in helplessly. Melsor is not among them, but Alex is.

Alex is looking in on the arriving equipment, his cheerful demeanor gone.

Two yellow front-end loaders are building a pile of scaffolding on the opposite side of the chain-link fence.

Bill and Alex shout over the roar.

"Rough morning?" Bill inquires.

"Looks like Bagram Air Base!"

"A lot of money being spent. Has the BOD approved a big project?"

"Board doesn't matter. This is *psikhicheskaya ataka*, psychiatric attack, to tell all of us that our votes will not count. Election results will be counted, but differently, like in USSR. You know Gogol, *Inspector General*? Don't lie, you do!"

"Okay, I do."

"That was cleaner time, nineteenth's century Russia. Crooks had fear there and then, so to say: they turned each other in. You know difference between then and now, there are here? Now and here nobody will turn in nobody. They aren't afraid. They don't care—and I don't care anymore. We lost everything—even before next assessment."

"We?"

"It was my daughter's apartment, she put it in my name before her husband went to prison."

"A hidden asset?"

"Your colleagues trapped him. All urologists take kickbacks, but he was caught. They had wire. They taped him, convicted him, disgorged him, mostly, except this apartment, which they couldn't find. Or it was more trouble than it's worth."

"They look for vulnerabilities."

"Apartment was paid for, but we didn't count on special assessments."

"Can't you sell it and move someplace else?"

"Tell your people they can take it now. Tell them Alex Bogomolov doesn't care anymore. No one buys apartments here, so it's not important. You can't pay assessments, you can't sell apartments, you are prisoner. They take your money and do what they want. It's triple fuck-your-mother: Fuck your mother! Fuck your mother! Fuck your mother!"

Another tractor trailer, spewing a cloud of black smoke, pulls up to the gate. Bill starts to cough.

When the cloud recedes, Alex is gone.

15

||||||||||||||||||||||||||||||||||||||||||||||||||||||||||||||||||||||||||||||||||||||||||||||||||||||||||||||||||||||||||||||||||||

MY CONTRACT WITH
THE CHÂTEAU

Checking his e-mail, Bill finds a note from his father.

The subject line, in English: "Your *Washington Post* email bounce-backed."

Why is this in the subject line? Should Bill acknowledge that his career is over, perhaps weep on Melsor's shoulder? That might make sense in another family, with another Melsor, on a different planet.

Bill moves on to the text of the e-mail: *"Perevedi pozhaluysta."* [Translate please.] The very existence of this document in English—i.e., the fact that it will appear below—indicates that Bill was, again, a very good boy, or trying to be one, which is the same thing.

Upon reading, you will recognize places where Bill would have proposed revisions—toning down reference to the Third Reich, for example—but, in a bow to expedience and conflict avoidance, didn't.

Preparation of this document was a three-step process:

(1) Melsor writes the original in Russian;

(2) Bill prepares a translation in the nonconfrontational manner he learned while preparing Melsor's Brief to the U.S. Supreme Court (importantly, he does this while eating *sardel'ki* and the Borodinski bread he had located in the freezer earlier in the morning); and

(3) Melsor carries out the final review, which involves restoring aggressive use of Capitalization, ALL CAPS, <u>underlining</u>, **bold face**, *italics*, font, and exclamation marks!!! All of these were present in the original Russian and reoccur in the translated version.

The decision to break the document into subsections—stanzas—must be attributed to Melsor.

This document would have looked different had it been bounced back to Bill for the final-final edits. He would have declared it way-the-fuck-too-long, meandering, and fundamentally unreadable—the Unabomber Manifesto.

Nonetheless, with the English mostly corrected, Melsor's declaration of candidacy for the Château's BOD is significantly more of-this-world than even his finest English-language *paskvil'*.

This thing even has articles, some definite, some indefinite:

MY CONTRACT WITH THE CHÂTEAU

By Melsor Katzenelenbogen

I, Melsor Katzenelenbogen, hereby Formally Announce My Candidacy for the Board of Directors (BOD) of the Château Sedan Neuve Condominium Association (CSNCA).

I RUN AS A LIMITED GOVERNMENT CANDIDATE.

Why do I run?

I run because I believe that the Fundamental Governing Documents of the CSNCA <u>and</u> Florida Statute 718 should be respected, studied, obeyed, and be considered in **EVERY RELEVANT DECISION** of this Condominium Association.

Fundamental documents are called "fundamental" because they <u>are</u> *fundamental*.

This is precisely *how* My Limited Governance will be Fundamentally Different from our past BODs—and **especially our current BOD!**—the Members and Vice President of which egregiously flaunted and continue to flaunt all legal constraints that should instead govern their conduct.

Here is what distinguishes me from *all other candidates*:

I—and no one but I—will ratify a **CONTRACT WITH THE CHÂTEAU:**

Should I at any point violate any obligation set forth in said Contract, I will—upon review of evidence by an impartial body—give my *a priori* consent to be <u>automatically recalled</u> from the BOD.

This Unilateral Contract automatically becomes Bilateral upon my election by Unit Owners and subsequent election to the **Post of Vice President** by my fellow Members of the BOD.

In the unlikely event I am NOT ELECTED to the BOD and appointed Vice President by its Members, I will RESIGN from the Board altogether, because under this Governance Structure there is no point to being in the Minority.

About Me:

I am a Russian poet, a veteran of the Struggle for Freedom of Soviet Jewry, a noted literary scholar and critic, and an American healthcare entrepreneur.

My past works of poetry are published by American Student Council for Freedom for Soviet Jewry [*PESNI O SVOBODE* (Songs About Freedom); Ann Arbor, Mich.: 1974]. My later works are published by the noteworthy Amazon.com and are exhibited prominently on www.stihi.ru, an important cultural website, where they are found side-by-side with acclaimed Masters.

I suffered from a long dry spell as a poet, but recently the "flood gates" opened, and I returned to writing.

"Why is Melsor setting aside important creative work for the sake of the administrative?" you might ask.

I answer:

"I run because I realize that—unless <u>fundamental</u> change occurs—I would not be able to live calmly and write here in this perhaps final stage of my Creative Career.

I have met with considerable success in my current work, as I finish a cycle of satirical folk rhymes dedicated to subjects all of us should regard as—yes—**Fundamental**. You may be treated to a benefit performance of these in the near future.

Today, as the very existence of Château Sedan Neuve is in

danger, as a Citizen, I have no choice but to set aside my poetry and turn my gaze to three Fundamental Documents:

- Declaration of Condominium,
- Condominium Bylaws, and
- Florida Statute 718.

I beseech you to join me in reading and studying these Fundamental Documents, because an *Informed Constituency* is the only proven safeguard against *Tyranny* and a mighty antidote to the *Culture of Kleptocracy!*

OUR BOD VICE PRESIDENT, THOUGH A JEW, LEARNED TRANSPARENCY FROM HITLER'S REICH!

Florida Statute 718.113 (2) (a) requires that "75 percent of the total voting interests of the association must approve the alterations or additions."

In the interpretation of the Florida Court of Appeals, approval is required for any effort "to palpably or perceptively vary or change the form, shape, elements or specifications of a building from its original design or plan or existing condition in such a manner as to appreciatively affect or influence its function, use or appearance."

This is The Truth! There can be no Disagreement with this Interpretation!

But our current Vice President Greenstein has declared: *"I am the Condominium!"*

We must shout back: *"No you are not!"*

He will shout: *"Yes, I can!"*

We must shout: *"No, you can't!"*

How do we MAKE THE CHÂTEAU GREAT AGAIN?

It will become great after We, the Unit Owners, *break the back* of his regime on this BOD.

The deeper you read our Fundamental Documents, the more convinced you will become that—like the Brezhnev Power, to which I courageously spoke the Truth—people to whom we are entrusting authority live exclusively by the laws they happen to like, discarding and ignoring the laws they don't like.

Today, our situation is very complicated, even **dangerous**:

Two Members are in Vice President Greenstein's pocket, one Member is a weak man who is on the verge of eviction because of Unpaid Dues, and one, whom I respect, is so disgusted that he doesn't attend meetings. (There is no reason to name names.)

I have always been a Limited Government advocate.

During the 2015 election, I posed a single question to all candidates: "Do you plan to be guided by Paragraph XIX of our Declaration of Condominium, which states that "Improvements and alterations costing in excess of $14,999 shall not be made without the approval of 2/3 of the entire voting power of the membership of the Association?"

No Candidate answered in the affirmative. All others REFUSED to ANSWER! **They IGNORED ME!**

Now you can see the consequences—without your approval or even your knowledge!—the South Pool Deck, formerly an Oasis, was turned into an uninhabited Desert where all dies.

Today, our contractor ICII—**like its near-namesake ISIS**—stands poised to warm its hands on a $19 million project!

Replacement of windows alone—how can you not call this a "material alteration?"—will cost more than $8 million!

One thing is Certain: the current BOD of CSNCA will not ask you to approve these changes!

- **LET'S Not Wait Anymore!**
- **LET'S <u>Ratify</u> my Contract with The Château!**
- **LET'S MAKE THE CHÂTEAU GREAT AGAIN!**

—Melsor Katzenelenbogen
January 15, 2017

Getting out his message and being noticed puts Melsor in an elevated mood. He loves the document enough to actually call Bill and compliment him.

"Tonight, we celebrate," he declares in English.

"Celebrate what? You haven't won."

Bill is in an irritable mood, irritable because he is doing nothing, not because he is lazy and wants to do nothing, but because there is genuinely nothing to do. At home, he was always busy, even after his job started to suck.

At the moment the phone rings Bill is watching a video in

which three bird-suited young men are flying off a cliff somewhere in the Far East. The music is irritating in a heroic the-devil-may-care sort of way, so Bill turns it off, relegating the young men to flying in radio silence.

"I no longer see situation where I don't win," Melsor continues, making Bill appreciate the advantages of watching videos of daredevil adventures while communicating with his father.

"I've seen enough surprise defeats," Bill continues, still watching. "First Bernie, then Hillary, more recently. I don't believe in celebrating early."

"I made reservation at Tbilisi—at six. We walk in just before end of early bird special and get free salad and free dessert."

"You and Nella?" Bill skips a few moments of the flight. He can repeat it later. Sure, this is all extreme, but he realizes that it's edited, curated. Bird-suited men die in real life, but on these videos flight is pure and life eternal.

"No, Nella hates Tbilisi. You and I. I pay for dinner, but if you drink, you pay for that. They can separate bills."

"I have dinner plans—sorry."

Melsor pauses. One of the young men on the laptop screen before Bill flies perilously close to the cables of a gondola.

"Is it woman?"

"Yes."

"What woman? Someone you met here?"

"Someone I've known for years—in Washington."

"How old?"

With a flap, or is it a turn, of his wings, the young man on the video averts collision with a gondola. Bill imagines what the collision would have looked like, especially to occupants of the gondola. The young man flies by safely and the gondola continues its climb.

"Maybe thirty-seven."

"Thirty-seven is good. Still hope, but self-reliance—more self-reliance. For how long do you know her?"

"Fifteen years."

"You are intimate, of course?"

"Depends on your definition of intimacy. She is young, too young maybe."

"There is such saying: 'You are as young as your youngest mistress.'"

The flight on the screen continues past otherworldly rock formations, toward peasant huts and rice paddies that look like they may be five hundred feet beneath. Looks roughly like the altitude equivalent to the forty-third story of the Grand Dux Hotel.

"Is she here for long time?"

"No, she just flew in for a day. Meetings."

The chute opens as the first of the three bird-suited men glides downward. The other two follow.

"Is she journalist?"

"Was. Now she runs a crisis management firm—public relations, sort of, with a tinge of private investigations."

That flight; it seems easy.

"Smart! I want to meet this one. I will call Tbilisi and change reservation to three. But we must walk in before early bird special or price goes up."

Bill hangs up, and before more images of yet another wing-suit flight appear on YouTube, he recognizes the magnitude of the intrusion he has just allowed to take place. He should have been on guard. Surely he knows that even blinking is hazardous when dealing with Melsor. An uninterrupted meeting with an emissary from his former life was the only thing Bill craved more than a proper—i.e., non-Kozachok—drink.

Now, Melsor has forced his way into his evening of sanity, perhaps even into his life. Why the hell did Bill have to admit that he was meeting a woman?

16

TBILISI

At the appointed time—5:45 P.M.—Melsor shows up wearing a double-breasted blue sport coat with the insignia of a yacht club that has only Ralph Lauren for a member. The pants are pristine white, as are the belt and the loafers. The polo—make that Polo—shirt is hot pink, the ascot an especially electric shade of lavender.

"I will drive," he declares. "Give me key."

Melsor gets behind the wheel, the white Prius turns on silently and lurches into the nearby white Cadillac Seville.

Paying no attention to the damage—it's quite a jolt; there has to be some—Melsor shifts to Drive, commanding the Prius to lurch forward.

"That's why God created bumpers," mutters Bill.

Their destination is Restaurant Tbilisi. Gwen would join them there sixish. Melsor has been assured that as long as two of the three people in their party walk in before six, the early bird pricing will apply.

"You wrote about science?" Melsor asks.

"On occasion."

Silence.

"Do you think they would have cured her if she got sick today?"

"Hard to say, but things wouldn't have gone the way they did. She didn't die of her disease. She died of treatment, and that treatment is no longer performed."

Why spare this tyrannical geezer from having to confront his role in the travesty he had orchestrated? This cop-out—this lie—is worse even than Bill's maintaining the fiction of his continuing employment.

Could his mother have been here, in this well-bumpered white Prius, sitting in the front seat *right now*?

Not likely, but possibly. Bill would have been happy to take the backseat, be the kid again.

"Did you find singers for *chastushki*?"

"Afraid not. Talked to one woman, she wasn't interested."

"Just as well. I think I have."

"Can I ask you what happened after my mother died? I understand insurance refused to pay for the transplant. Is that what started that ambulette business?"

"I had sixty thousand in debts to hospital, technically, and I was prepared to announce bankruptcy, but Alter said I didn't need to. He said, 'You are respected in Russian community—just see all these people who came out to cemetery.' So, I stopped working for pittance and started ambulette business, which he co-owned with me, secretly, of course."

"It was not entirely legal . . ."

"What I did was not so wrong. I didn't write prescriptions for ambulettes. Alter did."

"Is he still living?"

"Living, living. Should be getting out of prison in about a year.

"Enough unpleasant conversation! I do only pleasant conversation. Imagine big, stinking garbage truck going by. I don't look at it, I don't smell it. I let stream of consciousness take me away to pleasant things: I am in mountain stream, I am surrounded by daisies.

"That's the difference between you and me: you choose to smell garbage, I choose to smell flowers."

Tbilisi is a massive, brightly lit joint. The cuisine is nominally Georgian, but *zakuski* are Russian, salty, fatty, smoky—excellent.

The drink Bill craves is of the sort no self-respecting painter would use for cleaning brushes. A real drink, the kind that gives strength to confront, or at least evade, adversity. A real drink, not swill, not rotgut. A real drink, not Kozachok.

He wants a TB—badly.

Just as badly, he wants to avoid discussion about the physician Melsor was once enamored with. Werner Bezwoda was the name. The fucker indeed was later found to be a fraud. He collected no data—it was all falsified. He had no regimen. He made shit up and put it on slides. But it's over, who cares—she is dead.

The waitress has a pad and a sharp pencil. She stays on message, offering minimal guidance and no recommendations: "It takes the kitchen thirty-five minutes to make kabobs."

"Can you please ask whether they have Tito's and Bombay?

Tito's is a vodka. Bombay is a gin. I want it mixed one to one, shaken, with an olive."

She offers to check at the bar.

The tables at Tbilisi are configured in a way Bill has never seen before. Usually, at least in Washington, a table for twelve is a rarity. Here, a table for twelve would be laughably small. He sees a few tables for groups of four or so, but the bulk are set for enormous banquets. Eyeballing, Bill sees a table for thirty and a table for sixty. A third table, which takes up a corner of the restaurant, seems to be set for at least ninety.

The waitress returns with a tray with two small carafes, one of which contains one hundred grams of vodka, the other one hundred grams of gin—presumably Tito's and Bombay.

Also on the tray, there is an empty five-hundred-gram carafe, a soup plate full of ice, a salad plate with an assortment of olives, and two lowball glasses.

"Do you have a way to mix them?" Bill asks.

The waitress looks at Bill vacantly, shrugs, turns around, and leaves. She did her best.

Bill's thoughts of the logistics of TB-mixing are quickly thwarted by Melsor, who drinks all the Tito's, leaving only Bombay behind. Bill sets aside his Washington nostalgia, drinks up the room-temperature gin, and orders a 750 of chilled Russian Standard—because fuck it.

After doing what he did to his mother—after insisting on the worst, most brutal, and completely discredited treatment—how can Melsor see himself as a medical maven?

He placed his trust in Werner Bezwoda. Now he places his trust in Donal'd Tramp.

Introspection was always a luxury Bill couldn't afford. Tuning out, walking away for years, seemed less perilous—and was.

The Katzenelenbogens gave up on Washington and moved to Brooklyn in 1985. There was no point in staying. The U.S. Information Agency had no plans to employ Melsor. The language schools at the Department of Defense and the National Security Agency were still hiring people who could teach. Alas, Melsor wasn't being offered employment. It's possible that the U.S. Supreme Court filing, which Bill translated against his will, went from the clerk's office to be filed in a dossier kept by another arm of the U.S. government.

On one occasion, Melsor did get as far as a voice test at the Voice of America. He had to read some stuff into a tape recorder. According to a story whispered to Bill by his mother, Melsor read a paragraph, then added: "All of you know that I can speak Russian, that I speak well. So why don't I read you a few selections from the works of Akhmatova, Gumilyov, Tsvetaeva, Blok, and Mandelstam—and, of course, myself."

This quickly turned into a recital of Melsor's works in Russian and English, spilling from the cassette's Side A to its Side B. In the end, Melsor sang. His song was Georgian: "Suliko," a favorite of Stalin's. Did Melsor believe that he was responding to the prompt?

But why wouldn't he discern the opportunity to do better than the prompt and, if the gods smile upon him, seize the day?

After the move to New York, Melsor edited a Russian shopper, sort of like the South Florida *Machta*, which he mostly filled with unauthorized translations from the *National Enquirer*.

To keep his mind agile, he adjuncted at Hunter College. Rita had an office job at an insurance company that was making inroads into the Russian immigrant market. She didn't seem especially bored.

Her diagnosis came down on June 8, 1999: stage III breast cancer; four positive nodes, a motherfucker. A doctor, whom Melsor found through Russian contacts, said that high-dose chemotherapy with a bone marrow transplant was her best bet for long-term survival.

Bone marrow transplantation made sense logically: (1) you harvest the bone marrow and set it aside, then (2) use a massive dose of chemo to kill the disease and the remaining marrow, and finally (3) reintroduce the marrow you had reserved.

There were anecdotes of success and anecdotes of failure, but the procedure made so much sense logically that few women agreed to join randomized trials.

Sixteen and a half years later, at Restaurant Tbilisi, Bill is reconstructing that spring's events.

"She has breast cancer," Melsor told him over the phone.

Bill was in the newsroom at the time. There was no pause, no time to adjust to this devastating bit of news. Melsor jumped straight into what he planned to do about it: "I have excellent doctor who promises to cure it, Jewish man, orthodox: Alter. He is follower of South African doctor who found best treatment."

Bill listened:

"The most important thing is finding highest dose that doesn't kill patient. Alter, her doctor here, told me that this doctor Bezwoda, Werner Bezwoda, used Negro women to find it. Then he started giving it to white women. Now Alter has license to use exactly same treatment as Bezwoda.

"It's difficult regimen, but she is strong."

Actually, Bill knew quite a bit about Dr. Bezwoda and his amazing cancer cure. A week earlier, he was in Atlanta, in the front row at the plenary session of the American Society of Clinical Oncology, watching a presentation of four studies that showed that bone marrow transplantation provided no better survival than conventional chemo. Also presented that day was a study by Werner Bezwoda, the guy who developed the most toxic regimen of all.

While four studies screamed "Don't do it," Bezwoda cheerfully presented results showing that the treatment was just great.

How would Bill explain all this to Melsor? Hasn't he already made up his mind?

Bill heard his mother crying in the background. He knew what was transpiring in that apartment; he felt as powerless as he did the day his father forced him to translate his Supreme Court filing.

Melsor's choice of treatment may be indefensible, but there is logic to it. With him in charge, why would anything other than high-dose chemo with bone marrow transplantation rank high enough to be considered?

All the elements were present:

- The chemotherapy regimen was strong and crude. If that battle-ax wouldn't teach cancer a lesson, nothing would.
- Racist ideology was present, too, at least in Melsor's mind. The therapy was allegedly tested on *untermenschen* in South Africa—without their knowledge, and with good results.

- A conspiracy theory completed the package: the establishment is out to destroy Bezwoda. Why are they out to destroy him? Ha! Imagine the money that could be lost by hospitals and drug companies if breast cancer were cured.

Bill's first question was to himself: Does it make any sense to argue with this guy? Will he be able to recognize that the world that exists outside him doesn't always operate in accordance with his rules, that it's far more complex than it would have been had Melsor been its God and king?

His mother was about to get a brutal—murderous—treatment. Should he have made an effort to inject reality into this situation?

He did make an effort: "I know quite a bit about this treatment. I want you to be careful. I was there, in the front row, in Atlanta, when group after group of top-tier researchers presented the data from randomized clinical trials—that's the gold standard. Their data showed that this is a barbaric, killer therapy."

"They have jobs to protect."

"I know these people. They are honorable. Your Bezwoda was there, too. I saw him up close, presenting results that were diametrically different from everyone else's."

"They were ordered to sabotage trials. Insurance companies will go bankrupt if they keep paying for Bezwoda's cure."

"There was something odd about Bezwoda, a certain kind of smile on his face. You learn to trust this instinct when you do this long enough . . . Please don't do it."

"He will win Nobel Prize after they prove him right. I am absolutely convinced that this is right thing to do. There is nothing you can say that will dissuade me."

"You know, after these randomized trials, insurance companies are refusing to pay for transplants."

"I don't care. We must save her. I will fight with them later."

"Can I speak with my mother?"

"No. You are going to try to convince her not to do it."

"And you will kill her. For nothing."

"They will start procedures tomorrow. You will not speak with her until it's over and she is cured."

Bill didn't get to say good-bye to his mother.

Rita Katzenelenbogen was a 10-percenter, one of the casualties of the procedure. She developed a killer infection after the harvesting of her bone marrow. She slipped into a coma, and died before Bill could get to her bedside. He arrived in time to see her body wheeled out of her hospital room.

What would he say to her if he had a chance? You fucked up, you trusted your husband—my father—following him as he ignored another in the series of red lights he'd ignored in his life?

Bill attended the funeral. Standing silently before his mother's grave at the Mount Carmel Cemetery in Queens, he fought the admittedly Freudian/Shakespearean urge to avenge her death by killing his father and the Great Humanitarian, Dr. Mordechai Alter, the asshole who administered the cure.

He could imagine the headline in the following day's edition of the *New York Post*: KADDISH PICKAX MURDER; *WASH-INGTON POST* JOURNO HELD.

He could have beaten both Galich and Ginsberg in the "Kaddish" game. He could have owned "Kaddish."

———

Bill looks up and sees Gwen enter the restaurant.

In heels and a white dress, she looks like a swan making a pond landing. He waves, she waves back.

There is a hug, a quick kiss. An introduction to Melsor leads to a courtly kissing of the hand. She expects nothing less, clearly.

Melsor holds her hand in his a little too long for Bill's comfort, but apparently not hers. She flashes a delighted smile in Bill's direction.

Melsor raises his glass as Bill pours vodka into Gwen's.

MELSOR: I have toast! TBL!

BILL: Which means?

MELSOR: It means: to beautiful ladies!

BILL: *Oy vey.*

GWEN: Why didn't you tell me your father is cute?

MELSOR: Thank you for making my son happy.

GWEN: I don't know whether anyone or anything can accomplish *that* . . . Are you happy with the outcome of the elections?

MELSOR: Donal'd Tramp?

GWEN: Trump; yes.

MELSOR: Very, very happy. I live in America since end of Carter, and things always get better. With Reagan they got better, with Bush they got better, with other Bush they got better again. Now, finally, they will get very good. Only Donal'd Tramp can end political correctness.

GWEN: I don't understand that.

MELSOR: That's because it's everywhere, like air. You don't understand air until you start to cough. Political correctness needs to be taken out, like poison from atmosphere, and only Tramp understands that.

GWEN: So, Trump is like an editor with a red pen? Everything that smacks of what we call the pursuit of equality and social justice, he will take out with a stroke of his pen. Do I understand you?

MELSOR: I know this country. I lived in Washington, I lived in New York, I was editor, I was writer, I was businessman. This country is built on strongness of people and free market. Everything else sucks its blood.

BILL: You are starting to sound like you are a fan of Putin's, actually.

MELSOR: What's wrong with Putin?

GWEN: Meddling with our presidential election?

MELSOR: In this world, everyone spies on everyone. Why is this spying worse than other spying? Because it was effective? Because it helped Donal'd Tramp?

GWEN: I don't want to put you on the spot, but do you think you would have left Russia now?

MELSOR: No. Definitely not. I would have become oligarch. Probably in health. I would build best hospitals in biggest cities and instead of patients going to best hospitals here, best doctors would go there and give best treatments.

BILL: A medical entrepreneur. A hospital oligarch. Of course.

Waking up from silent reflection, Bill turns to Gwen: "How did your meetings go, Gwen, not to change the subject? It was NFL—right?"

GWEN: Team owners. You know, I do crisis management. Well, the players have been beating up their girlfriends a lot lately, and the press has been eating it up.

MELSOR: Managers of football teams? American football?

GWEN: Owners . . . Yes . . .

MELSOR: What did you tell them?

GWEN: The only thing you can do is cut and run. Don't defend the indefensible. Women don't ask to be beat up. Express remorse—and move on as fast as you can. In this climate, you can't afford to look like you are defending this kind of behavior. Violence against women has to have consequences. A wise friend once told me: "Nobody has ever gone wrong by taking too much responsibility. Own your guilt, own your unmooring, reach for more, more, more."

MELSOR: The players who beat their girlfriends, are they black?

BILL: You didn't hear that. I would strike it from the record.

GWEN: Never thought about that. An abuser is an abuser—pigmentation doesn't matter.

MELSOR: Woman is the most perfect creation of nature . . .

GWEN: And?

MELSOR: Feminists take it too far. Let me give you example: an old Jewish man who had sport team, in basketball, not football. He had affair with young woman. She made recording of their conversation in bed, publicized it on Internet, and government makes him sell his basketball team! What kind of country we have if you can't speak honestly in bed with your lover?

GWEN: Hmmm . . . Interesting . . . Isn't wife-beating still considered more or less okay in Russia?

MELSOR: There is saying in Russian villages: "He who beats his wife loves his wife." It means you have to love woman enough to beat her. If you don't care, you will not hurt her when she hurts you. I never beat anyone. Never loved anyone enough, maybe.

BILL: This is not going anyplace good.

GWEN: What's actually happening here, in this restaurant? I don't think I've ever seen tables this long, or this many people at the same table.

MELSOR: You don't understand?

GWEN: Not at all.

BILL: Neither do I.

MELSOR: These are birthdays—eightieth mostly. Mine had forty people three years ago. It was in Klub Susanna, which is better. It has show.

BILL: That table over there will bill ten thousand dollars, maybe more.

MELSOR: That's why they put tips on bill.

GWEN: Who pays? The birthday boy?

MELSOR: No. You invite people, they give you one hundred dollars, and you do deal with restaurant to give you good menu that still costs less than one hundred each. What you don't spend you keep.

BILL: People paid you to attend your birthday party?

MELSOR: You bring checks and maybe postcard. I had forty people and ended up with five hundred dollars left after tip.

Usually at Russian restaurants you worry about the havoc wrought on your food by heat lamps and microwaves, but the Tbilisi kabobs are spectacular, not dry at all.

Alas, with this conversation, Bill will not be able to swallow another bite.

Bill's mother would be eighty now. It would have been nice if she could have seen her sixtieth birthday. It would have been better than being killed by a two-bit crook at a community hospital in Jersey.

Bill looks at the faces of the old people around him. Maybe these folks are happy inside. It's possible that they are rejoicing at their friend's eightieth. But if they are, their faces do not reflect their exaltation, or, for that matter, much of anything at all. No one seems to be talking to anyone. The age spread seems to be from seventy to ninety, give or take. Where are the children, grandchildren, great-grandchildren? Will there be toasts, the wishes of health and happiness to the birthday boys and girls? Or is everyone just waiting for the musical numbers to begin? Will there be anyone around to say good-bye to them when they die?

GWEN: Sorry to eat and run. My flight is at nine forty-five. I can take an Uber.

MELSOR: No, no, I'll drive!

BILL: Actually, no, I will.

MELSOR: Are you sober?

BILL: This is relative. Thank you for your concern.

When the check arrives, Gwen grabs it, but Bill deftly wrests it away. Melsor makes no gesture to reach for his wallet.

There is another kissing of the hand as Melsor is dropped off at the Château, and Bill and Gwen take off for the airport.

"I have two things to say," Gwen begins.

"Shoot . . ."

"First, this was the most silent I've seen you—ever."

"And second?"

"Second, I don't know what to make of your wardrobe upgrade. What happened?"

"Complicated."

"Let's see, you are fucking an eighty-five-year-old widow who dresses you up?"

"No. Can you miss your plane?"

"Can't. A meeting tomorrow morning. Going after the NFL business."

"I am getting used to making out at curbs."

"I can return this weekend, if you want me to. We need a door, perhaps even walls."

Parked at the curb, they make out like teenagers until a police officer, using his cruiser's PA system, suggests discreetly that they get a room.

Gwen gets out of the Prius, straightens her dress, shakes out her hair, and leaves for Washington.

17

FRAU MÜLLER-GREENSTEIN'S BIRTHDAY

On the way back, Bill gets a text from his father: "Be here at 9:30."

"Why 9:30?"

"Birthday of Greenstein wife."

Is Melsor throwing a party for the wife of his nemesis?

When Bill comes in, Melsor and Nella are listening to the "transmissions" from the Greenstein apartment.

There is a call from the front desk: "Mr. Greenstein, two gentlemen are here to see you."

"So, it's true!" shouts Nella.

"So, what's true?" Bill asks.

"Rumor is—he pays two men on her birthday!"

"Pays two men for what?"

"What do you think?"

"I called Johnny already," says Melsor. "He will like to listen to this. It will keep him from shooting his Bushmaster at ocean. Pour vodka in bottle!"

"And get *zakuski,* I know. You think I don't know?"

Melsor is giving orders, ever the corsair, Captain Blood or Captain Bloodsucker, depending on where you happen to be in relation to his blunderbuss:

"Get vodka!"

"Cut herring!"

"Call comrades!"

"Turn on generator!"

"Find ruler for opening slice door!"

Nella's growling is muffled, its message always the same: "I don't need your damned commands. Don't shout! I know what to do. Better than you do."

If this isn't a partnership, what is?

Johnny Schwartz looks like he ran through the hallway and up the stairs. He wears Desert Storm camouflage fatigues and an orange Miami Dolphins T-shirt depicting a dolphin jumping either to the sun or through a ring of fire. Tall, lanky, muscular, he looks like he spends a considerable amount of time at the Château's gym.

MAN ONE: We are from Craigslist.

GREENSTEIN: Come in, please.

MAN TWO: Who are you?

GREENSTEIN: Think of me as a director.

MAN ONE: Director? We don't do filming. I don't want filming! It wasn't in the deal! What if my wife sees it?

MAN TWO: The Craigslist ad said: Casual Encounters: "mm4w," which mean two men for woman. There's nothing about film. Film is more money, and we don't do it.

Nella returns to the kabinet, carrying a bottle of Grey Ruse, four shot glasses, and a plate of pickles and tomatoes.

NELLA: What did I miss?
MELSOR: Two men walk in . . .
NELLA: From escort service?
MELSOR: From Craigslist, maybe escort service also. They are agreeing on price.

MAN ONE: Right, and with another "m" here it's "mm4mw." That's not what was advertised. You need somebody else. You'll find it.

MAN TWO: That's right— "mm4mf" is two men for couple. We don't do couples.

GREENSTEIN: I will not be joining you, no worries.

MELSOR: Are they Mexicans?
JOHNNY: *Schwartzes.*
BILL: Please . . . Terrible word . . .

JOHNNY: What's so terrible about *schwartzes*? Means black. Like my name: Schwartz. Want to call me a racist? Call me a racist.

MAN ONE: Okay. We don't give our price on Craigslist, but our regular price is three eighty. We can do three fifty. For one hour.

MAN TWO: You can be in the room if you have to.

MAN ONE: That's another hundred bucks, usually, but you can be there. But don't try to put nothing up my ass, cause if you do, I'll turn around and slug you. I don't like it, and it's not part of the deal.

GREENSTEIN: Your full three hundred eighty dollars is in line. But I want each of you to take this. One for you, and one for you.

JOHNNY: What do they want?

MELSOR: Who? Men? They want money. Herr Greenstein wants Frau Greenstein to get satisfied by two men, I think.

NELLA: Shhh!!! Quiet!!!

MAN ONE: What's this?

GREENSTEIN: It's Viagra.

MAN TWO: I don't take no Viagra. I have high blood pressure. Fortunately, I don't need none, haven't yet.

MAN ONE: I took it when I agreed to be filmed once, for a screen test. It looks like a little blue football with sharp edges. This one's red and round and has a *C* and a star in the middle.

GREENSTEIN: It's a crescent, and there is a little star that looks like a dot. It's the same Viagra, but it's from Turkey.

MAN ONE: I don't care. I am not taking it.

NELLA (TO JOHNNY): He wants her to get satisfied by two young men. When I heard rumors, they said he doesn't stay in room. He sits in living room and reads newspaper or watches Fox News.

JOHNNY: Why can't he do it?

NELLA: He has micropenis.

JOHNNY: Does it work?

NELLA: I don't know. He has a *protez* . . . How do you say it?

BILL: Prosthesis.

NELLA: It makes him look normal. But his *prostite* falls out. I saw it fall out of his bathing suit and float in ocean.

JOHNNY: I don't understand. Does he have a *schlong* or doesn't he have a *schlong*?

NELLA: They say he does, but it's micropenis—small.

JOHNNY: Small like rabbit-small?

NELLA: I don't know. I didn't see it. But he wears rubber penis, like lesbian. Look in literature. And it floated to surface when I talked to him when he was swimming in ocean.

JOHNNY: It floated away?

NELLA: I don't know. He looked like he didn't notice, but after I left he caught up with it, if he swam fast.

JOHNNY: Caught up with it and put it back there?

NELLA: If he caught it. I am sure it's expensive.

JOHNNY: I hate him as much as the next guy, but I don't see what the big deal is. When you get old, things fall off. How is it different from, for example, dentures?

MELSOR: *Sha!* I want to listen!

MAN TWO: Are you telling us she is so ugly that we need this Turkish stuff to get going?

GREENSTEIN: This is different. It's a natural product. It will not hurt you.

MAN ONE: In the e-mail you said MILF . . .

GREENSTEIN: Beauty is in the eye of the beholder.

MAN TWO: A MILF would have to be your daughter's age. Is she your daughter or something, because if she is, I am going home. I am not going to be a part of this, unless she is of legal age or older. I don't even know how Craigslist's calling this . . . Man gets off on watching two studs ram his daughter.

MAN ONE: And I am not taking any of this Turkish stuff, either, even if she isn't pretty. I say blindfold me and I'll think about my wife.

GREENSTEIN: No . . . She is not my daughter. She is my wife. And she is of legal age.

MAN ONE: So it's straight mm4f, not some weird-ass mm4mf shit, with guys doing shit to us we don't usually do?

GREENSTEIN: Accept my assurances.

JOHNNY: What is that word, MILF? I've been seeing it for eight or ten years.

BILL: Since the McCain-Palin thing in 2008?

JOHNNY: Something like that.

BILL: It's an abbreviation for Mother I'd Like to Fuck. It's a demeaning term for middle-aged women who look good.

NELLA: Wilfreda Müller-Greenstein is not MILF.

MELSOR: Quiet!

NELLA: Aren't you recording?

(Melsor nods.)

MAN ONE: Okay, I'll take this Turkish stuff. You seem okay.

MAN TWO: Okay, I'll take it, too, may need it, from what you are telling me.

GREENSTEIN: I am letting you in on something of a family tradition. There is something of a play involved: I take her out to an early dinner at a German restaurant.

She goes to bed to take a nap while I pretend to watch the news. Then two men walk into the bedroom, and she opens her eyes slowly, and you take it from there. Can you do that?

JOHNNY: After we helped mop up the Battle of the Bulge, we pressed on. I was a mortar man in the Seventh Army Forty-fifth Infantry Division. We went up and down and around Munich, liberated Dachau and a bunch of its satellites, one camp after another, and, believe me, I got to see that country as well as anyone. So correct me if I'm wrong: he has hired two guys and he wants them to do his wife while he is watching?

NELLA: I don't think he sits and watches it.

JOHNNY: My buddies and I had a one-word explanation for all this . . . Just one word . . .

MAN ONE: You want us to wake her up?

GREENSTEIN: Yes.

MAN TWO: Okay, we'll do well by you, man.

GREENSTEIN: I have full confidence . . .

NELLA: I can't tell what's going on in bedroom.

JOHNNY: Seems kind of quiet. Not a good sign.

BILL: Ominous—concurred.

MELSOR: What do you expect? Screams? The girl is having good time.

NELLA: Girl? She is grandmother! I tell you what's going on. She is in bed, pretending to sleep. They walk in on their toes, really quietly, they pull back blanket by a little, and she pretends like she is waking up.

JOHNNY: Is she buck naked?

NELLA: No! This is not like that. They start slowly, but then things go faster. Normal, except there are two of them.

MELSOR: How do you know?

NELLA: I have friend whose husband treated her like that once a year after his *prostitektiny.*

BILL: Prostatectomy.

NELLA: Greenstein is vicious animal to everyone else, but to his wife he is considerable.

BILL: Considerable may not be the right word.

NELLA: What word is right?

BILL: Considerate, maybe.

NELLA: What's the difference?

JOHNNY: If he were considerable, he wouldn't have to pay two guys to do her. He has a micropenis; right?

BILL: Actually, considerable in this case would refer to size, not performance. It could be large, but not seaworthy.

NELLA: Considerate, considerable, I don't care which one it is. He is animal to everyone else, but he loves her.

MELSOR: And she him?

NELLA: And she him.

MAN TWO: Hey, my buddy just passed out!

GREENSTEIN: What happened?

MAN TWO: He was mounting her from behind while she was working on me up front, and he just fell back.

GREENSTEIN: Is he breathing?

WILFREDA (*shouts from the other room*): Yes, he is breathing, he started up again.

MAN TWO: Call the ambulance! What if he dies? He is barely breathing, but his thing is still strong. What was in that Turkish stuff?

GREENSTEIN: Natural ingredients. Nothing that will harm you.

MAN ONE: Hey . . . What happened there . . .

MAN TWO: You went out cold. How are you feeling, bud?

MAN ONE: A little woozy still, did I just pass out? Hey, let's get the fuck out of here . . .

MAN TWO: Hey, dude, look at his eyes, they are bloodred, he's blown all the capillaries in there.

GREENSTEIN: I see no point in continuing then. You are free to go.

BILL: Okay, I get the idea.

NELLA: Sh-sh-sh. I am listening.

MAN ONE: What about our money?

GREENSTEIN: What money? You failed to perform.

MAN TWO: But he passed out, almost fucking died, all because of that Turkish shit you gave us. Now that I think of it, I am feeling light-headed, too.

GREENSTEIN: You were paid to perform a service, and you failed to complete it.

MAN ONE: But we got going, man.

GREENSTEIN: You were paid to provide a complete service. Getting started is of no value whatsoever. It's detrimental, even. You don't buy three-quarters of a surgery, or a quarter of a car, or half a cat.

MAN ONE: We'll report you, man.

GREENSTEIN: To whom? The vice squad? Craigslist? FDA?

WILFREDA: Thank you for your efforts, now get out of here.

MAN ONE: Hey, the cunt has a
gun. What the fuck!
GREENSTEIN: It's a Glock 43,
and my lovely wife knows how
to use it.
(The door slams.)

JOHNNY: Now are you ready
for a one-word explanation for
all this?
BILL: Yes, why not . . .
JOHNNY: Just one word says it all,
from one who's been there . . .

GREENSTEIN: Thank you, gentlemen.

BILL: Shoot?
JOHNNY: Germans . . .

Wilfreda's rant—in German—follows. Amused as everyone
else in the room seems to be, Bill doesn't understand anything
about what he has just heard. He catches a few German words
that sound mildly intriguing, but, ultimately, who cares?

Wilfreda is a mystery. She is in her seventies. Septuagenari-
ans fuck—yes. Bill can easily accept the notion of Wilfreda
having an affair, sanctioned or illicit, with, say, the octogenar-
ian heartthrob Johnny Schwartz.

But the thing he hears transpire makes no sense to Bill. It's
as puzzling and undeniable as Florida itself: yet another form of
exploitation; yet another form of devastation—Bill hears it, as
do others in the room.

"Germans . . ."

That one-word explanation is good enough for Johnny, but not for Bill.

Marriages are complicated things. Fascism is more complicated still. You do either for a while, revel in happiness or in the glory of Deutschland-first, Russia-first, America-first, and then you pay and pay and pay, for decades, for centuries. Bill finally gets around to his vodka.

Here in Florida nothing is what it appears to be. Rubber cocks float into the ocean, husbandly duties are not husbandly duties, fiduciary responsibilities are not fiduciary responsibilities. Folks pay one hundred dollars to attend eightieth birthdays out of fear that no one will come to theirs. Casual encounters are not casual encounters, mm4w is not mm4w, idiots are not idiots, Viagra is not Viagra, Grey Goose is not Grey Goose, everyone has an angle, everyone has a fraud.

Bill reaches for a pickle to deactivate what by now has become the familiar taste of Kozachok.

At least a pickle is a pickle.

18

PANI CONSUELA RAMIREZ-WRONSKA

Gwen broke no laws when she fabricated the open fly and the Washington parties, and being summarily, humiliatingly fired by the *Post* dealt with the matter completely.

Bill's misdeeds at this point are, any way you look at them, classifiable as felonies of the sort that may require atonement at one of the facilities operated by the Florida Department of Corrections.

After eavesdropping on the Greensteins' sexual episode, Bill consults a table on the Web site of the Reporters Committee for Freedom of the Press. He clicks on a summary of Florida laws covering recording. Florida Statute chapter 934.03 reads: "All parties must consent to the recording or the disclosure of the contents of any wire, oral, or electronic communication in Florida. Recording, disclosing, or endeavoring to disclose without the consent of all parties is a felony, unless the interception is a first offense committed without any illegal purpose, and not for commercial gain. These first of-

fenses and the interception of cellular frequencies are misde-
meanors."

Planting a bug in the apartment of his father's rival candidate for a seat on the condominium board of directors is an act
committed for commercial gain. It's a felony.

As a guardian of the public interest, Bill appears to have
crossed to the enemy side. He acknowledges this. It's possible
that this is temporary and that there is a way back. It may
very well matter that the couple he eavesdropped on was
the enemy, that he was doing to them what they would without hesitation do to him, that this was an element of broader
struggle, an experiment in using criminal tactics to fight crime.

Kozachok continues to go down smoothly, likely because Bill has
relocated it to the freezer.

Scribbling in his reporter's notebook reads: "Journalism — Eunuch at a gangbang. You observe, you don't do. I want
to do." The fact that only four pages in this notebook contain
any writing or drawing makes this entry significant. Here is all
that exists:

Page 1—The question-mark drawing done in the course of
his flight to Florida,
Page 2—The table listing the makes of cars he sees at the Château parking lot,
Page 3—Zbig's street address/license plates of the Lexuses
belonging to the Château board members/addresses of Klub
Susanna and Restaurant Tbilisi.

The observation about eunuchs is on page 4.

It should be noted that the entry continues:

"Task 1—Find meaning in Zbig's death. Task 2—Stop ISIS. OK to use criminal means to stop criminal activity."

Now there is decidedly nothing to do. Bill picks up a pen and composes a poem, his first in Russian:

Резиновый пенис ушел в океан,
Его подхватила волна.
А я наливаю водки стакан—
Как много на свете говна!

Not bad for a debut. The English translation is admittedly imperfect:

A rubber penis went off to sea,
It was picked up by a wave.
And I am filling my vodka glass—
There's so much shit in the world!

Like a mule who knows how to get his drunken peasant home, the computer takes Bill to BASE jumping videos.

In Washington, he thought of himself as the guy who trained bartenders at Martin's to produce perfect TBs.

Now, alone, surrounded by porny oil paintings of Luka Mudischev, compulsively watching videos of people jumping from great heights, chugging ice-cold Kozachok straight from the bottle, Bill focuses on the design features of the bottle at—or, more precisely, *in*—hand.

On a video, a young woman in a bathing suit prepares to dive off the side of a Norwegian fjord. Clearly, she is not seasonally dressed.

Bill's mind continues simultaneously on two tracks.

On Track One, he wants to know why it is that half-gallon containers of milk have handles while half-gallon plastic bottles of vodka usually do not.

On Track Two, he zeroes in on the young woman's preparation for a BASE jump—her commitment to the jump.

Taking a swig of Kozachok, on Track One, he acknowledges the thoughtfulness of the men and women of Kozachok Distillery Inc. of South Philly, who cared enough about their clients' convenience to decant their product into a handle-enabled container.

On Track Two—the video—the young woman takes a leap into the abyss. What follows is of little interest to Bill.

Bill scrolls back, making the image freeze at the instant the jumper's beach-sandaled feet part with the edge of the cliff, her breaking point. This is it—the precise point of departure, the point of commitment, the point of *doing,* as opposed to the point of *writing. No mas* gangbang eunuching!

He notes that these are questions he wouldn't have thought to ask had he remained in Washington, the place now referred to as "the swamp" in Trampenese.

The moment of departure—this instant of commitment to the leap, this breaking point—has to be the principal element of his obsession with watching these BASE-jumping stunts, this irresistible draw of the eye candy of death.

How could he have not thought of it?

The phone rings. It's Gwen. Fuck it! She isn't entitled to know what he is about to do.

Inspector Luftmensch reaches for the car keys.

It's 1:30 A.M. and not even a stray Lamborghini can be spotted on Ocean Drive. The white Prius tentatively piloted by the undeniably inebriated William "Ilya" Melsorovich Katzenelenbogen is the only moving object in sight.

Police cruisers await, poised to attack from the canopies of flowering bushes and palm tree groves of shopping centers. Bill sees them all, or at least believes he does. He remains calm. The word "philosophical" might be used, given his pre-Prius intellectual journey, the one that produced a debut poem in Russian and derived a monolithic theory that unified journalism, the packaging of vodka, gangbangs, eunuchs, and commitment to BASE jumps into a single entity.

A handle of Kozachok rolls gently on the floor of the front passenger seat.

Yes, police cruisers await, and within them danger lurks, but a wheezy hybrid doesn't make their list of top targets. A gentle weave can be observed in its trajectory—granted—but this is South Florida, officer, be pragmatic. In these parts, everyone has a cause to weave, with explanations falling into a complex cluster of categories of etiology: geriatric, psychiatric, emotional, neurologic, pharmacologic, and multifactorial. If you start pulling over everyone who momentarily deviates from the tyranny of white lines, you will be stopping every soul on Ocean Drive, especially at this late hour.

It's 2:07 A.M. and the lights at the Wronski home are out.

Bill rings the bell, but there is no answer. Consuela isn't home, or she would have at the very least yelled at him, thrown things at him, or made good on her threat to call the police. Fuck it! Bill doesn't care.

This is not just another stiff. This is Zbignew Stanislaw Wronski, M.D., the Butt God of Miami Beach! His college roommate! His friend! Why did he fall into that abyss, forty-three floors below, through the atrium's glass ceiling? Did he fall, or was he pushed? Why? Why? Why? No one, no one is more committed to this story, more entitled to it. This is Bill's leap and his alone. This is his boundary, his end of the old, his beginning of the new, his vote of confidence in his pack and his canopy and every meter of string packed inside it. In jumps, in falls—in everything—all you can do is summon the courage to make your feet abandon the edge. The rest is up to the winds, up to the gods.

Bill sits down on the white marble steps of his late friend's home, grabs onto the plastic handle, and takes a modest-sized swig of Kozachok. God bless South Philly. Sleep, if sleep is what it is, descends slowly, invisibly. He lets go, ascending to the universe of chutes, fly suits, great heights, protruding boulders.

Bill is awakened by a tap on his nose.

The object is inanimate. It is, in fact, a stiletto heel.

"You are drunk," says Consuela.

She is in a black silk sheath dress. It's so classic that the word "short" is all you need to describe it. She seems to wear no jewelry other than a wedding ring.

"Afraid so."

"You had to be drunk to come back—after that scene. With you playing paparazzi. What do you want?"

"It would be paparazzo. Singular. I was alone."

She doesn't look like the paragon of sobriety, either, but Bill is clearly worse off, bad enough to correct her Italian.

"I am here because I want to know what happened to my friend."

"That night?"

"And before."

"Do I even matter to you?"

"You? Yes."

"What do you think about me?"

"You are very beautiful."

"Come in," she says, opening the door. "Bring your bottle. We will need it."

The living room of the Wronski home is aggressively white, cliché white: white marble floor, white furniture.

It's not clear why Bill recognizes the two white leather sofas as the Charles, by B&B Italia. He looked it up once, when he was covering a story about the offing of a lobbyist in his home in Chevy Chase. (The brains, alas, ruined that sofa.)

Bill went through catalogs for that story. It's simple: to begin to understand the stiff, esthetic choices are a good place to start. Objects guide you into the inner world of their owners. It's Anthropology 101, or something like it.

At the Wronskis', a massive painting of a nude woman reclining on the beach hangs over the sofa. At first, Bill thinks it's a photograph, then realizes it's a painting. Super-realism. Bill respects super-realism.

"Do you think it's me?"

"Is it?"

"Could be. Or not. Zbig talked a lot about you, about your friendship."

"Which aspect of it?"

"He said you understand stories the way no one understands stories."

"I am flattered."

"You were the one who told him that a shape is a story, shaping is storytelling, reshaping is, too. He credited you with shaping his career. What were you drinking?"

It's her in the painting, of course. The purpose of art is to provoke. Bill hands her the bottle.

"Out of the bottle?"

Bill nods. She takes a swig, grimaces, takes another.

"This, too, tells a story: a rough remedy for a rough time. What did Zbig tell you about me?"

Bill thinks back. "Nothing, really."

"That's a story in itself. Do you think I am, say, Argentine?"

"Are you?"

"I could be. Do you think Ramirez is my real maiden name? I could be Slovenian for all you know. My name could be Malaria."

"Is it? Are you?"

"Possibly. Did he say I was his patient?"

"Were you?"

"I could have been. Did he say I was a model?"

"Were you? Are you?"

"Could be true."

"Are you going to tell me anything?"

"No. Not now. I never told anyone anything. What they don't know, they make up. I don't talk. Not even the homicide squad."

"They were involved?"

"Maybe."

"Why are you agreeing to be on that idiotic reality show?"

"Because they invited me. Others didn't. Zbig was pushing me to do it, said it was good for business. *Real Housewives* said they already had a plastic surgeon's wife, the wife of the Boob God. And now it's gone, and Zbig is gone."

She takes another swig.

"Are you going to tell *me* how Zbig died?"

"No."

"Forget me—you might owe *him* the truth, unite him with his story."

"It's not useful to pressure me. I will do what I will do—on my terms."

"Have you told the story on this *Merry Widows* thing?"

"Not yet, but I might. Should I?"

"Stories are for telling. I think. I believe—or believed."

"What if they—the audience—aren't equipped to understand?"

"That's not your problem. Your responsibility is to come up to the edge of the cliff and leap. The rest is up to the gods. That's Rule One of storytelling."

"What about the truth? Does it matter?"

"The truth is the thing that sets you free. At least that's what I've always believed."

"Do you believe this still?"

"I think I do. Maybe."

"Why do you waver?"

"Because lies bring victory. Look at Trump. He lied. It worked."

"Hillary never lied? Like George Washington?"

"Hillary lied—but it didn't work. Imagine what Hitler could have achieved if he had social media. You no longer have to imagine."

"Are you getting lost, Bill?"

"I might be—blame the vodka, always blame the vodka. All I am saying is, let me formulate it . . ."

She hands him the bottle.

He takes a swig.

"The truth doesn't fucking matter—not anymore. Do you accept this notion?"

"Yes."

"It is our duty as human beings, as citizens, to be truthful. A 'virtue' is the old word for this. Do you accept?"

"Maybe."

"So: the act of telling the truth is predicated on our rejection of the truth's irrelevance. Think of it as an act of civil disobedience. Am I talking out of my ass?"

"A little."

"Okay, you might extend it to say that telling the truth in the pre-Trump world was already a Fuck You to the system. Yes? Now, in the Trump world, it's a bigger Fuck You—a Fuck You, Fuck You, Fuck You. A triple salute. Are you with me?"

"No."

"I am shitfaced. Sorry."

"No apologies warranted. I needed to hear all this . . . I think. Thank you. You may have helped me more than you know."

"I hope so, but I don't believe I helped you one bit. Or myself, for that matter."

"Rest assured. But I am tired now—ciao. You can sleep on the sofa, if you wish."

"I'll make it home; I am good. The Prius knows the way."

Bill turns to leave but pauses and turns again to face her.

"Does it mean you'll tell the story, anywhere, ever?"

"I might."

19

THE FORUM

The Gulf Stream Room was mostly spared in the past deluge or deluges that had devastated the Château's lobby. It's a former library—former, because the books are almost entirely gone. The shelves that line the four walls stand bare.

In better days—four decades ago—someone had applied thought here. The floor is the same paisley design, except here it's smaller, the shades of marble lighter. With Lapidus at the helm, this was not some stuffy high-goyish men's club library.

Before he ensconced himself in Miami, Lapidus did many commissions in New York and Chicago—including, in fact, shoe stores. He knew many things, and shelves were among them.

These shelves are white, laminated, with little paisleys that remain as gold as they were the day they were made.

The ceiling tiles in the Gulf Stream Room, alas, are gone. Only the steel grid remains. Since there is no natural light—which is just fine for a library—Lapidus used Poul

Henningson PH5 fixtures—eight of them—to provide peripheral light. In the center, he used a Henningson Artichoke chandelier.

Bill snaps a photo and sends it to Gwen, causing a predictable exclamation: "I want!"

It's 6:30 P.M., January 16. Folks begin to trickle into the Gulf Stream Room for the start of the annual ritual of election to the BOD of the Château Sedan Neuve Condominium Association. The stakes this year are unusually high, but power is locked in. Election is two days away.

The math is simple: five seats on the board, a three-vote majority required to make *any* decision involving the Château's $4 million annual budget, and a virtually unlimited ability to levy special assessments.

It's all about candidates.

Vice President Greenstein is running again, for his sixth term. Micropenis aside, he is a lucky man. Had the misdeed that led to his disbarment also led to a felony conviction, he would have been precluded from serving as a fiduciary of a condominium association.

Two board members in his coalition are unchanged—Igor Roytman and Sergei Kushman.

Greenstein-Roytman-Kushman is an undefeatable coalition of Russians and Americans. Theirs is the perpetual winning ticket.

When Roytman is not engaged in water sports, at least one item of clothing he wears is always red. Today he wears red shorts. This choice of color is a play on his last name: red man. He is a former licensed construction engineer who lost his license for a misdeed no one at the Château has taken the trouble to investigate. There is no reason to look into this. The loss of a professional license, even for cause, doesn't preclude you from serving on the BOD.

Kushman wears black, mostly in order to distinguish himself from Roytman. He is a chemical engineer who once produced paints and furniture lacquer at a facility staffed by prisoners—a Gulag enterprise. Like Roytman, he was a deeply satisfied Soviet citizen who nonetheless took the opportunity to get the hell out as soon as this became possible.

He did end up with a minor felony conviction—paints, fraud, Jersey—but his civil rights were restored more than five years before he was duly elected to the BOD.

Some years, the board is completely harmonious—i.e., all five members vote with Greenstein-Roytman-Kushman. In recent years, as special assessments mounted, troublemakers got as many as two members to the board. With three being the magic number, the presence of two naysayers on the board can do no harm.

It should also be noted that no one knows what happens after all the votes are cast and tabulation commences behind closed doors. By decision of the BOD, this process is entrusted to Frau Müller-Greenstein, the wife of the vice president.

The fourth member of the board—President Aleksandr Bogomolov, a historian—is being forced to relinquish his BOD seat, because he has fallen into delinquency. He has attempted to trade information for dues forgiveness—something Greenstein has reportedly done in special cases in the past—but in this case the vice president saw no point in making a deal.

Though disgraced, BOD President Bogomolov is in attendance at the candidates' forum, sitting in the corner, his arms crossed. It is not publicly known whether he is present in order to bear witness or out of masochism.

The fifth member—Johnny Schwartz—keeps getting elected because he is popular with the ladies. He is also popular with men who go to the gym, where he freely dispenses workout advice. Schwartz hates the Greenstein-Roytman-Kushman triumvirate, but doesn't attend BOD meetings, having determined that this activity is pointless.

But this year, as has been established, the order is being challenged by one Melsor Y. Katzenelenbogen, a former dissident, a poet and retired "medical entrepreneur."

Naturally, this naysayer, this nutcase, this professional renegade, this out-of-touch boob, this narcissistic pariah, has no chance of being elected. Frau Müller-Greenstein will see to that.

No surveys of the Château have ever been taken, but based on observation—Bill's—the voters do not split strictly based on their country of origin. Americans seem to vote for the ruling troika, even though two of its members are Russian. Conversely, Johnny Schwartz may be receiving more than half of the Russian vote—the women.

It is often noted that Schwartz is a doppelgänger for Sean Connery. This is correct, though, absent rigorous polling, it is unknown whether Johnny Schwartz actually gets the votes of *all* women or just the vote of Frau Müller-Greenstein, which could well be the only vote required for ascent to the BOD.

If you wish to find Bill in a room—any room—face the audience and look in the direction of the leftmost seat in the back row. He is either sitting in that seat or standing behind it. This is an instinctive preference, his pursuit of journalistic Feng Shui, perhaps. Also, nothing beats standing up inconspicuously and getting the fuck out. Bill takes his customary back-row-leftmost-seat position. Alas, being the youngest person in the room by two or three decades precludes him blending in.

Rumors that identify him as an agent of an unspecified agency—perhaps FBI, perhaps DBPR—make him even more noticeable—the inspector general, traveling incognito, with secret orders.

Having lost his actual authority, Bill is starting to find himself at ease with the fictional.

People continue to arrive; two and three at a time, arranging themselves in clusters—the Russians, the Americans. Melsor plans to make his entrance in the middle of Greenstein's opening remarks. This would demonstrate his contempt for the existing regime. Nella is in the room, in the front row, across the aisle from Wilfreda Müller-Greenstein. Her mission is to text Melsor and give him the entrance cue.

Four tables are set up in the front. These are the same Milo Baughman tables that can be found crippled throughout the Château. Each is roughly thirty inches by thirty inches by thirty inches—perfect little cubes.

The ruling triumvirate is in place. Greenstein in the center, Roytman on his right, Kushman on his left. Mrs. Roytman is next to her husband, Mrs. Kushman next to hers. To consolidate the GRK bloc, both wives are running for the BOD. Under Florida law, a husband and wife can serve on the same condominium board if they own more than one unit. The Roytmans own three. The Kushmans own five and are preparing to put in a bid for the soon-to-be-vacated Bogomolov unit.

Johnny Schwartz shuffles in like a superannuated GI. His fatigues are pressed; his Dolphins T-shirt, too. Either Mrs. Roytman or Mrs. Kushman stands poised to replace him on the board. Whether you support the GRK bloc or oppose it, Johnny

Schwartz is so ineffective on the BOD that he will not be missed when the GRK bloc transforms itself into the GRRKK bloc.

No place is reserved for Melsor Katzenelenbogen.

"Thank you, and welcome to the 2017 candidates' forum. I am Jonah Greenstein. I am a six-term vice president of the Château Sedan Neuve Condominium Association, and I once again humbly seek your support.

"I am happy to report that, in addition to our proven leadership, we have a new, reinvigorated slate of exciting candidates. You will hear from all of them tonight. This has been a very positive campaign so far, and with your unwavering support, I plan on all of us working together. Together, we will make the Château great again!"

Greenstein pauses—it's a cue for applause, and Wilfreda Müller-Greenstein applauds as expected.

"Though this year has brought setbacks, such as three separate floods that have devastated our lobby, our able contractor, Dr. Murthy, has been able to mitigate the damage," Greenstein continues. "I remind you that these are acts of God, something none of us foresaw or could foresee. Nonetheless, we have completed the rebuilding of South Pool and have improved the South Pool deck. We have begun removal of the antiquated and inefficient cooling system and the spaghetti-like clusters of pipes that were installed four decades ago.

"First, we want to make sure that you hear what all of us—your BOD—have done for you."

"You got more rich!" shouts a rotund woman in the third row. She is shorter than an average twelve-year-old, her hair out-of-the-bottle red. She wears a sheer tropical-print muumuu over a gold-colored bathing suit. "Answer questions about your nineteen-million-dollar deal with ISIS! How much they give you?"

Others—Russians—echo her questions, with all of this being blurted out at once:

- "You signed contract in secret!"
- "It's our nineteen million, not your nineteen million!"
- "When do we get copy of contract?!"
- "Did they give you second Lexus?"
- "What will you tell to DBPR when they come to investigate?"

Greenstein retains his composure. "I can confirm that a contract is on the table, and that following this meeting this board will decide on its ratification," he says. "We have an absolute right to ratify the contract and the financing package, and until such time when the contract is duly ratified, we will answer no questions. You are welcome to comment, but we will answer no questions. Does anyone have any opinions?"

Hands shoot up, but no one seems to see any reason to wait to be recognized.

- "Did you have competition bidding or did you just give it to ISIS, as always?"
- "How many contractors bid and how much did they want?"
- "Did you meet on yacht outside U.S. territorial water?"
- "Did you bid the rigs?"
- "What will you tell to FBI when they come?"

"First, these were all questions. And second, I assure you that this board is committed to the principles of transparency and that we did not, as you say, 'bid the rigs.' Your duly elected board doesn't rig bids! I want everyone here to recognize that we are all in it together, I want everyone to be friendlier, or at least more polite. And that's the problem here: no one smiles!"

"Thanks to you!" shouts the woman in a muumuu. "You smile when someone stick big knife under your ribs!"

Greenstein looks directly at her. "No, Mrs. Falk, I can't imagine you smiling, or even being courteous, like a normal retiree."

"Glad you understand," shouts a woman next to the muumuu-clad Mrs. Falk. She is somewhere between seventy and eighty, short, zaftig, wearing a peach-colored velour warm-up suit with matching-tinted glasses.

A tall, bespectacled man next to her shouts: "How can we have opinions when you don't give us documents and say *Don't ask questions?*"

Muumuu says, "It's from Kafka!"

"A lot of angry faces here," Greenstein observes. "This makes me sad, truly. I guess there are no comments. All we heard was questions. Since not everyone here speaks English well, let me explain: an opinion doesn't end with a question mark. A question does. Again, we will not be taking questions at this time. Does anyone have any opinions?"

At this instant, Melsor Katzenelenbogen walks through the double doors, producing a double-loud slam.

He is wearing checkered green-and-white trousers and a double-breasted jacket with what appears to be an emblem of a yacht club. The polo shirt is canary yellow.

MELSOR: Enough!!! It's time to drain swamp! I am candidate for BOD! Where is my seat at table?!

GREENSTEIN: We expected nothing less than sloganeering populism from our opposition candidate. Please make space for Mr. Katzenelenbogen . . .

Stepan and his two security guards do not budge.

GREENSTEIN: Excuse me, we should all scoot over one seat to make room for my friend.

Still, no one budges.

MELSOR: Then I will stand! I don't want to be on pictures sitting at same table with you!

Melsor moves to tower over the seated Greenstein and Roytman and Kushman.

MELSOR: With crooks like you, I *prefer* to stand!

Greenstein and Roytman turn around, look up at Melsor, exchange nods, and move apart. Johnny Schwartz grabs the extra chair in the audience and inserts it between Greenstein and Roytman.

Though a chair has been made available for him, Melsor remains standing.

"Sit down!" shouts someone from the audience. It's Wilfreda Müller-Greenstein.

Melsor settles into his chair and lets his gaze look over the audience, making eye contact or at least seeking it.

MELSOR: I believe the future former vice president was speaking. His time ended, but I will let him make farewell address! And, to his lovely wife, I hope you had enjoyable birthday.

SCHWARTZ: I join Melsor in that hope. Wilfreda, I hope your birthday was filled with love, joy, and excitement.

Half of the Americans in the audience show no emotion. The other half show disgust. Half of the Russians roll their eyes. The other half applaud enthusiastically.

GREENSTEIN: I am here to lament. This used to be a friendly building. People greeted each other with smiles, stood up for each other, were neighbors in the best sense of the word. Now this has changed.

WOMAN IN MUUMUU: Thanks to you!

STEPAN: No interruption! *Ne perebivat'!*

GREENSTEIN: That's right, we can have you removed.

WOMAN IN PEACH: And evict me? So your satraps will buy my apartment chip?

MELSOR: Now let's watch Mr. Greenstein's tugs remove this grandmother. Think about it when you vote.

GREENSTEIN: It's "thugs." Th . . . Not T. We say "thugs" in English, Mr. Kazenelenbogen. Tugs are boats.

MELSOR: Yes, tugs!

GREENSTEIN: What happened to politeness? Decorum? What happened to all of us? I wish all of us could take the high road! What would it take to make the Château flourish as the jewel it once was? I think our first step is recognition that we are in it together. I don't care what country you are from, I don't care what race you are, I care what kind of a neighbor you are. I want to see more smiles!

WOMAN IN PEACH: You want us to smile as your tugs throw us out?

GREENSTEIN: We have hard choices to make. Millions of dollars will need to be spent . . .

NELLA: How is Lexus running?

MELSOR: You say you want to make Château great? Here is what you do: abduct!

GREENSTEIN: Are you trying to say "abdicate"?

MELSOR: Your time is over, villain! I do not afraid your tugs! What's the difference between Greenstein and Katzenelenbogen? Greenstein has tugs that will throw you out. Katzenelenbogen has singers who will sing for you! Give it up for South Florida Russian Women's Folk Choir! Let's go, girls! *Davayte, devochki!*

The doors swing open again, and three old women in Russian folk costumes—headdresses and all—burst into the room.

One of them has an accordion, another a balalaika, the third two wooden spoons, an authentic, widely used percussion instrument. The singers take position in the middle of the aisle, between Nella and Frau Müller-Greenstein.

Now Melsor shouts over the sounds of soft-playing accordion: "ISIS is on our doorstep. Their machines will start demolition—demolition that these crooks, these adventurists, will make you pay for!

"In my first act as your vice president of your BOD, I will fire ISIS! Together we will defeat ISIS! No more destruction! No more kickbacks! No more Lexuses! Together we will make Château great again!"

WOMAN IN PEACH: Melsor Katzenelenbogen, you will not be elected! The commandant's wife decides who get elected!

MELSOR: Their time is over! Let's shout, all together: Make Château Great—Again!

No one shouts. The accordion plays on, providing soft background music. The audience—the Russians and the Americans—look on in bewilderment. Greenstein is on his feet; his coalition members, too.

One of the singers—the wooden spoonist—emits a guttural sound, the sort that makes *chastushki* what they are. She begins to sing:

Гринштейн гонит в ад из рая
Нас по адской лестнице.
Как оброк с нас собирает
Спешиал ассесменты.

All three women carry sheets of paper, which they throw at the audience, like propaganda leaflets from a plane.

The second woman, the one with the balalaika, takes a turn, singing the English translation:

Greenstein shoves us from heaven to hell,
Down the Devil's staircase.
Like a ransom he is collecting
Special assessments.

She makes room for the accordionist:

К нам приехал ревизор—
Сволочная гадина.
Ни хрена он не найдет!
Всё уже украдено.

Now, the spoons player steps in with a translation:

The inspector has arrived,
Poisonous and bastardly.

He won't find a single thing,
All was stolen long ago!

"Podpevayte!" beckons the accordionist. Then in English: "You sing, too!"

"Remove them," shouts Greenstein as the Americans and a large number of the Russians look on in catatonic silence. However, about half of the Russians, including Nella, Alex, and the woman in peach, pick up the *chastushki* song sheets and sing along:

Протекает в лобби крыша,
Дуба дал эар кондишен,
Здесь нам братцы не до песен
Расползлась повсюду плесень.

The Americans aren't singing, but some of the Russians are, even in English, wooden as it is:

Roof is leaking in the lobby,
Air conditioner has kicked off,
We have no time to sing
Mold is climbing on the walls.

The security guards have their orders, but they seem to have no idea what to do. You can remove one lunatic, but not dozens of people as they sing along in what has the look of a cultist observance.

Что Флоридский нам закон?
Нет на нас здесь правил.
Без балконов и окон
Жить нас борд заставил.

Florida law means nothing here,
There are no rules for us.
With no balconies and windows
The board made us live.

As the guards stand in confusion, Bill notices a drop of water appear on his notepad. Another drop lands on his arm, another on his forehead. Is it raining? Indoors? The singers are undeterred.

На борду сидят подонки
И отдачи требуют.
А нам хочется скорей
Чтоб их больше не было!

Lowlife sits on condo board
And demands a kickback.
And all we want
Is for them to go extinct.

What the fuck? Has someone turned on the sprinkler system? If so, why is the water coming out of air ducts? Has something gone completely, wildly awry? The singers don't care . . .

Мой милёнок не убийца,
Мой милёнок не бандит.

Он не просто так ворует—
В кондо борде он сидит!

My beloved's not a killer,
My beloved's not a thug.
He doesn't need to pick your pocket,
'Cause he sits on condo board!

The water comes down in streams, and some of the folks—Russians, Americans—are trying to fight their way to the doors, but it's slow going. The singers' costumes are getting soaked, people are rushing past them, but they keep going:

В гараже у нас давно,
Мыши-крысы бегают!
Оставляют нам говно,
Вот как нас преследуют.

In our garage for a long time now
Rats and mice are running amok!
They are leaving us their turds
That's how we are persecuted.

Bill gets out of his chair to snap some photos, but before he is able to capture these events, he feels excruciating pain across his upper back, in the exact same spot where he was hit before the onset of all this madness, on his first day in Florida. Has she been released? Does the *Dzhuyka* Loony Bin release its inmates so soon after admitting them?

Bill gets out of the way just in time to evade a second blow, which crushes on the chair. The old woman in a soaked nightshirt regroups and runs toward the candidates as they scramble to evacuate. Her crooked cane poised, she runs past the singers.

Her battle cry hasn't changed after days she spent as the ward of *Dzhuyka*:

"*Fashisty! Svolochi!*"

The room is emptying fast, but the singers are oblivious to the flood and the attacking old woman.

Раз в неделю в лаундремате
Забирают доллары,
А в козну их не сдаёут—
Воровать здесь здорово!

This *chastushka* is especially heinous in translation. Bill cringes, but he has no one to blame.

Once a week at our laundry,
They take the money
But it doesn't go to the condo—
Stealing's so easy here!

The final *chastushka* is actually the only one Bill likes, sort of. Just two lines:

Есть у нас четыре бида
Перестроить пирамиды.

We already have four bids
To replace the pyramids.

The existence of these *chastushki* in the English translation constitutes strong evidence that the New Bill—as opposed to his Inner Child—is very much in evidence in Hollywood, FL. As an adult now, Bill has the capacity to pick battles, and this capacity is what distinguishes him from a child.

Did Bill actually translate these?

He did.

Fuck the Inner Child.

The water makes a swamp of the rug, then, in gentle waves, escapes into the taupe and white marble floor of the hallway, hiding in every seam, seeping into walls, where, in the damp darkness of wooden studs, it will unleash the spread of mighty black mold. The damages could cost millions; the kickbacks, even more.

The more vigorous of the hundred or so people in the room walk out rapidly; others hobble as water keeps pouring out of the air ducts, rising to shin level. The singers press on, wet, loud, diving deep into their repertoire, improvising. Melsor is dancing. Bill has never seen or even imagined Melsor in any situation that even tangentially involves music, yet here he is, undeniable as life itself, stomping away like a drunken peasant.

As water keeps rising, the singing stops, the accordion grows softer. They sound like partisans at a bonfire, enjoying the well-deserved respite after a glorious day of Nazi-killing.

The old woman with a crooked cane is the first one out. Bill imagines her running with the glee of madness, a crooked-cane-bearing majorette leading a hobbling procession.

The board members are presumably directly behind her. Fortunately for them, the presidium table was close to the doorway.

Somebody slips and falls. It's the Russian woman in the muu-muu. Bill is in intense pain; two strikes of an aluminum cane will do that. Why does she choose him? Is it madness, or is it a dare, or is it both? He bends over the woman in the muumuu and extends his hand. She is prostrate, helpless, but she grabs his hand, grabs it hard. She is too heavy for one man to lift.

"Oy, spasibo vam," she says to Bill, and he pretends not to understand that he is being thanked, profusely at that.

In English, he tells her to place her feet against his, then to sit up, and as she struggles upward he wonders what his mother would look like now, at eighty. He was unable to help her, to save her from *her* Great Flood, from murderous high-dose chemo, from Hurricane Melsor—but he will help this woman, and he will help her now.

"Careful, walk slowly," he tells her, and they wade forth.

Theirs is a slow, stumbling, grumbling procession that moves with the speed of the slowest walker-assisted burgher.

"Thank you," she says as they reach the elevator door. The floor is wet here, too, and water keeps coming. He grabs a chair and places it in front of her, to stabilize herself as she awaits the elevator that will evacuate her to the dry land of a higher floor.

She switches to Russian, adding that she has heard people say that they know why he is here and that she is certain that he is able to understand her.

"Vy iz FBR. Vy nasha yedinstvennaya nadezhda, poslednayya, yedinstvennaya. Spaside nas. My praymo stonem ot etoy korruptsii. Kak v plenu zdes' zhivyom v etoy proklyatoy Floride."

He understands her perfectly: "You are from the FBI. You are our last hope, our only hope. We are groaning under the weight of this corruption. We live like prisoners in this cursed Florida."

"I am sorry, I don't understand you," he replies, turns around, and wades back through the stream rushing over the marble floor.

On the way back, he runs into Johnny Schwartz helping a stooped man with a walker reach dry land. Not a surprise: surely, the Battle of the Bulge had lessons to teach. You don't abandon the wounded and the vulnerable.

"We must help them even if they voted for Donal'd Tramp," Bill says to himself, then, recognizing the thought for the cheap shot it is, perishes it.

After saluting Johnny, Bill returns to the flood zone.

The room is empty. The singers are gone. The dancing Melsor is gone, too.

The air vents have run dry.

After the flooded forum, there is a vodka-drinking (*vodkopitiye* is the term playfully derived from *chayepitiye,* a tea party) at Melsor's. The apartment is filled with people—maybe fifty, most of whom now look vaguely familiar to Bill.

Six bottles of super-chilled Grey Ruse stand in formation in the center of the table. Plates of herring, sardines, heavy spreads from a Russian store as well as odd, salty items from Costco are positioned around them.

Bill spots the only person who doesn't speak Russian—Johnny Schwartz. He stands alone beneath an especially large oil painting of waves breaking on a rocky and therefore un-Floridian shoreline. He has the look of a man sizing up the scene.

Though he is presumably looking for just the right younger woman, he greets Bill with a warm "How do you do, young man" and a handshake.

He places his hand at the corner of his mouth and motions to Bill to bend toward him.

"Your father came back to see me the other day," he whispers. "He told me not to mention to anyone that you are related. What's that about?"

"He didn't explain?"

"No."

"He wants everyone to keep thinking that I'm an FBI agent or some such, staying at his place, at his beck and call."

"Are you?"

"I could be."

"I really love your father, not in a *faygeleh* sort of way, but as much as one man can love another."

"Careful there."

Bill catches shreds of a conversation between the three *chastushki* singers, septa- or early octogenarians, obviously Jewish women in Russian peasant garb.

He lobs a question at Johnny—"I understand you fought in Germany . . ."—while continuing to listen to the women.

They are discussing the report that President-Elect Trump had a team of hookers perform "golden showers" in his hotel suite in Moscow.

"We trained for jungle fighting," Johnny begins. "At first, they were going to ship us to the Philippines, but I guess they needed us in Europe more . . ."

Bill engages in one conversation while simultaneously listening to the other.

"*A chto oni vidayat etikh zolotykh dushakh? V chem tut prelest'?*" [What do they see in those golden showers? Where is the delight in it?]

"I was young—seventeen—I lied about my age, but others weren't much older. I was the only Jew in my unit."

"Oy, Olya, dazhe ne sprashivay; ne ponimayu—muzhiki. Chert ikh znayet." [Oy, Olga, don't even ask. Who knows what they like—men.]

"Vot by my mogli dlya nashikh samodeyatel'nost pokazat'. Tol'ko vot pomerli." [We could have shown our husbands some action. Except they died.]

"Ne govori." [Don't even say it.]

Johnny opens a can of Budweiser. "What are they talking about? Do you understand Russian?"

"Golden showers," Bill whispers.

"I can't hear so well anymore. You have to speak louder . . . The Battle of the Bulge . . . We were fresh troops, young, the grass was green, got there at the very end, mopping it up after all the hard work was done. After that, they sent us toward Munich. They didn't tell us jack shit about Dachau till we found it."

"Ty znayesh, ya pryamo tri mesyatsa prazdnuyu." [I've been celebrating for three months straight.]

"Ya tozhe. Pomog nam Putin. A ya o nem tak plokho dumala." [Me, too. Putin helped us—and I once thought so badly of him.]

Meanwhile, Johnny's story proceeds to the concentration camps. "I saw a shot-down Messer, and I salvaged the camera from its wing. It survived the crash. All I needed to do was fill it with fresh film."

"Kak mne eta Obamacare ostopizdela." [I am so sick of their Obamacare.]

"Nelzya ikh vsekh k vracham vodit', Negrov, nelegalov." [They needed to take them to doctors—the Negroes, the illegals.]

"A nam v ocheredi zhdat'." [And we have to wait in line.]

"There was a guy from Iowa in my unit. He hated Jews, but by the end of it, after he saw what he saw, it got under his skin. There was one time we lined up all the SS at a camp. They surrendered, but we shot them one by one anyway. Are you listening?"

"I am," Bill responds truthfully, more or less.

Listening to two narratives in two languages is not for the meek.

"Vy znayete, ya ran'she ne verila v evolutsiyu. Dumala chto my proiskhodim ot inoplatetyan." [You know, I used to not believe in evolution. I thought we were brought here from visitors from other planets.]

"A teper' poverila?" [Have you started to believe?]

"Da, u nas u vracha recipshonistka sidit. Negritynka. Nu pryamo obez'yana." [At my doctor's office, there is a receptionist. A Negress. I look at her and think: an ape.]

"It was my friend from Iowa who did the shooting. It changed him, the awful things he saw. Then a lieutenant showed up, made us stop. Took my camera, never saw it again."

"What do you think of the election?"

"Not much."

"Does it remind you of anything? You've actually been there; others are imagining, fantasizing."

"What? The war? Nazis? No . . . I don't know much. I was dodging bullets. They shot at us, we shot at them. I got back and voted a couple of times."

"Who was the last guy you voted for?"

"Last guy . . . I voted for Ike. You know what, there are women here. I think I am going to find me a widow—you should, too."

The three singers are basking in post-performance bliss. So much so that they haven't bothered to change out of their wet costumes.

The ensemble was started by a woman named Faina Fainberg, an ethnomusicologist, who once collected folk songs in Russian villages. Faina was a perpetual adjunct professor in the U.S., living on a modified starvation diet—until she was diagnosed with advanced breast cancer.

She was advised to sue the guy who did her last mammogram a few years earlier, and she won big. Now she lives in a condo in Sunny Isles.

"You can teach anyone to sing Russian folk songs, engineers, even FBI agents," she says to Bill flirtatiously.

"I don't know about engineers," Bill retorts.

"Actually, my two ensemble members. Bella was a civil engineer, Natashka was chemical."

The appalling conversation he heard between Bella and Natashka—the two widowed Jewish engineers in Russian folk garb—was not okay, but it was an overheard conversation. He was not a party to it. Nothing he could say, nothing he could do.

There was something deeply attractive about Faina, and that something was her art. What he saw in that performance wasn't a clowning Jewish intellectual or a professional entertainer pretending to be a Russian peasant.

This wasn't Soviet-era "folk" adapted for stage. Condo board content, the setting (the Gulf Stream Room), and Bill's idiotic English translations notwithstanding, this performance had the sound of genuine folk music.

He approached Melsor from the side and whispered in Russian: *"Ty byl prav. Gde ty ikh nashel?"* [You were right. Where did you find them?]

"Na Craigsliste—120 baksov." [One hundred twenty bucks on Craigslist.]

With this, Melsor drains his glass of Grey Ruse and bows.

———

On January 17, at 6:49 A.M., Bill gets up in time to watch the sun rise over the ocean. A thin rose-colored stripe appears beneath blue clouds, growing, reddening, its boundaries cutting through the grayness of the water. He notes that for the first time since his arrival he isn't hungover.

What happened last night? It seems he imbibed sparingly, slowly sipping Kozachok posing as Grey Goose, then again sparingly, under its own label. He recalls being amused by seeing Johnny Schwartz slip away with Faina, the ethnomusicologist.

After the party, he surfed the Web, catching up on the latest golden shower cheap shots and Trump's absurd pissing match with the civil rights icon John Lewis, who'd had the gall to question his legitimacy. (Bill has met Lewis at many Washington events over the years and regards him as a prince of a guy.)

He recalls dipping into Florida condominium law and speaking with Gwen. They both noted that their conversations are acquiring the feel of a budding long-distance romance. The Princess of Style has blossomed into the Queen of Remorse, and their dance has changed. The moves are slower, more intense, less comedic—a different feel altogether. Their airport curbside makeout sessions at National and Fort Lauderdale felt different, too. Is that what "right" feels like?

On the morning of January 17, before resuming his duties, Bill decides to go for a run.

No one seems to have bothered to rope off the Gulf Stream Room and the surrounding hallway. Since Lapidus never foresaw repeated flooding, he didn't spec any floor drains and about an inch of standing water remains in the Gulf Stream Room. The artichoke chandelier is on the floor, bent, destroyed by streams of water that came down through the air ducts. Three of the six PH5 lights are destroyed, too.

This had to be an awful lot of water. There was no rain. It had to have come from somewhere. Bill turns around and heads toward the elevator. He is back on the second floor, walking through the plaza toward the South Pool. The pool has ceased to be a speck of intense blue in the middle of a fascistically grand plaza, that bit of other—that unmistakable touch of Benito Mussolini in the realm of Morris Lapidus.

The pool is still there, but the water is gone—every drop.

At the curb, Bill sees a gondola-shaped sofa. A massive breakfront rests on its side, one of its glass doors broken. The sofa-sized seascapes are still in their heavy gold frames, prostrate on the pavement. Massive black trash bags are piled up on top of each other a lifetime of treasures steaming inside them, family photos, china, crystal, documents—everything.

It's not the sacking of the Winter Palace. It's the sacking of Alex Bogomolov's apartment.

Alex sits on the sofa, looking as comfortable as he did on the night when he and Bill pounded Russian Standard and expressed deep thoughts. In fact, a bottle now rests on the pavement next to him.

"Please join me in the final toast," he says, pouring vodka into a stemless crystal champagne flute and handing it to Bill.

Bill takes it from his hands.

"*Chtob oni sdokhli,*" says Bill, raising the flute skyward like a sacred chalice. His Russian is clear, as Moscow as the church bells of the Kremlin.

May they all drop dead.

We know who they are—nothing is hidden. Everyone knows who they are. Even they know who they are. Especially they.

Has a more perfect toast ever been made?

The truth feels satisfying. This never fails.

"When did they throw out your stuff?" asks Bill.

"Last night, when I was at Melsor's party, they came and threw my things in street."

"I am sorry. Where did you spend the night?"

"Here, on mattress."

"Where do you go next?"

"*Ne znayu, no mne pora.*" [I don't know, but the time has come.]

"*Uvy,*" says Bill, switching to Russian. [Alas.]

"*A ty smozesh eto opisat'?*" [Will you be able to describe this?]

It's from Akhmatova, loosely; the prologue to the *Requiem*: she stands outside the Kresty prison in Leningrad, trying to get a food parcel to her son Lev, who is inside. Injustice has no motherland. It has no time limit. It is a constant, a polarity. Theft is a polarity, too, as is betrayal.

"*Dumayu, chto vste-taki smogy.*" [I think I can.]

"*A otomstit' smozhesh?*" [Will you be able to avenge, too?]

"*Postarayus'.*" [I will try.]

"Thank you," says Alex, getting up slowly. "I don't know who you are, but I believe you."

He nods to Bill, and begins a long descent down the ramp of Château Sedan Neuve.

PART III

||||||||||||||||||||||||||||||||||||||||||||||||||||||||||||||||||||||||||||||||||||||||||||||

I play to people's fantasies. People may not always think big themselves, but they can still get very excited by those who do. People want to believe that something is the biggest and the greatest and the most spectacular. I call it truthful hyperbole. It's an innocent form of exaggeration— and it's a very effective form of promotion.

—DONALD TRUMP
The Art of the Deal

||||||||||||||||||||||||||||||||||||||||||||||||||||||||||||||||||||||||||||||||||||||||||||||

20

THE REICHSTAG

As we reconstruct Bill's activities, the remainder of January 17—the entire blessed day—comes up utterly blank. Yes, there is a curbside morning shot of vodka from a crystal flute, a farewell to Alex, an acknowledgment of his Russianness. There is an attempted run on the Broadwalk, but after the run—nothing. Not a big, dark, secret nothing—those are honorable—but an even more malignant nothing: small, empty, the sort that masks the utter absence of pursuits of any sort. Not reading, not writing, not drinking even, the sort of nothing that drains the soul and by comparison makes a bender acquire redeeming qualities. An entry in Bill's reporter's notebook can likely be traced to that day: "Jesus, have I retired? Am I a Floridian now?"

On January 18, a note, written on a hardened, yellowed, fat-stained strip of paper, is taped to the elevator wall:

(so ignorant)

Don't throw Anything Over Balcony.
Security Informed
(orange peels etc.)

Unspecified objects are being tossed. These may be food-related: a smattering of peels, rinds, seeds, shells. Containers that had formerly encapsulated edible items, and, of course, bottles, may be thrown over balconies as well. Possibly also items of clothing, pieces of furniture, television sets, other electronic devices. Some of these objects could have been ignited prior to being thrown. The author is silent on this point.

"(so ignorant)" bespeaks contempt, but may also suggest that the thrower was careless in selecting items for throwing and has therefore unwittingly provided clues about his or her identity. Was an addressed envelope or a credit card statement among items tossed? If so, this was a cry for help, and help is on the way: the authorities have been informed.

"(orange peels etc.)" may tell us about the author's interpretation of the psychodynamics of this form of aberrant behavior: the perpetrator begins by throwing citrus peel over railings. This may be done innocently, out of laziness or for thrills, but this act sets the thrower on the path of an insatiable pursuit of the pleasure of watching shit drop. Orange peel is then a gateway projectile.

Tomorrow, on January 19, 2017, the thrower and the critic will cast their votes in the election to the BOD of Château Sedan Neuve Condominium Association, CSNCA. And on January 20, a gentleman whom many of the Château residents call Donal'd Tramp, the presidential candidate who received enthusiastic support here, will be sworn in as the leader of the free world.

This note differs from the one that Bill saw on this elevator wall before. The first one bespoke defeatism, futility. This one has the law-and-order swagger of America First. It trumpets our triumph—greatness regained.

A day and a half after the flood, the marble in the Château's lobby is still submerged under an inch of water. The wall-to-wall carpet in the Gulf Stream Room has turned into a purple paisley swamp. The few cardboard tiles that remain encased in the suspended ceiling are sagging under the weight of the waters that had rushed through the air-conditioning vents the day before.

Water from the pool doesn't ordinarily travel through air vents, but the Château is a place of many pipes; anything can happen. The timing, of course, is odd, and Bill wonders, "Could it be sabotage?"

As Bill stands observing this devastation, a single sagging tile drops heavily to the floor, unwieldy like a plastic tub of water, sloshing in its clumsy descent, joining its fallen brothers on the drenched floor eighteen feet below. There is no glory in this sound. It is the sound of prostration. Inner corruption has completed its journey.

The light fixtures are destroyed, all but two of them are dead on the floor. Most of the tiles have landed on the floor as well, but some are draped like wet pillowcases over chairs.

Bill picks up a soggy tile and hangs it over the lectern. Call it an installation, call it a composition: it tells the story. The lectern is a symbol of pompous, empty promises. A wet, dislodged ceiling tile is a symbol of falling Zbig-like from great heights. The Confederacy fell thus. The American democracy is making a heavy, creaking, waterlogged sound as we speak.

Bill snaps a picture, then runs a quick search for "hollywood fl television news," and www.local10.com pops up.

It's an ABC affiliate, and as the name suggests, its Web site oozes with local Florida news: grainy black-and-white surveillance videos of home break-ins, images of snakes in toilets, alligators in the sewers, blood-soaked pit bulls who have been very, very bad, and interviews with folks who thought they really knew those three freshly arrested teenagers who took a fun new designer drug called Bath Salts, gouged out the eyes of an elderly neighbor named Fisch, and ate his tongue raw over sushi rice. On a related note, you can look up restaurant inspections—by county!

Bill sends his staged photo of the lectern and the tile to the news tip desk. His note: "hey, just thought you might want to know: there was a flood at the Château. pool drained into this meeting room—through the ducts!—during [here the phone switches to all caps] WILD CONDO BOARD MEETING"

Bill lets the caps stay. He happens to have a sketchy address with a name he uses when contacting sources whose browsers might get searched as part of a leak investigation. Everybody needs an alias sometimes. His is "alex," followed by a long string of numbers and letters, @mail.ru.

He doesn't want his name associated with this piece of shit. He isn't even sure why he is doing this. His initial plan was to go jogging, as he did the day before, and he believes he still will.

After brief reflection, he adds: "I hear the VP of the board is a disgusting crook—will make good TV, I promise."

Which phone contact should he give them?

"You should contact Melzor Kazzenelenboggen (I can never get the spelling right; name too long). He is trying to unseat corrupt board and has all the dirt."

Bill taps in Melsor's cell phone number, hits "Send," and,

without giving the matter further thought, walks out into the dark, chilly morning.

Bill passes the security gate at 6:17 A.M.

He is not the first inhabitant of the Château to step out into darkness.

Three others—sad-faced men circa seventy-five, plus/minus ten—stand outside the building, waiting patiently as their little white dogs contemplate emptying their tiny bladders and bowels.

There is a joke about such men:

Why do Jewish men die before their wives?

Because they want to.

It's possible that these men are goyim, but the joke still stands. Goyim are people. This is about dogs. These dogs aren't dogs. All three—no, wait, there are four . . . All four are well under the weight limit of fifteen pounds specified in the condo "dos and don'ts" Bill noticed on the Web site. He happened to click on "pets"; he has no idea why.

These dogs don't apprehend tiny bad guys, they don't sniff out little explosives or baby cadavers, but they do have a mission: they substitute for the grandchildren who don't come to visit.

They aren't especially good at breathing, which is why they sometimes ride in baby strollers. They spend their days listening to complaints, about "mommy," about "daddy," about the sadly deteriorating physical and (allegedly) mental health of both, about doctors who overcharge while failing to acknowledge the obvious signs of mini-strokes and myelodysplastic syndrome, about Obamacare, about unappreciative, rude family members, and, of course, about crooked condo boards. *Svolochi* . . .

The dogs listen and they wheeze. If they could kill themselves, they would. When you are smaller than a cat and lack opposable thumbs, it's hard to pull the trigger.

Why do these dogs get Prozac?

Because they need it.

Bill runs past the silent, scooper-wielding sentries at the Château's gates and heads north on Ocean Drive.

It seems all the buildings around him are shedding their balconies. Steel rebar protrudes from their sides, awaiting encasement in concrete.

Imagine replacing all the balconies on one of these forty-year-old high-rises. You don't do it through competitive bids. You do it pursuant to local customs. Deals are concluded on chartered boats 12.1 miles offshore, outside U.S. territorial waters.

Bill has done his homework. He has enhanced his considerable prior knowledge with assistance from Messrs. Google and Kozachok. He has read up on local business practices and, what do you know, Melsor's stories check out. Out there, in open sea, with only Flipper as their witness, contractors harmonize to make a $2 million job into a $6 million job with another $3.7 million hiding in change orders. You can make a lot on the main job, but don't neglect the change orders. You don't bid out those; they are a layer of cream on the pasteurized dullness of milk.

New balconies that have replaced the old shine with chrome and glass—airborne aquaria. The logistics and, for that matter, economics—and let's not forget political economy—of balcony replacement are transparency itself.

You knock down the old balcony, you jackhammer the floor inside the apartment to bury new rebar, you leave it up to the folks inside to refloor—if that's a word. The windows get pitched. Time to refenestrate. The storm screens get shit-canned, too. Half of them don't work anyway. With this simple maneuver, you have just spent $80,000 on the balcony and forced the poor bastards in every apartment to spend at least another $40,000 on floors and windows.

With the subprime credit line the condo board took out (without anyone's approval) from a friend at a local bank, the out-of-pocket for each apartment is $150,000, depending on how long the board decides to keep the credit line gushing—and how much it wants to spew out.

With all the multipliers accounted for, with all the line items considered, Bill has just run past a couple billion dollars' worth of economic activity spread over less than a linear mile of Ocean Drive.

Let's say you devoted your life to screwing other people. You break no more laws than you have to. You avoid being disgorged. You build up a goodly stash. You move to Florida. You get fucked by your condo's BOD. Your stash gets drawn down. You try a new fraud, but it fails. The world is changing; you are losing your touch. You move on to a lesser place, or you start whacking people across their backs with your crooked cane until *Dzhuyka* carts you away. You might die in the middle of it. You might want to.

You will make room for fresh, idealistic sixty-seven-year-olds to take their turn at the good life by the sea.

Sunrise this morning makes the ocean purple. It's orderly, well-behaved, a good boy, waiting in its proper place, separated from the Broadwalk by one hundred feet of sand.

A tractor drags a sand plow to groom the beach much like one brushes the little white dogs Bill just saw ambulating, wheezing.

The Broadwalk lies a foot above sea level, maybe two. One big wave and this Hollywood Health Spa, which happens to be a Russian bathhouse; this Hollywood Grill, an Armenian restaurant that actually looks intriguing; and this Italian joint called Sapore di Mare, will wash away into said *mare*.

Bill tries not to blame the glum-faced people around him for having triggered a host of political disasters, the most recent of which is the rise of King Donal'd I, who tomorrow will be crowned. Forget xenophobia, forget the wall, forget making fun of the handicapped, forget the FSB prostitutes, forget the golden showers, whether or not they flowed! Here is the biggest incongruence: Floridians voting for a climate change denier are akin to concentration camp inmates embracing the ideal of racial hygiene. At least that's what Bill thinks, and his beliefs and his speech are protected by the First Amendment.

Massive towers are rising along the oceanfront, some bearing the Trump name. Twenty-story buildings like the Château were once thought to be tall; now, forty floors is about right. These towers contain apartments costing tens of millions, money that seems disposable to so many people. Do they recognize that they are building in the path of something far more ominous than the biblical flood?

That flood came and went. This one will come and stay.

There was a story Bill read in *The New Yorker* a bit more than a year earlier, in December 2015. The point: Florida is Ground Zero of global flooding. It sits as low as Kansas—about six feet above sea level. A drained swamp, it is cursed with a high water table. Its buildings, big and small, sit atop water-soaked limestone, and it takes pumps to keep this territory from drowning.

Bill read this piece in Washington. He read it the way most of his elitist friends read it, all of whom reached the same conclusion: let the fucker sink. With their chads hanging, they gave us George W. Bush, who gave us the invasion of Iraq in search of imaginary weapons of mass destruction. That was before *this thing*, this Donal'd F. Tramp. Let the waters come down, God, flood the place at your earliest. Maybe swimming with the fishes will make these *kakers* realize what they have done. Make sure you extract proper repentances before they drown. *Oh Lord!*

But now Bill is here, in Hollywood, running on this preposterously named Broadwalk. Should he hate the people who are starting to show up in this under-caffeinated darkness? Can he hate the red-haired grandmother who shouts in Russian into her cell phone? That word again: *"Svolochi!"* It's omnipresent. Might as well make it English.

Can Bill hate this life-battered, middle-aged couple emerging from the place Melsor calls Margarita Will? They were born Caucasian, presumably, but their skin has acquired the texture of distressed cordovan leather. They stand silently, staring at the ocean, dragging on their Camels, getting their early-morning pick-me-up, saying nothing. They are a bit older than Bill, or at least they seem to be. Theirs was a one-night stand or a thirty-five-year marriage; either way, nothing to talk about. If they couldn't drink, they would all go insane.

And here comes an overweight gentleman on a rusted, squeaking, folding bike with little wheels!

In the past, people came to Florida to die. They still do, but now they insist on stuffing the planet into the coffin with them. If death is boring, the end of the world is the most boring thing imaginable.

Bill is unable to blame these people for getting distracted by something else, anything else, even this Donal'd Tramp.

Every night in Moscow, Bill's parents took walks. This was their escape from the communal flat on Chkalov Street, at its intersection with Karl Marx Street, on the Garden Ring. The place is called Zemlyanoy Val, the Earth Berm.

They walked past the Pokrov Gates—Pokrovka, named after the shroud, the one thrown over still-dead Christ. These nightly journeys through the heart of Moscow were his beginning, his Jerusalem. Sometimes they walked farther, past Arkhipov Street, where the Great Moscow Synagogue stands. It wasn't their destination, at least not in the beginning.

Bill listened the way only children can: intensely, like a finely calibrated recording device, immortalizing the turns of phrase, the details. He was too young to understand every aspect of everything he heard, but he learned to recognize the importance of it all.

His parents spoke about the government's attacks on the intelligentsia, about disasters at work. When you teach Russian literature at the college level, as Melsor did, it's hard to keep from being reported to the ideological hacks. How do you cover the Decembrists' revolt without bringing back the echoes of contemporary dissidents? Can you steer away from the political minefields of today when you teach Akhmatova? That's even if you don't mention her *Requiem*, which you can't.

His parents spoke about the political trials—Yuli Daniel and Andrei Sinyavski, Aleksandr Ginzburg and Yuri Galanskov, the Leningrad poet-parasite Iosif Brodsky, the Pushkin Square Demonstration, the incarceration of Alik Esenin-Volpin in an insane asylum. They spoke about the Six-Day War, the invasion of Czechoslovakia, the Red Square demonstration, the tax on education levied on Jews who seek to emigrate, the Leningrad airplane hijacking. He grew up amid the evening crackle of the BBC Russian Service, the Voice of America, Deutsche Welle, Radio Liberty, the Voice of Israel. There was a world out there, pulsating with its separate life, watching his country with concern. Increasingly, his parents spoke about emigration, especially in the early '70s, when the synagogue on Arkhipov Street came to life with protests.

The U.S. embassy was nearby; he often went there by himself, to linger near parked cars. One Chevrolet—it was a Bel Air—became a vector in his escape fantasy. It was long, wide, golden. He contemplated its dashboard, imagining being inside.

He didn't root for the USSR, didn't refer to its sports teams as "we." Instead, he plotted desertion, mutiny, treason, defection, emigration. War fantasies set in well before he was ten: he is in the army, the USSR is at war in Europe, and Americans are involved. He crosses the battlefield—he surrenders, switches sides. They take him: he is already one of them.

He understood the meaning of the expression *figa v karmane*. *Figa* is the Russian version of a "fuck you" sign. You keep it in your pocket. With a *figa*, you are ready to listen to nonsense of any sort. It can't touch you.

It's all here, hardwired into Bill's skull as he runs on this Broadwalk, pondering the shroud of darkness that is about to descend on his new land, the land he loves—his first experiment with that face of love. He served this land valiantly by—pardon newsroomspeak, which is not a cliché—empowering its afflicted and afflicting its powerful.

Of course, he became a reporter because of those conversations on those nightly walks to Pokrovka. He is who he is because of those Moscow conversations that imprinted on his soul.

Melsor has changed in America, hardened, mastered the craft of deception. Perhaps America was gentler on Bill. He didn't have to change his orientation from honesty to fraud. He became a reporter, he kept the struggle alive. And now he is a reporter no more. It's possible that he will not be able to root for America in the next Olympics. It's almost a certainty that a *figa* will once again take up residence in his pocket.

In Moscow, he had a place to run, but not here. This is the end of the line. He is no longer passive. Observers observe. He will resist. Act. All those jokes about emigrating to Canada—he finds them offensive, cowardly. This 240-year-old democracy is worth fighting for. He will act alone if he has to. He will become a soldier-poet, a soldier-storyteller, an army of one. He will fight by all means at his disposal. He will correct every wrong in his path, in this Florida, at this Château, even in Washington, upon return.

At 7:48 A.M., when Bill returns to the Château, he sees a television truck with the Local News 10 logo on its side. The truck's antenna is up.

Achtung: state-of-the-art South Florida journalism is being practiced. Someone is being unmasked, confronted, chased. Of course, it might also be an animal story: alligator eats *svoloch'*, or, more likely, *svoloch'* eats alligator.

After a contemplative seven-mile run, Bill has momentarily forgotten that he had anonymously, blindly reached out to his colleagues at this Local News 10, giving his father's name as a contact for a flood story.

Perhaps he should have consulted with the old man.

"Oh hell," Bill concludes with abandon you would expect from a cultural Slav. "What's done is done."

Melsor is in the midst of an animated conversation with a reporter, a big guy of roughly Bill's age, whose name is also Bill—Bill Boyle. Bill had glanced through his mini-profile earlier that morning.

Sometimes Bill thinks that he should have stayed on the police beat all his life. The cop beat always goes to the young, but seasoned reporters like Bill Boyle, who make it a career-long pursuit, do it with the sort of grace that comes from deep knowledge. Bill—Bill Katzenelenbogen, that is—should have switched to television, too. There, the chase is raw—gushing blood, foamy brains on the gleaming white terrazzo. Freed from the bog of words, it's all visceral, all important. Sometimes you need a specialist—a board-certified sleazeologist—especially in South Florida.

For the first time, Bill K recognizes that his father gives good TV. Being a dissident poet was good media training, it seems.

"Off record . . . ," Melsor begins, "I do not exclude such possibility in which crimes of this condominium board are getting investigated by government at *highest* level."

What a fucking lie! Does he actually believe it?

Four decades earlier, an American with a camera—a kid who lucked into an important documentary about the Soviet Jewish movement—had come to their apartment in Moscow, and Bill watched his father recite poetry in Russian. That performance was staged—it's now on YouTube, probably.

This performance, today, is impromptu, in the moment, full of give and take.

Nella stands six feet to the side, near the glass doors to the apartment building. Bill nods silently to his father and steps behind her.

"We are *on* record, Mr. Katzenelenbogen," Bill B notes without much enthusiasm. "Am I pronouncing your name correctly?'"

It's basic housekeeping. You want to make sure that you are talking to the right weirdly named dude and that he knows that all the shit he spews will be hung on him.

"You may call me Melsor. You have my permission to broadcast everything I say then. Just cut film where I say 'off record.'"

It's hard to miss this trick. When he says "off record," he is making sure that the point will, in fact, get on the record. "Don't go there" means "Go there."

It's a little clumsy, unnecessarily desperate, but what the fuck, it works. Bill K would have simply noted the point off the record, off camera, and told his colleague how to get the rest of the story elsewhere.

Being manipulative is too much work. It's easier to be up front. But Bill Katzenelenbogen is Bill Katzenelenbogen and Melsor Katzenelenbogen is Melsor Katzenelenbogen.

"Could you repeat what you've just said, this time on record?"

"I do not exclude possibility, Bill, that crimes of this dishonest condo board are investigated by *highest* government authorities."

"Do you *know* this?"

"Ask yourself question: Would serious person like I say it if he does not know? I fought against KGB. I won. I was persecuted by Justice Department in America. I won. Now I tell you: yes, there is investigation."

This is pretty good: he is planting innuendo, and watching it take root. Would the old man have done even better on camera had Bill—Bill K—remembered to give him a heads up?

THE CHÂTEAU

Alas, for television, especially South Florida television—this is bullshit. No pictures, no story. Real stories are being missed. Cops are shooting black guys, fires rage, floods flood, pit bulls, boa constrictors, and alligators are on attack. The camera is about to stop rolling, the antenna outside will come down, and this van will drive away.

"Two night ago, at forum for candidates for condo board, these tugs endangered lives of unit owners. They *deliberately* caused swimming pool to break and pour into Gulf Stream Room through air ducts, costing unit owners hundreds of thousands dollars in damage and almost killing hundred old people! I can take you there in one minute. People of Florida must see this dangerous situation!"

"Are you saying they *deliberately* flooded the meeting room in the middle of the candidates' forum—to scare you?"

"No. I don't say this. I don't know exactly *why* they did it, because I don't speak with them. I am ballotating against them in election today. I don't expect to win. This system here is rigged, too. The night of forum—*during forum*—water from swimming pool started to pour into Gulf Stream Room exactly as I was speaking! I am saying—for quotation!—'Follow money, Bill.' It's for their advantage to have swimming pool break, because they now have excuse to get bigger kickback from contractor."

"I see," Bill B cuts in. "Do you have any information to indicate that they are getting kickbacks on construction contracts? On insurance money?"

"Of course, insurance money counts toward kickback!"

"But deliberate sabotage—come on . . ."

"You should see Gulf Stream Room. You will see devastation from flood!"

309

"We will do that in a minute. Just making sure, you are saying that this was a *deliberately set* flood that endangered the lives of senior citizens living in this building? And they did it in order to scare off dissent?"

"I'm not able to exclude this possibility."

"And you are saying that a high-level federal investigation of activities of this board is under way?"

"I am not at liberty to answer, Bill. You should ask them. I am told to say that I have no comment. FBI will say they can neither confirm nor deny existence of federal investigation. It's standard practice for them, except if your name is Hillary Clinton. Here, I have telephone, you have telephone. You can call FBI, or I will call chief tug here at Château: Obersturmführer Greenstein! I will call him in front of you."

This is getting better, but it's still just a garden variety condo board brawl—not a story.

"Are you calling the president of the board?"

"No! I am calling Greenstein, *vice* president of board. He is too smart to be president of board. President of BOD is fall guy. President goes to prison, president gets disgorged. *Vice* president is man with real power!"

Melsor sets the phone on speaker. Amazingly, Greenstein picks up. Melsor must have had his identity masked.

"Hello . . ."

"Villain! I have Channel 10 here!"

"Melsor? How did they get past security?"

"*I* got them through. They are *my* guests! I can still have visitors in your concentration camp!"

"No comment."

"Your chief tug—Russian—dived under security desk when he saw camera was filming. He is undocumented alien; yes? You should be careful with Donal'd Tramp becoming president in one day!"

"I am not going to dignify these unsubstantiated aspersions with a response."

"Sir, this is Bill Boyle, I am a reporter with Channel 10 News. Would you come out and talk to us?"

"Bill, I've seen your stories."

"Would you be willing to come down and talk with us, sir?"

"No."

"No?"

"If you are speaking with Katzenelenbogen, you are engaging in fake news."

"Then you should come down to the garage and set me straight."

"I said no."

"Are you declining to comment, sir?"

"I am going to comment: according to articles of the condominium of CSNCA, to be considered legitimate, *any and all* communications must originate from the board of directors. I would not put it beyond this splinter group of malcontents to sabotage this building."

"Are you making an accusation, sir?"

"Not yet."

"Is this all you are going to say?"

"If you are speaking with that indicted criminal, you are fake news."

"Is this your comment?"

"You are fake news. You don't deserve a comment."

With this, Greenstein hangs up.

The quality of sound of that conversation is as bad as it gets, traveling through the air from the wheezy cell phone to the microphone of a television camera. You could probably still rescue it if you absolutely had to—but why would you?

This is a brawl like any other in South Florida. Walk into the lobby of any of these balcony-shedding high-rises, and you will see exactly the same thing. Laws are easier to enforce when you have deviations from the rules. Here in Florida there are no rules. Here in Florida there are only deviations.

"Now you see how criminals operate!" shouts Melsor.

Bill K, had he been a television reporter, would have given the photographer the kill signal long ago.

It's possible that there is something captivating—"mesmerizing" might be the word—about Melsor's ravings. Having grown up with them, Bill K is in no position to know.

"It's very, very simple. This is very typical tactic for which fascists get credit. It's called Reichstag fire. Nazis themselves burn down German Reichstag and blame Communists so they get applauded, so to say, when they go kill Communists. Anyone can do it. This is how Putin came to power, they say. I do not exclude possibility that he had his secret police blow up two houses in Moscow so he could blame Chechens and start war. It's good, tested *tryuk*."

"*Tryuk?* What's that?"

"Lie."

"Oh, a trick . . ."

"It's standard tactic. They do it and blame us, malcontents. Reichstag fire is very, very effective tactic. I do not exclude possibility that this is something Donal'd Tramp will do in four years, if he is smart. And he is very, very smart. I will recognize it, of course, but will not tell you."

"Interesting. You two will have a secret."

This is a cluster of wild, unsubstantiated aspersions, sure, but Bill B is having fun watching his feisty geezer trample European history in a heavy-hoofed gallop. But this is Local News 10! Flashing lights and snarling animals are their stock in trade, and this shit—whatever it is—will not cut it. Time to go . . .

A mighty sound, heavier than a head-on car crash, but with a flash, makes all heads and the camera turn north, toward Fort Lauderdale, toward the spot where the swimming pool's hulking sarcophagus-like bottom rests atop the parking deck.

A cloud of smoke and dust dissipates quickly, drowning in a stream that rushes out of a long crack, a broken seam, bursting like an improbable constellation of fire hydrants uncapped, spewing out a white, chlorine-scented torrent. An eight-foot chunk of concrete drops squarely on top of a white Lexus, pinning it to the parking deck. Water comes down with flash-flood force, aiming it point blank at another white Lexus, an SUV, which begins to budge, smashing into a white Lexus sedan, then making a beast o' three backs with a silver Mercedes convertible, and on, and on, and on, a man-made pileup triggered by a man-made flood. Bill K, Bill B, Melsor, Nella, and the camera-wielding photographer press against the side of the building, watching the mad demolition derby, as cracks in the pool widen, and the waters gush until there is no more—until sunlight comes through the missing section of the pool's bottom.

Bill B breaks the silence.

"Holy fuck! Did you get that?"

The photographer, a young Hispanic guy, nods. He has seen many unbelievable things here in South Florida. And now this.

21

THE USUAL

Bill is pleased to see that the warning to the thrower of projectiles is still taped to the elevator wall. Someone at the Château cares passionately about justice.

He attempts to make sense of the morning's events:

It's possible, of course, that the South Pool had spontaneously drained into the Gulf Stream Room. But the timing—during the forum—is highly suspicious.

The Greenstein faction could have arranged the draining of the South Pool to point the good burghers toward thinking that this was the work of the Katzenelenbogen faction.

The Katzenelenbogenites could have started it, too. Their goal would be to make it look like the Greensteinians were trying to make it look like the Katzenelenbogenites were making it look like the Greensteinians did it.

Two general principles are observed in this war of illusions:

- **LEVEL ONE:** The Katzenelenbogenites want the Greensteinians blamed, and the Greensteinians want the Katzenelenbogenites blamed for the *actual acts* of destruction of the
  Château's pools.
- **LEVEL TWO:** The Katzenelenbogenites want the Greensteinians blamed for *creating the illusion* that the Katzenelenbogenites had committed the acts of destruction and, by the
  same token, Greensteinians want the Katzenelenbogenites
  blamed for *creating the illusion* that the Katzenelenbogenites had committed the acts of destruction.

This is classic. Not much time is needed to unpack it.

When you consider the collapse of the North Pool, events
gain nuance quickly. Statistically, it's remotely possible that the
North Pool would burst spontaneously the day after the draining of the South Pool into the Gulf Stream Room.

However, it's fallacious to assume that the collapse of the
North Pool was facilitated by the same faction that triggered
the draining of the South Pool. The copycat effect cannot be
ruled out, i.e., hypothetically, the Greensteinians could have
caused the draining of the South Pool and the Katzenelenbogenites could have busted the North Pool. Or the other way
around.

Assume for the sake of argument that the collapse of the
North Pool is spontaneous: after forty years of dedicated service,
the pool's wall bursts. But what are the odds of this happening
in front of rolling cameras not quite two days after a mishap
involving the South Pool?

The sound of a blast that preceded the collapse of the North
Pool raises questions too. Yes, it could have been the sound of rebar bursting and concrete cracking. Bill hasn't seen anything of

the sort before. An explosion seems more likely, or so they, whoever they are, want you to think.

Wasn't Melsor talking about the Reichstag fire, praising it as a method of seizing power? And then—presto—the North Pool bursts! Does this make Melsor a suspect, or does it make Greenstein a suspect?

The right answer seems to be both and neither.

Bill's initial analysis assumes two possible groups of perpetrators. What if there are others? And what if some of them are acting in unison? Oy . . . He might need to do something he has never done before—put up one of those ridiculous whiteboards and cover it with notes, clippings, and photographs. There is no better way to get bogged down in bullshit.

Would anyone even investigate the swimming pool collapse he has just observed? A fire truck showed up, sure, but there was no fire and thus nothing to do. By then, the Channel 10 crew was gone. They had great stuff and needed to process it. The cops showed up as well. They spoke with Melsor for a few minutes and moved on, their demeanor saying, "Fuck it."

Technically, a crime or crimes have been committed, but if you want to find out whether explosives were used to blow up the North Pool you will need to load a wheelbarrow with little pieces of wet concrete and rebar and send them off to the FBI lab in Quantico, Virginia. You'd need to convince the FBI that you are dealing with a suspected act of domestic terror. The two police officers on the scene at the collapse of the North Pool show no signs of desire to make this case.

There was a fucking massacre at the Fort Lauderdale airport two weeks ago. Now *that's* a real case! Grainy images, corpses on the terrazzo floor.

And what do you have here?

Here you have people with strange accents saying crazy shit. Let them figure it out, settle it among themselves. It's tribal. Sometimes an investigation is just not useful. Even if they are blowing shit up.

The pools will be reconstructed, water damage corrected, mold removed—again. Bids will be rigged in open sea, and kickbacks will accrue to the board without regard for race, color, religious creed, national origin, ancestry, sex, sexual orientation, age, genetic information, military service, or disability. Fuck all that! All the more reasons to get on the board!

Bill returns to the apartment, takes a quick shower, and puts on his naturally distressed Carhartt jeans, his time-honored Top-Siders, and his fully depreciated Duke T-shirt, which doesn't look a day over thirty.

He is in no mood to play South Florida dress-up.

He is feeling the urge to get home, to Washington, to the world, to figure out his next step, to start his life anew.

The word "Resist," which has popped up on social media, resonates within his soul.

He is fucking nowhere with the Zbig project—doesn't even know whether there *is* a project. And now there is shit to be done here, at the fucking Château. He can't just leave; can he?

Not today at least.

He will crack this fucking case, thinking globally, acting locally—resisting. What was that thing Martin Luther King said: "Injustice anywhere is a threat to justice everywhere"?

It's true.

He will right these wrongs, and then and only then will he leave.

———

Bill has a couple things to check out, urgently. Alas, his first step would be to talk with Melsor.

It might say somewhere in the Diagnostic and Statistical Manual of Mental Disorders that Melsor Katzenelenbogen should be avoided for at least two hours following television exposure, and that four hours is probably safer.

"Do u have time 2 talk?" Bill texts his father at 8:59 A.M.

"*Menya v Machte opublikovali,*" Melsor responds. [I was published in *Machta.*]

Not exactly a response.

This is a fine morning for Melsor. He is already on to his second narcissistic event.

Three dots flash ominously on Bill's screen. A "request" is coming, and Bill knows it. It's more like an order, of course:

"*Novyyee chastushki. Srochno nuzhen perevod.*" [New *chastushki.* Translation urgently needed.]

"Why urgently?"

"*U menya repetitsiya. Devochli poyut.*" [I have a rehearsal. The girls are singing.]

The dots flash again. Shit! Melsor has more to say.

"*Vot link Machty. Perevedi. U tebya eto poluchayetsya.*" [Here is a link to *Machta.* Translate. You do it well.]

This is—what?—a compliment? From Melsor Yakovlevich Katzenelenbogen? The first? No . . . Is the fucker well?

Bill follows the link to *Machta,* which has indeed published *chastushki* by Melsor Katzenelenbogen, composed on the occasion of the impending inauguration of Donal'd Tramp.

Bill reads the first *chastushka.* It's not too awful, actually, in that certain post-apocalyptic way, which on the eve of the coronation strikes the younger Katzenelenbogen as appropriate:

Нам, ребята, не страшны
Мусульманскиые орды.
Трамп теперь нас в бой ведёт.
Заряжай! Стреляй! Вперёд!

Bill copies it, and—maybe it's because he doesn't give a shit—the translation emerges quickly:

Don't you worry, don't you fear!
Muslim hordes stand no chance here.
Long live Donald! Hooray Trump!
Load your AR-15!
Onward! Watch them fall! We win!

The second *chastushka* has the consistency of a parody, which it probably isn't, strictly speaking, but with humor being the bedrock of this genre, there is no way to know:

Ай да Вовка, ай да Путин,
Дал нам президентика!
Никогда бы Трамп не выиграл,
Подсобили хакеры!

Bill isn't embarrassed by this one. He actually agrees with the message, albeit from the opposite end of the political spectrum:

Way to go,
Brother Putin gave us quite a president!

No way Trump would have won,
FSB hackers got it done!

The third *chastushka* is even better than the one that preceded it:

В Вашингтонском да в болоте
Крокодилы плавают.
А народ им говорит:
Будем с Путиным дружить
И болота здесь сушить.

Bill has two simultaneous, interrelated points to make:

- It's too early for Kozachok, either in its own bottle or in
  the Grey Ruse disguise, and
- Occasional poetry always sucks, because it does.

However, these *chastushki* keep getting better, which makes
translation easy:

The Potomac swamp of late,
Big green crocodiles populate.
Our Putin and our Trump
Will soon drain that stinking swamp.

The final *chastushka* is sort of okay, too!

Как в Техасе-Аризоне
Вырастет рубеж-стена.
Хорошо нам станет жить

Рассветёт моя страна!

Bill gives it what it deserves; no more, no less:

Soon in Texas-Arizona
Border wall will rise from sand.
Life will get much better then,
As our country flourishes!

Bill shoots the translations over to his father—the whole thing takes twenty minutes tops.

He opens the window—the physical window, that is—to let a warm breeze enter the apartment. The wind is stronger than it was when he ran on the Broadwalk. Bill's gaze sweeps over the ocean.

What will the end of the world look like? We could be mowed down in a single event, or it might come in gentle waves. Like these, below. Pelicans may still be overhead, and they may or may not be on fire.

A cruise ship may be on the horizon, a small plane may be dragging a banner advertising an all-you-can-eat special at some god-awful joint.

Actually, the world could be ending right now, and Bill is growing increasingly certain that it is.

If it's comforting for you to believe that he is going mad, be my guest.

Bill would be of no use in helping with this determination.

Like the rest of us, he would see no reason to distinguish madness within his skull from madness around him.

Bill calls Gwen.

Is she still coming here, to Florida, tonight?

He gets voicemail and one of those fucking "I can't talk to you right now" bounce-backs via text.

Bill knows how his parents survived in a totalitarian state.

They had each other, they had him, they escaped into their lives. It's less clear to Bill how he will survive today, in this transformed world, with his mother gone, with his father bowing to King Donal'd.

They say Jews don't bow to anyone but the construct they call "G-d," but a vote for America First, a geriatric goose step, and a crypto-fascist salute are obviously within the range of possibility.

Whom does Bill have today, as darkness descends?

Gwen? Maybe, kind of, sort of.

He wishes she were here, in Florida, in a large bed, sleeping peacefully.

Is she his Beatrice now?

He has had relationships, but never with Beatrice.

Maybe now . . .

Stealing a girl from Dante is a risky move, granted, but maybe Beatrice will be his just when he needs her—now.

Bill arrives in Melsor's apartment at 10 A.M., as the last of the *chastushki* singers leaves and Melsor settles onto the porny white sectional to watch MSNBC.

"What? No Fox News?" Bill asks in English.

"I watch MSNBC. I want opposite point of view. I already know what I think."

"Oh . . . I need to interrupt you nonetheless."

Rachel Maddow says something truly scary about Trump: the link between his close associates and the Russian banks. She laughs nervously—who wouldn't?

"*Ona lezbiyanka. Ostromnaya baba,*" says Melsor. [She is a lesbian. A humorous broad.]

"That's what I hear . . ."

"*Yevreyka. Po dedushke.*" [Jewish, on grandfather's side.]

"I really do need your attention for a moment."

"I am listening."

"Do you remember that rant, where Greenstein's wife chased out the two guys from Craigslist—where she screams in German?"

Melsor looks quizzically at Bill.

"Do you have it recorded?"

"Yes, I record everything from transmissions."

"Can you give it to me? Now . . . Please . . ."

"*Zachem?*" [Why?]

"I thought I heard something useful. My German sucks. I want someone else to take a listen."

As Melsor gets up to get the right recording off his computer, Bill changes channels to the ABC affiliate.

"We interrupt this program to bring you a special bulletin: a deep swimming pool cracks open at a luxury ocean-side condo in Hollywood!"

The anchor, seated at the news desk, is dark-haired, young, leggy.

"Our reporter is on the scene."

This is followed by images of water bursting through a widening crack, a chunk of concrete dropping on top of a white Lexus, and rushing waters creating a pileup of Lexuses and a Mercedes.

The deep, heavy thud and Melsor's equally explosive words are picked up, too: "Reichstag fire is very, very effective tactic. I do not exclude possibility that this is something Donal'd Tramp will do in four years, if he is smart. And he is very, very smart."

"Our reporter, Bill Boyle, was on the scene. Bill, what did you see?"

"To be honest, Claudia, I was focused on an unrelated story. Suddenly, there was what sounded like an explosion."

CLAUDIA: Explosion? Is it terrorism?

BILL B: Could also be the sound of the swimming pool collapsing on its own.

CLAUDIA: We have a graphic here. This was a very deep aboveground pool that is essentially embedded in the parking structure. How were you able to film it, Bill?

BILL B: As you can see, Claudia . . . Could you run it again? As you can see, the stream is very narrow at first, but the pressure is extreme, because of the sheer depth of the pool. It was more like a powerful fire hydrant than a flash flood at first, and then—you see here—a section of the swimming pool drops out and lands on top of this car. It was very concentrated still. You can see it sweep other cars—at least a dozen of them—out of its way.

CLAUDIA: What was the story you were working on?

BILL B: Just basic condo board turmoil, the usual in South Florida. Accusations of malfeasance flying back and forth. These are basically multimillion-dollar enterprises that operate without any fiscal controls.

CLAUDIA: The usual turmoil then?

BILL B: The usual.

As a child, Bill knew that his father's outbursts started softly, with a hiss.

"*Sv-volochi . . .*"

Melsor spent time with that son of a bitch, that idiot reporter, gave him an interview, explained the Reichstag fire even. What he got for his efforts was a story that described his struggle—his struggle for justice!—as "the usual," something that you might as well accept!

Imagine that: Melsor Yakovlevich Katzenelenbogen was being trivialized!

"*Yego kupili, tvoyego Billa.*" [They bought him, your Bill.]

"He is not 'my Bill.' I don't know him. And, for what it's worth, what he did was anything but unprofessional. He had unique images of the swimming pool collapsing, causing a flash flood in the garage—destroying some really expensive cars—before your eyes. It's amazing footage. I'd do the same thing."

"This is dishonest! He could show injustice! Lawlessness!"

"That guy is not a *svoloch'*. He is a pro."

"Then you are *svoloch'*, too."

"Thanks for the insult. You might want to try to see the world as it is, just this once. You were trying to sell him on a story, and you were upstaged by a big bang. There was an explosion! Or whatever the fuck it was. That's it! Nothing else to it! Collapsing swimming pools will always trump a struggle for justice, if that is what it is."

"Don't bring Tramp into this . . ."

"I didn't. I said trump, like in cards. Did you hire some asshole to blow the thing up? Did you have it done?"

"If I said I did or no I didn't, you wouldn't believe me! Would you?"

"No. I certainly would not."

"And if I did, would you turn me in to your FBI?"

"It's not *my* FBI. I am not with the FBI, as you know."

"You are a conformist!"

"You are a narcissist!"

"You are unemployed. I called and found out."

"First time you gave a fuck about me. Thank you, Father."

"You are ungrateful."

"At least I am not a felon!"

"Neither am I."

"You are guilty as fuck, and you know it."

"Don't pretend that you understand me!"

"Theft! Fraud! Snitching on your accomplices! No remorse that I can see. And a stash of ill-gotten money very much intact. Look at all this! It's all built on fraud! I wouldn't know how to explain it in a way that you would give a fuck about. I'll fucking do it anyway . . ."

"Fuck, fuck, fuck. Do you know more words than 'fuck'?"

"I've been called many things. *Svoloch'*, for example. By you! I don't give a fuck about that. If you want to insult me, tell me I am not a gentleman. Tell me I am not behaving as a decent human being—the way you used to. In Moscow. Remember? Moscow?"

"You were child!"

"You made me into who I am, and then you stopped being who you were! How is that fair? What did this fucking country do to you?"

"Fuck, fuck, fuck . . ."

"What made you give up on decency? You threw it out like a used condom. What made you so smug? Do you even under-stand what I am saying?"

As Bill leaves, slamming the door, a familiar epithet is the last thing he hears:

"*Predatel'*." [Traitor.]

"You still don't understand, do you, asshole?" Bill mutters in the hallway. "*You* are the traitor."

———

As Bill slams the door, he believes that he will leave this place and not speak to the fucker for another decade or two.

Maybe it's better this way.

Strike the "maybe." It is better this way.

When he checks his e-mail a few moments later, he has received a recording of Wilfreda's rant.

It comes through—sans message—just as he enters the apartment.

The geezer is softening, accepting the notion that standoffs aren't always in his best interest.

This could also mean that the other side—the Greenstein assholes—is guilty of wrecking the building. Or that his side—the Katzenelenbogen assholes—is.

Somebody is feeling secure about their smoke screens, or halls of mirrors, or whatever you call rat-fucking in this new America.

Maybe at some point Bill was thinking of helping his father, repairing the things that went wrong, but no more. Now his loyalty is to the truth.

Whatever it is, Bill will find it.

He will—what is it our president-elect says?—he will drain this swamp. And if he finds real, indictable fraud, he will burn them, all of them. He taps out a quick e-mail to a friend who once covered Germany, before being shit-canned by the *Post*.

This dude was the best reporter Bill ever met. Let's call him Subodh. A Brahmin who grew up in India, he used "Subodh" as a pseudonym when calling sources at the White House a generation ago.

The name somehow got out into the newsroom, and it stuck.

Subodh is freelancing now, mostly for *Bethesda Magazine,* or maybe *Washingtonian.* Bill reads neither.

A text message from Gwen announces itself.

"Can't wait to see you."

"Mutual."

He does want to see her—that's true.

He thought about her last night, tossing on his cot, finally getting his computer and turning to videos of bird-suited jumpers launching themselves off cliffs and tall buildings.

"What's on your mind?"

"What's a man to do?"

"????"

"Fundamental question of Russian literature."

"Relevant here/now?"

"Relevant as fuck."

"Brooding?"

"Brooding."

"Gotta run. A sweet deal about to come through. Drawn to you."

"Mutual."

"Let's stay sober this time."

Bill walks up to the refrigerator to look for something edible, and by the time he is done toasting frozen Borodinski bread and smearing it with something that purports to contain cream cheese, an e-mail from Subodh comes in.

It's like a gentle breeze bringing the comforting scent of home:

Bill! Dude!

Nice to hear from you, you old sheep-plugger. Heard about your shit-canning. For insubordination! You de man. Go team! Hope vicissitude sits lightly on your shoulders.

Hearing from you brought back pleasant memories of broomsticks shoved. You still have the scale; right? Now, with this new White House, it will be possible to shove entire brooms without anyone noticing! I hate Bezos as much as the next guy, but the Post *is producing excellent fodder for SNL these days.*

Having considerable difficulty imagining you in Florida, even for a day, even for an hour.

As you know, I am blessed with free time, so I was able to give you ultra-quick turnaround. You will find the transcript and the translation in separate attachments. It's disturbing on more levels than I can count.

I realize that you are not asking for advice. Still, I suggest that you bring in the constabulary. At the very least, notify the nearest Holocaust museum. I can guarantee that when you deal with this shit, guns are involved somewhere down the line. Stay safe. You owe me a TB at Martin's. Make it two—or, hell, three.

Yours,
Comrade Subodh

P.S. Never mind advice . . . You will do what you will do.
P.S.S. Is this a book? Dude!

Bill first clicks on the German transcript and reads the thing. Yes . . . just as he thought. It's amazing how far you can get with a little Yiddish and having watched *The Marriage of Maria Braun* and *Das Boot* with subtitles multiple times while your brain was forming.

FRAUENSTIMME: Du knauseriger, perverser Scheisskerl! Kannst du nicht an irgend etwas anderes denken als an deinen kleinen Schwanz? Glaubst du wirklich, dass ich mir zum Geburtstag wünsche, von zwei fremden Männern gefickt zu werden? Mit zweiundsiebzig Jahre! Stell dir vor mit siebenunddreißig . . .

Ich hätte dir nichts erzählen sollen! Höre zu: "Wenn ich drei Mal nächtlich hätte vögeln wollen, hätte ich keinen Mann ausgesucht, der ein Stück Gummi in der Hose trägt!"

Glaubst du, ich möchte wirklich Verkehr mit einem ganzen Zug haben? Oder geht es eher darum, dass du insgeheim von all diesen Männern gefickt werden möchtest? Oder glaubst du, dass alle Deutsche so etwas wollen? Willst du mit mir abrechnen dafür, was meinen Vater getan hat?

Er rettete das ganze für uns. Er kämpfte am Fließband gegen einen Hungerlohn und verkauften keinen einzigen Zahn.

Nur zur Kenntnis: Ich will Schmuck zum Geburtstag, du mieser, perverser Hurensohn! Ich will einen Ring wie Ida Kruger und alle anderen jüdischen Frauen haben. Ein Jubiläumsring von Tiffany!

Du muss es nicht unbedingt von Tiffany kaufen, du kleiner, schwanzloser Untermensch! Du muss dir nicht vom Geld des Sponsors unbedingt trennen!

Nimm noch einen von dieser kleinen blauen Taschen, entleere das Gold, und lass Dir wieder eine Stange fertigen. Worauf wartest Du? Du bist ja siebenundsiebzig Jahre alt! Du leidest unter Herzschwächen! Ich überlebte Krebs zweimal. Nur Gott weiss, welche Krankheiten ich sonst habe.

Du, Schwein, nimm diese Tasche! Nimm sie in deiner Hand! Geh zu einem deiner Juden! Lass es schmelzen! Und kauf mir was ich tatsächlich will!

MÄNNERSTIMME: Ja, Geliebte.

Just to be sure, he clicks on the English translation.

WOMAN'S VOICE: You cheap, twisted bastard! Can you think about anything beyond your little dick? Do you really think I wanted to get fucked by two men on my birthday? I am seventy-two years old! Maybe at twenty-seven . . .

I should never have told you anything! Listen to me: "If I wanted to be fucked three times every night, I would not have chosen a husband who wears a piece of rubber hose in his pants!"

Do you think I really want to have relations with a platoon? Is all this happening because secretly *you* want to be fucked by all these men, or is this what you think all Germans want? Are you getting even with me for what my father did, you ungrateful rat?

He saved all this for us. He struggled on his assembly-line salary and never sold a single tooth.

Just so you know: I want jewelry for my birthday, you cheap, twisted son of a whore! I want a ring like Ida Kruger and all the other Jewish women have: an anniversary ring that they have at Tiffany's!

You don't even have to get it from Tiffany's, you little, no-dick subhuman. You don't even need to part with the money from the sponsor!

Just take another one of these blue velvet bags, empty out the gold, and have them make you another bar. What are you waiting for? You are seventy-seven years old! You have a heart condition! I had cancer twice. God knows what other disease I have now.

Here, swine, take *this* bag! Take it in your hand! Go to one of your Jews! Have it melted! And buy me what I actually want! For once.

MAN'S VOICE: Yes, beloved.

22

ŠVEJK

By 10:30, the video of gushing water slamming a white Lexus broadside into its sibling, then slamming both into a Mercedes convertible, is trending on Twitter.

How often do you get to see a deep pool collapse, making a Rube Goldberg spectacle out of expensive white cars? The fact that the video made it possible to suggest that terrorists were involved makes the thing sweeter still.

When Bill K calls Bill B, he has no idea that the latter records suspected crank calls, nor does he care. A transcript of their conversation follows:

BILL K: Hey, that was quite a story.

BILL B: Thanks. Who is this?

BILL K: Bill Katzenelenbogen. I used to be with the *Post*.

BILL B: The New York *Post*?

BILL K: The Washington *Post*.

BILL B: Sure. Name sounds familiar. Any relation to that lunatic I spoke with?

BILL K: Son.

BILL B: I am sorry. I bet he is pissed about the story.

BILL K: Furious. He doesn't understand that the flood is the thing.

BILL B: True. The flood is the thing.

BILL K: I was the guy who sent you that e-mail. Worked out well for you, dude.

BILL B: Now you are going to say I owe you one?

BILL K: I am!

BILL B: Shoot!

BILL K: Tell me what you know about the plastic surgeon who went splat.

BILL B: The Butt God?

BILL K: Zbig Wronski.

BILL B: What's it to you?

BILL K: He was my college roommate. Thinking about doing a book. Did you cover his death?

BILL B: I did, just one story. We had a computer simulation. Sick. The cops closed the case, called it an accident. Pervert shit, so weird you can't touch it. Never learned what the fuck it was. That's really all I have. Except . . . I think the cable TV assholes were pimping a tape—his wife's interview on some reality show.

BILL K: Can I have it?

BILL B: If we have it, it's under an embargo. Our word of honor. I can't be caught at it, but—shit—I owe you one. Checking, checking, checking—yes, it's here!

BILL K: Can you show it to me?

BILL B: Heading out on an overturned vegetable truck story. Tossed lettuce all over southbound I-95. Want some salad?

BILL K: Not that kind . . . Fatalities?

BILL B: Two or three. We actually have a video of that thing *happening*. You see the driver fly out headfirst and hit the pavement—instant death! Then you see lettuce fly. Call me on my cell in two hours.

Four calls are all it takes to locate Roza Kisel'. There are only so many places for the Jewish community of South Florida to store its demented indigent brethren.

Bill ventures a guess, then another, and thirty minutes later, he parks Melsor's Prius in the parking lot of the Beth Shalom Home for the Aged.

The place has the look of a small hospital.

His initial guess is that Mrs. Kisel' would be kept in a rubber room, where she surely belongs, but as he introduces himself as her nephew, the middle-aged woman at the desk looks at him with approval.

"It's so nice to have a young person visit," she says, and points him to the hallway. "Mrs. Kisel is in room 312. Take the elevator around the corner, hon."

The first time he saw Roza, she wore a housecoat, carried a crooked cane, and screamed about *svolochi* and fascists. She had a point, as Bill now knows.

Their second encounter, in mid-flood, also entailed physical pain. His shoulders and his back hurt still, especially in the early mornings, when he begins to contemplate getting up.

Expecting to get whacked again, Bill is surprised to see Mrs. Kisel' seated in a chair, reading a Russian translation of Jane Austen's *Emma*, a book Bill regards as ghastly. Roza is dressed in a comfortable blue pantsuit and sensible sneakers, the sort nurses wear. She looks up over her thin reading glasses, exuding a sense of comfort, like a professor holding office hours.

The picture on the wall looks vaguely familiar. It's clearly Washington; Georgetown, in fact. The C&O Canal. There used to be a restaurant there. Port O' Georgetown it was called—few people remember it, but it had a killer terrace.

Clearly not a personal item, clearly not Roza's, that painting has nothing to do with anything. Eye candy for the demented, it's a part of the room, the representational counterpart of a hospital bed.

"Mrs. Kisel', thank you for agreeing to talk with me," Bill begins in English.

"*Oy, eto vy! Prostite, chto ya vas dvazhdy udarila,*" she responds. [Oh, it's you! Forgive me for having whacked you twice.]

Bill shrugs. It's a painful motion, thanks to her. Compared to other setbacks in his life, being whacked across the back with a crooked cane by a madwoman is a minor inconvenience.

With that motion—the shrug—he has blown his cover—fuck it. Yes, he speaks Russian, and very well at that.

"*Eto ya vas tak dlya maskirovki, prostite uzh starushku. Vizhu, krasivyy molodoy chelovek—kak palkoy ne udarit'?*" [I did that for cover, forgive the old lady. I see an attractive young man; why would I not hit him?]

Madness is gone from Roza's eyes, and how does she know that he speaks Russian? Thanks to Melsor's propensity to see an enemy behind every tree, his Russianness was to be kept secret.

"*Nu eto nichego,*" he responds with a slight wave of the right hand, a dismissive gesture that reveals something they can't teach at the FBI academy—the Russian body language. [It's nothing.]

"*Prezhde vsego, kak vas zovut?*" [First of all, what is your name?]

"William."

"Vil'-yam? Da bros'te vy. Kakoy vy tam Vil'-yam? Khoroshiy Moskovsky mal'chik, khorosho vospitannyy. Nevooruzhennym glazom vizhu. Kak vas vpravdu zovut?" [Vil'-yam? Please . . . What kind of a Vil'-yam are you? You are good Moscow boy, well brought up. I see this with the naked eye. What is your real name?]

"Ilya."

The sound of his real name rolling off his tongue feels as comfortable as wearing his own Carhartts after days of masquerading in Florida costumes.

His mother would be Roza's age now, give or take a year or two.

"A po otchestvy vas kak?" [And what is your patronymic?]

"Melsorovich," he replies with hesitation.

"Melsorovich. Nu togda vsyo ponyatno. Nu, mozhet ne sovsem vsyo, no mnogoye. Nash Melsor—tot chto zhulik?" [Melsorovich . . . Then it all becomes clear. Maybe not all of it, but many things. Our Melsor, the one who is a crook?]

"Roza Borisovna . . ." He pauses long enough for her to appreciate that he knows her patronymic.

She nods.

"U menya slozhilos' vpechatleniye, ves'ma vozmozhno lozhnoye, chto vy v etom ikhnem Shato basseyin v zal spustili," he says softly, Russianly, letting his Moscow elocution kick in. [I have formed the perhaps false impression that you are the person who flushed the swimming pool into the meeting room of that Château of theirs.]

She smiles.

Had this been her apartment, she would be pouring tea into those orange made-in-Czechoslovakia polka-dotted cups, the ones Bill saw smashed up, in bags, on the curb, during her eviction. In better days, there would have been sweets in a colorful cardboard box depicting roses, the Kremlin, or both. He should have brought her one of those boxes, he realizes. He is certain you can buy them at a place called Matryoshka, in Sunny Isles, God knows. Maybe he will make a stop there before he leaves. He wants to.

"*A vy kto po spetsial'nosti?*" she asks. [And what would your profession be?]

"*Byl zhurnalistom. Teper' ne znayu.*" [I was a journalist. Now I don't know.]

"*Mozhno skazat' vam doveritel'no, Ilya Melsorovich?*" [May I respond in confidence, Ilya Melsorovich?]

This question, short and to the point though it may be, bears unpacking.

Admittedly, "in confidence" is a weak translation of "*doveri-tel'no.*" "In trust" would be better, as it conveys respect, the sort of respect he hasn't felt since Moscow.

There is something wonderful about being addressed formally as "*vy,*" as opposed to "*ty,*" by an older person. This would be the manner in which a Moscow professor would address her students. Having left as a boy, Bill was forever familiar—"*ty.*"

Holy shit! That's what's missing in this fucking Florida: respect.

Would it be too late for Bill to abandon his American nom de guerre and resurrect his former self—Ilya?

As Ilya, he would start from scratch.

He nods. Of course, Roza Borisovna, you can respond in confidence.

"*Po sekretu, na ushko?*" [Secretly, whispered into your little ear?]

He nods again.

"*Chest'yu poklyatnites', pozhaluysta.*" [Swear upon your honor, please.]

"Chest' shtuka vazhnaya, osobenno seychas, v nashe idiotskoye vremya," he responds. [Honor is an important thing, especially in this idiotic time.]

"Imenno po-etomy ya vam takoye usloviye stavlyu." [That's precisely why I am setting these conditions.]

"Da," he says. *"Chest'yu klyanus'."* [Yes. I swear upon my honor.]

"Nu, togda—da, vy pravil'no vycheslili. Ya flexible payp vrezala nedaleko ot nasosa basseyna—s odnoy storony, i v vozdushnyy dakt s drugoy. I basseyn, predstav'te sebe, zaprosto spustilsya." [Yes then. Your calculations are correct. I cut a piece of flexible pipe into the swimming pool drain, near the filter, on one side and the air ducts on the other. And the pool—imagine that—simply drained."

"Tak—eto Severnyy Basseyn. A Yuzhnyy?" [So, this takes care of the South Pool. What about the North?]

"A etot ya dinamitom." [I did that with dynamite.]

"Kak vy yego dostali; dinamit?" [How did you get it, the dynamite?]

"Kak, kak . . . U menya chetyre funtika posle raboty ostalos'. Ya zhe vzryvnik." [I had four pounds left over from work. I am an explosives expert.]

"Professor v Gornom Institute . . . V Moskve . . . A do togo, inzhener-vsryvnik v Soyuzvsryvprome," Bill adds. [A professor at the Mining Institute in Moscow. And before that, an explosives engineer at Soyuzvsryvprom.]

She looks at him quizzically, and he explains that Roza Kisel' is an uncommon name, and that it figured on the list of refuseniks. The Orwellian name of her former employer, *"Soyuzvsryvprom"* is from that list, too. It stands for "the enterprise of explosion-making."

She wants the details. How did Bill get that list, that bio?

He called the YIVO Institute for Jewish Research in New

York. The place has an excellent archive and, more importantly, excellent archivists. In this case, he scored a direct hit: a list of refuseniks put out by the Anti-Defamation League. Roza was in the 1982 edition—one of the longest: almost one thousand names.

Next, he ran a pedestrian Google search, and her name popped up again in the *Las Vegas Sun* in 1998. It was in a piece about a Russian restaurant that was opened by a former Moscow engineer, an explosives expert who by then spent more than a decade working for gold mining enterprises in Nevada.

Cirque du Soleil performers regarded that restaurant as their home away from home. The story was about a bunch of clowns.

For that crowd, the place had to be very good.

"Rasskazhite mne pro vashe . . . kak eto skazat' delikatno . . ." [Tell me about your . . . how do I put this politely . . .]

"Moyo buynoye pomeshatel'stvo?" She smiles. [My violent insanity?]

"Ono samoye." [That very thing.]

"Ilya Melsorovich, vy so Shveykon znakomy?" [Ilya Melsorovich, are you familiar with Švejk?]

Is Bill familiar with *The Good Soldier Švejk?*

Švejk is his hemoglobin! Švejk was read to him before he was old enough to handle a book that thick. It was the yellow tome with illustrations—and don't forget those cartoons, those incredible cartoons.

Melsor is wrong. It's Švejk's creator, Jaroslav Hašek, not Donal'd Tramp, who is the oracle of our times—and he lives on, producing recipes for dealing with madness. "I have the honor to report that I am a complete idiot," Švejk states with a salute that bespeaks mental health in the feebleminded world blown apart by the Great War.

Švejk stands shoulder to shoulder with Don Quixote, Young Werther, Onegin, and Huck. Švejk is immortal. Brecht extended Švejk's adventures into World War II—literally. Joseph Heller did the same, but figuratively. Without Švejk, there could be no *Catch-22*. Even *M*A*S*H* stands on Švejk's blocky shoulders.

Bill's mother wouldn't part with that well-worn yellow tome. It traveled to America in a suitcase, next to a stack of the Katzenelenbogen family photos. Surely the brave soldier exists in a box in Melsor's apartment. Bill should dig him out, liberate him on the occasion of the encroaching reign of King Donal'd I, the Sun King who ate Washington. Actually, fuck it. Bill knows Švejk by heart—the parts that matter.

Švejk's mystery is what matters: is he genuinely extremely feebleminded, or is he pretending to be extremely feebleminded in order to liberate himself from the feeblemindedness around him?

"*Da, so Shweikon ya znakom,*" Bill responds. [Yes, I am familiar with Švejk.]

No shit.

"*Togda vy vsyo ponimayete?*" [Then you understand everything?]

"*Nachinayu . . .*" [Starting to . . .]

"*Smotrite, yesli vy skazhete khot' komu-nibud' ob etom nashem razgovore, vam prosto ne poveryat. Skazhut, chto eto vy psikh.*" [You see, if you were to describe our conversation to anyone, you will not be believed. They will say that you are the one who is insane.]

Bill nods.

"*Po-etomu, poymite, drug moy, ya sovsem ne volnuyus' o tom, chto vy znayete o moyey podryvnoy deyatel'nosti. Vy im vyskazhite vsy pravdu, a oni vas v yebanatiki zachislyat.*" [So, my friend, you understand why I am not worried in the least about you knowing about my sabotage, my work with explosives. You could tell them the truth, but they will say that you are the one who is insane.]

"*Da. Eto absolyutnaya zaschita,*" Bill agrees on reflection. [Yes. This is an absolute defense.]

"*Ona samaya. Chto-b vy ne skazali, oni vam otvetyat, chto Roza Kisel' psikh, yebanatik—ya slyshala, chto tak menya v Shato nazyvayut.*" [Indeed, absolute. No matter how you frame it, they will tell you that Roza Kisel' is a psychopath; a, pardon me, fucking lunatic they call me at the Château, I hear.]

"*Vy znayete, molodoy chelovek, mozno vas poprosit' sbegat's k kontsu korridora i prinesti mne Ginger Ale iz mashiny etoy proklyatoy. I zaplatite pozhaluysta, u menya posobiye esche be oformili,*" she says. [Please, young man, may I ask you to run over to the end of the corridor and grab a ginger ale from that cursed vending machine. My subsidy here hasn't been determined.]

A few minutes later, laden with four cans of ginger ale and an assortment of vending machine offerings—he got the entire lineup of sweets: M&Ms, Hershey bars, Three Musketeers, Oreos, and Reese's—Bill returns to Roza's room.

He has a point to make on the subject of Švejk.

Švejk didn't demonstrate much initiative during the Great War. He was moved around, passively, and much of the time he was simply lost and looking for his regiment.

The good soldier didn't flood any meeting rooms, didn't blow up pools with dynamite. Bill couldn't remember whether Švejk ever discharged his rifle. One of his war buddies gets shot in the ass, Bill recalls. Does Švejk have a "fuck you" sign in his pocket, like all the people Bill loved during his Moscow childhood?

Hašek provides no answers, because, clearly, he doesn't want to.

"Ya ne sovsem s vami soglasen naschet Shveyka. On idiot, a vy, sobst-venno, terrorist," Bill counters. [I am not entirely in agreement with you about Švejk. He is extremely feebleminded, and you are, essentially, a terrorist.]

"Chisto teoreticheski, ya, konechno, za neprotivleniye. No eto zhe fash-isty, grabitely, svolochi! To u nikh special assesmenty, to u nikh zuby. Mimo etogo prokhodit' nel'zya." [On the purely theoretical level, I am all for passive resistance, of course. But these are fascists, robbers, *svolochi*! They have their special assessments. They have their gold teeth. This cannot be ignored.]

"Ah . . . Vy tozhe pro zolotyyye zuby znayete?" [So you, too, know about the gold teeth?]

She nods.

"Znayu, znayu. Vot vam i, kak govoryat v narode, quod erat demon-strandum. *Fashisti. Svolochi."* [I know, I know. And so, to use a folk expression, *quod erat demonstrandum. Fascists. Svolochi.*]

QED indeed.

One last question: *"Kak vy tuda, v Shato, dobirayetes'?"* [How do you get there, to the Château?]

"Ahhh, oni zdes' dumayut, cho menya plemannitsa k vrachu vozit. Na samom dele u menya net nikakoy plemannitsy—eto moya studentka byvshaya." [They think that my niece takes me to the doctor. Actually, I have no niece. It's a former student of mine.]

Bill glances at his watch. It's time to go, but Roza disagrees.

There is a book-sized chess set—she saved it from her eviction. It's no use to lie to her, to argue that he doesn't know how to play.

Ridiculous! Good boys like Ilya Katzenelenbogen know how to play chess, and even now, in her golden years and in the care of the South Florida *Dzhuyka*, Professor Roza Borisovna Kisel' will not be beat.

23

MERRY WIDOWS

It takes an hour for Bill to lose one chess game and, surprisingly, win another. It's 12:30, dammit. On the way out, he calls Bill B:

"Dude . . ."

"Meet us in front of Juicy Gyro, 6900 block of Collins. We're in front, in a van. You're buying."

"Sure, it's not far, get the food now. Give me fifteen."

"What do you want?"

"Shwarma and diet something."

"Suit yourself. Their gyros are better."

"Remember the ground rules—you can't tell anyone. An embargo until this piece of shit airs."

Bill nods. Sure. How would he, a fired journalist, break an embargo? With what?

Stepping into the van, Bill hands a twenty-dollar bill to the photographer, the same young guy who filmed the swimming pool collapse.

"Give him another five," says Bill B, clicking on a file on the screen in front of him and taking a big first bite out of the gyro. It is, as advertised, a juicy one.

There is some video static, followed by the image of Consuela, long-legged, resplendent, in a little black dress and dangerously tall pumps, reclining on the shrink's couch.

It looks like she is in a real shrink's office, in real analysis, with the patient on the couch, facing away from the analyst. The analyst is straight out of central casting; poor man's Freud.

Freud argued that laymen could be analysts, but that was before reality TV. For all anyone knows, today he might have argued that, with public exposure being the norm, it would be fine to Webcast analysis to the people. And with judges and doctors (especially plastic surgeons) playing the reality TV game, why should shrinks be left behind?

In any case, shrinkage is what's being done, here, now, for the benefit of Consuela Ramirez-Wronska.

They seem to be somewhere mid-session.

> **BILL B:** Look at those fucking legs!

ANALYST: You were saying, Zbig was hypertensive . . .

> **BILL B:** So fucking what?

CONSUELA: He was. It was under control. He took drugs for it.

ANALYST: Did that create prob-lems with your lifestyle?

> BILL B: "Lifestyle" . . . always a loaded word. Do you think they are real?
>
> PHOTOGRAPHER: Legs—yes. Boobs—no.

CONSUELA: It did. He was un-able to take enhancing drugs that he needed if he were to have a vigorous sex life. We could still have sex—when it was just the two of us. But he wanted more.

ANALYST: And you?

CONSUELA: I did. But when we wanted to have others in bed with us, well . . . he would have needed some . . . help.

> BILL B: So that's what the cops were saying . . . Shit . . . How do you like your shwarma?
>
> BILL K: Good. Did we get any fries with that?
>
> PHOTOGRAPHER: No.

ANALYST: How did it make you feel? Having sex with multiple people?

CONSUELA: I never thought about it. It's just what we did. Some people are straight, some people are gay. This was our thing.

ANALYST: Did he find a way to deal with this problem, this need for a substitute for these drugs? Some people take these drugs anyway. And some people swear by nutraceuticals.

PHOTOGRAPHER: Are they going to talk about fucking iguanas next?

BILL B: Them and boa constrictors. Reptiles are the thing.

PHOTOGRAPHER: Gross.

BILL B: Why gross? They are reptiles and they consort with reptiles. It's godly.

PHOTOGRAPHER: Fuck you.

CONSUELA: He found something better than drugs. Danger. Heights.

ANALYST: Do you like it, too?

CONSUELA: One day, in Colorado, he took me by the edge of a gorge. It was very nice.

ANALYST: Fear, pheromones, adrenaline—there could be a link. At least many people think there is.

BILL B: Do you think he's doing her, the TV shrink?

PHOTOGRAPHER: Sure, why not? I don't care.

CONSUELA: It was bigger for him than it was for me. Sometimes we would get a room on the top floor of the hotel, and he would use the balcony to . . . I told you already.

BILL B: I hope they made the estate pay for fixing those glass panes at the Dux. That was reckless behavior, in my book. Standing on the railing with his dick hanging out. Unnecessary.

ANALYST: I see, he stood close to the edge of the balcony and looked down?

CONSUELA: That, and sometimes he would let his hands go and stand balancing on the railing.

ANALYST: Fully dressed.

CONSUELA: Not always.

ANALYST: How did that help?

BILL B: Remember the time they found a sixteen-year-old kid hanging by the neck on a playground swing, with his pants down and, on the ground in front of him, a photo of two broads fucking a guy?

PHOTOGRAPHER: Yeah. I was on that story. What's it called, that thing they do?

BILL K: A ménage à trois?

PHOTOGRAPHER: No! I know that one!

BILL K: You mean what the kid did?

PHOTOGRAPHER: Yes, that.

BILL K: Autoerotic asphyxiation.

CONSUELA: It helped by giving him a powerful, lasting erection—the closeness of death . . . I am not a doctor . . .

ANALYST: But he was . . .

CONSUELA: But he was . . .

ANALYST: Did this work?

CONSUELA: Yes. I can tell you that.

ANALYST: So what happened that night?

PHOTOGRAPHER: What's auto-erotic asphyxiation? I forgot.

BILL K: Constricting the flow of oxygen to the brain to get a more intense orgasm. If you do it in a noose and you pass out, you fucking die. It's not suicide. It's an accident. I heard of cases, in small towns, where they call it murder— and they go out searching for the killer. And sometimes they make arrests. That's the scariest part.

PHOTOGRAPHER: And you know so much about this because . . .

BILL K: Because Fuck You, that's how.

CONSUELA: We were in a hotel room . . . On the forty-third floor.

ANALYST: Who is *we*?

CONSUELA: The three of us—a patient of his was with us, and Zbig walked out on the balcony.

PHOTOGRAPHER: Was there a golden shower? Who does he think he is?

BILL B: Who *did* he think he *was?*

ANALYST: This is a violation of medical ethics, of course. The patient . . .

CONSUELA: Her husband didn't mind.

ANALYST: Hmmm. And . . .

CONSUELA: And what?

ANALYST: What happened?

CONSUELA: We made love, then realized that he wasn't there. And I got out of bed, and he wasn't on the balcony anymore.

ANALYST: Could you see the atrium panels from up there?

CONSUELA: No. It was dark, but I could see the ambulance driving up, with lights on.

ANALYST: Dr. Wronski was prominent here in South Florida, as are you. Do you see any meaning in what happened that night? Any lesson learned? People want to know.

BILL K: What a great fucking question!

CONSUELA: What do you mean?

ANALYST: Is there anything this big life of this big man, Dr. Wronski's, can teach the rest of us? Is there meaning?

BILL B: Give me a fucking break . . .

CONSUELA: Zbig lived for beauty, he gave all he had.

ANALYST: And that's all?

CONSUELA: That's all.

BILL K: That's all? This is not even an answer! Where is the mystery? Is there anything left? Just porn? Threesomes, four-somes, hookers, golden show-ers?

I thought she was okay for a while. But she's like Trump in a skirt. Better legs, I give you that.

BILL B: Don't forget the butt. *Much* better than Trump's.

PHOTOGRAPHER: You seen Trump's?

BILL B: I needed that—thanks, asshole.

BILL K: The man lived, the man died. There has to be more to it.

BILL B: I can tell you the only meaning I derive from this shit: It's going to take quite a dance number to get this on the news.

BILL K: Even in South Florida?

BILL B: Even in South Florida.

24

THE TREASURE OF THE CHÂTEAU

Bill K says good-bye to Bill B and his Sancho Panza. Their camaraderie, the zingers they let fly as they watched the embargoed preview of that preposterous interview, made him fathom the magnitude of his loss. What a horrible time not to be a reporter.

It's akin to missing your boat to Spain, leaving the fascists unopposed. Here today, with Democrats having neutralized the progressives, the battle lines have been drawn: the rampaging dinosaurs vs. the press. It's us versus them, the lying white men in suits versus defenders of justice, accuracy, and truth.

Bill loves the drive on Collins Avenue—always has. And he is probably not the first man to ponder fascism along that route.

It feels like Tel Aviv, just bigger, and still very Bauhaus. Very German, but good German. Our German.

There was a time when Holocaust survivors—folks with numbers on their forearms—lived here. Isaac Bashevis Singer walked these streets, exchanging nods with people he knew, speaking Yiddish, Polish, English, taking Nobel Prize–worthy notes, thinking Nobel Prize–worthy thoughts, muttering Nobel Prize–worthy mutterings, and, in addition to all this, trying to get laid.

Here, on the right, is the Fontainebleau, a landmark now encumbered by an extra tower, that appendage that annoys Bill. The great white Fontainebleau, a creation of the great Morris Lapidus, who had a vision of building castles up and down this strip—castles that included, less famously, Château Sedan Neuve, the castle fated to fall.

Bill really should stop and go in, to see the Fontainebleau's lobby, to marvel at its curves, its whiteness, its Staircase to Nowhere. Of course, he should do it because good design is good, but also because a design nobly executed is a weapon against fascism: a Katyusha.

Piloting the white Prius north on Collins, he is a man in a hurry. Whatever it takes, he, William M. Katzenelenbogen, must get on that boat, he must join this fight, he must strike anywhere and everywhere, fighting by all means at his disposal.

Bill knows exactly what he can do.

In the eternal fight against fascism, "can" equals "must."

It's 3:30 P.M., the Russians have left the ocean, and only a small figure—a man—is bobbing in the waves.

Bill walks up to the chaise—the only chaise on the beach—picks up a pair of black-and-purple plaid shorts, reaches into the pocket, and finds a set of keys and a cell phone. The figure out there, in the ocean, starts a journey toward the shore, and seeing no reason to conceal his actions, Bill turns around and walks toward Château Sedan Neuve.

He walks up the steps, past the scorched, dry, empty pool, finally entering the building from the pool deck. He pushes the elevator button to the ninth floor and heads slowly along the corridor to the Greensteins' apartment.

There, he walks up to the disgustingly painted breakfront, opens its doors, and—one by one—takes out the velvet bags. There are six bags altogether. There could be more, he should look around, but time is short. He reaches inside one of the bags—it's gold. Crowns. Taken out of the mouths of dead Jews, or perhaps Jews still living.

Chills run up his spine and down again.

Greenstein can't be far behind. It doesn't matter. If Herr or, for that matter, Frau Greenstein gets in his way, he will kill them with his bare hands. Hands in which the Treasure of Château Sedan Neuve is now safe.

"Ruki vverkh!" commands a man Bill recognizes as the Russian security guard.

"You really should be using German," Bill says calmly. "Repeat after me: *Hände hoch.*"

Then, for good measure, he adds: "Asshole."

There is a gun pointed at him. Bill doesn't know his calibers and doesn't give a fuck. If he is ordered to give up these bags, he will do no such thing. After years of humiliation, they are in his hands, safe. This is it.

"Hey, in English we have an expression. You may not have heard it, so pay attention: Fuck you."

Dropping five of the bags on the floor, he takes the sixth, and, swinging it, whacks the gun-wielding guard across the face.

"Yob tvouy," the man shouts, and reciprocates by throwing a

left, getting Bill under the chin, then following up with a whack with the handle of his pistol.

Bill falls to the floor, his body shielding the five bags. He is thinking of the right word to describe what's just happened . . . "Pistol-whipped." No hyphen, one word: "pistolwhipped." That's what he is, pistolfuckingwhipped.

He has no idea how long he has been out, but he is comforted to realize that the five velvet bags are still beneath him. He has not been moved.

Good thing—he will not let these bags go. If he can't liberate them, he will sanctify them with his blood. Looks like he already has. He doesn't want to move . . . The bags. He must protect the bags.

Somebody throws a bucket of water on him. Fuckers. He will kill them, or he will try.

"So, you went for it . . ." It's Greenstein. "You give us no choice."

"How do you know I am not with FBI?" Bill responds, thinking of the bags.

"Because you are not. I did some research—not much is needed these days. A few little guesses, face recognition, this and that. It's not nice to waste FBI agents, but you are not an FBI agent. It's not good to kill reporters, but you are no longer a reporter. You are a *former* reporter. Your father might care, a little bit, but frankly that, too, is uncertain.

GREENSTEIN: Stepan, would you make this gentleman disappear?

STEPAN: How?

GREENSTEIN: Do I need to explain?

STEPAN: Shoot him here, now?

GREENSTEIN: Not in my apartment, idiot. He will ruin the rugs.

STEPAN: I can take him in bathroom and shoot him in back of head.

BILL: You will need to move me. And take these teeth.

WILFREDA: These are my father's teeth.

BILL: No. They are actually *Jewish* teeth. Your father was a Nazi.

WILFREDA: My husband is a Jew!

BILL: So?! You can be a Jew and a Nazi. Why is this so fucking hard for people to understand?

WILFREDA: I want my teeth!

STEPAN: I need clear orders.

WILFREDA: Kill him!

BILL: Go ahead, see if I give a fuck.

GREENSTEIN: Hold off on that. What will we do with the body?

STEPAN: Can I kick him at least?

BILL: Be my guest. I am not moving.

STEPAN: What if he screams?

BILL: Wouldn't you? That's the problem with you Nazis. You talk a good game, but when it comes to implementation, you fuck up big. Look at Franco. Look at Mussolini. Look at your Hitler. Your Trump will fuck up, too. And we will remove him.

GREENSTEIN: Pistolwhip him again, this time for real, and carry him out in a big duffle.

STEPAN: Do you have one?

BILL: See what I mean? Implementation.

STEPAN: Give me bags now. I am warning you.

BILL: Fuck you.

———

Pain is the last thing Bill remembers, together with this thought: "They killed me. Cowards."

When consciousness returns, he is covered with shards of glass, as is the room. He checks whether the teeth are still there, and they are. He has not been moved—means he has not been out long.

"How are you, *bubbie*?"

It's Johnny! The blind man with his Bushmaster.

"*Molodetz!*" It's Melsor. [Good lad.]

Good lad? Please . . .

The shards around and on top of Bill are from the "slice door," as sliding glass doors are known in the dialect of Château Sedan Neuve.

BILL: Johnny, I want you to take these bags. All six of them. You will take them to the Holocaust Museum. Can I trust you?

JOHNNY: I liberated Dachau. You know that.

Bill looks at Greenstein.

BILL: I know. And, you, Herr Greenstein, it's time for us to talk. You almost killed me, you Nazi asshole Jew. Would you like to be arrested on charges of assault with intent to kill—and, while you are at it, disgorged?

GREENSTEIN: What do you want?

BILL: The envelopes with the condo board ballots are being steam-opened right now. I know the results.

GREENSTEIN: What are they?

BILL: There was a write-in campaign, it appears. A movement. Frau Greenstein, write this down.

WILFREDA: Yes, dictate.

BILL: The winning slate: Roza Kisel', president. Melsor Katzenelenbogen, vice president. Nella Katzenelenbogen, board member. Alex Bogomolov, board member. Johnny Schwartz, also a board member.

And I want Roza Kisel' brought back here in a fucking black stretch limo. No, make it white. This is Florida.

WILFREDA: Yes?

GREENSTEIN: Yes. What choice do we have?

STEPAN: I have to go now.

BILL: Indeed, you do—you'll catch the next plane to Russia, douchebag. God save the czar!

25

BEATRICE

Gwen comes out of the gate wearing a polka-dot dress and an unbuttoned green Barbour coat, a messenger bearing greetings from a different universe.

They embrace, her hand running over the bruise on the back of his head.

"What happened to you?" she asks, pulling away for a moment. "You're bleeding."

"Nothing to worry about. Just pistolwhipped."

"Should we turn around and return to D.C.? I want you alive."

"In a couple of days, yes, let's return, maybe."

They kiss again. Gwen is here—his, for him. They will survive this in each other's arms, he is certain of this, like his parents did, taking walks through the darkened city—theirs.

She pulls back again.

"Were they trying to kill you?"

"They were. They failed."

"You didn't kill anyone . . ."

What can Bill possibly say to this? How is it relevant? I found my Don't Give a Fuckness, I stared down a gun without flinching, defanged the Evil Dwarf, restored justice in a corner of South Florida. And, yes, I got the girl; did I not? Is this not worth killing for? What difference does it make whether I did or didn't?

"I don't like this pause—please say no."

"No. Let's just say I won—and they lost."

It's 7:05 P.M., January 19. The burghers of the Château are in a meeting, feverishly counting the ballots. When it comes to ballots, Frau Wilfreda Müller-Greenstein is an exceptional, experienced cook. There will be no surprises—no reason to babysit the meeting.

Bill doesn't have to manage that thing anymore. He can be here, at the airport, holding Gwen. If such measurements had been taken, it would be revealed that they stay joined in an embrace longer than any other couple upon that gleaming terrazzo floor over the preceding three and a half hours, and those other contestants were much younger, indeed neither was of legal age. Also, they were boys.

They part, but his right arm remains on her, held in place by her left hand. He feels her beating heart. He feels the possibilities—all of them at once—ranging from the physical—the taste of her mouth—all the way to the existential—his rebirth as a writer, perhaps.

No, this will probably not happen, not with this Zbig thing, but with something else, something urgent, something political.

He stops for a moment in the darkness of the parking garage, and they kiss again, briefly this time, but long enough to chase away the thoughts about the story that brought him here, to Florida.

They kiss again and again in the Prius, and as the car starts silently, his hand drops to her mid-thigh, coming to rest beneath her hem and her hand. He keeps it there.

They drive in silence, drinking it in, looking at the lights.

"How is the book?" she asks as the ramp takes them to Ocean Drive.

His hand is on her knee. It feels to him like a greeting of sorts, the ringing in of an era. What will he do in this new era? Books perhaps, though not about the reptile-fucking rich. He has been looking into this thing, but no aspect of it has drawn him in. You need that if you are to get cranking.

So, no journalism, unless he finds a way in.

Perhaps crime reporting for a television station would be the thing. Opposition research comes to mind, too. Public relations, even that narrow field called crisis management, is clearly not an option the way it was for Gwen. Not for him. He couldn't possibly.

Or maybe he will do what so many others have done— become a PI. William M. Katzenelenbogen, Existentialist Investigator of the Gold Coast, Inspector Luftmensch. You have to admit, there is panache . . .

The pondering of career options when your hand rests upon your lover's knee is frowned upon, even in Washington. But in Bill's case, an exception is warranted. The guy has never had a job. He has had a place in the universe—it was inseparable from other aspects of his existence.

You will see: when this Trump madness subsides, retreats,

dissolves, because this is, after all, America, Bill and Gwen will be together still, made stronger by their adventure.

Readers are encouraged to mobilize their memories or imaginations to reconstruct what happens before dawn. We will skip over all this.

The sun is yet to rise, and Gwen is in Bill's arms.

She begins to talk:

"I haven't had a chance to tell you, that deal, it's big. It's for a PAC. Republican this time, probably channeling money for the Trump organization, on the private side, so it's very hush-hush. There will be more revelations, and they will want me on their crisis team, running it."

Bill takes a deep breath. He sits up in the bed.

"I hope you don't mind."

"What right do I have to object?"

"I hear you thinking: 'A Faustian deal.'"

"No. You are not a reporter—not anymore. You represent no interests but your own."

"And you, Bill? You are not a reporter, either."

"No. I am not."

"What will you be? Are you capable of making a deal?"

"Faustian?"

"Is there another kind?"

"I could become a PI."

"That's Faustian in my book."

"I've been thinking of hanging out a shingle: EXISTEN-TIALIST INVESTIGATIONS L.L.C. William M. Katzenelenbogen, Inspector Luftmensch."

"Clever. That's you."

"But there is something I must do first. Finish the unfinished business. Understand something big."

"Honor your art?"

"My former art."

His Carhartts, his T-shirt, and his Top-Siders on, Bill leans over the bed and kisses her brow.

EPILOGUE

At the Château, Melsor's parking spot is occupied by a new white Lexus GS F with temporary plates.

On his cell phone, Bill looks up the starting price: $84,000.

Melsor's payoff arrived the morning after the election. Not a bad way for returns to start trickling in. As the vice president of the CSNCA BOD, Melsor Y. Katzenelenbogen is entitled to a first-class ride. The good men of ISIS have seen to that. ISIS works fast.

Bill leaves the dirty little white Prius in front of the gleaming white Lexus.

He needs to run in for a moment, to get something. He does get that something—two items, to be exact, and as he leaves, he notices an ISIS eighteen-wheeler unloading scaffolding in front of the Château.

Regime change or not, the balconies will come down.

Back at the Grand Dux parking lot, Bill considers drafting a note to his father, but quickly rejects the idea. Has he not expressed his thoughts on multiple occasions without being heard?

Fuck it, Melsor is the only family he has. He starts drafting an e-mail, but stumbles immediately. In previous e-mails—there were few—there was no need for salutations. It was all business. You would think that after a half century the Katzenelenbogen men would have ironed out the problem of salutation, but it is what it is, or, to translate a Russian expression, "When it's fuck your mother, it's fuck your mother, but when it's fuck your mother, it's fuck your mother."

It's all in the inflections. Isn't everything always?

A text comes in as Bill exits the elevator on the top floor of the Grand Dux:

"Bill, you are uncooperative! This is your THIRD AND FI-NAL REMINDER. Why are you dragging this out? Just let me go!"

He starts on a response, weighing the idea of answering, and as three dots surely blink on Lena's phone, he keys in "GO!!!" but erases it.

On the rooftop of the Grand Dux, the alarm, in winding, howling waves, braids with the wind. A light cloud has descended, grazing the roof, a smoky tangent. The wind is oceanbound, the cloud is its ward.

Winded from the run up three flights of stairs to the roof— the forty-eighth floor—Bill waits for his heartbeat to settle. His T-shirt sleeves flutter, like banners, like petite blue wings. His *W* cap begins to move, the wind has entered it, an unseen wedge inserted, it quakes. The hat, it takes its leap. The hat, it rises. The hat, above him, a flying instrument with buoyancy all its own, the visor down, like a parachutist—a jumper—beneath the canopy, his sail. It rises, turns a somersault, then, in a leap, surfing the invisible currents toward the sea, disappears completely. Bill may believe he sees it still, but it is out, gone, free.

He looks into the ocean. He turns around, letting his gaze sweep across the inland marshes, high-rises, channels. Pelicans above invite him to join their silent patrol. The wind will show him how silly it was to fear, introduce Bill to the world Zbig fathoms fully, uniting them in knowledge. Roommates again. Absurd, but true.

Infinity is a concept, but it's a feeling, too. It takes a leap— just one. One leap, toward imprisonment or liberation. Commit, commit, and rush to penetrate the spheres. Life/death is a dichotomy of outcomes, and is there anything more boring than outcomes, I ask? Is retreat possible? A stupid question. The edge—that's all there is. It's all about the edge. To fathom Zbig, to catch him by his feet, you grab his final moment, his Zbigness. No other way exists.

They will be here soon—security, rent-a-cops in blue, armed, dangerous even if you are white. He must make his resolutions quickly and act forthwith.

Bill's thoughts:

The cloud's content, its gentle fog. I could attach myself to it, Inspector Luftmensch in his magic dirigible. It's porous, the boundary between the spheres. This is my story. My cloud, my dirigible. It's lifting, lifting fast, and I remain below.

The purple band on the horizon brightens, orange in its core. Dawn nears, my dawn, the first I've ever owned. This narrative is mine at last. I didn't get to choose my material, my smarts and deficits—none of the attributes, mental, physical. I didn't choose those precious intelligentsia sensibilities. I didn't choose those cold, dark streets. I didn't volunteer to be a carrier of my father's criminality, the cancerousness of my mother's breasts.

I was a journalist once. No more of that. I had a Beatrice, I thought. No more. I had a book to write, I thought. I may—or not. It rides on this. The quest is not to understand. It's to explore, which means to feel. There's nothing harder. The method of elimination is all I ever had, I see this now. Commitment to the narrative does not mean having to relate. It is okay, it's noble to bottle in. Inspector Luftmensch has no loyalties, he has no obligations, and he has nothing to explain. With firmament beneath me still, I make my choice with open eyes. What difference do eyes make when there's a leap?

I'll set my gaze upon the rising sun, this orange streak on the horizon. It pulls me, eastward, through air, clouds, ocean. To tell your story, you become it. Inspector Luftmensch knew this all along. Now I know, too.

I haven't seen the edge, the very edge—not yet. Would it be cowardly to stand and peer, to let prior knowledge fuel my fear? I'll see it soon enough; I'll take my leap, my flight. The concept of the final step seems old and quaint. The edge is of no consequence—I see this. The final step—it's of no greater consequence than the first—and damn those stallions. The song— irrelevant. The edge—romanticism of the unknown. What does it matter? Trajectory is my metric now, my neopedestrian vector in my new realm.

I check the buckles on my pack. Where is the rip cord? A brave man never checks; a coward—always. This is not suicide. This isn't what ascetics call mortification of the flesh. Glorification is the word, and it's about meaning, not flesh. There's time to think about the rip cord, about the pilot chute. I will do no such thing.

"Here I come!" I shout, setting my course into the wind, and then I leap.

There is a strip of sand beneath—the beach.

Melsor begins the morning of January 20 the way he begins all mornings. On the balcony, staring into the ocean.

He is not the sort that waits for sunrises or sunsets. He is on this balcony for a reason. Fifty push-ups today, like every day. He used to do these on the concrete floor. He still has the breath, the heartbeat, the musculature, but some errant nerve caused pain. He tried to elevate, doing his push-ups off the edge of a plastic chaise, and that worked fine for a few weeks.

Now, Melsor places his hands on the balcony's aluminum railing; this is hardly a push-up, you might as well be standing upright, but the pain announces itself, shooting up from the small of his back.

Melsor is not the sort that surrenders. He faces south. Up, down, up again, counting. One . . . exhale . . . forty-nine to go . . . inhale. He pauses on top of the second push-up, looking up at the twin towers of the Grand Dux.

Three . . . Forty-seven to go . . . He will do every single one of them, gulping down the pain. Up-down, up again, counting, because life is not a handout. Life is a privilege, life is what you defend, life is the thing you conquer.

Melsor is naked except for his white boxer shorts. Fruit of the Loom; the only brand he has worn since coming to America. To people who inhabit the skyscraper aeries a few hundred feet away, he is a figure bopping up and down anonymously on the balcony. He could do this completely naked if he so chose.

Push-ups on the balcony speed up his blood's journey through his calcifying arteries, his constricting veins. It gushes through, like breath through a whistle. This is his private moment, a send-off to a day in a life that is, once again, becoming public. He was a poet once, a bard of freedom, a voice of moral authority, a weaver of verse on the world's stage. He is a leader now, a vice president, the de facto king of his Château. Has he changed? No. Never. The world is the one who has changed, matured, wizened to the point of accepting his leadership, offering itself to Melsor Yakovlevich Katzenelenbogen. Here I am, Melsor Yakovlevich—I am yours. Take, reap, rule, do as you please.

Melsor has worked up a sweat, enough to wipe off with a cold, wet towel. He had soaked it in the sink and brought it out in a Walmart shopping bag to keep it from dripping on the white tiled floor. It's a sponge bath really, something you learn to appreciate in a cold-water communal flat in Moscow, the kind of place where the corridors are long and where there is no shower. The public bathhouse is too far for daily or even weekly visits—a basin filled with water and a wet towel is all you get.

Melsor runs the towel beneath his armpits, sending streams of cold water down his chest, past his core, down to the band of the boxer shorts, letting it stream through the subtropical jungle of coarse hair behind what is technically known as a "functional fly front."

He walks inside the apartment, pulls on a pair of cargo shorts and a striped T-shirt.

The instant he steps out of the Château's gates, his body takes over, running itself past the glum white men with their glum white dogs. They stay behind him, unaware of their surrender.

Note his elbows, they are bent, a bit arthritic perhaps, but stiffer than granite. Winglike, they speed him up as he rushes north toward his destination—the Broadwalk.

There, at the Broadwalk, he pauses, looks back, past the Châ-teau, past the Diplomat, past the Grand Dux. It's a cloudless morning, the beginning of a cloudless day. More than anyone, Melsor knows that sometimes, sometimes you must look back, to measure the distance covered, legions defeated, lands conquered, nations subjugated.

Usually, he can get all these thoughts packed like proverbial sausage into proverbial *kishke* of a single instant. He will touch the mezuzah next. Unlike his *nebesh* son, Melsor is not in the least perplexed by the mezuzah's presence here, its hiding place on the back of a rotting fence post.

Its purpose is to send Melsor on to his daily triumph over age, to protect his launching pad from unwanted intruders. Should some overly eager city maintenance worker find it and pull it off with a crowbar, Melsor will buy a new mezuzah and affix it to another rotting post, and if they dig out the posts, he will use trees, for this is the place that needs protection; screw the apart-ment. Nella takes care of that.

Before his hand gets to the mezuzah, Melsor pauses, turning around to consider the view, squinting to increase the resolution of the sweeping picture before him—the ever-rising skyline of the South Florida coastline. He lingers a bit, questioning whether he is actually seeing an intensely orange dot pop up next to the Grand Dux. What can it be? A parachute? Sometimes speed-boats drag parachutists along the coast; it's hard to fathom why. Those fools—and fools they must be—are never more than a few meters in the air.

This one is near the building's top, too close to the building

to make any sense. There is no boat that Melsor can see. No airplane either. Suicide maybe. Two weeks ago, on Local News 10,
Melsor heard about a plastic surgeon, the Butt God they called
him, who fell to his death. It was at the Grand Dux. Here in
Florida you do what you want. If you are crazy, be crazy. If you
want to jump, well, knock yourself out—jump.

The orange dot is gone. Perhaps it was never there. It could
have been triggered by solar activity, or—and this is unlikely in
the extreme—it's Melsor's mind playing tricks, conjuring images,
lying.

Melsor kisses his hand and reaches behind a post, where his
fingers find the hidden mezuzah that shouldn't be there, but, the
rabbis be damned, is.

ACKNOWLEDGMENTS

The disintegrating hulk of Château Sedan Neuve cannot be found on any map of South Florida. The building is my homage to the great Morris Lapidus, the creator of Miami modernism, whose Hotel Fontainebleau is one of my favorite buildings anywhere.

I urge you to refrain from going on the Web to reserve a room at the Grand Dux Hotel in Hollywood, Florida. Someone may take your credit card number, but you will not get a room. Like the Château, the place exists only in my imagination.

My biggest debt of gratitude is to my father, Boris Goldberg, for not being Melsor Katzenelenbogen.

Boris has taught me everything I know about being a journalist and a novelist. While I am his creation, Melsor is mine. You might say they have me in common, and, importantly, they are both poets. Melsor's principal mission is to help me play out my fascination with dishonesty—political, economic, intellectual, artistic, personal.

ACKNOWLEDGMENTS

I accept full responsibility for the Russian poems attributed to Melsor and Bill. English translations are mine as well. I composed this oeuvre while sitting on my father's sofa in South Florida. I feel obligated to disclose that he declared my poetry to be beyond awful and generously proposed edits, which I rejected.

The idea for this book was tossed to me by Susan Keselenko Coll, a comic novelist whose ideas I took seriously even before we were married. My literary agent, Josh Getzler, thought the idea was a hoot, and my editor, James Meader, suggested that this could be not just one, but a series of novels—a fucking career!

As I dug into the material, I became fascinated by the institution of a condo board. In the context of the United States, it's difficult to imagine a political structure less accountable, less transparent, and more open to abuse. The problem is especially acute in Florida, where laws governing these entities are as weak as the stakes high.

Florida, I learned, is a land of opportunity to defraud thy neighbor. Sunburn notwithstanding, Nikolai Gogol would have struck gold on Hollywood's Broadwalk. (That's Broadwalk, not boardwalk—it's an actual place.) Should you find yourself there, you might want to listen in to the narratives glum-looking passersby pour out into their cell phones. My informal survey suggests that condo boards are their chief complaint, followed by deteriorating health and America's predatory health care system. The inadequate level of attention from children comes in fourth.

As I wrote, I became obsessed with the Russian culture of South Florida. I hung out at Russian restaurants and Russian clubs, navigating rivers of vodka, and listening, listening, listening. Chunks of this novel are lifted from these overheard conversations.

My Washington friends Ellen and Gerry Sigal were generous with their time. Gerry, a builder who knows from Florida, helped me devise the disasters that befall the Château and has allowed me to shadow him at work.

In Florida, I often consulted with my *Duke Chronicle* friends Davia and Jim Mazur. Nina Gordon, a *Chronicle* friend as well, was immensely helpful and encouraging, as was her law partner Arvin Jaffe. I will continue to pick their brains as this thing rolls on.

As always, I turned to my friend and (on occasion) co-author Otis Brawley with questions involving medicine. Omer Mei-Dan, an orthopedic surgeon and BASE jumper, answered my questions about the mechanics of this extreme sport. Kate Whitmore translated Frau Müller-Greenstein's lament into original German. Julius Getman walked me through legal perils faced by those who hold loot from the Holocaust.

The list of friends and family members who offered guidance or looked over the manuscript includes Amin Ahmad, Jeff Altbush, Marilyn Altbush, Peter Bach, Alan Bennett, Joel Berkowitz, Laura Brawley, Ken Crerar, Claire Dietz, Slavik Dushenkov, Anna Dushenkova, Richard Folkers, Graydon Forrer, Vladimir Frumkin, Peter Garrett, Galina Goldberg, Tom Grubisich, Gardiner Harris, Dudley Hudspeth, Jonathan Keselenko, Marian Keselenko, Steven Lieberman, Richard Liebeskind, Julie Lloyd, Patricia Lochmuller, the late Mike Madigan, Harsha Murthy, Amanda Newman, Matthew Bin Han Ong, Alexei Pervov, Caitlin Riley, Gregory Rolbin, Lela Rosenberg, Kara Sergeant, Angela Spring, Jon Steiger, Dave Stephen, Valerie Strauss, and Mel Tomberg.

ACKNOWLEDGMENTS

I've also benefited from advice from the talented younger generation of my wonderful blended family: Sarah Goldberg, Katie Goldberg, Max Coll, Emma Bivona, John Bivona, Ally Coll Steele, and Rory Steele.

After considering thanking the semi-fictional character the Château residents call Donal'd Tramp for giving this book urgency, providing the macrocosm for my microcosm, and inspiring me to write like the wind, I decided to do nothing of the sort.